ALSO BY TYLER GEIS
Scyphozoa

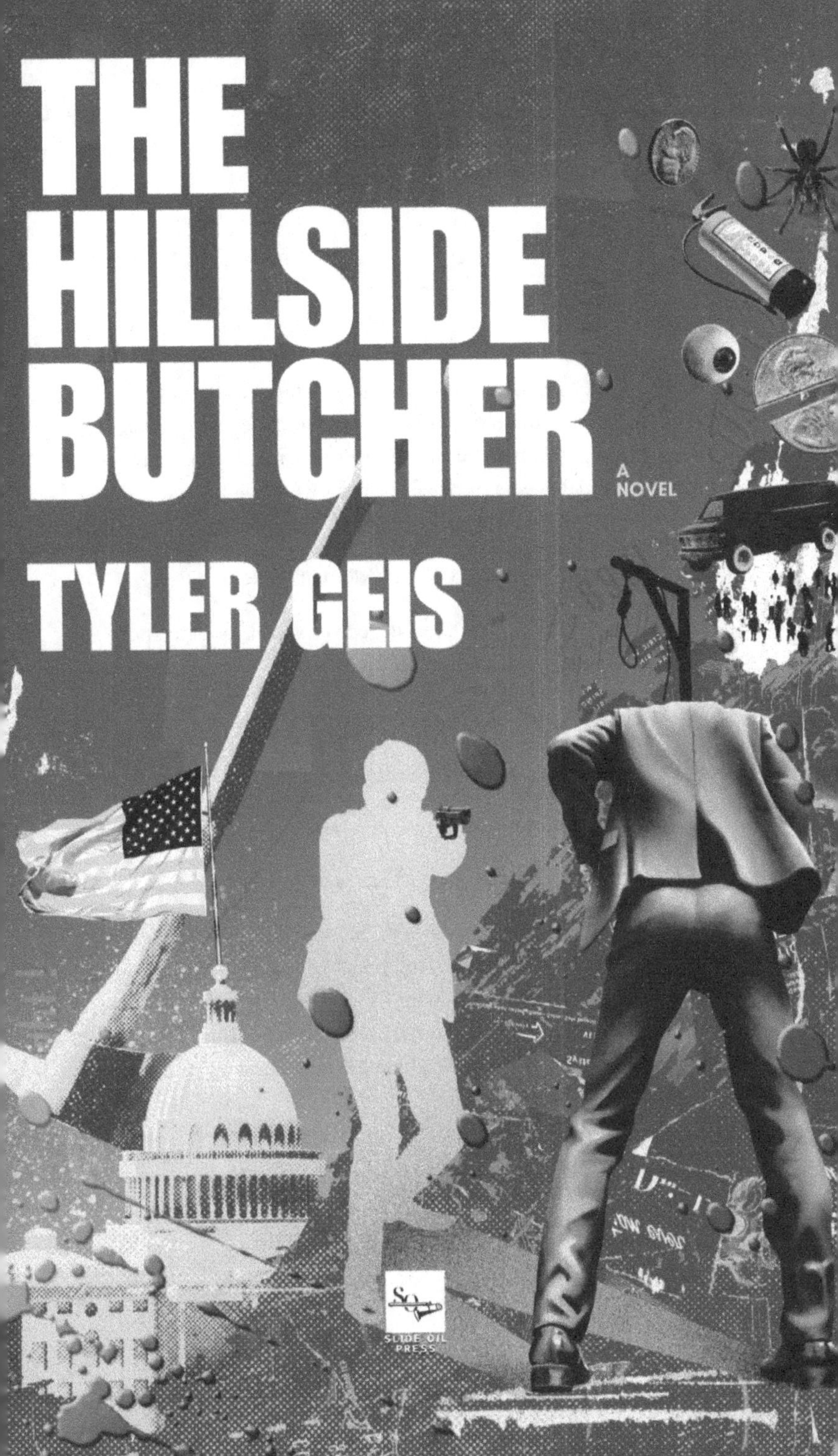

THE HILLSIDE BUTCHER
A NOVEL
TYLER GEIS
SLIDE OIL PRESS

Slide Oil Press

For Kamilo

THE
HILLSIDE
BUTCHER

Free
OHIO
RUM COCKTAILS
YERS'S
UM

PART ONE

CEMETERY HILL

CHAPTER 1

★ ★ ★

Mark Smith knew he was getting old the moment he threw his back out while pulling an axe from Mrs. Reagan's skull.

He'd been suspicious of that fact for months now. The bright colors of his childhood had slowly faded as the years rode on by. The Mecca that was his local McDonald's had shifted from lush yellow brick and a textured red roof to a dry, gray building that harbored no joy. The lake behind Mom's house just didn't shine the way it used to. The grass had changed from lush greens to the beige of discarded hay.

But when the axe refused to dislodge itself from Mrs. Reagan's head—and when Mark had pulled with all his might—the looming presence of the brutal passage of time came into full view. He tugged on the handle a bit too hard and instantly felt it. The pain. That shooting sensation that rocketed through his nerves and turned his legs to jelly. He stifled a scream and tumbled to the chevron rug next to his latest victim. The axe handle wiggled as if telling him, "No, no, no. Don't you even think about trying to get me out. I quite like the way this broad's brain feels on my blade."

Mark applied pressure to his lower back. Another spasm of pain exploded there. His leg twitched. He squinted his eyes.

He couldn't give up now, though.

There was too much work left to be done.

Mark bit his tongue and got to his knees, then his feet. He stumbled back, took a good, long look at the remains of one Mrs. Reagan, managed a smile, and propped a foot on her ass. He grasped the axe handle once again and pulled, ignoring the low hum of pain ringing inside him. He twisted his grip, prying Mrs. Reagan's skull apart.

The bone cracked beautifully. A harsh, uneven split. Blood gushed from the wound like a fountain in a kiddie pool. He pulled again, and the axe came up with him, almost hitting the popcorn ceiling above. Mark sighed deeply as he let the axe head rest on the rug. He gazed upon his work. Another job well done. The ravine that had once been a perfectly functioning skull spewed red as Mrs. Reagan's heart thumped its last beat. He leaned over and placed two pristine pennies in the crevice, squishing them down for dramatic effect.

Mark washed his hands in the Reagans' kitchen sink. He picked bits of congealing blood from under his fingernails as he applied a ridiculous amount of soap. There was a stain on his dress shirt just below the chest. He rubbed it with tap water as best as he could. *Why did you wear white tonight?* he asked himself. He knew the answer, though. All his black shirts were at the dry cleaner on East Monroe Street, as were his ski masks and black khakis. Mark hadn't felt so free as he did on this night, walking into the Reagans' home with his face unmasked and his hands ungloved. The front door had been graciously left unlocked as if the matriarch of the house had just been asking for it. Mark smirked at the thought as he dried his hands and hobbled toward the living room.

He turned on the family's television, which had already been tuned into FOX News. Some overly botoxed man with slick black hair complained about another minority group while the four others at the table with him were appalled, agreeing, or both. Mark raised the volume, grabbed the axe, and headed upstairs.

He peered through multiple doors left ajar. A half bathroom here, a linen closet there. A room deeper down the hall, aglow with soft lamplight. He pushed the door open and saw tiny Louella Reagan bundled underneath her butterfly-patterned bedsheets. The lamp emitted shapes onto the ceiling. Silhouettes of those same butterflies along with puppies and kittens and whatever else children liked nowadays. Mark tilted his head, wondering what little Lou Lou was dreaming about. Sweet dreams set on an open meadow where sentient jellybeans danced on the grass? Or nightmares where a masked killer broke into her house and hovered over her sleeping body? Luckily for Louella, Mark wasn't wearing a mask tonight, so it wasn't *that* scary.

After taking care of her, Mark moved onto the next room. Late Louella's older brother, Seth, laid sprawled on the floor, earbuds dangling from his ears, a handheld gaming console on the carpet a few inches from his open palm. Seth was able to pause the game before the looming presence of sleep took over. Another lucky kid, it seemed. Mark raised the axe and did his business.

He checked the rest of the house for any stragglers. He had heard rumblings of the Reagans having to put down their precious German shepherd of twelve years due to kidney failure a few weeks back. Grief was imbedded throughout the home. A basket of dog toys sat in the corner of the small playroom at the end of the second-floor hallway. He had noticed a few rubber bones in the living room, but thought nothing of it then. It took a lot for a family to reckon with the death of a loved one, so much so that they usually forget to get rid of the departed's belongings. Almost as if they would come back to retrieve them.

Mark liked to think he did the Reagans a favor. Not only were they saddened by the euthanizing of their beloved pet, but Mr. Reagan had also left the missus for a much younger, much hotter woman only a few months before. There was sadness in every square foot of the house, and Mark had extinguished that fire before it could burn the home to the ground.

When Mark returned to his apartment, he threw his stained clothes into the hamper and submerged himself in a steaming hot bath. The Reagans' blood turned the clear water pink. Mark tapped the faucet with his bare feet as he massaged his aching shoulders. There was a tenseness there that made him more uncomfortable than anything. Ten years ago, when he had committed his first murder, Mark had been in the best shape of his life. Bulging biceps and pecs from chopping firewood in the backyard. Toned legs from walking the dog nearly every day. While some of that muscle remained, Mark couldn't help but notice how those lumps of meat inside him were beginning to lose definition. Hard creases that he once was able to slide his fingers under were reduced to soft angles. That single vein down his left bicep had receded as a layer of fat grew over it.

Mark was getting older, he had to admit. He wasn't the spry 25-year-old that had murdered his father in a fit of passion. He was in the middle of his thirties with aches in his joints and fat over his stomach. He pinched a chunk of skin on his arm, dug his nails into it, and watched as blood pooled in the thin crater.

Refreshed, he climbed into bed but couldn't fall asleep. A thought nagged at the back of his mind. The thought of aging, dying, and being forgotten. Mark wanted to live a life of importance, one that would guarantee him the satisfaction of a world that would remember him.

He was the Hillside Butcher.

★ ★ ★

Walmart was the perfect place to scout for his next victims. The tortured looks on the customers' faces, the utter disdain shown from the underpaid cashiers. There was an aura of hurt inside those grocery store walls, and Mark lapped it all up.

He garnered some stares from passersby. A violent glare from Anthony Ratchet, a sorrowful glance from old Mrs. Donahugh, a nervous peek from a group of teens he still hadn't clocked the names of. One of them—the tallest girl with straight bleach-blonde hair—was definitely named Kayleigh or something similar. She giggled as the posse sauntered by. It was a Thursday morning, and they were certainly skipping summer classes, but Mark paid no mind. He was just shopping for his next kill, nothing to see here.

After covering up his suspicious activities with two loaves of French bread and a head of lettuce in his cart, he went through a self-checkout kiosk and exited the store. He packed the groceries into his trunk and zoomed out of the oddly full parking lot for a weekday. As he drove down Main Street toward his apartment, a squad of police cars rushed by in the opposite direction toward the Reagans' residence. Mark was surprised the bodies had been discovered so soon, considering the Reagan family lived in a more secluded area of town. Maybe he left a window open by accident and the stench of death wafted to their next-door neighbor. Who was he to guess? He was used to people finding the bodies so soon. It wasn't the first time they'd been found within a day. Nothing out of the ordinary.

Later that day, Mark sat on his sofa and turned on the news as he snacked on one of the French loaves. "FAMILY OF THREE DEAD IN RURAL ARKANSAS," the headline splashed across the bottom of the screen said. The news anchor, a ginger man named Noah McCarthy, explained the local devastation in further detail. "Police intelligence believes the culprit premeditated this attack, and that it was no accident," McCarthy summarized. "Melissa Reagan, a schoolteacher at Bernard Elementary, and her two young children were allegedly murdered in the late hours of last night. No murder weapon was left at the scene, but police theorize that it was something with a medium-sized blade, such as a cleaver or an axe. A candlelight vigil will be held for the family outside Bernard Elementary on Saturday evening. No suspects have been identified in the attack, yet many Bernard residents claim it to allegedly be the area's notorious Hillside Butcher."

Mark held a lot of hatred for the word "allegedly." He understood that news stations such as this were obligated to use the word when talking about sensitive legal topics, but it was all the more infuriating when *he* was the one who "allegedly" committed those crimes. Without fail, all of Mark's murders have been alleged, almost as if they had never occurred at all. How was he supposed to earn his recognition if the people responsible for covering his story were too scared to acknowledge that the killings actually happened?

He ripped a fluffy chunk from the bread loaf and threw the rest onto the coffee table. An empty mug slid from its coaster and tumbled to the floor, shattering into dusty ceramic fragments. Mark groaned and headed for the broom closet. But just as he grasped the doorknob, the doorbell rang. Well, "rang" is a bit generous. The doorbell screeched like a crow being crushed by a rather large boulder. Mark winced and peered through the peephole. Any hint of a smile vanished from his face when he saw who was on the other side.

With all three deadbolts unfastened, Mark let Abel Watterson into his apartment. Before the door could close, Abel was already spewing private information, the crook. "That was you last night, right?" the kid asked. "No one else could wipe out a family of three and get away with it like that."

"Yes, Abel. That was me," Mark said, wishing Abel would discover the miracle of deodorant someday.

"I *knew* it! You're so cool, man."

"Why're you here, Abel? Shouldn't you be in school?"

"I graduated two years ago."

Mark raised his eyebrows. How had he forgotten that Abel had turned twenty a few months back? That Abel had graduated high school at nearly the bottom of his class with no awards of merit to show for it? Mark had been at the graduation ceremony scouting for new people to relieve their lives. He had chosen a lovely woman in a tight maroon dress that day, a Samantha or Sandra. Something like that. That death had been especially cathartic. Mark had taken her to a nearby motel and slammed a clothing iron into her nose before turning it on and melting her face into an amalgamation of burnt skin and oozing cartilage. The police didn't find her for a solid three days. By the time they did, ants had picked her face clean until there was nothing but bones and two loose pennies left.

"I completely forgot," Mark said. "I'm very sorry."

"It's alright, Mr. Smith. I forget I graduated sometimes, too. School was *such* a waste of time."

Try telling your teachers that, Mark thought.

"Anyway," Abel interjected, "could I help you with your next one? I know this town like the back of my hand."

The boy showed the front of his hand instead of the back to Mark and wiggled his scrawny fingers.

"So do I," Mark said. "I've lived here longer than you have. Beaten you to the punch by fifteen years, apparently. You ask me this every time I kill someone, and *what* do I tell you when you do?"

"'Fuck off,'" Abel recited, sighing.

"Good. I'm glad you remember. Now, would you kindly leave my apartment? I have a lot of work to do, and I can't afford any distractions. You understand?"

"I guess so."

Mark hated how much Abel thought the killings were just a game. They were more than that. Cleansing darkness from the world one death at a time was hard work. Required work. Something that was necessary and something that only Mark had the courage to do.

Abel lowered his head in defeat. The kid was too enamored by the idea of committing premeditated murder. Surely he could have allotted some of that brain activity toward learning algebra or chemistry or how to take a damn shower, right? Mark swore he saw a bead of oil drip from Abel's greasy, black hair. He coughed and carefully rested a hand on the boy's shoulder, making sure to avoid the mustard stain splattered near his armpit.

"If I ever need you, I will let you know," Mark assured. "But for now I need to continue my work as a solo operation. Everything works better that way, and I don't intend on changing it for a while."

"Alright. I guess I'll see you around, then."

Abel left and Mark closed the door behind him. Before he thought about doing anything else with his day, Mark made sure to disinfect every surface Abel had touched. New species of germ were born every day. Millions and millions of disgusting specks that live in our walls, in our bodies, clogging our minds. But Mark's mind was clear. Free of blockage. After using up yet another bottle of Windex, he chucked it into the open trash can and rested on the sofa as a news story about "alleged" zombie deer played on the television.

* * *

Mark spent the entirely of the next day planning the weekend's murder. He slightly messed up his schedule by murdering the Reagan family on a Wednesday night instead of his usual Sunday evening affair, but this upcoming weekend would help steer him back on track.

He perused the Bernard community page on Facebook, sifting through posts that announced local restaurant deals and thanked young boys for mowing their neighbor's lawn from the goodness of their hearts. All that sappy stuff never led to the right victims. Some people were too joyful to deserve a grisly end. No, what Mark needed was someone who held nothing but resentment for the people around them. Someone who complained, complained, complained about the most unnecessary things.

His eyes widened as he locked onto a post from a disgruntled older gentleman by the name of Arthur Guthrie. It seemed like there was no relation to the classic folk singer, since the post on Mark's laptop's screen was full of hateful rhetoric and condescending phrases. Guthrie's post read:

im fed up with this town.

to start could you new parents please shut your fuckin kids up? they get off the school bus and yak yak yak until you

wurthless idiots decide to walk them home. i yelled at a kid the other day and he/she/it told me to 'shut the hell up, cracker.' EXCUSE ME??? since when r kids allowed too talk to they're elders like THAT???

2nd, could we stop with the dei hiring in bernard? I went to joe's tuesday morning and ordered my usual, but the black server fcked up my coffee! how do you burn coffee?? just by lookin at her i knew she was not quantified

Mark knew that last word was supposed to be "qualified" instead of "quantified," but the rest of the post was generally so poorly written that he let it slide.

and 1 last thing. if you r going to let your dog shit in my lawn, dont be surprised when i blast your head off for trespasing. its my God given right to bear arms and im not afraid to use them!

The only tidbit of information that worried Mark was the mention of a firearm, but the thought waned when the realization that he lived in deep-country Arkansas hit him like an obvious freight train. Everyone had a gun, even Mark did, despite hating how lazy he felt killing with it.

Mark spent the next day resting for the most part, taking advantage of the cool Saturday afternoon to walk around the block Mr. Guthrie inhabited. The old man lived in a quaint cottage between two newer houses. The juxtaposition of his dingy home against the two clean, furnished homes on either side made Mark chuckle slightly, his voice suppressed by the light breeze whispering by.

He slid into a tall bush and surveyed the house. The roof was missing some slate; the bricks were worn by years of thunderstorms and strong tornado winds. But the house remained standing despite its many trials over the decades.

A light flickered on in what Mark guessed was the home's singular bathroom. It had the only glazed window on the whole exterior. The dark blur of Arthur Guthrie waddled around inside the room, the bottom half of him disappearing as he sat on the toilet. Mark continued to search the exterior for anything he would need for the next night's adventure, but that was until he heard the muffled click of a lock and the bathroom window sliding up a crack.

Mark smiled a clean grin and tiptoed toward the window. The light turned off, and the door shut inside. He picked up a tiny pebble from the grass and gripped it tight in his palm. Underneath the open window, Mark pinched the pebble between his fingers and gave it a kiss. The salt of the earth graced his lips. He would sanitize his face later, but now was the time for fun. He had his in. Mark placed the pebble in the corner of the sill and walked away.

Sunday morning, he felt the healthiest he had ever been. The aches and pains from his stint with Mrs. Reagan's skull were all but a memory. Mark felt as young and free as he had been when he had started this job. The sun shone its rays onto his bed as he stretched and let out a hapless moan. The natural light fell neatly into the lumps of his remaining musculature. A thin field of chest hair began to run from nipple to nipple. That wouldn't do. Not at all.

In the time that followed, Mark shaved every inch of his body besides the hair atop his head. He would need to drive out to Little Rock to get that professionally trimmed, but that was a tomorrow issue. A deep clean in the shower followed. Intricate lathering of shampoo, followed by moisturizing conditioner, then the exfoliating body wash that smelled like cherry blossoms and tickled when applied but kept his body silky smooth throughout the day. He applied a facial cleanser, rubbing extra deep today to check if there was any hair left on his face. Thankfully, there was none, and his face would be acne-free another day as a bonus.

His sets of black clothing were still at the dry cleaner, but he thought he'd spice his outfit up a bit tonight. He rummaged through his neatly organized closet and retrieved a gray polo, beige khakis, a leather belt, and a pair of moccasins. Each item of clothing slid over his smooth skin perfectly, accentuating the curves of his body. He had his father to thank for the ass poking through the back of his pants. Mark's mother had been flat as a bone.

He pulled a royal blue beanie from the top shelf and slid it over his wavy hair, getting it over the top of his head until all sides were ideally aligned with the shape of his skull. Mark did a final pat-down of every square inch of his body, and when he was satisfied with tonight's garb, he lifted the floorboard under his bed and acquired his axe. The Reagans' blood was still crusted on the blade. Mark sighed and washed it with dish soap and water in the kitchen sink. Dark red flakes circled down the drain like a penny dropped in one of those spiral wishing wells. He remembered visiting a science center in Missouri when Aunt Lauren had died in a traffic accident. He had dropped a penny in that large, plastic funnel and watched it go round and round and round and round until the copper coin disappeared into the abyss at the well's center. It was such a fun experience that he dropped every coin in his Dexter's Laboratory wallet into the well. Thirty minutes later, he sauntered over to the main reception desk and asked the teenager working if she'd seen his parents. No tears, no worries that his parents had abandoned him in such a strange, wonderful place. At the ripe age of eight, Mark had felt mature enough to live on his own. Getting lost in that children's museum was nothing to him. They found him eventually with tears in their eyes. His mother hugged him as tight as her frail body would allow while Dad stood behind and scowled. Disappointed, he was, and for good reason, too. Mark had been a bad boy that day, and that truth was only further accentuated by the lashings he received in the hotel room hours later.

Mark felt a stinging sensation. He blinked through watery eyes and saw a single bead of red blooming on his fingertip. He must've scrubbed the blade too hard. A little disinfectant would clean up the wound in no time. He still had a few hours to kill before sundown. There was no use in bashing himself for this bout of incompetence. Everyone makes mistakes.

Some more than others, he thought.

★ ★ ★

Mark checked his watch. Twenty minutes past eleven. The sky was absurdly clear that night. He peered up through the tall bush and spotted the Big and Little Dippers, split eternally from each other by that scheming snake, Draco.

He checked his watch again.

11:30pm.

Time to work.

Arthur Guthrie had fallen asleep an hour before. His windows were completely dark, offering nothing to hint at the old geezer's whereabouts inside. Mark maneuvered from the bush and toward the bathroom window. He planted his ear on the glass and listened. Nothing except for the hum of the air conditioning unit. With a grin, Mark slid his fingers under the window and lightly pushed up. The pebble had kept it from locking, but the real challenge was opening the window high enough to crawl through. The pane scraped against the frame, squeaking against decades of grime and dirt between the cracks.

With the window as open as it could possibly go, Mark lifted himself into the house. His foot came to rest on the yellow-stained toilet. He silently thanked the metaphorical Lord that he was wearing shoes. Both feet planted on the tile, Mark slipped his axe out from the makeshift sheath at his side (which was just an extra bit of leather belt that he had attached in a loop to his waist).

As soon as his eyes were able to adjust to the pervasive dark, floorboards moaned a room or two over. Mark quietly got comfortable in the shower basin and closed the floral-printed curtain with the utmost delicacy.

The footsteps grew closer. Mark crouched on his toes. The light flickered on. Arthur needed to get that bulb replaced. The thought of Mr. Guthrie never being able to replace it now almost made Mark give up his position with a giggle. The old man hummed as he shuffled toward the toilet and relieved himself with short, succinct dribbles. Mark hoped he'd never have to deal with a weak bladder. Imagining such a scenario in which his body didn't work like it used to sent a shiver down his spine.

The toilet flushed, Arthur turned on the tap, lathered his hands with lavender-scented soap, all while continuing to hum a nonsensical tune. Mark wondered if now would be the best time to strike. Reverse *Psycho* style. The helpless victim outside the shower while the killer laid in wait just behind the curtain. Mark felt an erection tugging the crotch of his pants. He used his hand as a rolling pin and flattened it out.

The light turned off, and Mark was left in silence once more. However, that silence was fleeting. The television came to life in the living room. The glow of its screen shone into the bathroom with a blue aura. An unmistakable saxophone solo blasted from the dusty speakers. *"Live from New York, it's Saturday Night!"* Mark never took Arthur Guthrie for the sketch comedy type, but *he* wasn't completely perfect himself, believe it or not. Everyone makes mistakes, even people as flawless as Mark Smith.

He climbed from the tub and made his way to the living room, axe tight in his grip. The SNL cast repeated an overdone joke from years past, cueing paid audience applause along with a snide chuckle from Arthur. His wispy white hair was combed back in thick clumps. Purple blemishes dotted the scalp underneath. He held the television remote in his left hand, a half-empty beer bottle in his right. Never too late in the night to get a little buzz.

Mark sneered, the wrinkles at the corners of his eyes folding from years of creasing. He lifted the axe above his head. He revved up his engine, pulled the axe farther while silently counting down.

3... 2... 1...

He must've pulled back a bit too far. The axehead tapped the ceiling with a dull thud. Before he had the chance to let it fall into the old man's skull, Arthur Guthrie bolted upright from his recliner. Mark had never seen someone so elderly move so fast. The shock of Arthur's quickness overwhelmed his senses. Just enough to distract him from the shotgun that suddenly appeared in Arthur's arms.

"Who the fuck are you?" the old man shouted.

"I'm just a worker."

"Working for who?"

Mark breathed but was cut off before any words came out.

"Nevermind," Arthur said. "Don't say another fuckin' word. Put that down and get out of my house."

"You've been unwell, Mr. Guthrie," Mark said, lowering the axe. "I was sent to help you."

"I don't need your damn help." Arthur cocked his shotgun. "And I thought I told you to shut your mouth."

"It seems like you wish everyone would just be quiet, then. That's exactly why I'm here, Arthur. I can make them quiet. I can make everything quiet. You just have to trust me."

How could he have been so stupid as to not think Arthur would keep his gun on him at all times? If the Facebook post was anything to go on, Mark should've known. A bead of sweat formed over his brow. The television flashed reds and greens and blues. A bright light hit like the morning sun as an Ozempic commercial aired. The shotgun rattled in Arthur's tired grasp.

The shaking subsided and the old man's eyes widened.

"Oh, wow," he sputtered. "You're… You're that Smith boy. Sophia and Mark's boy. Yeah, I remember! Shit, I thought you'd have gone out of town to join the Navy after what happened to those poor lovebirds."

A twinge of anger and the subtle lowering of the shotgun were the perfect recipe for mayhem. Mark screamed and drove the axe into Arthur's hip. The blade sliced through thin skin and stopped abruptly.

Through Arthur's pained cries, he managed to mutter, "Hip replacement." The old man tumbled to the carpet and wheezed like a bike tire losing air.

The following few minutes were a blur. Mark grunted as he lifted the axe and bore down on Arthur. He chopped and chopped until nothing solid could be chopped. He had to give it to Mr. Guthrie, he was a fighter. After ten gashes all across his torso, the man was still breathing despite the tears in his lungs. He coughed blood in a sad dribble that streamed in pink bubbles down his wrinkled cheek. Mark cleaved straight into Arthur's sternum. A loud crack echoed, only suppressed by the television speakers as

Saturday Night Live returned from its commercial break. Splatters of blood rose from the wound. Arthur's entrails peeked from beneath his flannel shirt like raw chicken laying on a picnic blanket. There was another whole person inside him. One that wriggled and writhed as the man on the outside drank and complained himself to death. The muscles and tissues and organs looked so fresh, so perfect. *Good enough to eat*, Mark thought bemusedly. Drown the kidneys in avocado oil and season them with rosemary and thyme. Mark's mouth watered as he planted the final blow into Arthur Guthrie's head, right between the eyes and splitting his nose in two. Blood drained from the lesion and formed a scarlet veil that poured down his neck.

Mark fished into his pocket and presented two clean pennies to Arthur's remains. He kneeled and stuck both coins inside the abrasion splitting the man's rib cage. The fractured bones scraped against the front and back of his hand. He dropped the pennies and propped himself on his feet.

Clink.

He whirled around and noticed something in the pale light illuminating the kitchen. A woman stood in the darkness, her eyes wide.

CHAPTER 2

★ ★ ★

She turned on the kitchen light. The bulb flashed, clicked, and burst to life with that signature fluorescent buzz. Mark suddenly felt the sensation of liquid on skin. Arthur's warm blood started to cool as it soaked through his shirt and pressed against his stomach. The woman—who was no older than Mark, he assumed—glanced up and down. She huffed and flung open the fridge, rummaging for a late-night snack.

Mark was breathing heavily. Low bursts of air crashed in and out of his lungs. But the woman was as calm as a puppy taking an afternoon nap. She shut the fridge and popped open a can of Coke. She took a swig, her shirtsleeve lowering to reveal a tattoo of a snake slithering on her tricep.

"I see you were busy tonight," she said, her voice raspy at that late hour.

"Who are you?" Mark asked despite himself.

"I don't see why that matters."

"It surely matters to *me*."

"But I don't care. That's the issue. Well, it's not an issue for me, but it's definitely an issue for you."

That comment made Mark aware of how hot his cheeks were burning. He wiped them as if the pressure would remove his blushing, but he only made it worse by smearing Arthur's blood all over his face.

The woman took another sip and leaned against the marble-laminated counter.

"You can leave through the front door," she said nonchalantly. "All I ask is that you lock up behind you. There's a spare key under the welcome mat."

"I could've just used the front door?" Mark asked. He felt nothing but flustered with how embarrassing the situation was for him. What kind of killer of the night was he if he was too stupid to think that an old man wouldn't primitively leave a spare key right outside his front door? Goddamn idiot.

"I mean, I would have," the woman said with a smirk. "But I also wouldn't have killed my father. He wasn't the *worst* person in the world, but he was getting old. It was only a matter of time."

"You're—" Mark hesitated. His embarrassment morphed into confusion. "You're not mad that he's dead? That *I* killed him?"

"Well, not really. I've been telling him to leave Bernard for years now. The high mortality rate in this town was making me nervous for so long, but I've kinda just accepted it at this point."

"What?"

She stepped closer, her bare feet treading from the kitchen tile to the living room carpet. She grabbed the remote from the recliner's armrest and turned the television off. "I said: 'I've just accepted it at this point.' You know, the killings."

"I still don't understand," Mark muttered.

She was so close now that Mark could feel her breath on his neck. He physically had a good four or five inches over her, but she was figuratively towering over him. He felt small. Weak. This woman stood before him without any fear. The Grim Reaper visited her father's home, and she could do no more than smile in the face of death.

"My name's Ashley," she said.

"I'm—"

"Mark Smith, I know."

"How did you—"

"Everybody in this town knows who you are, Mark. You've been terrorizing everyone for close to ten years now, is it? Picking people off one by one. Always avoiding the police, not that Bernard PD is anything to be scared of. We went to school together, you and me. I was in the year above you, from what I remember. Little Markie Smith trundling through the halls of Bernard Community High School. Didn't think anyone noticed you? We *all* noticed you. Everyone's had an eye on you since your father opened that paper mill, and then since your dad passed in that... How did they describe it?" She raised her hands and used finger quotes. "A 'freak accident.' That's what they called it."

Mark was having trouble processing any of the words coming out of Ashley's mouth. He was too enraptured by her breasts peeking through the collar of her loose V-neck shirt. A necklace hung there on a silver chain, a spider encrusted in gold paint dangled in the pocket of her cleavage.

His ogling was interrupted by a sharp slap across the face.

"You come here uninvited, kill my father, and think you have the right to stare at my boobs?" Ashley asked. The question had its fangs bared, but her tone sounded bored and uninterested. "You really *are* something."

"I wasn't—"

"Get out."

"Would you please let me explain?"

Pleading was something new for Mark. The words felt gross and wet on his tongue.

"Explain what?" she asked. "I can see what you did right here! Now I have to call the coroner and get this carpet cleaned. Do you know how much it costs to get bloodstains out of a carpet? I wish you'd just laid a tarp down before he noticed you were here."

"What?"

"Get the fuck out!"

Mark picked up his axe and went to the front door. Before he could open it, he turned and watched Ashley stare hopelessly at her father's fresh corpse. This had to be the fastest anyone had ever discovered his murders. In fact, he had never had a witness. If Ashley Guthrie had been standing in that kitchen for longer than he assumed, she would be the first. All her talk about everyone in Bernard noticing him and knowing he was behind the murders and not giving a damn about the destruction and pain he caused. It was insane, truly. What kind of small American town would stand for a serial killer on the loose?

He opened the front door and planted his shoes on the welcome mat. A chunk of Arthur's muscle tissue squelched underneath his foot. He scraped it off, leaving a pinkish smear, and knelt to find the key under the mat.

With the door locked, Mark breathed out and let the summer night air wrap him in a billowing blanket.

Everything was going to be alright.

★ ★ ★

Everything was not alright.

Mark was under the impression that Abel Watterson was the only abnormal resident of Bernard, Arkansas. But after his confrontation with Ashley Guthrie, the whole town seemed to have devolved into insanity.

As he perused the aisles of Walmart the next morning, he elicited more glances than he was used to. Usually, it would be the older women that would give him fawning stares in the bread aisle. They seemingly couldn't resist the allure of an attractive younger man. But today was different. Customers of all ages and genders would walk by and give Mark the stink eye. An elderly couple, a mother and her two infant twins, that same group of crazed teenagers. He was even side-eyed by the cashier, an acne-riddled high schooler who didn't seem to look like the type to be judging someone based on their outward appearance.

"$56.89," the ugly fucking cashier said with a yawn.

"Here you go," said Mark, handing him 3 twenties and a dashing smile.

The cashier ignored him and hastily gave him his change. Mark scowled, checked the clerk's name tag (*Winston Albright… interesting*), grabbed his bags and left the store.

Even the people walking toward the building wouldn't stop giving him looks as he trudged back to his car. There was a deep disdain behind those eyes. But there was also a melancholy to them. The faint gloss of tears over eyes that wished they didn't have to see. Almost as if the entirety of Walmart's shopping population hated the idea of shopping at their establishment.

Mark knew they weren't dreading a simple shopping experience, though. He knew the eyes were all trained on him. As if *he* had done something wrong. What a joke. No one other than Abel and Ashley knew that he was the one relieving these poor people of their burdens. The thought that everyone in Bernard knew about his escapades made him shiver, but it was only a cool breeze passing by. That thought was nonsense. How could a town not want to put a man in jail for murdering at least one person every week? Mark mused on that absurdity as he packed his two loaves of French bread, head of lettuce, and pack of drill bits into his trunk.

He couldn't follow basic traffic laws on the short drive back to his apartment. If he focused too much on a stop sign, he could be missing another pair of eyes glowering at him. The weird, accusatory stares that could remain enshrouded in mystery. He ran another stop sign as he peered through the passenger-side window. Homes splattered with rotten tomatoes, likely due to the criminal at large slinging them like David to Goliath. Two-bedroom homes with rusted mailboxes and gaudily painted shutters leered back. There were people behind those walls. Were they thinking about him? Had Ashley leaked his identity online after the coroner picked up her father's body? Was she telling the truth? Did everyone know he was the Hillside Butcher?

Did they even care?

Mark was about to run the last stop sign when his body jolted violently to the left. His car door crumpled and the window exploded into white frost. The pain in his back resurfaced as the car tumbled and fell on its roof. The impact crushed the windshield. A spiderweb of cracks formed on the sleek glass. Mark hit his head on the top of the cabin, the seatbelt digging into his collarbone with the weight of a hydraulic press before the weight became too much and the bone shattered.

Car horns blared.

(*Honk honk honk HONK HONK HONK.*)

"Turn that down," Mark mumbled.

The world had turned upside-down. He hung suspended in his upturned seat, the only thing keeping him from falling being the seatbelt pushing his collarbone into the meat under the skin. Breathing was barely an option. He smelled Sharpie ink. That arid stench of whiskey ilk. No, that was gasoline. Someone must've hit the tank. Mark remembered the smell of gas as his father refueled the family pickup truck. He had never paid attention to how Dad had put the fuel in the car; just noticed the smell. His head would usually be buried in his hand-me-down GameBoy or—if he was grounded from playing with electronics—a weathered *Goosebumps* novel.

(*HONK HONK HONK*)

"TURN THAT DOWN!"

"Get out of the fucking car, man!" a voice shouted.

No more GameBoy, no more *Goosebumps*. No more Dad.

Back in the present, Mark looked to his left and saw a pair of dirty sneakers. Dazed, he unbuckled his seatbelt and fell on his head. Everything hurt. Pain exploded from every nerve in his body, the epicenter being right below his neck.

He clenched his jaw and bore the pain as he crawled through the broken car window onto the hot asphalt. The sun had finally come out on that gloomy morning. Mark struggled to his feet and met the mystery man face to face. Out of all the people in their twenties left in Bernard, he couldn't recognize this one. But the Black man recognized him, his eyes wide in a fluid mix of terror and indifference.

"Oh, uh," he stuttered. "I… I think you should call an ambulance. If you need it, of course. I'm not saying you do."

"Kid, I'm bleeding," Mark spit. "I think I need one. My phone's in the car. Could you call for me?"

"Sure, Mr. Smith."

Mr. Smith? How did he know Mark's name? And why so formal? Had he become a local celebrity overnight? Was Arthur Guthrie really that bad of a person that his death warranted this kind of mass reaction?

As the kid dialed 9-1-1, Mark staggered to the other side of his car. Less damage there, save for a few minor scratches on the grey metallic paint. Nowhere near as mutilated as the driver's side. On top of all the aches and pains from the crash itself, Mark felt a headache coming on. The sudden heat wasn't helping his situation. The sun, combined with the day's high humidity, instantly made him feel drowsy. Blood dripped from under his untucked shirt and splatted on the paved intersection. Other cars began to crowd the spot along with people walking from their homes to check on the carnage.

Those eyes again. Every resident of the north side of Bernard seemed to be here. They were watching, perceiving... *noticing*.

We all *noticed you.*

And that was just it: They were noticing him.

They were all recognizing him for who he was.

He was a hero among a stagnant town. The savior they all needed. Someone who had the willpower to do what was right, to rid their world of the suffering and misery that seemed to come as naturally as the sun rising and setting each and every day. *That's* why Ashley had dropped that bomb on him the night before. She recognized his talents in person and couldn't resist propping him up on a pedestal. After ten years of working for the people, Mark was finally gaining the recognition he so rightfully deserved.

On the verge of tears, he collapsed.

★ ★ ★

Ashley Guthrie could still smell her father's rotting corpse as the pallbearers hoisted his coffin above the grave. It felt surreal to see that empty space next to her mother finally filled. "Finally" might not have been the proper word, but it was the correct one. Because if you lived in Bernard, Arkansas, the sweet release of death came at the most inopportune times. Whether by natural causes, car crashes, or an axe to the head, everybody died eventually. There was a finality in death, but that finality was a comma at the end of a sentence instead of a period, the comma signifying "Yes, but also…" before the rest of the page is left blank.

No explanation, no desire to carry on.

Ashley recalled her last years in high school. She never thought of that period of her life while away from her hometown, which was essentially all the time. But leave it to Mark Smith to make her rare visit to her father so memorable. Her last family member was dead, stuck with so many wounds that his body would've been unidentifiable if she hadn't seen the immediate aftermath of the carnage. Arthur Guthrie had been so loving. Never deserving of the grisly death that had befallen him.

There were times when she would come home from school with various bumps and bruises. Students bumping her shoulders in the hallways or targeting her during dodgeball matches. It seemed to happen at least once a week, when she would hop off the school bus and rush into her father's arms. He had been stronger then, more rigid. His hugs had been like a weighted blanket, warm and heavy. He would kiss her forehead and say, "I know what'll cheer you up."

What had cheered her up every time—without fail—was a trip to the custard shop down the street. It got to the point where her father would order for her, and she'd be greeted with her usual. She'd wipe tears from her eyes and dig into that vanilla custard with rainbow sprinkles and Oreo chunks as her father would watch with the biggest smile on his face.

The world had been brighter then, more colorful. The blue above the clouds was so untainted by age. The trees swayed to the rhythm of life. All was good in the world until she entered high school.

There was always something off about Markie Smith. The way his eyes would dart around as he walked in a perfectly straight line. The way his smile petered out toward the edges. The way he would return from summer breaks a few inches taller and with ten more pounds of muscle mass. By his junior year, he was basically unrecognizable. A spitting image of his father, Mark, who owned the paper mill on Mulholland Avenue. Handsome, dashing, but a little off-putting. When his eyes would finally stay still, they were hollow pits. No life behind those pupils, just a hunger. A need to… to do what?

That question and many others had lingered in the minds of everyone who knew him. Why was the Smith boy like that? What is he so nervous about? Is he watching me? No, look over there! That perv's *definitely* fucking staring at me.

It wasn't Mark Smith staring at her, but it was Uncle Drew. He had just been released from prison three months ago after serving a sentence brought about by his debilitating porn addiction. Ashley didn't want to think about the specifics of his case; it was bad enough watching her father's coffin being lowered six feet under. A wave of every emotion under the hot sun struck her like an airplane on the tarmac. The thought of laying herself to the runway and waiting for the plane to squish her into meaty chunks crossed her mind, but only briefly. Before she could sob for the first time that day, Ashley breathed through her nose, held all her air in her lungs until they were ready to burst, and breathed out.

There was no eulogy at the wake because Ashley didn't want to speak in front of her extended family. They didn't deserve her words, and they sure as hell didn't care for the deceased. Generations upon generations of Guthries came to the wake with dry faces and dinner plans afterward that made them rush through the general proceedings. There were at least 100 visitors, both family and local friends, but only fifteen came for the burial.

The cemetery was eerily quiet. Her father had requested no music at both the wake and the funeral itself. He was never the type of man to put on a record or CD while he did his business around the house. He preferred the quiet until his later years, reminiscing about everything from farmers' salaries to Ashley's days at school to what he was going to cook for dinner tonight. Her mother, dying so young, left a gaping void in the Guthrie house, but Arthur had persevered. He carried on with grace and dignity, and Ashley eventually came to appreciate that. She wouldn't be in the position she was without him.

But that's what made the whole situation so unfair. Arthur Guthrie was a good man. Sure, he became a bit grumpier as the claws of old age dug their nails into his psyche, but he was still the same proper family man deep inside. Her trip to see him was one she'd been planning on for a while. She finally had a week off from work in D.C., and he had been ecstatic when she called him and told him the news.

"*Oh, sweetheart, that's wonderful!*" her father had said.

"I'll have to spend two days traveling there and back, but that leaves five days for us to spend together. Does that sound okay?"

"*Okay? Honey, I've been seeing you on the television for too long. Of course it's okay for you to come home. I'll whip up some sweet potato pie for when you get here. I may be a bit rusty, but your mother's recipe isn't.*"

"That's okay, Dad. You don't have to."

"No. I need to."

After laying a bouquet of red and white chrysanthemums atop the new soil, Ashley kissed her fingers and laid them on the headstone. "He's with you again, Mom," she whispered. "Save me a spot."

She accepted hugs from whoever offered, being sure to keep the ensuing small talk to a minimum. Uncle Drew was the last to come in for one, but Ashley stepped back with a pained grin. He dropped his arms and went to his car without a word.

As for Ashley, she thanked the cemetery workers and stepped into her car. The air was hot and humid in the cabin. She was sweating through the folds of her black suit. She unpinned the flower from his left breast pocket and chucked it at the dashboard with a bellowing scream. She leaned her head on the steaming steering wheel and started the engine. The A/C kicked in, drying any tears that attempted to escape her eyes.

She entered an address into her phone's GPS and started her drive to Little Rock Memorial Hospital without taking another look at her parents' graves.

CHAPTER 3

★ ★ ★

Mark Smith clung to consciousness by a weak thread.

He'd spent the entire week after the crash in and out of a comatose state. He would wake from his dreamless sleep, peer around at the sterile hospital room, feel something pinch his arm, then go back to sleep. His brain wasn't working hard enough to count how many times this happened. But when he was finally well enough to use his five senses, he guessed around twenty.

Conscious and alert, he took in the room with unblurred vision. A teal curtain separated him from the rest of the room. A heartbeat monitor beeped to his left. An IV tube slithered from the crook of his elbow up to a bag of clear liquid on a thin, metal pole. The air conditioning made him feel as if he'd been dropped by a helicopter to the middle of Antarctica. Mark shivered, vaguely aware that underneath the blanket, he was wearing nothing but a paper gown. He wanted to itch his balls so bad but thought better of it. For all the killing he'd done, Mark didn't want to find out what a hypodermic needle felt like if the tip snapped and became lodged in his flesh.

A nurse trotted in holding a clipboard and pen. She glanced at Mark, started to turn away, and halted. Turning back to him, her mouth dropped into a faint smile. "Good morning, Mr. Smith," she said coolly. "Can you hear me alright?"

Mark nodded.

"Excellent!"

She performed an arduous physical examination on him, testing his eyes, reflexes, and the like. He felt a burdened sense of rage because her hospital wear was covering her cleavage. Better yet, it covered everything. Not a single distinct curve could be identified. A shame.

The nurse jotted something down on the clipboard, gave Mark another half-hearted smile, then vanished behind the curtain.

Mark lay back and stared at the paneled ceiling. He heard mumbled voices in the hall, a female and male chatting about something unimportant like the adults in those old Peanuts cartoons. *Wah wah wah, wah WAH,* Mark thought with a chuckle that produced a faint ache in his shoulder.

A doctor came in. Mark knew it was a doctor because he was a man. He walked around the bed and pulled up an empty visitors' chair. "Hello, Mr. Smith," he said with that same feigned grin the nurse had worn. "How're you feeling? You've been out for quite a while."

"I…" Mark hated how scratchy his throat felt, but he pushed on. "I feel fine. Where am I?"

"Little Rock Memorial Hospital. Do you remember anything about the traffic accident that brought you here?"

"I remember getting flipped upside down. I hit my head pretty good."

"Yes, alright. Well, my name's Dr. Connors. It's nice to finally meet you awake." The doctor offered a hand, to which Mark shrugged. Connors' brows furrowed as his hand slid away from view. "You *are* right. You hit your head pretty good. You then hit your head *again* when you fainted outside the car. We diagnosed you with a simple concussion. You also suffered some minor scratches and a bruised collarbone from the initial impact."

"How's the car?"

"I'm not a mechanic."

Their conversation continued until Connors looked visibly annoyed and left without another word.

★ ★ ★

Ashley made her way past reception by convincing the person at the desk she was a family friend of Mark. She was fully aware that friends of the family did not count for visitation in most cases, but the receptionist wasn't.

She took the elevator to the fourth floor. When she exited, she was greeted by a flock of police officers. A nurse who looked like she had much better things to do leaned on an empty gurney and watched the cops' holstered guns like a hawk. Ashley sighed lightly and walked toward the group. Above them hung a sign reading: "Intensive Care Unit."

"Excuse me, miss," one officer said, stretching his hand toward her. "Please step away."

"Can I ask why?"

"We're here on very special business," another officer interjected. "So, for your safety, we advise you to back up and let us handle the situation."

Ashley rolled her eyes and reached into her purse. The two officers twitched at what they assumed would either be lipgloss or a pipe bomb. One had his hand over his holster, the nurse on the gurney ready to scream. Ashley instead held up her identification papers, to which the cops relaxed. "I need to see the person you'll be apprehending. It's important."

The first officer chuckled while the second blushed and turned away. "Appr—? Sorry for the confusion, congresswoman," the first one said. "Right this way."

The group of blue uniforms parted like the Red Sea as the first officer guided Ashley through the badged crowd and into the ICU.

"He'll be in the last unit by the window on your left."

Ashley nodded and proceeded. She didn't like how her funeral heels clacked against the white tile, how the sound echoed like rocks tumbling in a quarry. There were multiple patients in different states of duress behind each curtain. An old man breathing through a ventilator. A mother holding her husband's shoulder as her children watched her puked into a container. A teenage girl with all her limbs except a stub of an arm wrapped in swathes of bandages. Ashley gave the girl an empathetic smile, and was pleased to receive one back.

Ashley came upon the final curtain and pulled it so hard it almost came off the rod holding it up. Mark Smith lay in the hospital bed with his eyes closed. "I don't need anything, thank you," he mumbled. Well, at least he was awake.

"I'm not your nurse, Mark," Ashley said.

Mark opened his eyes and lifted his brows. There was barely a wrinkle in his forehead to signal any surprise.

"Oh! Ashley, right?"

"Yes, that's my name, thanks."

"What're you doing here? I thought you'd still be back in Bernard all sad about your father. Speaking of, how was the funeral? Or was he one of those people who would rather be cremated?"

"People can have funerals even if they're cremated." Ashley scoffed. "You'd think someone in your line of work would know how funerals operated."

"I don't attend. I just cause them."

"That you do."

Ashley pushed her hair over her shoulder and sat on the bed, being sure to apply pressure to Mark's leg underneath her ass. She hoped the fucker's leg was broken under there. It'd only be a fraction of the pain he inflicted on her father, but any amount was worth it to her. He didn't understand the gravity of his actions, but she could nudge him in the right direction. She just needed to nudge him there.

"The funeral went well," she began. "Everyone was nice and sad about Arthur's passing. Just how you wanted, correct?"

"I didn't want *him* to be nice and sad. Didn't you pick up on that? I put him out of his misery like you put down a dog whose kidneys are failing. It's the same principle."

Ashley felt a fire growing in her belly. Her eye twitched before she continued.

"It's not, Mark. I need you to understand that what you've been doing for the past ten years hasn't gone unnoticed. What you're doing—without consequence, I should add—is inherently wrong. No, it's worse than wrong. It's downright evil. Don't you get it? Murdering people in cold blood doesn't solve the world's problems. If someone is truly hopeless, the best we can do is rehabilitate them."

The words over two syllables didn't seem to be registering in Mark's head, so she tried dumbing it down even further. *Talk to him like Dad would to you when you were five*, she thought to herself. *If it got through to me before I gained a conscience, it'll get through to this goddamn idiot.*

"How many people have you killed?" she asked.

"A little over 200," Mark said without a moment's hesitation. "Maybe 250."

"And how many of those people did you save?"

Mark scoffed. "All of them."

"Right. And where are they now?"

"I don't understand."

"Where do these people go after they die?"

Ashley leaned closer, her spider necklace dangling from her dress shirt. She could smell the rot of his teeth, presumably unbrushed for the past week while he was penned up in this hospital. She wanted to puke—both from the funeral and the knowledge of what this man has done—but she persisted.

"Where did *you* take them?"

"A better place, I suppose," Mark shrugged. "What're you getting at?"

"How do you know?"

"I guess I just believe that's where they go. No more suffering, no more pain."

"Except for the pain you give them right before they leave."

"Exactly."

Ashley slapped him. His heartrate monitor beeped faster, either from fear or arousal. She had seen him staring at her tits again while she reprimanded him. She hoped he didn't think he could hide that from her. She had enough trouble with her coworkers ogling her breasts. The last thing she wanted was to add a soon-to-be convicted serial killer to that last.

Footsteps clattered from behind. A sneer graced Ashley's face. The cops were coming in. Finally, this freak would receive justice. In a country as dire as the United States of America, true and swift justice was still possible. She got up from the hospital bed and dusted herself off before being overwhelmed by a camera crew.

* * *

"You fucking queer-ass faggot bitch!"

Abel Watterson ripped the headphones from his ears and chucked them to the floor. He was convinced the person he was fighting against online was hacking. You can't just punch through blocks like that and still deal damage. Just another fucking awful loser who had to resort to cheating to gain… what? More experience points? The game didn't even have level progression based on XP. Really, winning matches didn't give you anything substantial.

Abel looked at the remains of his latest headset on the floor. Cracked neon green plastic mixed with soft felt and a tangle of rubber cords. He'd just have to ask his mom for another set. Contented with that idea, Abel rose from his desk chair and headed upstairs.

"Mom?"

The kitchen was empty. He poured himself a tall glass of Sprite, left the rest of the bottle out to go flat, and walked to the living room.

His mom sat on the leather couch watching the news. Ignoring the latest story of a rescue dog being saved from a pound in Little Rock, Abel leaned behind her and tapped her shoulder until she turned.

"What, Abel?"

"I might need a new headset."

"Again?" She scowled at him, her angry wrinkles deeper than ever. "What did I tell you the last time you asked me to buy you those headphones?"

"Not to break them?"

"Yes! So I'll give you another chance to ask your question."

Abel perused around the couch and sat a comfortable distance from his mother. The unmistakeable scent of tobacco was embedded in the cushions. He set his glass down on the coffee table and clasped his hands together.

"Please, Mom," he begged. "It'll be the last time, I swear."

"Oh! You swear?"

Before he could say yes, she was already laughing up a storm.

"Just like you swore to turn in those college applications when I asked?"

"Mom, that's different."

"No, Abel! It's not. Arguably I think their the most important thing you *should* be thinking about right now. How many times have I told you to make something out of yourself? Oh, it doesn't matter. As long as *I* comply and let you freeload in this house, it doesn't matter, right?"

Abel had graduated from high school just about two years ago. Since then, he had been promoted to a managerial position at the Circle K down by the highway. Well... he *had* been. After a single failed health inspection, Abel was promptly fired. That was a year and eleven months ago.

He tried his hardest to please his mom, but no matter what Abel did, it was never enough. Surely his presence would be enough for the woman who literally birthed him twenty years ago? Wouldn't most middle-aged mothers be ecstatic to keep their children at home forever. Abel undoubtedly thought so. But here was good ol' Linda Watterson sitting across the couch from him, hounding him once again for something he had no control over. All he wanted was for her to order another headset off Amazon. Literally two clicks and *BOOM*, it would appear on their doorstep.

Every conversation after high school devolved into this. The same innocent start always turned for the worse, inviting the accusations of Abel being a lazy fuck, a freeloader. You're just like your father. Why can't you be more like your sister? You should have applied to Harvard; they always take a few retards for diversity's sake.

"I'm sorry," Abel said. It was all he could muster.

"That's good, sweetie."

An empty acceptance, same as ever.

The commercial break wrapped up and it was right back to the news. Abel didn't get why older people were so glued to the news. There was nothing interesting to watch on those stations. The same, tired stories about local heroes and stock prices dropping and political decisions that made little to no sense.

"Our top story of the day comes from the town of Bernard right here in Arkansas," said the heavily-botoxed male anchor. "We take our coverage to Mandy Miller for the scoop."

A blue graphic slid over the screen and revealed a reporter who looked as if she'd been caught in a tornado before clocking in. Her bleach-blonde hair hung in wisps from her scalp, her eyes wide with fanaticism.

"Thank you, Brad," said Mandy as she and her cameraman weaved through a throng of cops. "We're here at Little Rock Memorial Hospital for an exclusive interview with a *very* special patient who has just come to from a week-long coma."

Abel leaned forward in his seat. Mark hadn't been responding to any of his texts all week after that crash. Could he be…?

"Hello, Mr. Smith," Mandy said, shoving the microphone into a hospital patient's face. Abel immediately recognized that glorious face. His mom watched his wonderment with disgust. "Are you aware of how much trouble you've caused?"

* * *

"I would guess a lot," Mark said, shielding his sore eyes from the beaming camera flash.

There was the reporter (who looked worse for wear, to put it lightly), the cameraman (a scrawny intern with a hunched back only rivaled by Quasimodo), and a photographer snapping pictures from behind the two pests. *No*, Mark thought with a smirk, *they aren't pests. They're fans. My fans.*

"You could say that again," the reporter said with a forced chuckle. "What all have you heard about your case?"

Was this a set-up? With the curtain finally drawn, Mark could see police officers crowding around the doorframe some yards away, all their hands either hung in their pockets or hovering over their service pistols. He would hate to see a decade of good-hearted civility go down the drain with a tumultuous arrest. But being arrested on live television? Mark could work with that.

"I'm not sure I've heard," he said. "I've been sleeping for the past week, if you weren't aware."

"Oh, we're *well* aware, Mr. Smith," the reporter nodded. "Everyone's been waiting for your input on the situation with bated breath. But since you aren't aware, now would be the best time to fill in anyone at home who is just as confused."

Mark was more enamored by the reporter's frizzy hair than her incoming exposition dump, but he couldn't help but listen with a dumb grin splashed across his lips.

"One week ago, on July 11, 2028, an alleged criminal suspect going by Andre Williams fled the scene of his investigation," the reporter stated directly to the camera. "A recreational marijuana farm was found within his residence, a farm that yielded approximately 25 kilograms. That's more than *20 times more* than the chargeable possession of four ounces. Luckily, this brave gentleman before me attempted to stop the suspect by blocking him with his own vehicle, an act that landed him in a hospital bed for seven days due to the physical trauma."

"What happened to Williams?" Mark asked.

"He's at the state jail here in Little Rock, silly! Where else would he be?"

She had a point there. Mark was still a bit groggy from the medicine.

"Now that you're caught up," the reporter continued, "please share with us your experience as a local, small-town hero."

Hero.

It was a loaded ask, talking about himself in such a positive light. Mark wasn't accustomed to the moniker of "hero." It didn't roll off the tongue as naturally as *hullabaloo* or *flabbergasted* or *razzmatazz*. That word, though, felt good. There was an aura to it that was indescribable, a feeling of grandeur, of grace, of power. He'd never dare see himself as a villain no matter how many people like Ashley Guthrie would want otherwise. They were wrong, plain as that.

Despite that, he thought it would be best not to mention his frequent murders. Something deep within him felt it more professional to disregard all that. Hundreds—maybe thousands—of eyes watching him as he lay in a hospital bed. An apparent hero who helped stop a drug dealer from evading the law. Time to continue keeping up appearances, even for just a little while longer.

"I don't want to brag," Mark bragged, "but my father always said I had the smarts of a thousand men combined. When I was driving down that road, I wasn't thinking about stopping a criminal dead in his tracks. No." Pause from dramatic effect. 3… 2… 1… *Perfect.* "I was rushing home to help my poor, old neighbor

Mrs. Carmichael up the stairs to her apartment. I always make sure to get there right after work to see her up."

A mingling of *"Awws"* came from the hallway. A tougher look-ing police officer slapped the weakest one he could find, and the rest of them shut up quickly after. The reporter attempted to straighten her frizzy hair off camera before the cameraman piv-oted back to her.

"That's a beautifully sweet sentiment," she said. "The people of Bernard must think you're a saint!"

"Some would say that, I guess," said Mark, smirking.

"But in that moment—when Williams' car slammed into yours—did you think yourself a martyr?"

"Not in the slightest."

"Very humble," the reporter said as an aside to the audience.

"I just hope Williams is alright."

★ ★ ★

Ashley couldn't believe what she was seeing, let alone what she was *hearing*.

No doubt the new station's fact checkers would confirm that the Mrs. Carmichael he had mentioned had been dead for three months. She had been close friends with Ashley's father, being sure to bring a tray of warm brownies to the Guthrie residence every week or so. That all went down the drain when her mangled body had been found lodged underneath the arm of an oil rig some five miles out of town with a penny stuck in both her caved-in eye sockets. "Another case of the Hillside Butcher," as Arthur had mentioned it. "I sure hope the police catch that sick fuck before he gets even more of us. It's gotta be hundreds now."

It *was* hundreds now. Over *two* hundred if Mark Smith's words were to be believed. But for all the times Arthur Guthrie had been correct in his long life, he was wrong about one thing: Hoping the police would catch the Hillside Butcher before he killed more people was a foolish wish. They weren't going to do anything about it. Even Little Rock's police force wasn't in this hospital to arrest the sick fuck. They were here to celebrate a local legend in the making. A man who "bravely" sacrificed his Chevy Malibu to stop an alleged criminal.

And that was just it. Andre Williams was most definitely tending to a marijuana farm inside his apartment. That much was clear. His actions were illegal under the laws of the state of Arkansas. However, his crimes were child's play compared to the crimes of one Mark Smith. Ashley wished she'd been recording their little talk before the reporter barged in. Audio evidence would be the best way to get Mark convicted and sent behind bars. The town of Bernard had had enough, and the world didn't need him in it.

The reporter carried on the interview with annoying vigor. "As I stated previously, Andre Williams is being held in detainment until a trial date it set," she said. "Is there anything you'd like to say to the people who may be watching back at home?"

"I'd like to say that I love every last one of you," Mark said, stealing the microphone from the reporter. "You've always been good to me, and I'll continue to be good to you. I'll see you all soon."

With that, the interview was over. The camera's flash dimmed, and the reporter snatched her mic back from Mark's red hands. He winked at her and her face flushed. Ashley felt a thin stream of bile rise in her throat. There was no way someone as vile and depraved as Mark would be able to sink his claws into anyone. But also, this reporter had the aura of someone who didn't have proper brain activity, her only directive being to look pretty for the camera and say her lines. Anyone with Mark's background could manipulate someone like that; shallow and willing.

Ashley left the hospital and hopped into her car, started the engine, and began her arduous drive back to the East Coast.

★ ★ ★

I love every last one of you…

Those seven words repeated over and over again in Abel's head. *That* was the Mark he knew, that beautiful, charismatic, charming man who had always been there for him. However, for how long Abel had known the man, he had never heard him say "I love you" before. Not to him, especially.

Abel had taken it as a sign that Mark was unable to express his feelings in a succinct manner. Abel was the same way. Throughout high school, he always had a tough time talking to his peers. Maybe it had to do with his looks, maybe it had to do with his bug obsession. Through it all, though, there was a constant: Abel didn't know how to talk to people. Sure, he could smile and wave and say the rare "Hello," but that would be the most he could muster at a single time.

It was different online. Using voice chat on *Valorant* and *Counter-Strike* and *Overwatch* and *Warzone* gave him the freedom to speak his mind without sets of human eyes monitoring his every movement. He could call someone a faggot without being punished for it. He could fantasize bombings and shootings and all the other fun things without actually doing it. Abel could admit he was a bit strange, but he was also a follower of the law.

Well, mostly.

"Turn this shit off," his mother said, lighting another cigarette. "I can't believe they'd let that Smith boy on the news without a background check."

"What do you mean?" Abel asked.

She took a drag and blew the smoke into his face.

"Let's just say I don't want you to ever be near him," she said, her eyes narrowing. "He's always been trouble. I don't want his influence to rub off on you."

"I don't even know who that was."

"You don't have to lie. You do that enough as is."

His mother rose from the couch and held her hip so it wouldn't pop out of its socket again. Before she could disappear into her bedroom, she turned, pointed the lit cigarette at Abel, and added, "Apply to more damn colleges, please. Watching people like *that* make it in life by doing nothing valuable makes me sick. And also, I don't want you meeting up with that Eddie freak this week. He's from California for Christ's sake. You can be better than that, Abel."

She shut the door, leaving Abel alone in the living room with nothing but his thoughts and a lone ninety-nine cent lighter. He sipped his Sprite and toyed with the little plastic lighter. Dazzling specks flew as he pushed down the spark wheel. A small flame grew from its orifice.

Abel remembered the week before his high school biology class was to dissect frogs. He had never been more excited for anything in his life. He could hardly contain himself thinking about all the ways he'd poke and prod the fortunate animal. He imagined how the eyes would burst as he plunged a needle into the socket, how the leg muscles would tear as he removed them from their hips, how their intestines would smell when held at just the right angle from his nostrils. A week before the big day, Abel and Macy, his unwilling group partner for the quarter, were working on a vocabulary worksheet about the parts of the body. Macy's dad was a doctor, so all the words came naturally to her.

While she had busied herself with filling out all the blank spots on the paper, Abel was lost in his thoughts, as he was wont to do. Limbs and bone and tissue floated around in his head. His toes curled at the thought of digging his scalpel into that frog.

He couldn't wait. No, that was too long. Seven days? You've gotta be shitting me. Abel had to do it now.

With as much sanity as Abel Watterson's brain could comprehend, he had driven his sharpened pencil into his group partner's neck. She hadn't screamed at first. The immediate adrenaline from the shock had hidden the pain for just a brief time. Macy was in the middle of writing "veins" in a blank space before her own pencil fell and she began to scream.

Abel wouldn't let go of the pencil. It was his tool of power, his staff of destruction. He had the power to harm, to maim. He removed the pencil from Macy's neck. A river of scarlet poured from the hole like the brownish water from the water fountain just outside the classroom.

"MIH-UH AR-EYE-CULL!" Macy choked.

Mr. Carmichael's eyes went wide as he jumped over his desk, ungraded papers flying, and cupped his hand around Macy's gaping neck wound.

The teacher shouted something at Abel, but he hadn't heard. Blood had splattered all over his lap. It seeped into his jeans as his bladder released with pure euphoria. The warmth of both her blood and his piss made him feel as if he were soaring through the clouds. The world around him was a blur. He raised the pencil again and jammed it into Mr. Carmichael's hand, piercing straight through the palm and reentering Macy's new neck hole.

I love every last one of you...

It hadn't been his mother that bailed him out of the local jail. It was a rich benefactor who went by the name Mark Smith. Abel had been sure the name was some sort of alias, something so bland and stupid as to easily drop off the law's radar without anyone noticing. But no, that was his name. And Abel liked that a lot.

I love… you…

Now Abel reminisced about that violent day, soiling his pants on the dirty couch in his mother's home just as he did back then in that biology classroom, soaked in a pretty girl's blood. He wasn't going to let Mark down. Not ever. Because there was one thing Mark had told him on that day outside Bernard City Jail, one thing that had stayed with him ever since.

"You have spirit, kid," Mark said. "I could use someone like you."

CHAPTER 4

★ ★ ★

Dr. Connors came into the room immediately after the reporter and her cameraman lackey shuffled out. He handed Mark a clipboard and a pen with shaking, wrinkled hands and asked him to sign the bottom of the wordy paper. "We've cleared your physical report," the doctor stated without looking Mark directly in the eye. "You're free to leave."

"That's such a relief, doc," Mark said. "Thank you."

Dr. Connors ignored the gratitude and bent down to unplug the heart monitor. A different nurse came in and hastily removed the IV tubes from Mark's arms. The two of them were as silent as a rock garden. They were simply back to get Mark out of the hospital and reset the room in a way that didn't hint that he had been there in the first place.

With the final needle out of the crook of his elbow, Mark rose from the bed and planted his bare feet on the ground for the first time in seven days. There was a loose wobble in his knees that subsided before he could register the imbalance. The nurse didn't come to help in case he had fallen; she straightened out the thin blanket and fluffed the pillow that had about half its feathers missing. Dr. Connors stood upright with his hand outstretched. Mark went in for a handshake, to which the doctor lightly slapped his hand away. He pointed to the clipboard, Mark signed his name, handed it to the doctor, and walked out of the room.

Another nurse caught up to Mark reminding him to pick up his clean clothes before he left. Mark hadn't noticed he was still wearing the hospital's provided paper gown, but it made more sense that his testicles were swinging back and forth with a lot more velocity than usual.

Once he was dressed in his tight-fitting tee and dark brown khakis, he left Little Rock Memorial Hospital and was greeted with the familiar humid warmth of Arkansas summer. The cloudless day gave him a slight headache. He squinted and spotted a woman in a formal suit standing in the parking lot.

The news reporter was screaming unintelligible nonsense at her cameraman. Her hair blew in the wind, the frizziness reminding Mark of a plasma ball with its lightning tendrils spewing in all directions.

He walked across the asphalt, the reporter's words growing louder and more distinct with every step.

She screamed a series of increasingly dire threats:

"Why couldn't you have woken me up sooner?"

"I didn't have enough time to get ready before this!"

"You *ruined* my big break!"

"This was *my* story and you fucked it all up!"

"I hope they fire you."

"I hope you lose your fiancée and house and kid and everything else you love. You ruined my life, so it's the least you deserve."

Only a few yards away now, Mark put up both his hands and said, "Whoa whoa whoa. What's going on here?"

The cameraman hid his eyes under his blue flat-brim cap and continued packing his lenses into a sleek black bag. The reporter whipped around, straightened her hair with clawed fingers, and giggled innocently.

"There's our local hero!" she laughed as if rage wasn't in her vocabulary.

"Yeah, that's me," Mark guessed. "You know, I don't have my car with me right now. The hospital discharged me without offering transportation. Do you think you could call a cab or something for me? I don't have my—"

"Oh, don't worry," the reporter said, waving her hand. "We're actually on our way to Gum Springs to report on some stupid gas station explosion. You could hitch a ride with us."

"Do I need to pay a fare?" Mark jokingly asked, knowing money wasn't an issue for him.

The reporter laughed. It was the forced chuckle you would hear from a parent at the Thanksgiving dinner table after their geriatric father says something offhandedly racist. She nudged a wisp of her hair over her ear and said, "You're just something, Mr. Smith."

"Mark is fine."

"Mark, then. Our ride is your ride."

The cameraman sighed and lifted himself into the news van's driver's seat, slamming the glossy black door behind him as the engine started. The reporter opened the sliding back door and motioned for Mark to enter. He did gladly and was greeted by the largest array of technology he had ever seen localized inside one vehicle. An entire corner of the hollowed-out van was adorned with monitors and thousands of flashing buttons that Mark didn't know the uses for. They were sitting upon desks with no chairs accompanying them. Mark was surprised by the sheer amount of clutter in such a small space. There was a fire extinguisher, three backpacks, crumpled candy wrappers, and hundreds of folders stacked on the floor filled to the brim with discarded documents and the latest scoops.

The reporter climbed in and slid the door shut. The interior didn't seem to lose any light now that they were cut off from the outside world, save for the small aperture dividing the driver's seat from the back of the van. The reporter guided Mark to two chairs sat directly opposite of each other. Mark climbed in and buckled the seatbelt, and the reporter did the same. She slapped the wall twice, and Mark felt the weight of the van lurching forward from the parking lot toward Bernard, Arkansas.

"Don't mind Justin," she said. "He's a bit of a fucking idiot."

"I don't really mind," Mark said. He couldn't stop surveying everything inside the van. There was a boom mic in the corner, a case of Ozarka wattle bottles, and even more stacks of useless folders. "He seems like he just wants to do his job."

She scoffed. "If only he was good at it. He always makes me look white as a ghost with that bright fucking flash."

"I noticed."

"I'm sure you did, Mark."

"I don't think I caught your name."

"It's Mandy. Short for Amanda, but my dad named me after his mom, and I'm not a fan of either of them. So just call me Mandy."

"Noted."

Mark was taken aback by how miserable this woman came across as. Her entire life seemed to revolve around nothing but running around capturing as many newsworthy moments as possible. Justin the cameraman didn't seem to be too terrible at his job, but Mark decided to continue humoring Mandy. Agreeing with people was the best way to make them lower their guard. It was the easiest trick for him to pull when scouting for people at Walmart. No reason why it wouldn't work in any general situation.

"Do you hate your boss?" Mark asked.

"I don't really hate anyone," said Mandy. "Why are you going after my boss? Do you know Reynold?"

"No."

"Then why did you ask?"

"Everyone hates their bosses," Mark said, flashing a smile. "I was just wondering if you were like everyone else."

"Well, I guess I'm *not* like everyone else. I quite like my boss, and he quite likes me."

"Is that so?" Mark crossed his arms and leaned back in his chair. To keep Mandy talking, he needed to pretend to care about her. There was a smidgen of care in his heart. Mark cared deeply about everyone in his life, even the people who weren't here anymore. He was doing all the dearly departed a favor, but he found it hard to care for them outside of that fundamental love buried in his chest. Something always held him back, tugging at him with the might of a boa constrictor tying itself around him and squeezing the air from his lungs. Suffocating, yet unfeeling. That's what bothered Mark. He put his reputation on the line to see that everyone was happy, but why did he ache?

"Yes," Mandy said. "I only started at the station three months ago. But Reynold promised that he'd give me a promotion if I stayed on top of things. I think that's pretty reasonable, don't you think?"

Mark nodded and said, "You know my dad owned a wood processing plant just outside Bernard?"

"Oh really?"

"Yes. They would pump trees through the processors and cut them down into lumber for houses and paper for… well, whatever all *that* is over there."

Mark waved a hand over the amalgam of folders lining the van walls. Justin hit a pothole and the cabin jolted for a second before continuing its incessant hum down Interstate 30. "Sometimes he'd let me come by and watch the employees work. He'd sit me down in his little office that had a window overseeing the whole operation. Sometimes I would get bored and just draw on blank sheets of paper from his office printer, but other times I'd prop the chair up by that little window and watch the workers do their thing. And I'll tell you, they were no slouches. Always at the top of their game. Operating small cranes and lifts, adjusting the logs for trimming, pouring bleach into vats so that the paper would come out as pristine and white as possible. It was like watching ants steal some of your crumbs and hurry them back to their hill. It was all so meticulous."

"Now why didn't you mention any of this in the interview?" Mandy asked. "It would have been nice to here some more personal stories other than that Black kid getting arrested."

"Sorry. But there was this one day—"

"You know they're going to charge him with everything they got, right?" Mandy asked. "Sorry to bring the accident up, but that Williams is going to be locked up for a long time. He had a wife and two little daughters. I got to talk to them a little bit yesterday. They're absolutely torn up."

"I'm sorry to hear that. They must be good people."

"Some of the best," Mandy said. With a long pause, she continued, "They don't deserve to have Andre taken away."

"He was a drug dealer," Mark said matter-of-factly. "That's serious in this state."

"Not as serious as murder."

Mark took a second to process that offhanded comment. The unkempt news reporter with the cute nose and blushing cheeks seemingly vanished from across the room. Sitting in her chair was someone with a vendetta, not a hopelessly adoring fan who happened to also be a journalist. The wideness of her eyes faded as they morphed into hollow slits. Mark felt a small tickle at the nape of his neck. Had Justin turned off the air conditioning? His pits were beginning to sweat.

"Why so sad, Mark?" asked Mandy. "Something bothering you?"

"I just wasn't expecting you to get so serious all of a sudden," Mark said with a desperate chuckle.

"I'm not like everyone else, like you said. I'm serious about my work, but I'm more serious about what's right."

"I am, too."

"Right, Mark. Of course." Mandy slapped her forehead and shouted a "duh!"

"I'm serious."

"That's what they all say, Mark. You're so naive, you know that? There's a lot I could say to you right now, but I'll keep it brief: You're the Hillside Butcher, aren't you?"

How did she know? Who *was* this woman and how could she be so smart? The only people who knew were the people he had killed… and Ashley Guthrie. Had she let slip his secret before the interview? No, there wouldn't have been enough time. So how did Mandy—this prim and proper news rat fresh out of college and with seemingly endless amounts of undeserved job opportunities—figure it out?

"I don't know who that is," Mark said.

"Could it be a split personality we're dealing with?"

"No."

"But it *is* you, Mark. There's evidence to prove that. There's even evidence proving you didn't intentionally stop Andre Williams from evading the police. Residential surveillance cameras for multiple blocks caught you running stop signs. You weren't going to stop until you crashed into something, but I guess you were just lucky enough to get run *into* instead. Where were you heading, Mr. Butcher? *That's* the story I want."

Deny deny deny, his father had parroted for years, especially after Mark's mother had died. Mark wanted to deny these claims, he really did. But he was still a little woozy from the pain medication, and the words in his head didn't necessarily translate well to his tongue.

"I was heading to my apartment," he said, lowering his head. "I was going to plan my next kill. There was a cashier who looked down in the dumps. Near suicidal. I was going to look him up on Facebook and plan accordingly. That was until I got into the accident. Really put a damper on my plans."

"And how many times have you committed murder?"

"Hundreds."

Mandy didn't gasp. That was good. Maybe there was a bit of understanding left in that small lady brain of hers. She should've known better than to stick her nose into other people's business. Reporters were just socially acceptable paparazzi, though, so Mark took that thought back. Mandy was a real bitch.

"And you've never been caught?" Mandy asked.

"Not until recently."

The van swayed as Justin veered into the passing lane. Mark noticed the small hole in the wall that looked out into the driver's seat, the vast highway stretching beyond. Justin was tapping the steering wheel with his thumbs as he hummed a noiseless tune.

"Do you feel as if the world is caving in?" asked Mandy. "Do you just wish you could make everything better?"

"Yes."

"Then why don't you? The local media's making you sound like a vigilante. A doer of good. A smalltown superhero who stops the bad guys and lives to tell the tale. I know that all isn't true, but that doesn't matter to everyone. They want to feel warm and safe. If there's one less drug dealer off the street, they'll be happy." She hesitated for a brief second. "But that begs the question: Why hasn't anyone done anything about you?"

Mark knew the answer, so he blurted out: "Because I'm doing the good thing. Fighting the real fight."

"Against what?"

"Suicide."

"Is that right?"

"Yes."

Mandy put a hand to her mouth and snickered. "That's just rich," she said. "I've never heard of a serial killer justifying their actions like this."

"I'm not—"

"But you *are*. A serial killer is someone who kills with a pattern. You tend to kill people you believe to be dangers to themselves, people who you think would contemplate suicide. Then when you finish your business, you stick two pennies in their bodies and leave. This is all common knowledge among local police, Mark. You have to understand that much."

"You're lying."

"You don't even wipe down the crime scenes! Bernard PD has identified you too many times to count, but they do *nothing*. I had to do some digging for a story to find any records linking someone to Bernard's abnormal murder rate, and I found you.

That's only because the police have hidden everything so well. Why?"

"This is the first I'm hearing any of this."

"Are you paying them off? You've been living off your parents' life insurance, right? You have to be paying them. There's no other explanation."

"I'm not," Mark said through gritted teeth.

Mandy unbuckled her seatbelt and lunged at Mark. His seat jolted back with her added weight, which was a lot more than he had expected. He attempted to unlatch himself from the seat, but the reporter slammed her heeled foot on his sandaled one. He groaned as she gathered a clump of his hair in her hand and tugged.

"Then how the fuck are you doing it?" Mandy hissed.

"With an axe!"

"Cute."

Mandy pulled his scalp until he felt some strands tearing from their follicles. The van chugged along the highway without stopping. Mark thought Justin should consider ditching the news gig and focus his efforts on ridesharing.

"I guess I'm just so good they don't bother to stop me," Mark babbled, wincing as the words tumbled out. "I'm doing everyone a favor, aren't I?"

"No, you fucking idiot," Mandy sneered. "What did my brother have to do with your false sense of justice, huh?"

"Your... brother?"

Mandy groaned and let go of his hair.

"You murdered him in the spring of 2023," she said, stepping back. "Chopped him into little pieces and left him to rot in the heat. They found chunks of him in a soybean field."

"There's no way of knowing that was me," Mark said.

"You stuck two pennies in whatever was left of his torso."

Fair enough, Mark thought.

"Why do you deny everything when the facts are plain to see?" Mandy asked. "Why not admit it if you feel what you're doing is right?"

"Because the truth can be scary. I don't want to scare my neighbors."

"Well, you fucked up that opportunity. You've been fucking that up for damn near a decade now."

Mark didn't have to listen to this bitch blabber on and on about things she didn't understand. The whole point of ending people's lives was to do it before they had the chance to do it themselves. Bernard's suicide rate had plummeted since Mark began enacting his civil duty. People like this damn news reporter didn't know anything about anything. The only thing in their skulls wasn't a brain, but a single housefly, zipping and buzzing at the skull walls, tapping away at the bone with nothing but the idea of escape fueling them. They were worthless, these media people. They crawled under your skin with a false sense of comfort before revealing their true selves and bogging you down with "facts and logic." Well, sometimes facts were wrong, and logic was wrong. Mark didn't "allegedly" kill all those people; he *did* kill them. The news twists words to better fit their own self-image.

But Mark could stop it.

He had the power, and it would be a waste to leave it untapped.

Mark unbuckled his seatbelt and leaned forward, his hands clasped on his knees. "You didn't let me finish my story about the paper mill," he said, his tone darker in the digitally lit van interior.

"I'm not sure I want to hear it."

"My father would let me sit in his office and watch the

workers do their jobs. He would tell me all about their personal lives. Their hopes, their dreams. Even their grievances and woes. I mean, why wouldn't he? I was just a boy. Was I going to tell them that their boss knew everything about them? That he hated them all and wished he could fire them and leave their families to starve? No. I never did. He would tell me about how Stephen beat his wife, how Jessica abused diet pills to stay skinny, how Weston sold his kid to a foster home. These were all such miserable people. Every last one. Did I feel bad for them?"

"I would guess no," Mandy said, crossing her arms.

"I *did*, though. That's the kicker. I felt awful for Stephen and Jessica and Weston and Delilah and Roger and Blake and the rest. They were just shuffling their feet through life, living off my father's dime so they could continue being miserable sacks of shit." Mark stood slowly and craned his head down to meet Mandy's. He didn't blink. Blinking would spoil the surprise. "Not unlike you, Mandy. I don't think you quite like where you are in your life. You do a great job covering it up, I'll admit, but you can't hide the truth." Mark went to the window overlooking the highway ahead and slowly slid it shut. The country music on the radio died as the last bit of sunlight drained from the room. "Not from me, any-way."

Mandy had that look of a dog who had just been caught tearing a pillow to shreds. White feathers and cotton strewn about the carpet like Christmas in July. The van jerked to the side. Mark placed his hand on a desktop monitor for support. The young reporter's eyes were wide in fright. She had been dead set on luring Mark into a state of calm before bringing down the hammer.

Only, Mark had the hammer now.

His cards were in play.

"I've already contacted all the police departments surrounding

Bernard," Mandy said as smugness infected her features. "Arkadelphia, Knoxville, Joan, Friendship, Donaldson. All contacted with your records. Once you leave this van, it's over. All those years of senseless murder. Done. How does that make you feel?"

"I feel like you're bluffing."

"And why would I do that, Mark? I'm a journalist. I only care about the truth."

"Oh yeah? The truth?"

Mark couldn't help the wavering of his tone. The prospect of the law finally catching up to him was impossible to ignore. The walls certainly *were* closing in. A hole had ripped in the ozone layer, sucking all the oxygen from Earth to the deep vacuum of space. The lights were going out. His fingers twitched into claws. A vein popped in his temple. No way would he let his fucking cunt ruin all the good he's done. No way.

"The truth is that I love killing," Mark said, walking toward the fire extinguisher hanging on the wall. "I witnessed my first death when I was sitting in my father's office. Stephen the wife beater was aligning logs with the timber chute when his finger got caught on the line. I watched as his body was sucked into that machine inch by inch. First the finger, then his arm, then his torso. The force was so great that his head ripped from his neck as his body was turned into fish chum. It took them weeks to get his meat out of the gears. No one helped him. No one cared. It was beautiful, that fountain of red and gore. Oh, so beautiful. I'll never forget that day."

"You're sick," Mandy spat.

"I can be much worse."

★ ★ ★

Justin Hightower tapped his thumbs on the steering wheel. Garth Brooks played on the radio. The road ahead went on and on without a destination in sight. He turned up the volume, letting the music envelope him, drowning out the sounds of Mark Smith bludgeoning Mandy Miller with a fire extinguisher just five feet behind the driver's seat.

The plan was a bit cobbled together. The news station had received word that the local warrior of justice from Bernard had finally woken from his coma. Mandy had been researching him since the car crash. She dug up so much shit on the guy that Justin simply couldn't believe it at first. Over two hundred people dead because of one guy's lack of boundaries. A kid who had received millions in inheritance funds after his parents died, using that money to stay in his hometown and kill without the risk of getting caught.

The irony of some undeserving, rich White dude getting away with multiple crimes wasn't lost on Justin. He'd helped a number of reporters cover stories about businessmen laying off employees due to budgetary reasons while also giving themselves lofty end-of-year bonuses. He'd seen families torn apart by domestic troubles almost exclusively caused by the husbands. He'd been there on the White House lawn when the president played with the economy like a spoiled brat dribbling a basketball, the stocks going up and down and up and down and up and...

When the call came from Little Rock's main news station, Mandy was raring to go. The story was first come, first serve for the station's reporting body. Mandy felt it was wise to come in looking disheveled and weary. It would make her seem more human, more desirable. After convincing Smith they were on his side, they would wait in the parking lot until he was discharged, which the disgruntled Dr. Connors had said would be immediate due to him wanting the patient out of his hospital as quick as fucking possible.

And so they waited, Mandy putting on a show as Smith exited the hospital. Justin had to admit that her comments hurt a lot, but he knew it was all for the greater good. He chuckled as the large green sign shouting "EXIT 78 CADDO VALLEY" came into view. Justin lowered the radio's volume and exited onto the ramp. Multiple towns' police forces would be waiting in Bernard to make their formal arrest. Complacency was a thing of the past for the quaint town at the center of all this. Mark Smith's terrible life was over.

The news van passed Fat Boys Fine Foods as Justin veered left into the Arkansas wilderness. Backroads twisted and turned through dense trees with gnarled branches, their fingers outstretched like eagles' talons. Justin couldn't help but wonder how an ambulance had managed to rush Smith out of Bernard without flying off the road and plummeting into a ditch.

He reached the town limits. A grandiose sign welcomed him to the township of Bernard, Arkansas. Founded in 1817. The jewel of the Land of Opportunity. Justin had a good laugh at that. A town so backwards it couldn't even bother changing its main welcome sign to fit with the times. Did "The Natural State" mean nothing to these people? All the people who remembered Arkansas' old nickname were probably murdered and buried by now.

The main strip of Bernard was eerily quiet. For a Tuesday afternoon, Justin had expected more young couples rolling newborns in strollers, more children playing hopscotch on the sidewalks, more cars and pickup trucks plowing through Main Street as if it were the interstate. Instead of the usual smalltown hustle and bustle, there was a gaping void of nothing. Everyone was inside.

Or dead, Justin thought.

He turned onto a side road that led toward the police department. He passed pastel-painted homes with green lawns and towering trees. Kids' toys and bikes lay dormant in the yards. Without the people, things were creepy, but Justin thought it would be nice to live someplace like this. You know, without the serial killer on the loose. He and Petra could move out of Little Rock and live in the middle of nowhere. No more traffic, no more worries, no more regrets. It all seemed a bit too nice. He was sure most of the families in Bernard felt the same way he did, living away from the city and all. It's just too bad they ended up here, stuck under the thumb of one Mark Smith.

Justin pulled into the parking lot and scowled. The department was empty. Mandy had made all those calls begging all the police in the area to convene at Bernard PD. There was a special type of criminal being transported there today, and they had a duty as officers of the law to apprehend him.

But there was no one. Not a soul.

He couldn't even tell if there were officers inside the building.

Justin parked the van and felt the low vibration of something rolling in the back. That damn fire extinguisher must've fallen off its hook again. He really needed to complain to his boss to get that fixed. He shut off the engine and hopped out.

"Opening up!" Justin shouted, banging the van twice with a clenched fist.

His heart skipped a beat.

As the door slid open, a gust of something foul singed his nose hairs. An overwhelming stench of metal, like the way your hand smells after holding onto pennies for a few minutes.

The walls were covered in blood, incarnadine and rank. Bits of bone and meat clung to the desktop monitors like wet socks.

The two chairs facing each other were bent from their floor sockets.

Mandy, in her dark gray suit and shining black heels, lay on the floor. Her body was relatively untouched, but her head… oh my God, her *head*. What was there to say? Any semblance of structure was gone. Her skull had been completely run through. Nothing but crimson gore where her brain had once been. An unharmed hazel eye looked at Justin. It was like a white meatball floating alone in a sea of marinara sauce. Wisps of her yellow hair tangled through the carnage like spaghetti.

Smith stood above her, panting like the rabid dog he was. The bottom end of the fire extinguisher was painted with Mandy's insides. Justin wanted to vomit. It was all too much. She had just been alive—his best coworker, his best friend—hamming it up to lure Smith into a false sense of security. And what had it been for? The police weren't here, and she was dead and gone.

The moment Smith locked eyes with him, Justin yelped and turned heel, booking it through the parking lot.

"Don't you think about leaving!" Smith shouted, his voice never diminishing.

An infinity of thoughts bombarded Justin's head. *Mandy. Oh God, Mandy. What did you do? What set him off? You were always so upfront, so blunt. Why couldn't you keep him calm for the whole ride?* And Petra. Petra, his beautiful fiancée, raising their baby boy Tommy in a high-rise apartment in Little Rock. Rocking his crib back and forth until the crying stopped and the kid began to snore. He'd be with them soon. He just needed to get away from…

Justin's foot snagged in a pothole, his ankle snapping as he plummeted face-first into the pavement. He howled in anguish, his throat on fire from the strain. Blood seeped through his white sock, a flowery omen harkening the things to come.

Smith was there, blocking out the sun with his looming silhouette.

"You really thought I'd stop with her?" the Hillside Butcher asked, wielding the fire extinguisher as if it weighed nothing. "You're all miserable, every last one of you media leeches."

"Please, man," Justin cried. "I have a kid. Here, I can show you."

Justin fumbled for his wallet and pulled out a photo with his trembling fingers. Smith stared past him, zoning out from the world. He'd seemed so human lying in that hospital bed. That wasn't the same man Justin saw before him. This was something much worse. Something all too familiar.

Smith laid a foot on Justin's broken ankle. Justin seethed, air bursting between his clenched teeth.

"I care deeply about your kid," Smith said. "I just wouldn't want him to watch his daddy kill himself." He leaned down and jammed the metal handle of the extinguisher into Justin's stomach. "I can do the job for you."

Justin wriggled like an earthworm in the hot sun. His broken foot wouldn't move from the pothole. Smith pushed the handle further and further, twisting with all his might to create a hole of satisfactory size. Justin thought of Tommy with his curly auburn hair and his mother's eyes. He wasn't coming home tonight. He'd accepted that.

Smith removed the handle and inserted the hose. Justin groaned (it was the only thing left he knew how to do) as Smith squeezed the handle and his stomach filled with toxic fumes.

* * *

Mark roared as he felt the cameraman's body fill with gaseous powder. He never saw the violence as the main event, more of a bonus. This bonus, however, was to die for.

He shook the hose, lodging it deeper into the makeshift, fleshy hole. White smoke began to pour from the cameraman's mouth, nostrils, and eye sockets. The man could only wheeze as the powder clogged his lungs and filled his throat.

After a time, the cameraman's entire torso was bulging with the stuff. His shirt ripped at the seams, revealing translucent skin swimming with pink clouds and mist. Mark smiled as more and more gas spilled from the man's mouth. He bared his teeth and howled.

The skin began to tear, revealing ravines of bright red.

Then, when the pressure became too much for the human body to handle, the cameraman popped like a balloon.

Blood shot in all directions, leaving a haze of scarlet in its wake. It coated the concrete, the stray police cars, and the windows of the empty department building. Mark spit some from his mouth and chuckled as he removed the hose and wiped his blood-stained eyes. This is exactly what he had needed. A week spent in the hospital, just rotting away until he was well enough to fuck off. All of that without having killed a single person.

Sat with his reward for a week well fought, Mark reached into his pocket and found his wallet. Oh, what a joy it would be to stick his two cents into the pile of entrails at his feet. The squelch of wet tissue enveloping the coins as he shoved them in. He could barely contain himself. The smile that crept across his face was maniacal but warranted.

There were only a twenty in the wallet's folds. No pennies.

Had the nurses stolen them as a precaution? Was he so well known that they knew his signature?

Mark couldn't stop the hyperventilation once it came. He was out of pennies. How the fuck did he run out of pennies. He had had a roll's worth in his wallet before the crash. *Oh God. Oh my God. Fuck fuck fuck fuck.* Where the fuck were his pennies?

A tomato splattered onto Mark's face, the rank stench of rot seeping into his pores. Angered, he scanned the area for the culprit. The snide jeering of a child caught his attention, but they were gone before he could retaliate.

Instead of admiring his day's work, Mark laid in the moist crater that had once been Justin Hightower, crumpled into the fetal position, and wept.

CHAPTER 5

★ ★ ★

Abel Watterson tugged on the fancy golden pen at the main desk. The bank seemed to have downsized over the years. Back when he was in elementary school, his mom would bring him along while she took money from her savings account. The teller would lean over the desk, give him a smile, and give him a lollipop. Abel always liked the grape-flavored ones.

He was thinking about those purple lollipops as he waited for the same bank teller to come to the front desk. The little metal basket of lollipops was gone. The high ceilings of the past were filled in. Abel couldn't tell if he was just taller, or if they simply lowered the building's roof.

He rang the brass-coated bell again, its *ding* echoing through the vacant hall. He sighed and continued tugging on the pen, its gold chain anchored to the desk. He knew Mr. Quincy was in today; he saw the old man's blue sedan in the parking lot. Abel didn't appreciate being ignored, but he decided to let things be and simply wait. There was no reason to start a ruckus.

The front door swung open, the force nearly sending it off its hinges. Abel whipped around and saw a grisly sight. Mark stomped toward him, blood dripping from his clothes. Abel smiled, but Mark kept that stoic face he so often wore. He came up next to Abel, grunted, and shoved him aside, leaving a red handprint on Abel's gray sweatshirt. Mark leaned over the desk, looked left and right, muttered something under his breath, then proceeded to slam his hand down on the brass bell over and over again.

DING DING DING DING DING DING…

"Alright! Alright! I'm coming!"

The bank teller Mr. Quincy hobbled from his office at the back of the building. He zipped up the fly of his pants and waved his free hand. Abel felt a sense of dread wash over him seeing how old the man looked. The last time he had seen Mr. Quincy, he'd been lively and full of joy, a smile as permanent on his face as a tattoo. Here though, his jet black hair was graying, his posture was more hunched, and that smile was nothing but a memory. He squinted through wire-rimmed glasses and rolled his eyes.

"Another roll of pennies, Smith?" the old man asked.

"As many as you can give me," Mark said, the sentence seeming to scratch his vocal cords.

Mr. Quincy opened his palm. Mark reached into his pocket and presented a twenty-dollar bill, brown from that mix of blood and green cotton. Mr. Quincy snatched the bill and wandered back to where he came from, shutting the door behind him.

"What… What happened to you?" Abel asked.

"Not now, kid," Mark muttered. "I'm sensitive right now."

"Sensitive? *You?* No way, man."

"Do you think I've been found out, Abel?"

Abel looked Mark up and down. His clothes were damp with

blood and gore. He looked so goddamn tired, his eyes sunken with ginormous, lavender bags hanging down from the sockets. No telling how far he walked to get here; Abel didn't hear a car pulling up. Did anyone suspect him of being the Hillside Butcher? As much as Abel idolized him, he couldn't deny that the jig might've been up.

"No, I don't think so," Abel lied. "I think you'll get off scotch-free."

"Scot-free."

"What?"

"It's 'scot-free,'" Mark said, "not scotch. Do they teach you anything in school?"

"I don't go to school."

"Right."

They sat in silence, the only sound coming from the back office where Mr. Quincy deposited hundreds of pennies into small paper sleeves. Tiny metallic clinks mixed with the metallic stink of whoever's blood was glazed over every inch of Mark's body. Abel felt enamored by the scene, a faint rumbling of an erection peaking in his sweatpants. He rubbed a hand over his crotch to tame the beast.

"If you really need to know," Mark blurted, "I smashed some bitch's skull in with a fire extinguisher, then used the same extinguisher to blow someone up like a balloon."

"That's amazing, Mark," Abel said with wonderment in his eyes.

"It was. They were both absolutely miserable sacks of shit, so I gave them an easy out before they could do it themselves. But I didn't have my fucking pennies. Some nurse must've taken them when they booked me."

"I'm sorry, sir."

"Don't call me that."

"Sorry."

Mr. Quincy burst through the back door with a plastic Walmart bag. He dropped it on the front desk and gave Mark a long, hard look. No words, just contempt. Blazing walls of fire burned behind those aging pupils. He gave a passing glance to Abel before sauntering off, disappearing into his office.

Mark took the bag, checked its contents, and made his way out the door. Abel disregarded being blatantly ignored by the bank teller and followed Mark.

His hunch was right: Mark had walked here. Abel could make out wet footprints on the asphalt.

"You must've walked a long way," Abel said, trailing behind Mark like a lost puppy.

"The police station is six blocks away," said Mark.

"You did all that at the *police station?*"

"That's where they dropped me off, yes."

"Sick."

Mark swiftly turned and stared Abel down. Abel jolted back, startled by the suddenness of it all. Underneath the hardening blood caking Mark's face, his mouth wore a scathing frown, highlighted by deep creases shooting down from the sides of his nose.

"Abel, what the fuck do you want?"

"I just wanted to know how your day was."

"Is that right?" Mark stepped closer. They were in the middle of the road. There wasn't a car in sight, just the empty stores dotting Monroe Street. "Well, I already told you. It was fine until I found out my coins had been stolen. Do you seriously think my day would be going well? Now I have to walk back to the station, plant the pennies, then haul ass back to my apartment before anyone notices the mess. So no, maybe I'm not fine. Stop fucking following me."

Abel hadn't felt genuine shock like this since he found out his father hadn't actually gotten lost at the store while shopping for a gallon of milk and a pack of Marlboros. Ever since the Macy incident, Mark had been by Abel's side, granting him something he never granted anyone else. Mark had trusted Abel so much as to let him in on the fact that *he* was the Hillside Butcher. Since that night, Abel felt a strange sort of attraction toward the man. No, not sexually. That'd be gay. But he had felt an inseparable bond. Thelma and Louise. Bonnie and Clyde. He would hear of the previous night's escapades, come to Mark's apartment, get the rundown, and gaze into that man's eyes with nothing but amazement. He felt like a real part of some master plan. Sure, there were definitely holes in the logic leading up to those murders, but the killing itself was the real treat. The idea of breaking into a home of unsuspecting residents and hacking them to bits was enough for Abel to keep on going. Life at home was a drag, but listening to Mark's ramblings nearly every week brought him immense joy. There was a power behind the man's voice, a vicious tremor only a father could provide.

How could Abel stand being reprimanded by his idol? The same way many others did, of course. They took the punches without feeling the pain. The wounds were physically there, but disregarded in terms of anything important. They were thankfully abused, turning a blind eye to the obvious signs of disdain. Because why else would Abel Watterson think Mark kept him around for pity's sake? There was no reason to think such awful thoughts.

For all Abel knew, Mark was God.

His savior.

★ ★ ★

Not a single minute back at her office, Ashley heard a knock at the door. She didn't get to begrudgingly say "Come in!" before the door swung open.

Congressman Shaw walked in, but his usual overly-wide grin faded when he saw how dim the room was. Ashley had the curtains pulled and a single lamp turned on, basking her office in a faint, orange glow. She was exhausted from her roadtrip back to D.C. from Little Rock, even if she managed to shave two hours off the drive by speeding, paying exuberant amounts of tolls, and avoiding the flooding around the Chesapeake Bay Area. Not to mention that the grief she thought she was required to feel during the funeral caught up to her as she crossed the Tennessee-Virginia border, keeping her car on the road while her eyes were drowned in thick, running tears.

Shaw didn't seem to catch any hint of this, so he turned on the overhead light and made himself comfortable. Ashley squinted as a new headache erupted, her temples throbbing from the brightness.

"How was the trip, Guthrie?" he said, that trademark smile erupting like a jubilant volcano.

"How do you think?" Ashley asked, crossing her arms and laying her head there. "It was a fucking funeral."

"Oh, I bet."

She lifted her head. "You bet? It literally was. What the fuck are you on?"

"Zoloft and two shots of tequila," he said.

It wasn't out of the ordinary for Shaw to clock in with a little buzz; half of Congress could barely string together a coherent sentence regardless of whether there were toxins swimming around in their bloodstreams. Ashley always tried to keep herself clearheaded during days under the rotunda, but the last two years—

and especially the last week or so—were making her reconsider her workplace sobriety.

"This Government Protections committee is kicking my ass," Shaw said. "Needed to up my dose. That's enough about me, though. Did you hear the news?"

"I haven't been on my phone, no."

"It's very big news. Do you want to find out yourself, or can I spoil the surprise?"

Judging by the smile still on the congressman's face, Ashley knew the correct answer.

"The president is unwell," he said. "We've all known this. Forging physical and cognitive records didn't do much to cover that up. But when I say he's unwell, I mean he's *unwell.*"

"Dying?" Ashley asked, hating herself for the sudden joy in her tone.

"I appreciate the enthusiasm, but no. While you were gone, the president had a bit of an episode in the Oval Office. The Salvadoran president came in for a visit again."

"Don't tell me they were trying to start that deportation shit again."

"That seems to be the case. I don't know why they thought renegotiations would be a good idea. That's beside the point. During the meeting, the Salvadoran president made some kind of offhanded comment about how gaudy the Oval Office looked with all that gold. This rubbed our president the wrong way, so he choked the Salvadoran."

"Choked?" asked Ashley. She knew the president wasn't well in the head, but she never expected to hear of actual, physical violence occurring inside the White House. "Like, wrapped his hands around his neck and…?"

"Exactly that. This is all rumor now, though. The media was

barred from filming the negotiations, but a few photographers managed to snap some pictures of the Salvadoran president as he left the Oval Office."

Shaw presented his phone. The screen brightness was turned all the way up, so Ashley turned it down before seeing blurry photos of the Salvadoran president with gnarly, purple bruising around his neck. His face looked white as a sheet of paper from the senior Mark Smith's paper mill. *No Ash*, she thought. *Don't think about that fucked-up family. Don't think about home. You're back in D.C. Do your job.*

She handed the phone back and asked, "What happened after?"

"Our president's staff ushered him to a car and shipped him off to Walter Reed," Shaw said. "He's been there since Wednesday, but word is that the doctors diagnosed him with dementia due to Alzheimer's. Crazy fucking world, huh?"

"Crazy fucking world."

After her lunch break, Ashley attempted to get back to the dark cave that was once her office without being noticed. Unfortunately, there was a trio of Republican representatives outside the door. The oldest of the three twirled a withering finger along the tassels of the pride flag she had propped up there. The younger two scrolled endlessly on their phones. Ashley felt a rush of dread drain the courage from her body. She straightened her suit and proceeded toward them, feigning a smile as best as she could.

"Congressmen!" she said, putting out her hand. "To what do I owe the pleasure?"

None of them returned the gesture with a firm handshake, to which Ashley was grateful. Lord knew the last time they had washed their hands after a piss. The flu outbreak among the Republican side of the aisle last winter felt apocalyptic, with only the representatives from Maine and Montana being well enough to continue their work that week.

"We have questions for you, Congresswoman."

"Alright, shoot."

"This conversation would be better had in a more private area."

Their idea of a more private area was the janitors' closet down the hall. Ashley felt an immediate wave of jealousy with the space. Why the hell did a janitor's closet have more square footage than her own office?

The older congressman was Hughes, and younger men being Palmer and Fitzgerald. They wore their hair short, combed and gelled so smooth they looked as if they were wearing LEGO Minifigure headpieces. Ashley wished she had no ties with them, but they were the other representatives for Arkansas. She was fresh meat compared to them, having been first elected into office almost two years ago. That was chump change compared to Hughes, who had been serving his time in the Capitol since 1978. The elderly man coughed into an oily rag and returned it to a shelf.

"We need your input on something, Miss Guthrie," Fitzgerald said.

"It's imperative that you express complete transparency with us," Palmer added.

Those two were like two peas in a straight, White pod. Cut from the same cloth, only eight years of experience separating them. There was some light powder clinging to Palmer's stubble just under his nose. Ashley had no doubt that he and Fitzgerald had indulged in some of that sweet Delaware blow before meeting with her.

"What do you want?" Ashley asked.

"Information on Mark Thomas Smith," Hughes coughed.

"Our correspondents picked up a story about a man who stopped a drug kingpin from escaping the police down in Bernard."

Not a kingpin, just a dealer trying to get by, Ashley thought.

"And lo and behold, that's where our records indicate you are from," Palmer said.

"You and this Mark Smith went to school together, is that right?" Fitzgerald asked.

Wherever this is going, it's not going to end well.

"Yes?" said Ashley with caution. "What about him?"

"We trust you've been informed of the president's state," Fitzgerald said, sniffing as if there was a large blob of snot stuck in his nose. "We overheard your conversation with Congressman Shaw."

She wasn't going to put it past her fellow representatives to stoop so low as to eavesdrop inside the nation's Capitol Building. She dampened her shocked expression and continued the conversation. She was nervous, yes, but also morbidly intrigued.

"There's rumblings of using the 25th amendment against the president," Hughes said. "Try as we might to cover this up, this is too much for all of us."

"I don't see the problem," Ashley said, seeing all the problems. Namely, the fact that if the president were to resign due to mental incapacity, the vice president would assume his role for the remainder of his term. Just the thought of the vice president being the leader of the United States sent a shiver down Ashley's spine. "I know over half the country would be elated to hear he's stepping down. What does this have to do with Mark?"

"That's just it," Palmer said. "While the president will no doubt resign, that will leave a huge vacancy in the White House. The media doesn't know he's at Walter Reed right now. The public doesn't know their leader is ready for the nursing home at his old age." Hughes scowled his bushy, gray eyebrows. Palmer winced but held firm. "As long as they don't know, the president will be able to make decisions, and his next executive order will be to fire his entire cabinet, including his immediate successors."

"He can't just do that," Ashley stated.

"As far as you've seen from him in the past four years, you know the president can do whatever he wants. He can ignore Congress, the Supreme Court, and his entire minority of constituents. Yes, I'll admit we're in the minority currently, but we desperately need your help. We think we've found a worthy successor. Someone much better than Davey Robinson."

Ashley's heart dropped into her stomach and burst like the nuclear bombs their inept president had the launch codes for; not that he could remember the sequence. What were these men saying? Why would they insinuate letting Mark Smith outside of Arkansas? What did they see in a man who had dedicated his life to making a small town suffer for what happened to his mother two decades ago? Did these three even know about the murders, or were they just head-over-heels about the hero story?

"I'm not going to fucking help you," Ashley said. "If you men want to present a random citizen to the president and trick him into endorsing him as his successor, go ahead. I know your games. It's an election year, and you want to feel special before you lose your jobs. You cowards are never in the House any other year, but *now* you want to try to make something out of your useless terms? By all means, do what you want, but don't hire Mark Smith for anything. Keep him away from Washington."

The three men laughed, Hughes coughing so violently between chuckles Ashley noticed his dentures slide out for a split second. She left the closet without another word, and as the door closed, she heard Palmer yell to her: "This wouldn't be a problem if you liberals had let him run for a third term!"

* * *

Mark sat in the dark watching *Grey's Anatomy*. He liked to put it on after a long day. The plot and characters were boring as hell, but the gore was pleasant. The doctors sliced a patient open with a thin scalpel, revealing puffy layers of golden fat coated in wrinkles of red. He felt overwhelming disappointment when the show cut to the next scene without showing the rest of the surgery. He didn't want to hear about Meredith Grey's melodramatic, shitty life. Get back to the blood. He wanted to see them pull that tumor out, all pink and veiny.

When the sappy music started, Mark lost all hope for pleasure. He turned off the television and moseyed himself to bed. He didn't take a shower, didn't brush his teeth, didn't even take his clothes off. He laid atop the covers and squeezed his eyes shut. Sleep wouldn't come like it was apt to do. He rolled over, taking some sheets with him, but he felt worse than before. Aches and pains, all stemming from bruises turned invisible. Was this the end? Had the hands of time finally come to take him away? Was it his time to die? If everything that reporter had said was true, what *was* he? A shell of his former self? A killer who was better at getting caught than anything else?

And what about Ashley Guthrie? She'd mentioned that everyone knew. What did she mean by that? Was there a cabal of Bernard residents that knew about his role in the town's murders, turned a blind eye, and went about their lives without caring? How was Mark supposed to take that scathing information? As fact? No.

Mark rose from bed. It was one o'clock in the morning. He peeked from behind his window blinds. The harsh porchlight obscured the stars above. He cracked the loose floorboard in his closet and retrieved his new axe; new because his old one had been lost after the car had been totaled. He gazed into the shiny red metal of the head, ran his hand up and down the smooth wood finish of the handle.

He pictured the night he murdered Arthur Guthrie, the clean split of the old man's nose as he drove the axe through the top of his head. The intestines slowly spilling from his open torso like worms from a grassy knoll on a rainy day. What a perfect night that would have been if it weren't for Arthur's bitch of a daughter spoiling the fun.

Of course she couldn't keep the remorse focused on that one night. Let bygones be bygones. Oh, no no no. Ashley had to continue infecting his life, burrowing under his skin and festering there like a malignant case of ringworm. Ever since he met her in her late father's house, Mark's mind had been totally out of whack. Always so concerned with what others thought of him. Always looking over his shoulder. Maybe someone's looking his way. Maybe they know he's the Hillside Butcher. Maybe they don't give a shit.

Mark swung the axe in frustration and chopped the bedroom doorframe. Splinters flew from the divot. "No," he muttered, meaning to keep that to himself. "They do."

They all gave a shit about his work. Why else would he still be going strong after ten years of doing it? Did nobody feel the need to call the police? Mark knew that murder was inherently illegal in the United States, but did it have to be? All the good he's done—using serial killing as his tool—didn't have to be for nothing.

And then his phone rang.

Unknown caller.

CHAPTER 6

★ ★ ★

"Is this Mark Thomas Smith, Jr. of 1303 Monroe Avenue, Bernard, Arkansas?"

"Apartment 7, yes," Mark said into the phone. "Who is this?

"Wonderful! This is Congressman Finley Palmer from the United States House of Representatives. Would you care to have a little chat?"

Mark had an uneasy feeling that this was some sort of prank call, but the voice on the other end sounded so professional, almost too monotone for the joviality imbued in each sentence. He'd watched videos of politicians on various web forums, even went to a rally held by the current president. All politicians sounded the same expect for the president. Boring and matter-of-fact. This Palmer individual seemed to fit the bill.

"Why are you calling?" Mark asked, propping his axe on the splintered doorframe.

"I'll take that as a 'yes.' If you didn't already know, I am one of your representatives for the state of Arkansas. Congressmen Hughes and Fitzgerald

are the other two Republicans speaking for the state. They are also on the line."

Mark heard faint hellos in the grainy background as if the other two men were in the same room instead of simply intercepting the call from their own cellphones. Evidently, they technically weren't on the line.

"We wanted to express our deepest gratitude to you for your heroic actions down there a week or so ago," Palmer said. *"We understand how dire the drug trade currently is in our state, and it's people like you that keep the streets safe from the criminals and thugs."*

Mark couldn't help but smile. It had seemed as if no one would allow him to feel good about all he had done to heal the world. Stopping that Ashton or Andre or whoever from selling narcotics on the streets of his beloved hometown was just the cherry on top of his murderous sundae. More work was to be done, a concept that Ashley Guthrie and those freaks from the news station couldn't seem to grasp. But these three congressmen and their soothing words of praise. Oh, they were playing those chords just right, strumming the guitar strings of his heart with gentle yet thunderous plucks.

"It's really no trouble," Mark said. "I love Bernardans more than anything, and I'd do anything for them."

"You've made that abundantly clear."

Mark blushed and expressed his gratitude.

"With the pleasantries out of the way, I'd like to veer the conversation toward a new direction," an older fellow shouted, definitely not needing to with how close he was to the phone. *"We would like to sponsor you on a... tour, or sorts."*

"A tour?"

"Election years are always the worst for everyone up in Washington," Palmer said. *"So many things can go wrong, and most of the time, they* do.

This year is no exception. Our previous plans have had a slight detour in recent days, and we've been scrambling like deer with their heads cut off."

The mental image of deer hopping around a forest without their heads brought another smile to Mark's lips. Blood gurgling from thick, meaty stumps as they scattered through a bed of wild bushes, rustling leaves as they painted the greenery a thick shade of deep black. Mark suppressed a sudden burst of sexual moans, holding his mouth with an open palm.

"*And because our current president has essentially let go every potential candidate, we had prepared in case he didn't want to run again, we've found ourselves a bit lost. We're not saying we'll hand you the presidency. No, no, no.*" A wave of roaring laughter blasted through Mark's phone's speakers. When they diminished, Palmer came back on the line. "*What we're saying is this: We need to show the American people what we really are about. They need to see someone they can relate to. The past four—no, twelve—years have conditioned them to scoff at the older generation in power. Maybe we could show them that our ways of thinking aren't backward if the newer generation exhibits those views. Does that make sense, Mr. Smith?*"

Candidates. Elections. The presidency.

Mark was having trouble processing those words in such quick succession. He was far from tired, though. Drowsiness wasn't a factor in the confusion. The situation was strange. Why him? Why this? Why at one in the morning? Did these politicians have nothing better to—

"*Mr. Smith?*"

"Oh, yeah," Mark coughed. "Yes."

"*Fantastic! But, as we stated, this won't be something too involved for you. We simply would like for you to present yourself as a speaker for one of our grassroots candidates. Your speech does not need to be a certain length. It doesn't even need to pertain to our chosen candidate. All we ask is for your short time, and that you mention your community service, namely how you stopped that drug-dealing thug."*

"Sounds easy enough," Mark said.

"We'll keep in touch."

The line went dead.

Mark stared at the empty black screen and set the phone on its charging pad. He walked over to the wrecked doorframe and stuck his finger in the crevice. Rough pillars of sharp wooden fibers grazed his skin. He felt a twist of hot pain and looked at the damage. A splinter had lodged itself underneath a fingernail. Mark huffed as he pulled on the thin spire, wincing when it didn't budge.

Life seemed to be going too well lately. Sure, there were moments here and there that upset him, but the overall landscape was clear as a field of wildflowers on a sunny spring afternoon. After ten years of putting in the work, he'd finally gained the recognition he deserved. Only sheer fate brought his car into that intersection, only to be T-boned by someone who the general public held no positive opinion of. Through the simple action of throwing a Black man in jail, Mark had gained notoriety within the broader Arkansas community. And even farther than that, too. The congressmen of his beautiful state had reached out to him. Normally, Mark wouldn't give a shit about what a politician had to say, but this time was different. Special, even. The topic of discussion wasn't illegal immigration or transgender rights or COVID-19 or any of that boring shit.

It was *him* they were talking about.

And that was the great, big, beautiful thing.

★ ★ ★

Abel could barely contain himself as he walked through the glass double doors. The sweet aroma of Windex and gunpowder filled his nostrils. The sterile lights overhead brought a sense of belonging, strangely enough. Much to Abel's mother's probable dismay, Edmund Wright stood at the glass counter perusing the contents held within.

"My man!" Abel said, patting Eddie's back.

Eddie jerked his shoulder back and quickly whipped his head around. His hand had jolted toward the waistline of his black jeans, hovering over the pistol-shaped protrusion bulging from under his long leather jacket. Fear had embedded itself into his eyes, but his look softened when he recognized his old friend.

"Abel!" he shouted, throwing his hands into the air. "Bring it here!"

Abel let the hug consume him fully. Eddie smelled the same as he did in middle school. Still used the same ocean spray cologne he had nabbed from his dad everyday before rushing to the bus.

Eddie let go and beckoned Abel to look into the cabinet. Abel felt the urge to pretend he'd never been in Louis' Gun Emporium before. There was a weird shroud of embarrassment that came with sharing a common interest with someone you haven't seen since your face first started erupting with acne. Maybe he could stare quizzically at the handguns and simple rifles displayed within the glass box. Maybe he could ask Louis Hamilton behind the counter what... hmm... *that* one is. But Abel knew that it was a CVA Cascade coated in blue steel, and he also knew that hiding his love for anything that kills was a battle he'd rather not fight.

"Where do you think they keep all the good stuff?" Eddie asked, his nose so close to the glass he could practically smell the bullets.

"You know this kid?" Louis asked, gruff as ever.

The man stood five foot six, but for what he lacked in height, he gained in knowledge. Perfect, then, that his boundless knowledge was only tailored toward selling and buying contraband weapons off the black market.

"Yeah I know him," said Abel. "This is Eddie. We went to middle school together before he ditched me."

"Ditched you?" Eddie laughed. "My dad got stationed out in Nevada and we had to move with him. Wasn't my call."

That's the Eddie Abel knew. The kid who would always find a way to remind you of his military brat status. Abel remembered all of the hundreds of times Eddie had bragged that he'd been to Iceland before. Yeah okay, the Vikings were also there before, so it's nothing special. Abel had hated him for being able to move across the country, or even to *other* countries. Abel had spent his whole life in Bernard with no signs that his living situation was going to change.

"Oh, right," Abel said. "I forgot."

"Since you know my good friend here, I'll let you in on a little secret," Louis said to Eddie. The little man leaned over the counter, his salt-and-pepper scruff nearly scraping Eddie's bearded chin. "All the good stuff is in the back."

Eddie whistled enthusiastically. "Automatic?"

"Anything you can dream of, kid."

"Rocket launcher?"

"Maybe not anything."

Eddie went silent. With sad eyes, he mumbled, "I guess I have no business here, sir. I'm awful sorry."

Louis crossed his burly arms, confused. But Abel remembered this trick all too well. The old pouty-eyes technique. Eddie had used this many times at Bernard Junior High to get what a he wanted. An unwarranted trip to the nurse's office, another bathroom break right after he'd returned from the previous one, an extra serving of brown slop in the cafeteria line. Such plays on the heartstrings worked on measly middle school teachers, but Louis was a man of no empathy, skin as thick as he was short.

"How the hell do you think I'd smuggle a goddamn rocket launcher into middle-of-nowhere Arkansas?" Louis said, unimpressed.

"Could we just rent out two rifles from you?" Abel asked, pushing past his friend. "We'd bring them back by the end of the day. Promise."

"What're you planning on doing?"

"Going to the range past Cemetery Hill."

"Do they not provide firearms there?"

"Oh, I'm not talking about the gun range," Abel said. "The other range. The old wheat field."

"I see."

Louis raised a finger and scooted out the door behind him. Abel heard rumblings and clanging from beyond the wall, a moment here and there in which Louis would scream something in a garbled Italian/English word vomit. When the ruckus ceased, Louis reemerged with two standard hunting rifles.

"Winchester Pre-64 Model 70," Louis said, setting the classic rifles on the counter with a delicate ease.

Abel stared at the guns' smooth wooden finishes in awe, taking extra note of the years-worn sheen on the metallic bolt handle. The sights were similarly worn from age but seemed to be positioned correctly regardless. He'd only had mere glimpses of the pre-64 models online through various Reddit and 4chan threads, but seeing the full package in person was a wholly different beast. Eddie reached for the closest rifle and met with a vicious slap on the wrist.

"Promise me I'll see these beauties again," Louis commanded.

"If I don't see these Winchesters back in this store by sunset, you won't have my business anymore. Understood?"

"Understood," Abel and Eddie said in unison.

Louis clicked his tongue and set a box of ammunition next to the guns.

"Go raze hell," he said with a grin.

Louis would never see those beauties again.

* * *

Congresswoman Ashley Guthrie was fucking exhausted. Another terrible day of sitting in the House chamber, listening with gritted teeth as a meager amount of her Republican colleagues spewed the same non-answer bullshit they'd been peddling since the president took office again almost four years ago. When she had been elected in a close midterm race against Quentin Linklater two years ago, Ashley wanted nothing more than to serve the people of Arkansas on a grander, country-spanning scale. Bring greater education back to her home state, give the right to choose back to women and transgender men, relegalize queer love.

Her aspirations seemed attainable at the time. The approval ratings on the other side of the aisle was plummeting harder than the stock market. The American people were clamoring for change. Their mistake of electing the current president was quickly made prominent, one awful policy decision after another. Ashley knew she shouldn't have been elected; Arkansas was a historically red state. But District 4 flipped blue in her favor by a margin of a mere 500 votes, and the rest was history.

Life in D.C. was beautiful. The area surrounding the White House was decorated with monuments and memorials and glistening, blue ponds and well-kept green lawns. The city itself was bustling with people walking from place to place instead of driving a few blocks to grab a cup of coffee. The air was clean out there, a far cry from the persistent chemical smell of an old paper mill that infected her hometown. But all that beauty was purely a facade, a glimpse into a fantasy land where people got along and nothing was wrong. Inside those columned buildings, there were people on both major sides of the political spectrum that wanted nothing more than to make sure that fantasy land never came to fruition. Ashley felt nothing but an overwhelming sickness at the thought of not wanting to better the common man.

A soft stream of nausea crawled through her nerves as she walked up the three flights of stairs to her apartment. She knocked on the door and waited. *Tasha's not home.* "Dammit," Ashley whispered.

She fumbled for her keys and slipped the only silver one into the lock. Opening the door, she was greeted by the familiar scent of the honey and vanilla air freshener that Tasha refused to part ways with. Two years of being engaged and she still wouldn't budge. "Maybe ease into it with an apple scent or something," Ashley would pester, to which Tasha would respond, "I'm allergic to apples," and Ashley would retort, "They don't actually put apples in the damn oil."

The lights were out. Ashley had been in the House chamber so long that her brain was pink sludge. She couldn't remember if Tasha had told her she'd made plans tonight. No matter, though. Ashley would just take a hot bath and watch reruns of *Buffy* on the sofa while she awaited her beloved.

She flicked on the main hall's light. There was a lone red balloon in the living room beyond. It stood eerily still, begging to push past the ceiling and reach for the stars. Ashley crept down the hallway.

Then she heard whispers, a snide remark of the wind. Chitter chatter from behind the corner. There was no sign of breaking and entering. The front door had been on its hinges; the deadbolt was locked in place. The apartment smelled like it usually did. As Ashley reminisced on the sameness of the vanilla and honey air freshener, she noticed an anomaly. A minty, flowery perfume that Tasha would never be caught dead wearing. It didn't smell like anything Ashley would apply, either. It was familiar, but not in here.

Someone was in her apartment.

Ashley froze in place, keeping her eyes locked on the single balloon as she reached into her purse and retrieved her small can of pepper spray. She intoned a silent prayer. *Please God. I hope I haven't emptied this thing on my coworkers. Please oh please oh please oh FUCK!*

The darkness evaporated as the entire apartment was engulfed in bright light. The balloon swished to and fro as waves of movement absorbed the space. Colorful streamers adorned the ceiling, kazoos blared like malnourished trumpets, and people jumped from various hiding places screaming, "Happy birthday!"

A few feet in front of Ashley, a man emerged from around the corner. He was soaked in deep scarlet liquid, his white dress shirt dripped with the stuff. It was Mark Smith, no doubt about it. Fear enveloped Ashley as she screamed and sprayed him with her pepper spray.

The jubilation she hadn't noticed died down.

Tony Parvin laid before her, not Mark. Thankfully not Mark. When the realization of what she'd done hit her like that bus from *Speed*, Ashley bent down and apologized over and over again. "Shit, I'm sorry! Oh my God, I'm so sorry, Tony," she blabbered. "I completely forgot it's my birthday. I thought I was getting murdered. I'm sorry."

Other party guests—both Tasha's and Ashley's D.C. friends alike—began to gather around the pathetic scene. Tony's younger brother (a spitting image of Tony except for the lack of a few inches in height) brought a glass of milk, knelt down, and spilled it over Tony's reddening eyes.

Ashley felt numb. Tears of her own filled her eyes as she put a hand to her mouth and fled to the bedroom.

Tasha came in an hour later. Ashley had washed up, scrubbing the sweat and shame from her naked body until her skin was raw. She laid in bed above the covers with a towel wrapped in a spongy cone around her damp hair. Tasha gave a short sigh and sat on the edge. She placed a hand on Ashley's bare thigh, rubbing the tiny tattoo of a tulip inked there.

"Tony's better," Tasha said. "He's missing you out there."

"I'm just…" Ashley said, trailing off. Her mind could barely handle the pressures of her job, but the added stress of her colleagues possibly *contacting* a deranged serial killer for brownie points in the upcoming election really seemed to send her off the edge. "I think I'm going crazy."

"Going? Thought you were already there."

Ashley cracked a smirk and playfully shoved her fiancée.

"Work is hell," Ashley added.

"I'm aware. I thought I'd help ease you up a bit tonight. It's your birthday! The big 36! How couldn't we celebrate?"

"I forgot that was today. I've just been so busy."

"I know, baby."

Tasha kicked her legs onto the bed and squeezed tight next to her. Ashley smelled the shea butter in her hair, a warm feeling sprouting deep within her.

With her hand placed over Ashley's chest, Tasha asked, "They still trying to defund teachers?"

"No, it's not the topic of the week. Unfortunately there was enough people today to make legislation. They were debating whether to ban gay people from the military."

"Again?"

"Yes, again."

The two of them chuckled.

"I wouldn't mind if that was passed. I'd rather not be shipped off to Saudi Arabia to drill oil and bomb innocent children," Tasha remarked.

Ashley decided to not add her opinion on the matter, but she enjoyed the sentiment. No matter the topic, she loved hearing Tasha speak. That soothing yet confident voice, smooth as butter but tough as bricks. She combed her fingers through Tasha's curly black hair, scratching her scalp in all the places she knew she enjoyed.

"I just worry about you sometimes," Tasha said. "I've seen you stressed before, but I've never seen you outright scared to death. What else happened today?"

"Today? Just the same old shit."

"And before?"

There was an obvious blind spot in their relationship. Despite spending most of her childhood in backwater Arkansas, Ashley barely talked about those earlier years with Tasha. There wasn't much reason to; everything important in her life occurred after she left for Syracuse University. But the root of her problem, the malignant tumor eating away at her brain until it became a block of Swiss cheese, resided in that state. What would Tasha say? How would she react to hearing that her fiancée was squabbling with a hometown serial killer who was being considered as a piece of political warfare by her Republican colleagues? Ashley was too tired to care at this point, so she said fuck it, got out of bed, and poured her thoughts.

Tasha sat wide-eyed at the conclusion of Ashley's ramblings. The bedroom was silent except for the muffled sounds of an AI-generated Spotify playlist and the partygoers dancing through their living room. Tasha stood and made her way over to Ashley, taking her in for a hug.

"I thought Arthur died from a stroke. But he… *he* killed him?"

"Yes," Ashley said. It felt strange saying it out loud, the confirmation hanging in the air forever and ever. She began to sob. "And I didn't do anything."

"No. No, no, hush now." Tasha held her face in her hands, gently squeezing her cheeks as she stared intently into her eyes. "It's not your fault. It's that fucker's fault."

"You're not mad at me?"

"For what?"

"For lying to you?"

"No, of course not. Trauma comes in many ways. Some people take it and go on, but other people are normal about it, in a way. They block it. They keep it from others. I don't care that you told me he had a stroke. I'm just glad you're brave enough to face it now."

Ashley sniffled.

"I don't know what to do," she said. "I froze when he did it. I couldn't process it was real, what was happening. I let him *go*. And no one's going to do anything about him. No one."

"Did he hurt you?"

"What do you mean?"

"Physically, I mean," Tasha corrected. "Did this Mark guy hurt you?"

"No."

"Because if he did, I'd kill him myself."

"I want him dead."

Ashley was a little shocked by those four words coming out of her mouth. She'd never wished death upon another person before, no matter how deplorable their crimes, but Mark was different. She had never experienced someone so perverted by evil in her life. There were people in all three branches of the federal government that were guided by sin, but *none* as tainted as Mark Smith. Was she biased due to the personal nature of the whole thing? Yes, and she knew that as a fact, but that wouldn't change anything. The cycle of revenge and all that nonsense from her high school and college English courses felt like something rooted in fiction. But it was most certainly real, and Ashley sought nothing except Mark's downfall.

An eye for an eye.

Or in this case, a hacked-off limb for a hacked-off limb.

A life for a life.

"We can talk about this more tomorrow," Tasha said, sensing the rage boiling inside Ashley. "Why don't you cover up and attend your party? I bought carrot cake."

"You hate carrot cake."

"But *you* love it."

★ ★ ★

Abel lined up his sights and fired. The shot rang like a tremendous lightning bolt as the bullet drove into the archery target a few hundred yards away. The target nearly exploded from the force, wobbling back as a sharp cloud of smoke jettisoned from its back. Once the smoke cleared, Abel squinted and noted the hole seared into the yellow spot of the target.

"Bullseye," Abel muttered under his breath.

"Lucky shot," Eddie laughed.

"If it was lucky, it would've hit dead-center. Look."

Abel pointed toward the target. Eddie leaned beside him, close enough for Abel to catch another whiff of that ocean breeze cologne. It burned his nostrils, but the pain felt wonderful, maybe in the same way hot coals feel good when placed on your naked back despite the excruciating heat. Some pain was good. It was always good. Pain was necessary to feel, to live.

"Damn," Eddie said with a whistle. "I guess you're getting rusty."

"Oh, shut up."

"It's true! Remember when we broke into your dad's gun safe and took his revolver for a spin? You were knocking apples off that porch like no one's business."

Abel blushed. He was shocked Eddie would remember something from so long ago.

"Yeah, but those were apples, Eddie. They exploded on impact. Could never tell where the bullet landed."

"But you were in middle school, brother. Brain wasn't developed or whatever. And you *still* hit every apple we set up there."

"Dad was pissed after, though," Abel said.

"How's the old man doing these days, anyway?"

"He left."

"Like…" Eddie laid out a flat hand and walked two fingers across it. "Like, he went out for cigarettes and never came back?"

"It was actually for a whole grocery list. Mom still regrets sending him out for that pickup order. She was out like two hundred bucks because no one showed up to grab it."

"That sucks," Eddie said solemnly, scratching his beard.

"It's alright. I'm over it. How's your dad?"

"He died a few years ago."

"I'm sorry," Abel said. "In combat?"

"Suicide."

"Oh."

Eddie picked up his rifle, lined up a shot, breathed out, and fired. The archery target lurched back. Abel grinned maniacally as the target regained its footing and planted itself back into place, a burnt hole in its red ring, an inch off from the bullseye.

"I guess *you're* getting rusty," Abel laughed.

"And *you* look like shit," Eddie retorted, his face twisted with anger. "A *Star Wars* t-shirt? What are you? Four?"

"Okay, okay. I get it, man. Calm down."

Eddie set his rifle on a hay bale and wiped his forehead. He commented on how hot it was outside, to which Abel thought the notion was insane. It was an abnormally cool summer afternoon. He even had goosebumps from some of the sparse wind gusts. Eddie fanned himself and removed his leather coat. Underneath the coat was an equally black T-shirt. Way too tight for him, but just enough for Abel's eyes. The last time Abel had seen Eddie in person, he had been a scrawny little middle schooler with a mountain range of acne and mere hints of facial hair blooming in the pus-filled crevices. Now, Eddie was a fully bearded, fully muscled stud. Thick biceps bulged from his shirt sleeves; chest muscles popped like two balloons underneath the black cloth. He hadn't just grown in height, but length and width like an ever-expanding prism.

Abel shook his head, thinking that the physicality of the motion would somehow shake those feelings from his brain. Sure, Eddie was everything he wanted out of a person. Smart, confident, beautiful. The only issue was the masculine part of Eddie. He was a man, and a man loving a man was oh so very wrong. Why had Abel risked a night with his father's belt just so he could galavant around town with a revolver? Because Eddie told him to. And what Eddie said was sacred, even back then.

Another shot rang through the empty field. Eddie shouted something about fucking the target's mother and threw his rifle into the grass. Abel squinted and noted a new hole, this time burning in the target's blue ring. He winced at the implications of Eddie making such a terrible shot. Would he run away into the ether, never to be seen again? Would he pick that rifle back up and prop the barrel under his chin, pulling the trigger? Mark had mentioned why he chose to kill so many people around Bernard. They were sad, miserable. Unnecessarily despairing and dejected. He chose to take up the axe so that he could end their suffering before they could do something about it themselves. Abel had always taken Mark's words as holier than thou. But now there was something different, a new notch in his heart that simply said, "No." Watching Eddie stomp around that empty grassy field, his arm veins bulging with rage, Abel thought something new.

What if he's wrong?

The thought was horrifying. He couldn't simply ignore everything Mark Smith had taught him for the past few years. Negating those teachings would make Mark, well… nothing. Nothing but a murderer. A low-life. A deranged man operating under the guise of justice.

Eddie kicked a clump of hay into the air, screaming to the clouds.

"Hey, man," Abel said, walking over. "It's just one missed shot. Actually, you didn't even miss the target."

"Don't you fucking tell me shit!" Eddie shouted, pointing a nasty finger.

"I'm sorry."

"You were always so goddamn perfect at everything, man. Always fucking better than me. You had parents who didn't move you around the fucking country all the damn time. They *cared*. You had it all."

"No I didn't. That's not true."

"You know I was here for the longest, right? I actually had enough time to make friends. Two years! Before and after, my dad would get stationed at a new base every year. Utah, Illinois, California, Maryland, Guam. Oh, Guam was the worst. I fucking *hated* Guam. But I didn't have a choice! I was fucking stuck with my shit-eating dad and my weak fucking mom. Tearing me from being normal so they could live the lives they wanted. But no, no, no. I guess it *wasn't* the life my dad wanted, because he decided it was easier to stick a gun in his mouth and blow his brains out."

"My dad left me, too," Abel said. "Me and my mom. She hasn't stopped smoking since."

"My mom lives in San Francisco with some bum that wants me to call him Dad. He'll never be him. At least your dad is still out there, Abel. You can find him."

"I don't think I want to."

Eddie's face softened, his beard rustling with his quivering bottom lip. He had always been a loose cannon, but never a crier. Never, until today. He dropped to his knees and put his large hands to his face. Abel sat next to his friend, not minding the hay sticking to his ass. He placed a hand on Eddie's back, smoothing out the creases of his shirt. He could feel the tough ripples of muscle underneath the fabric as his fingers glided over the lumps between each body. Before his thoughts could take over, he brought his hand back into his lap, holding it there as if it were a rabid hamster trying to escape captivity.

"You know," Eddie began, combing his hair back, "I never wanted to leave this place. Not just because I was already sick of the constant moving, but I really thought life couldn't get better than this."

"Why's that?" Abel asked.

"The people. No matter where I went, the people from other places didn't feel real, but here they were real. Real people doing real people things. Not worrying about how they looked or how they acted or how others saw them. People here are so far away from big cities that they don't have that insecurity, I think. There's no need for it. When we packed the U-Haul and left for Utah, I knew the people up there wouldn't compare to the ones in Arkansas. And I was right. Nothing ever came close."

"Are you thinking about coming back? Staying, I mean."

"No," Eddie said. His knees cracked as he stood. "I have contacts to meet in New England. I told you that, right?"

"You might have mentioned it," Abel lied. Eddie had said he was in the area and wanted to hang out for a bit when he had called initially. No mention of what would happen after.

"Yeah, it's some serious business stuff. I was coming over from San Fran, and I thought I might as well stop by."

It made more sense to Abel that he was just a pit stop on Eddie's way to something bigger. Nevertheless, he was glad his friend was here, even if their time together would be cut short.

"What's the business?" Abel asked.

Eddie put a finger to his lips and said, "Top secret."

"Suuurrreee."

"I'm not bullshitting you! It's serious."

The two of them laughed. Eddie slapped Abel on the shoulder, the clap booming through the distant trees. They walked back behind the hay bale and reloaded their rifles. *BANG* after *BANG* after *BANG*. The target became as porous as a sponge, and as dirty, too. Covered in holes and smoke and gunpowder.

There was a rustling in the tall bushes beyond. A deer of some kind, maybe. Abel and Eddie felt a sense of euphoria so heightened that the world around them felt right and unreal. Reconnecting as old friends in arms, blasting away at a random archery target in the middle of some field. Abel joked that he'd shoot the deer behind those bushes over there. Right between the eyes, he said. Eddie said he'd bet ten dollars on it. Abel lined up, breathed out, and fired.

But he didn't hit a deer.

It was a woman.

Her scream—her final scream—as she tumbled from the green was deafening. It echoed through the trees, bounced from the shrubbery. Her body contorted as she lifelessly flopped into the dirt. Abel, wide-eyed, threw down his rifle and rushed over, Eddie in tow.

He knew this woman. No... this *girl*. She was only a few months younger than him. *Macy*, the girl he'd stabbed in the neck with a sharpened pencil during a vocabulary assignment. Yes, it was her. Beneath the abnormal bruising and fresh scratches, the half-an-inch circle of a scar stared back at him. He knew she'd survived the ordeal, but what was she doing out there? What the *fuck*? Here of all places?

The shock of seeing her again, the knowing fear of what he had done. Abel began to shake, anxiety taking over like a parasitic fungus worming into a helpless worker ant. This was it; this was his first kill. He'd been saving that day for whenever he would go on an excursion with Mark, but here it was. A corpse created by his own hand. His own finger on the trigger.

Before he knew it, he was crying.

Eddie put his hands to his head, muttering, "Oh shit, oh shit, oh shit."

"Oh my God," Abel blabbered. "Oh my fucking God."

Macy's lifeless eyes glared back at him, blasting laser beams through his skull. God, how his head hurt. It was unbearable. He'd always wanted to help kill someone, but not like this. Not as an accident. He wanted to pick the target and execute a plan, not shoot wildly at a mystery deer and somehow hit the shot through the thick brush on the outskirts of town. Abel was confused at his feelings. Something deep down told him to mourn the loss of a life, to feel nothing but a cavernous sadness at the life he had chosen. But another part told him to embrace it, to take this murder as a fact of life and live with it.

The bullet had sliced straight through her trachea and out the nape of her neck. If she were to have survived, she would have been paralyzed from the neck down. But she didn't survive, and Abel was to blame. Twenty years-old and a wanted murderer. Wanted by some form of law, whoever that would be.

"You need to come with me, Abel," Eddie said. "This is bad."

"Yeah, no shit."

"I can help you. It's my job. Come on, get up."

Eddie wrapped his arms around his old friend, unaware of the warmth Abel felt in his groin from the simple interaction. Once Abel was firmly on his feet, Eddie continued:

"We're far enough from town that no one will notice the body. Did you know her?"

Abel nodded.

"Did she have any family?"

"She did, but I don't know anymore."

"Will anyone miss her?"

Maybe, Abel thought, then said, "Probably not."

"Okay, that's good. Come on. We're leaving."

"I need to go home," Abel said. "Go to bed, maybe."

Eddie sighed and responded, "You need to go pack your things, but you can't stay."

* * *

Sorrow was something Mark was all too familiar with.

It festered like a great rot in his stomach. Today, of all days, was when he felt sorrow the most. The anniversary of his mother's death was never something to feel any semblance of joy over, and the rot enveloped him like an impenetrable shield.

As he stood at the base of his family's gravestone, he reminisced on all the good their deaths accomplished, his mother's in particular.

When she had received her cancer diagnosis, Mark's world had fallen to pieces. Shattered like a glass-pane window folding to the force of a rotten tomato thrown with as much force as a delinquent child could. His mother, poor Sophia Smith, had been a shining beacon. A warm presence in any room she entered, always ready to shine a light with that infectious smile.

There were points during Mark's childhood when he would be bullied relentlessly by his school peers. They made fun of him for his abnormal behavior, some even stooping so low as to make fun of the mole he once had just above his upper lip. Rumors spread about his sexuality, whether or not he went to the bathroom so often just to give Mr. Henderson a blowjob so he could keep an A in social studies. He had come home wet with tears. His mother—so full of life before the cancer sapped her dry—had taken him into his arms, rustled his hair in just the way he liked, and whipped him up a bowl of turkey soup. As he would slurp on the hearty broth and chew on the soft carrots, celery, pasta, and turkey chunks, Sophia turned on the television and switched the channel to Cartoon Network. After he would finish the bowl of soup, he would join his mother on the couch and laugh along to *Johnny Bravo* reruns. No matter the troubles ailing him at school, his mother would always be home to greet him with love. They sat at that couch, his head nestled within the crook of her neck, and watched his favorite shows until his father barged in from another long day of work.

Mark thought the beatings would stop after his mother had been diagnosed with stomach cancer. She had lost so much weight during chemotherapy, and lost a few extra pounds after she begged the doctors to stop. Her full features gradually hollowed out. She was weak and frail on the outside. Surely, Mark's father would have some sympathy and stop hitting her after work. How could you break what was already broken? But he continued despite it all. The belt would come off, the lashings would be dealt, and Mark Sr. would lay on the couch with a can of beer and bloodstains on his cheeks.

Sophia would never beg for mercy, even as the cancer ate her alive. She looked like skin and bones, but inside she was strong as ever. A heart encrusted in gold sat idly in her chest, even when her love wasn't reciprocated. Sometimes, Mark thought that was what pissed his father off so much. No matter how many times he would beat the shit out of his wife, she wouldn't budge. She wouldn't submit.

Well, until she made the decision for herself.

Mark had been thirteen, a ripe age for confusion and angst. Pimples rose, hair grew in weird places, and he wanted a girlfriend more than anything. There was a nice girl in his class named Erin. She was nice in the context of everyone else being utterly shitty, but nice all the same. He didn't have any wood to chop that day, so he sucked in his gut and asked Erin if she would like to get dinner with him later that night. To his shock, she said yes, grinning with a full set of hot-pink braces.

Mark raced home with the news. He wanted nothing more

than to see his mother smile again. If he told her out his upcoming date, she would surely show that infinite joy she held years before. When he entered the house, the air was eerily dense. Dust motes swam through the open foyer.

"Mom?" he shouted, setting his backpack on the welcome mat.

He checked every room on the first floor. Unwashed dishes clogged the kitchen sink, a track of mud ran through the living room carpet, an unused napkin was folded into the shape of a boat on the dining room table. All this, but no Mom.

He climbed the stairs and knocked on the bathroom door. No answer. He opened the door and was met with darkness. No one here. A thump emanated from down the hall, coming from the master bedroom. Mark asked for his mother again and was met with no response.

No child ever expects their parents to leave them so soon. It's the fatal flaw of anyone growing up carefree: taking parents for granted. One day they're here cooking you your favorite foods and giving you your favorite memories. The next, they're hanging from the ceiling, suspended by a rope tied taut around their neck. The pain had become too much for her failing but strong heart. The weight of the world seemed to be too much for Sophia Smith.

The same stepstool Mark had used when he learned how to brush his teeth all by himself was laid on its side beneath his mother's body. A red slipper had fallen from her limp feet. It rested unlaced on the floral carpet.

Mark didn't cry for her.

The funeral came around, the outside air gaining humidity from the tears of Mark's entire family.

Still, he did not cry.

But here and now, standing in the hillside cemetery his killer alter ego was named after, Mark began to weep for his mother for the first time. Before making his graveyard visit, he had murdered that snarky Walmart employee Winston Albright to blow some steam, but that didn't seem to help. Mark fell to his knees and laid a hand atop the headstone. *Loving mother, God's strongest warrior*, read her epitaph. Without her sacrifice, Mark would never have started his work. He would never let another person die by suicide again. He would kill them before the depression took them over. It was the only way to heal the world.

The politicians had called Mark again the night before.

"Is this Mark Thomas Smith, Jr. of 1303 Monroe Av—"

"Yes," Mark had said.

"Wonderful! This is Congressman Finley Palmer!"

"I know."

"I'm here again with Congressmen Hughes and Fitzgerald. We hope you're doing well."

Mark was unsure of the validity of that last statement, but he humored them by saying: "Couldn't be better, now that you're calling tonight."

"Amazing to hear!" Congressman Palmer sniffed aggressively over the line. *"We have more information regarding the rally. You remember the one?"*

Mark nodded on instinct despite Parker not being in the same room to see his agreement. He thumped himself in the forehead, feeling utterly stupid, and said, "Yes, I remember."

"The first rally will be held in Tulsa, Oklahoma," Palmer said. *"Talk about your journey in bettering your community, and connect it to what makes our candidate the best possible choice for this election."*

"We know you don't know him," another man, presumably Fitzgerald, added, *"but we'll arrange to have you meet him before the rally begins."*

"Great," Mark said. "How will I get to Tulsa, though? If you remember, my car was totaled when I stopped that thug."

"We'll send an email with a boarding pass for your trip," Palmer said, wrangling the phone from Fitzgerald. *"The rally is in three days. We hope to see you there."*

The line had gone dead, and Mark felt deja vu standing there in his dark apartment with the phone held in his hand. It was all so much, being in contact with people in Washington. His father had always complained about the regulations on the paper mill business coming from the White House. Between the moments of violence enacted on Sophia, Mark Sr. would violently complain about all the workers he would be forced to lay off. Budget cuts, mass layoffs, lack of modern uses for paper. Everything digital, nobody reads, every house that would be constructed had already been built. Why process more trees if no one needed the lumber and paper?

Standing on the mound of his parents' shared graves now, Mark had an awful feeling he would never set foot in Bernard again. It was a bittersweet thought, one that intruded in such a way he couldn't be angry about it, like a house robber that shatters your window, steals your belongings, but leaves a heart-shaped box of chocolates as consolation. Mark had done so much for his community, weeding out the pain and suffering killing person after person. Over two hundred, plus the Walmart cashier from a few hours before. No one would kill themselves again, not if he had any say in it. The haunting image of his dear mother hanging from the ceiling like a skeleton on a clothesline would forever be seared into his mind, hidden behind his eyes but just there enough to make an impression.

"I'll avenge you, Mom," he muttered, setting a bouquet of lavender and red cornflowers on his mother's side of the grave. "Whatever it takes."

Just as tears began to well in his eyes, something wet splatted on the headstone. Orange chunks exploded from the impact, some of them getting into Mark's mouth.

He heard giggles just out of earshot. What was inside his mouth was rotten and metallic, but slightly tasting of... *Tomatoes,* Mark thought with unbridled rage. He turned around and spotted a little girl, no older than six years. The girl was the culprit behind the rotten tomatoes strewn about random homes in town. The police had been after her whereabouts for weeks. And she was here, desecrating the grave of the most important woman in the world.

She laughed maniacally, the little shit, her pigtails bobbing from side to side with each labored chuckle. All color drained from Mark's world. He wanted to shout at the girl: "You fucking cunt! That's my mother!"

But he kept his mouth shut.

Instead, he reached into his suit jacket, brought out a pistol, and shot the bitch in the head, the sound mixing perfectly with a similar shot from a Winchester rifle a mile down the hill. Her little body jolted back from the blast and fell, tumbling flaccidly down the hillside.

Mark concealed the gun and followed the trajectory of the body. He stood over her, wanting nothing more than to stomp her head until her teeth exploded like shrapnel into the adjacent head-stones. But that would be too easy, so unnecessary. She was already dead, good riddance.

He took two pennies from his pocket and shoved them one by one into the bullet hole in the child's forehead, jamming them in after they hit bone. He grabbed her cheeks with a single hand and jerked her head to and fro, his back aching with age as he did. Her pigtails, decorated with bright pink bows that fluoresced under the cloudy sky, swayed with the motion.

Such a waste of a life, the miserable shit.

PART TWO

★ ★ ★

PAIN RELIEF

CHAPTER 7

★ ★ ★

Davey Robinson was the grassroots candidate for the Republican Party, if "grassroots" was even the right term to use in his case. One of Representative Palmer's biggest pet peeves was when swaths of government officials claimed to be for the people when they were, in fact, not. If you're going to be a corrupt politician bending to the wills of billionaire donors, own up to it!

The party was extravagant, both politically and physically. A glistening chandelier hung above the multi-storied ballroom. Donors, both millionaire and billionaire alike, dotted the room like the shining plates of a spinning disco ball. The main floor was full of them, full of money. They could drop a hundred-dollar bill on the carpet and not bother to pick it up; they made that money back in the time it took for them to bend over and grab it. Palmer stood at the top of the grand staircase, its railings encrusted in a gilded finish, and drank from a crystal champagne flute. The hot rush of alcohol blazed down his throat, and before he knew it, the champagne was gone. He was hopped up on so many drugs he'd forgotten what was swimming through his veins. After the third line, things began to blur into a mess of cigarettes, champagne, Pinot Grigio, marijuana (he had loved reintroducing a bill that would bar states from making it legal and loved it even more when the bill miraculously passed in 2027), and more cocaine. But through all that drug-infested fog, Palmer still had the drive to keep his attention solely on Davey Robinson.

The man had been a complete nobody in March, but he unfortunately made his presence known in April when he stormed into the Capitol with a briefcase full of blackmail documents with dirt on every Congressman in the Republican Party. Trips to sex islands, donations to South American dictators, sexual harassment cases from past jobs, generous gifts from Turkey and Qatar such as free hair transplants and luxury cars. That was his way of applying for a job, and he got it without question. Paid the big bucks to work as an acting advisor for the president.

When Davey Robinson walked into the Capitol with that briefcase, he looked like any other ordinary Caucasian you would find walking the streets of D.C. Trimmed brown hair, generally fit build, wearing a freshly tailored suit jacket no matter the weather.

In the three months since he barged into the legislative branch, he has slowly morphed into a spitting image of the president himself: Bleach-blonde hair, a faint spray tan, navy blue suits with red or pale-yellow ties depending on the occasion. His overall tone of voice became more nasal as those months passed. As the new campaign barreled into view, looking at Davey Robinson was like gazing into a time machine and seeing the president as he was forty years ago. It gave Palmer and his colleagues the creeps, and they wanted Robinson gone.

Mark Smith was always in the cards; that's why Palmer, Fitzgerald, and Hughes contacted him, after all. A psychopathic maniac who evaded the law and saw himself as a martyr. Where had they seen *that* before? With a little bit of shaping, Mark Smith wouldn't be just another blip on the campaign trail. He could be in the running. There was immense potential in him, but the obstacle they all needed to overcome was Robinson. Despite becoming a near-carbon copy of the president, he was lacking one specific skill that further separated him from his idol.

Davey Robinson was the place where charisma went to die.

He sucked the air out of any room he entered; his presence quieting down any continuing conversations, replacing any reasonable talks with short murmurs and glances to the side. He could talk the talk, but he certainly couldn't walk the walk. There was an awkwardness that came with being near someone who was clearly trying to be someone else, and Palmer couldn't stand it. Mark Smith, on the other hand. Oh, there was something underneath the surface that they needed to keep the Democrats from stealing another election. Something primal and mean. Brutal and without remorse. Clearly confused, but successful, nonetheless.

Palmer grabbed another flute from an usher's passing tray. He swigged the contents in one massive gulp and descended the stairs. The door to the ballroom opened before him, and the basic silhouette of a man stood in the frame. The man stepped into the room, looking downright bewildered by the chic commotion occurring around him. Mark Smith didn't know a single soul here, but they would all know him.

Yes, oh yes. How they would know him.

Palmer quickened his pace and outstretched his arms. "Mr. Smith! Pleasure to finally make your acquaintance," he said, going in for a hug Mark absolutely was not in the mood for.

Mark stepped back, smelling the booze on the congressman's breath.

"Which one are you?" he asked.

"Finley Palmer. The one who made all the phone calls."

Mark nodded wordlessly. He was in awe of the extravagance embedded within every carved structure in the ballroom. A crystal chandelier he had only seen in the movies hung above. People of all ages sashayed across the red carpet below, some men bringing their women to private rooms past the staircase leading to a grand terrace. The largest room in Bernard had been the local high school's gymnasium, where homecoming and prom dances usually took place. Instead of the tacky suits and dresses high schoolers were apt to wear for such occasions, these adults were adorned in those same tacky garments, just with real diamonds instead of that cheap plastic shit.

"Must be some candidate," Mark said.

"In a way, yes," Palmer responded, trying his damnedest to not slur his words. "Most of the people here are Mr. Robinson's donors. But Fitzgerald, Hughes, and I are here since we're in charge of the Midwestern leg of the campaign trail."

"Oklahoma isn't in the Midwest."

"That's not the point."

A crescendo of strings entered the atmosphere of the night. Violins tickled the stratosphere while the sole cello provided a much-needed foundation. All the musicians were White, which Mark saw as the reason why the music was subpar at best. Palmer would have stated otherwise, but that impending argument wasn't part of the plan.

The two found Davey Robinson chatting up a group of women who looked much too young to be called women. Robinson's hand was around one of their thin waists, the other gripped tightly on another girl's shoulder. Palmer grew more jealous of the man, while Mark felt a twinge of disgust broiling in his stomach. He instinctually tapped the man's shoulder, to which Robinson's cheery demeanor dropping into a deep, dark pit. His shining eyes softened into matte rocks.

"Who do we have here, Palmer?" Robinson asked, a feigned rasp in his voice setting Mark on edge.

"This is Mark Smith from Arkansas," Palmer said. "He'll be one of the guest speakers during the rally tomorrow."

Robinson, despite his obvious dismay, offered Mark a hand. They shook with relative strength, Mark wanting to rip Robinson's arm out of his socket for some unknown reason.

"I don't know anything about you, sir," Mark said.

"You will, my friend," said Robinson, flashing a too-white smile. "You must be quite the tremendous young man to be speaking at my first tour stop."

Mark wanted to point out that Robinson was probably only five years his senior but instead took *young man* as the compliment he so desperately desired.

"He's the best of the best, you might say," Palmer said.

"Well, if he's the best of the best, what does that make me? *More* the best?" Robinson cackled like a rabid hyena, the group of young girls around him joining in with their own childish giggles as if on command. "They've been saying no one will be more 'best' than me, no one. I don't quite like that word, now that I'm thinking about it. Have you ever been out of the country, Mark?"

"N," Mark said.

"I've always said that you can never be the best if you never have that world experience; that X-factor," Robinson said, having never said that before. He paused, confused, twisting his tanned face. "You haven't been outside America?"

"No."

"Are you fucking crazy?"

"No."

"Well how about I teach you to live?"

★ ★ ★

Abel had never felt so terrified yet so numb at the same time. There was a deep, underlying anxiety that ate away at the inside lining of his stomach, but his brain was too weak to feel it. He was only subconsciously aware of what he had done, murdering someone in cold blood.

"You couldn't have known," Eddie said, driving the two of them into the night, destination unclear. "You thought it was a deer or something. I thought that, too! It's not your fault."

"Then where are you taking me?" Abel asked, gliding his finger on the passenger-side window, tracing the distant tree line as it rushed by.

"You can't live there anymore. Why're you asking me this now? Didn't it occur to you that you weren't going to live in Bernard anymore? We packed all your shit."

"Yeah, I know," Abel said, feeling the weight of all his belongings jostling about in the bed of the pickup truck.

"I hope you understand how serious this is. Within a few days, someone's gonna realize this Macy girl is missing. Then there'll be a search party. Then someone will find her, and they'll track the bullet residue back to Louis, and he'll tell the police it was us who had the Winchesters. It'll all come back to us."

"And we need to be as far away as possible."

"Exactly."

"But it was an accident," Abel said. "They'd pick up on that, right?"

"You have too much hope," Eddie said, stomping the gas pedal as he passed a rather slow Kia Soul on the highway. "Nothing's an accident anymore. Everything's intentional. If I'd let you stay in Bernard, you'd be fucked. So fucked. *Too* fucked, even."

Abel's numbness grew so dire that the tips of his fingers began to buzz with pins and needles. Thank God his mom wasn't home. Despite how much they'd grown apart in the past few years, she was still his mother. Through the wall of cigarette smoke, she would have spotted his intentions from a mile away. Leaving her alone after her husband had done the same thing. She was broken, isolated, unloved. But Abel loved her. She gave him a home, a safe haven to rely upon when things got rough. That home, though, was gone.

Physically, no.

Conceptually, yes.

Home was dangerous, home was hostile. Home was a ticking time bomb that was ready to detonate the moment a body was found in a shallow grave just past Cemetery Hill.

Poor Macy. Poor fucking Macy. Abel reeled in the passenger seat as the pickup truck veered from lane to lane, passing cars that were going over the speed limit anyway. He didn't understand it, his brain. He didn't get why he felt nauseous, why he felt an urge to spill his guts to the nearest police officer, the urge to grab the steering wheel and send himself and Eddie flying off the road and into a nice, sturdy tree.

All that inner turmoil went straight to his bladder. Fuck, he needed to pee so goddamn bad. Abel tapped his old friend on the shoulder and asked him to stop at the next gas station. Eddie refused, saying he was hungry and would rather have a good meal over a gas station hotdog that would give him the shits.

They eventually pulled into a diner called Fast Freddie's after

Eddie had missed the first exit that advertised a much cleaner establishment. Abel scrambled out of the truck and bolted into the building, holding his dick and balls with a tight grip as he awkwardly limped toward the nearest restroom. He relieved himself over a toilet bowl, its rim caked in curly pubic hairs and dried piss. Each droplet that exited his body felt like a one-pound weight being lifted from his shoulders. He tried to suppress a moan but was too weak to do so. He let it out as his kidneys pushed the last of the toxins from his system.

He zipped up his fly, a cold draft painting his brow. He felt lightheaded, as if the air in the musty restroom had been sucked out from under the door. Walking toward the mirror, he didn't see himself. He saw Macy in the reflection, staring back at him with a bloodied grin and a hole in her neck oozing the stuff like a high-pressure water fountain.

Abel rubbed his eyes, not caring that whatever germs were on the toilet's handle were raring to give him pinkeye. Once his vision cleared, he looked into the mirror once more. Macy, only Macy. But she was different than before. Her cheeks were less red, hollower. Her skin had cracked like dry dirt on a hot day. Maggots dug through the barrier and formed little holes, squirming about as a beam of light found the girl's decaying body.

Abel saw the police discover the body. He saw them clear the area, looking for clues as to who this poor girl was, and why she was dead barely outside the Bernard town limits. He saw detectives and forensics brush for fingerprints. They find the bullet residue in Macy's body. They trace it back to Louis, who tells the cops exactly who had his Winchesters last. They find Abel curled up on some dusty motel bed. They put him in cuffs, they take him to prison, they document his fingerprints.

He saw a trial, Macy's family weeping in the pews behind him.

The judge smacks her gavel down, sentencing Abel to death in accordance with Arkansas state law. He saw himself walking down the hallway to his doom. He saw an electric chair, his head placed into a metal bowl, his arms and legs strapped to the chair. The executioner says something, but the sweat dripping from Abel's temples drowns out all sound. The lightning surges through his body, setting his nervous system ablaze with white fire. His eyeballs melt from their sockets; his brain becomes charcoal.

Abel? a voice shouts through the chaos.

Abel saw his own death. It was what he deserved. Everything that he was passionate about—killing, violence, weaponry—was nothing in the void. His life would be up for forfeit. Nothing mattered, in the end. The electric chair, a firing squad, a needle filled with a lethal cocktail.

ABEL!

A slap woke him from his trance. Abel was on the floor of the grimy diner restroom, Eddie raising his open palm for another smack. Abel shielded himself with his own hand, becoming lost in the intricate details of his skin's wrinkles.

"I'm fine," Abel sputtered. "I'm fine."

"You were in here for half an hour. What the fuck happened?"

Eddie helped him to his feet, going in for a hug. Abel stepped back, a burning sickness rising in his throat. He needed space, more space than the universe could possibly offer.

"Nothing," Abel said. "Just dehydrated."

"I got a water pitcher for the booth," Eddie consoled. "Come on."

They sat together inside Fast Freddie's, Eddie devouring a double bacon cheeseburger with steak fries, and Abel staring hopelessly into a plate of ham and cheese-smothered hash browns.

★ ★ ★

A year since the rumors of the president's dementia diagnosis hit the news circuit, Congress still hadn't been able to pass any legislation, both the good and the bad.

Next to none of the Republicans would show up to do their jobs. One stunningly bright representative found a useful loophole within the Constitution that allowed people of both the House and the Senate to take paid leave for as long as required. All the absentees needed to do was claim they were working "in the field" and they were all set.

Ashley tapped her red pen against her legal pad, eventually trading the random tempo for the melody of some Kendrick Lamar song from before the current president returned to power. Half of the House was out "in the field" including the Speaker. In reality, most of them were in Tulsa preparing for Davey Robinson's banal rally, and by "preparing," Ashley knew that meant drinking and smoking and shooting up and snorting as many drugs as possible while fondling as many barely legal teenage girls as possible.

The Speaker pro tempore was at the podium, sure, but he was also a bumbling idiot. He spoke only to the empty side of the aisle while the Democratic representatives could barely hear him. He didn't know how to work the microphone because of his old age. Ashley thought amusedly about what would happen if the pro tempore heard his own soft voice amplified through expensive speakers. She envisioned him screaming and turning to stone, the light draft of air blowing him into trillions of dust particles.

Ashley always had full faith in the function of the United States government. The rules were sound, everyone was replaceable. If the president were to die, the vice president would take over. If the Speaker of the House were out partying in Oklahoma, the Speaker pro tempore would stay behind in Washington to do… well, nothing. Ashley's faith dwindled with every passing second, her ears straining to catch a morsel of coherent speech from the pro tempore. She continued to tap her pen, losing the structured melody in favor of an angry snare drum trill.

Things weren't supposed to be this way. America had celebrated when the House and the Senate flipped back to blue after the midterm elections. There was joy, not chaos, in the streets. Multicolored streamers, impromptu musical performances, voters shedding happy tears on their local news stations. Two years of terror under the rule of the current president had been handicapped, and Ashley Guthrie was part of that movement.

Almost two years later, she had her doubts. Without half the House, nothing could be passed. They were out "in the field," working with their constituents according to the rules laid out haphazardly within the Constitution. That is, the constituents who lined their pockets, provided positive campaign advertising, and dealt them exorbitant amounts of illegal drugs.

She walked back home in the dark, clutching a small can of pepper spray inside her purse. She held her breath in the abyss between each lamppost's light. Washington, usually bustling with life, was dead quiet tonight. She walked past an apartment complex and heard the metallic *clink* of a toaster three floors above. She thought of how she had simply cracked a Coke open in her father's kitchen while he was slaughtered like a pig. She saw his mangled corpse and did nothing. Nothing. Just stood there, made snarky remarks, and let the killer leave unscathed.

Weak, Ashley thought. *You're weak. You're useless. You're a burden.*

"Hey, Ash!"

Ashley screamed, turned, and sprayed the assailant. Luckily for Representative Shaw, Ashley was already too frazzled to think straight, let alone shoot straight. The contents of the pepper spray landed on Shaw's navy-blue tie, splattering in indistinct chunks on the white dress shirt beneath. Ashley swept a strand of her hair from her face, realizing her repeated mistake. She dropped the can onto the sidewalk and said, "Oh my God, I am *so* sorry."

"No, it's okay," Shaw said, doing his best to wipe the residue from his clothes. "I needed a new tie anyway. You wanna grab a drink?"

"I feel like I kind of have to at this point."

"Perfect."

The two representatives found bar seats at a local pub called the Irish Jig. The interior looked like a tsunami full of green food dye caused a catastrophic flood, leaving nothing but glittery clovers, Irish propaganda, and cardboard cutouts of cartoonish leprechauns in its wake. Ashley put an Amaretto sour on her tab, allowing Shaw to put his tequila old fashioned on the same bill out of pity.

Just as it was out on the streets, the Irish Jig was nearly barren of human activity. Grating traditional Irish tunes blared on the nearby speakers, but that was the only other noise outside of the bartender clinking glasses while pouring their drinks. Ashley and Shaw sat there, twiddling their thumbs. Ashley really needed to get back home and stuff her face with the rest of that birthday carrot cake. But more importantly, she needed to be back with Tasha.

"You hear about the rally tomorrow?" Shaw asked, breaking the silence as he usually did.

"Who hasn't? Robinson wouldn't shut the fuck up about it," Ashley said. "Our president's own spitting image, right?"

"I guess so."

The bartender presented them with their drinks. Ashley thanked her but didn't take a sip. Shaw downed half of his old fashioned and knocked it down onto a dark green coaster.

"I can't stand the fucker," Shaw said.

"None of us can," Ashley responded.

"'Grassroots' my ass. That man has more corporate sponsors than the government already has. ExxonMobil, Warner Bros., PepsiCo, Meta. They all want the same guy as before, just in a different font."

"It's their way of circumventing the 22nd amendment," said Ashley, finally taking a sip of her Amaretto sour. "Remember when the president's reelection campaign was based on that Project 2025 crap? Remember that it had plans laid out to get rid of the 22nd? They couldn't get that to work because this whole administration is stuck digging in their butts, but of course the perfect proxy fell into their laps anyway."

"I'd say *they* fell into Robinson's lap, frankly."

"Same difference."

"Mr. President Junior," Shaw joked, putting a saluted hand to his brow. "But in all seriousness, I'm terrified of how he's going to rile up that crowd."

"You think there'll be a crowd?"

"I'm not sure about much anymore."

Ashley raised her glass to that.

"He's got a lot of guest speakers padding out the time tomorrow," Shaw added. "People in government positions and regular citizens alike. I checked the speakers' list and I saw someone from your old stomping ground, believe it or not."

Ashley's stomach dropped.

"What do you mean?" she asked.

"Yeah, it was some guy with a really basic name. I guess it was so bland I already forgot! Clark, maybe… no. It was Mark something, I'm pretty sure."

But Ashley couldn't forget that name. She would never forget that name as long as she lived. The blood on her hands. No, *his* hands. Memories of murder, memories of regret. All of these flooded her mind like the green tsunami that once ravaged the Irish Jig. There was something else in there too. A memory of the three other representatives from Arkansas harassing her with questions in the janitor's closet.

We think we've found a worthy successor.

"Smith," Ashley muttered. "It's Mark Smith."

"Yes, that's the name. You know him?"

"Do I *know* him?" Ashley laughed without any joy. "Everyone in that damn town knows him. Fucking piece of shit."

"Wow. I've never seen you so riled up."

"You don't know the half of it."

Ashley downed the rest of her drink, feeling grateful for the sweet burn of alcohol rushing down her throat.

"I can't believe those stupid assholes managed to drag Mark out of Bernard," Ashley said. "Palmer, Fitzgerald, Hughes. What do they expect to happen having him speak in front of a bunch of low-life idiots? All he knows is death and decay."

"What do you mean?" Shaw asked.

"You really want to know?"

Shaw sipped his drink and nodded wearily.

And then Ashley told him everything. Every last goddamn detail. Her slightly drunken tale spanned from the moment Mark Smith first ogled her breasts in high school, took a turn for the worse with the deaths of his mother and father, and went straight to hell when she chronicled the onslaught of murders enacted by him over the past decade.

"You're joking, right?" Shaw asked, a faint glimmer of hope glossing over his eyes like fresh tears. "That's just some dumb Hicksville tall tale. No offense."

"None taken, and no. It's all true."

"But the police—"

"No, they don't give a shit," Ashley said sternly. "Bernard PD stopped caring after the first year or so. It's a small town southwest of Little Rock. They honestly never—and *will* never—have enough officers employed to cover every case Mark Smith drops into their laps. So that's why they started ignoring everything. They set their sights on petty theft and traffic incidents. You know, easier stuff. But the killings? No. They don't care. Mark's too quick, bloodthirsty. Even the coroners in the area don't care. They get these bodies one after another and simply write the causes of death as 'suicide' or 'fatal accident.' Could I get another drink?"

The bartender gave a wonderful customer-service smile and whipped up another Amaretto sour.

"Thank you," Ashley said, sipping the beverage violently. She turned back to Representative Shaw. "All this to say: Bernard, Arkansas grew too numb to care about hundreds of their neighbors being slaughtered. Death in that town is as common as the sun rising in the east, or lobbyists running the government. They grew complacent, even *I* did. And I'll carry the guilt of that for the rest of my fucking life."

"Because he killed your father," Shaw solemnly said.

"How'd you guess?"

"You've barely talked about it."

"People grieve in different ways, Chris."

"But you haven't had the time to grieve at all," Shaw said. "You've been in the Capitol every day since you got back from Arkansas. I'm grateful for the work you're putting in for our country. We *all* are. But you also need to take care of yourself."

Ashley drank the rest of her second Amaretto. That sweet yet bitter taste washed the implications of grief from her mind. In a split second, she weighed the benefits and consequences of quitting her job and becoming a full-time alcoholic instead.

"You're strong, Ash," Shaw said, "but leave some strength for the rest of us. You don't have to go through this alone."

The television set that hung above them was on mute, but a quick glance revealed a late-night news headline that read: "SEVERAL DEAD, MORE WOUNDED IN SOUTH CAROLINA NIGHTCLUB SHOOTING." Helicopter footage showed police vehicles flashing red and blue, many miraculously unharmed citizens leaving the nightclub in tears, carrying the unbearable weight of knowing there were bodies inside the building, festering with death. Arthur Guthrie sat next to Ashley then; his head split down the middle like a pomegranate hacked by a machete. She glanced back to the television, mourning the losses of more Americans. She wanted to scream to them: "I'm sorry I'm sorry I'm sorry." Death was natural though, but not these deaths. They didn't have to happen. She could stop it. She knew she could. Her reelection this November was basically secured, and the next two years of her life could be spent advocating for victims of gun violence or sexual assault or hate crimes. Maybe the representatives across the aisle would finally listen after the next president was decided on.

Shaw lifted his empty cup to the news station. As the number of casualties flashed across the screen, he said, "I know you have a lot of hatred for this Mark Smith guy, but surely he can't be worse than all this."

* * *

Mark woke up with the worst headache he had ever experienced. His temples throbbed, each pulse sending a shockwave of pain through his nerves. He crawled out of a bed that wasn't his. The room was dark, but he saw a sliver of light peek through the heavy curtains. He was dripping with sweat, but the cool air from the air conditioning unit froze him like a popsicle. He inched toward the curtain, squinted his eyes, and pulled the thick fabrics apart.

Once the light settled, he opened his eyes. The view was much grander than the inherent flatness of the Bernard skyline. Buildings tore into the sky, cars bustled in the streets below, and fireworks blasted in the distances.

Mark felt a slight cramp in his backside. He bent down to alleviate the sharp knife in his spine, but what he saw instead was gruesome. Sheets of red coated his legs like the glaze of a candied apple. Was that… *his* blood? He smeared some of the stuff on his fingers, redundantly so since his hands were also smothered in gore. He tasted the liquid, sensing hints of rot and metal. That was most definitely blood, but not his, right? He followed his scarlet footprints back to the bed.

He hadn't been the only one sleeping there. Mark limped back to the mattress and lifted the duvet. Underneath was a woman. Blonde hair, perky breasts, cleanly shaved all over. Her legs were gone, reduced to chaotic stumps. Her face was forever carved with fear, her lifeless eyes staring up to the ceiling, her mouth agape with fright.

"Damn," Mark said, as it was the only word that could come to mind.

Had *he* done that? After two seconds of contemplation, he surmised that—yes—he had probably done that. But why? Had this beautiful young woman been upset? Had she been thinking of killing herself? To ease his own mental concerns, Mark quickly decided that the mystery woman had told him she wanted to die, and he had done the deed for her sake. Was it the truth? For now, it had to be.

Mark cleaned up in the adjoining bathroom. His toiletries were placed underneath the sink's marble counter, so the room must've been his. He stepped out of the shower and wrapped a white towel around his torso, hiding his protruding belly in case anyone barged in a saw it. He could hardly perceive himself in the mirror, even with his stomach fat hidden. He hated the thinning of his scalp, the wrinkles forming on his forehead and in the crooks by his armpits. A faded splotch of pigmentation appeared under his left eye. Mark remembered the liver spots that had infected his late uncle before his untimely passing. He had been spotted like a fucking leopard. Mark now wondered with horror if the old man's genes had passed onto him.

An earthquake erupted in his stomach. Mark raced to the open toilet and let the vomit spew forth. Chunks of late night's food, alcohol, and drugs spilled into the basin. Something resembling a tooth floated within the mess.

A text message dinged from his phone on the bedside table. It was the last in a series of texts from that Palmer politician. It read:

robinson rally @ noon!! where the FUCK r u?

Mark frowned, realizing he was going to be late for the only reason he was dragged out to Oklahoma in the first place. It was 11:30 in the morning according to the digital clock next to his phone. Mark scrolled further back in the one-sided text conversation, breathing a sigh of relief when he saw that Palmer had pinged his exact location in case Mark was lost.

He slipped into his dress clothes, struggling to button his suit jacket as he squeezed the wool over his torso. Before leaving the hotel room, he stepped back to the bed and lifted the duvet. Curious, he spread the dead girl's top lip, surprised to see one of her front teeth was missing. He found two pennies and set them on her cold tongue.

★ ★ ★

The Village People's "Y.M.C.A." blasted on the speakers surrounding the perimeter of the outdoor rally space. Signs that screamed "DAVEY 2028" in big, bold white letters against red and blue backgrounds clashed with the Tulsa's rather drab skyline. People of all shapes and sizes piled into the stands. Well… the stands that the venue allowed to be used (only 20 percent of the venue's 50,000 people capacity).

Citizens found their seats, all sunburnt from the onset of a very humid summer. Their red skin matched decently well with their red hats, all of which were embroidered with slogans in white text that had become synonymous with the American Republican movement. In that sea of red, Representative Palmer couldn't find Mark Smith, and that worried him.

"Any sight of Smith?" Fitzgerald asked.

"No," Palmer seethed.

From their vantage point, it should have been easy to spot Smith. He was much taller than the average-heighted people crawling into the venue, and if his voting records were anything to go by, Mark Smith wouldn't be caught dead with a red hat atop his head.

"Should I call him?"

"I've already bombarded his number with texts," Palmer said, crossing his arms. He peeked at the sun from over his sunglasses. Damn, it was hot. Why the *hell* did he decide to wear a suit today? Everything was going to shit even before it started. "Lucky for us, he doesn't have a speech until a decent portion through the rally. That should give him enough time to get here, while we sit here and suffer through dozens of scripted sob stories."

"Not to make you more worried than I already am," Fitzgerald said, "but I also can't find Hughes anywhere. Have you seen him?"

"He's probably smoking in a porta-potty. Please go check those before he falls in."

"On it."

Fitzgerald composed himself and set off for the toilets.

Palmer continued to stare over the crowd like a stone gargoyle perched atop a gothic cathedral. Just as he thought "Y.M.C.A." would end, the song looped back to the beginning. Everything was a cycle, Palmer thought. Just as the audio engineer repeated the same tired song incessantly, the nation's conservatives wanted a repeat of the ailing president. A replica in every way except for the drive, the want, the need to be better than the country he served. Palmer couldn't let that happen. America was dying. She'd been dying in plain sight for decades. Identity politics and terrorism and mass shootings and foreign wars had been destroying the very foundation she was built upon: independence. The United States did not need to butter up other countries for its own gain. No, they needed a leader who would cut them off from the international lens. The current president had attempted to do so with obnoxious tariffs and morally incorrect political alignments, but his old age was showing, and he was never completely up for the task. Mark Smith, however, would be a force to reckon with. An extremely unlikeable man that would harken a new American age, one without immigration, legal or otherwise.

And there the man was, finally shuffling through the crowd of red hats. Palmer hadn't realized an entire hour had gone by. Numerous paid actors had said their pieces, complaining about illegals stealing their crops and transgender students sexually harassing their teachers.

Palmer smiled despite the sunburn beginning to form on his unprotected skin. *Here cometh the angel of death,* he thought. *Save us from ourselves.*

CHAPTER 8

★ ★ ★

"My freedoms were taken away by these last midterms!" a disgruntled white woman shouted from the main stage. "I voted for cheaper egg prices in 2024, but when 2026 came around, suddenly everyone wanted those fucking libtards back in office? Who's making the rules around here? A bunch of sissy liberals, or a strong army of red, white, and blue-blooded patriots?"

Mark waded through the crowd feeling less disgusted by his own body. There was a plethora of different body types here: Dangerously skinny people as well as severely overweight pigs. They all stood in awe of the useless drivel spewing from the center stage. American flags decorated the backdrop, with the backdrop itself being a ginormous projection that read "DAVEY 2028" in all capital letters, with the titular man gracing the right half of the screen in an image so large that Mark could see each and every one of the overly tanned man's pores.

He thought of the dead girl, the one from his hotel room. He hadn't stopped thinking about her. Even in the backseat of the Lyft, the image of her blonde hair streaked with deep maroon planted itself on his mind like a parasite. He tried to remember the events that led to her death. His hangover kept him from grasping the finer details of the matter. A damning mental fog covered everything. But that man's face—that Davey Robinson—was all too familiar.

They had talked at that extravagant party, not that Mark had willingly entered the conversation. Representative Palmer had introduced him to the man. Mark remembered the veneers Robinson wore, how they glistened in the yellow glow of the chandeliers like the shiny cheap plastic of McDonald's Happy Meal toys. He remembered the girls, too. Wow, they were young. *Way* too young. Barely eighteen, if even that. All blonde, some more naturally than others. Had Mark taken one of them back to his room? The thought shook him to his core, adding more misery to the cold sweats he already felt standing in that arena amongst some of America's most reviled citizens.

"Will you all stand up against the pedophilic elites?" the white woman speaker concluded. "Or will you lick their boots like the good, little slaves you are?"

The crowd chanted *fight, fight, fight* all in painful unison. Each booming amalgam of voices bashed Mark's skull in like a thousand sledgehammers to his temples. He continued to shove his way through the mass, tipping red baseball caps off people's heads as he passed. He did not excuse himself, he did not wait for gaps to form. No, he persevered. A simple fucking headache wasn't going to stop him from finally speaking to the country. If only the people who lived outside Bernard, Arkansas could experience the joy his actions brought to the people inside the town limits.

Mark eventually found a VIP entrance guarded by a burly

Black man. Mark was surprised to find someone taller than himself at this venue, but it was certainly a welcome surprise.

"ID?" the guard asked.

Mark felt for his wallet, but his pockets were smooth over his thighs. Time to improvise.

"I'm Mark Smith," he said. "I'm a guest speaker."

The guard didn't budge, simply lifted a brow that arched violently over the rim of his sunglasses.

"*SMITH!*"

Mark peered over the guard's bowling ball shoulder and spotted the weak frame of Representative Palmer running from beneath the stage toward the VIP entrance. He stopped behind the guard, tapped the big man's shoulder, and said, "He's with me. Let him through."

The guard huffed and moved out of the way. Palmer grabbed Mark by the coat sleeve and rushed him under the stage.

"Where the fuck were you?" the politician asked through gritted teeth.

"My alarm didn't go off," Mark lied.

"And neither did my hundreds of other messages?"

"I got them eventually."

"Almost too late, Smith. Almost too late. You're on after this next speaker."

Palmer led him up a flight of iron steps and back into the sunlight. Mark winced momentarily, then heard Palmer ask: "Do you remember what you need to say?"

"Mostly."

"That doesn't give me much confidence." The congressman lifted a bit of powder from his pants pocket and swiftly sucked it up his left nostril. He groaned, pinched his nose, and continued to speak with watering eyes. "You need to go out there and appease the audience. At this point, they're bored out of their fucking minds. Go out there and appeal to their sensibilities. Rile them up, tell a sad story, earn some sympathy. Just give them a small glimpse of who you really are."

"Who I really am?" Mark asked.

"Exactly."

Palmer grinned in the same maniacal way those bombers would before the explosions destroyed Grey Sloan Memorial Hospital for the fiftieth time on *Grey's*. There was an ugly plan lingering behind the politician's drugged-out eyes, but Mark didn't want to know. Palmer patted down Mark's suit jacket, wiping away Tulsa's atmospheric grime.

The current speaker complained about how few employees he had on his farm after the present administration removed all his Latino workers through their ICE protocols. He was immediately booed and led off the stage by another two guards that looked identical to the one outside the VIP entrance.

Watching from the side of the giant backdrop, Mark said, "Tough crowd."

"Whatever you were planning on saying, make sure none of it has to do with immigration," Palmer said with a laugh. "It's a bit of a touchy subject."

"Alright."

But Mark wasn't alright. He watched the two guards pick the speaker up by the back of his flannel shirt and toss him over the barricade. The man laid in the dry grass, unresponsive, baking in the hot sun like a crispy worm on asphalt.

Anxiety clouded Mark's judgement. How would the crowd react to anything he had to say? Would they even listen? He obviously wasn't the main attraction. They were all here to see Davey Robinson, the man who bore an uncanny resemblance to the current president, both in manner of speaking and in taste in females. They were infatuated with the idea of a caricature of a businessman continuing to lead the country, unable to open themselves up to more novel perspectives. If they somehow were to listen to Mark, would they boo him off the stage like the last guy? Maybe they weren't ready for the truth of their salvation, that the answer of life's greatest horror was written in blood.

An omniscient announcer shouted Mark's name. Palmer clapped him on the back and told him to break a leg.

He swallowed his pride, patted himself down, and introduced himself to the world. For better or for worse.

★ ★ ★

The House wouldn't meet that day due to more than the typical half of absentees being missing in action. Ashley wasn't sure whether she should feel elated or downright pissed about a day off from work, but she used the free morning to take an everything shower and clean up around the apartment. Tasha was out on a trip to a psychology conference in Virginia, so she had the whole apartment to herself, meaning she was responsible for vacuuming and scrubbing and mopping until the entire fucking place sparkled.

Around noon and soaking with sweat from a job well done, Ashley plopped down onto the sofa and turned on the television. She selected a random news station and watched as live coverage of the first Davey Robinson rally appeared on the screen. A disgruntled man had been thrown off the stage and over the fence for announcing his dismay for recent immigration policies. For a topic so near and dear to all Republicans' hearts, Ashley was surprised by how much they refused to mention immigration during any recorded events. Representative Hughes surely loved to shoot the shit—behind closed doors, naturally—about how undocumented people stole his third wife and ate his precious rat dog. They were embarrassed, all of them. They were embarrassed about how the botched mass deportation of Mexicans from the United States made their party look bad during the midterms. If she were in their shoes, Ashley would be flustered too, as much as she abhorred to admit it.

After a brief delay, an announcer heralded the rally's next guest speaker.

"Introducing an honored patriot from rural Arkansas," the voice rattled. "Mark Thomas Smith!"

Ashley awoke from her cleaning-induced stupor and quickly turned up the volume. She wanted to hear every detail of the embarrassment that would soon unfold in Tulsa.

Mark Smith walked onto the stage. He gave a short wave to the audience before reaching the podium. Was he wearing the same shirt he wore the night he'd murdered her father? Did blood really wash out of white fabric that easy?

Stock audio of a crowd cheering played on the news station (the actual audience looked deadpan and tight-lipped as the camera panned across them). As Mark planted his hands on either side of the wooden podium, he hunched his back and leaned toward the microphone. He looked nervous, just as nervous as he had been when Ashley caught him in the act in her father's home. She never understood why he was nervous to be caught murdering someone; he *had* to be aware that everyone knew he was the aptly named Hillside Butcher. *Three new graves added to Cemetery Hill… Search continues for the Hillside Butcher,* a headline from the Bernard Gazette had read after the brutality the Reagan family had endured. If anything, Ashley should've been furious watching her father's murderer live on national television, but she wasn't.

Frankly, the congresswoman was rather excited for him to bomb.

"Hello, Tulsa," Mark finally said, monotone. "How are we doing today?"

More audio clips of applause graced Ashley's speakers, despite the crowd remaining relatively still. Mark coughed into his jacket sleeve and tapped the microphone. The sharp din of feedback scratched Ashley's ears with razored talons.

"As you all know, my name is Mark Thomas Smith… the Second! They forgot to say that. I'm a daddy's boy, what can I say?"

"Holy shit," Ashley said on the edge of her seat. Mark seriously thought that was funny. When was the last time he had interacted with a human being? That night in her father's kitchen? Her unwelcome visit to him at Little Rock Memorial? She was enjoying every goddamn second of this train-wreck, regardless.

"I grew up in a little town an hour or so from Little Rock," Mark began. "The people were friendly, and the stray cats were even friendlier. As a… *patriot*… I've always been involved in the dirty work. After most days of school, I would come home, take the dog for a walk, and chop firewood ad nauseam until my father came home from work. Dad—who I'm named after, bless his soul—owned a paper mill in town. They processed timber into useful things such as paper, lumber, and other products. The entire town's economy hung in the balance of whether that mill succeeded or failed."

Ashley had to give it to the psycho; he was right. The Smith Family Paper Mill had been Bernard's top source of economic stability for years. The funds made by the mill were usually reallocated to school activities or park renovations. Recreational stuff, for the most part. But when the senior Mark Smith died, the paper mill died with him, and the current Mark took his family's inheritance and all their stakes in the business and hoarded the wealth. As far as Ashley knew, the only things Mark had spent those millions of dollars on were food, water, shelter, and weapons.

"But then my mother died, and I couldn't forgive myself for it," Mark continued from the Tulsa stage. "Suicide is a disease; you all must know. It's a raging sickness that infects all the sad, miserable people in our country. When I found my mom hanging from the ceiling, I vowed to make sure that no one ever killed themselves ever again…" There was a grand pause. Ashley held her breath. "So I kill them all before they can do it themselves."

Ashley felt the air suck out of the spotless apartment. Did he… did Mark Smith really admit to mass serial murder? On *national television*? Despite the implications of hundreds of deaths being brought to the public's attention, Ashley couldn't help but smile. *That absolute fucking idiot*, she thought amusedly. *Bernard PD let you off the hook, but would the whole country? I don't think so.*

"Suicide is an epidemic in our nation," Mark said. "I am the cure."

Ashley waited with bated breath for the same guards that hurled the previous speaker off the stage to do the same to Mark. Maybe something worse, if there truly was a God. But they didn't come. Ashley stood up and shook the flatscreen, unsure of whether the screen had frozen or if Mark was standing inhumanly still. Surely the newsfeed had been cut. Something as heinous as the dogshit spewing from Mark's mouth would warrant a stop to the live taping. Ashley searched her mind for a semblance of hope; another shrivel of faith in her country and her community.

The camera cut from Mark and panned once more over the crowd. They were dead silent, staring in shock toward the center stage. As the newsfeed cut back to Mark, Ashley saw him quickly glance to the back of the stage, nod toward someone, and turn back to the camera.

"And I know, with the help of Mister Davey Robinson," Mark amended, "our country will know no more suffering. Vote for Davey this November!"

The crowd immediately erupted into applause. They seemed to not have heard a single thing Mark had said before his endorsement of Davey Robinson for president. Every red-hat-wearing idiot in that audience was afflicted with an acute case of tunnel vision. It didn't matter what someone told them, as long as they were on *their* side.

Ashley turned the television off, nearly scaring herself when she saw her reflection in the black mirror.

"What… the *fuck*," she muttered.

She walked into the kitchen and opened the fridge, grabbing the Brita filter and pouring herself a glass of water. She downed the entire glass in just a few gulps, her throat burning as the cold ice water stung her insides. God, she needed a drink. A *real* drink. She wondered if Shaw wanted to meet again at the Irish Jig. Maybe Tasha was on a lunch break at that Virginia conference.

In the corner of her eye, Ashley saw her father, but not as she remembered his gruff yet bright face from her childhood. That same apparition that has haunted her since that fateful night, the image of him split down the middle that would be etched into her eyes for the rest of her life. She could hear the squelching of blood and muscle tissue hit her laminate floors. She kept her focus on the empty glass of water. A droplet swam down the inside like a lazy tadpole.

Ashley, baby, Arthur said.

She screamed and swatted the glass off the counter. It landed on the floor and exploded into thousands of dazzling shards.

It was all a lie, a fluke. Mark Smith could never rile a crowd like that. It was just because he mentioned Robinson that the audience shouted their praise. Affiliations were powerful things in the world of politics. They had the power to sway voters in the blink of an eye. She didn't know what games Palmer, Fitzgerald, and Hughes were playing, but their intentions were as wrong as ever.

If the United States were to continue living, Mark Smith could not be a part of its history. Not now, not ever.

★ ★ ★

After what seemed to be an eternity on the open road, Eddie finally took an exit off the highway and onto a paved road that abruptly turned into a gravel lane before Abel had time to process where he was.

Eddie had remained silent on absolutely nothing except for where the hell they were going. He had joked about a three-car pile-up, *oohed* and *aahed* at four separate deer carcasses, and asked Abel about what he'd been up to for the last few years. Yet none of the asides and conversations led to the answer of why Abel was in the truck to begin with. Where the hell was the road taking them? Why did he need to be there with Eddie? The questions were numerous, but one stood out most in his mind: How was Mom doing? Surely, she'd noticed that he was gone. The thought of her sobbing in an empty house, a cigarette burning into her fingers, tortured Abel to no end as the truck jolted him awake on the bumpy gravel path.

"Almost there," Eddie said.

"Almost *where*?"

"Stop asking that."

The arid sky disappeared behind a looming wall of dense trees. They rippled and swayed in the light breeze, allowing rays of light to glint through their branches. Abel squinted at a red speck hidden in one of those branches. A cardinal bird rested there before noticing the truck and flying off.

There was an open alcove within the woods. The gravel road expanded into a circle of dirt surrounding an isolated cabin. Abel was reminded of every single horror movie involving a cabin in the woods: *The Evil Dead, Friday the 13th, Creep, It Comes at Night, Hush, The Blair Witch Proj*—

"Abel, get outta the truck," Eddie said.

Abel shook out of his anxiety-riddled daze and exited the vehicle, nearly missing the step as he descended to the forest floor. Eddie grabbed his meager belongings, and Abel attempted to haul his own stuff along with the two Winchester rifles. They went up two steps and Eddie knocked on the door with a distinct pattern.

Th-thunk. Thunk. Th-thunk.

Footsteps echoed from behind the door before coalescing into the hinges creaking open. An extremely built woman appeared in the doorway with a violent scowl ripped across her face. A deep scar formed a ravine from her brow bone to the middle of her forehead. Abel instinctively took a step back, almost tripping over one of his multiple backpacks.

"Long time, no see," the woman said to Eddie, her voice as husky as cigarette ash.

"Could say the same," Eddie said. "Sorry for the holdup, though. I had some complications on the way up."

"Taking a visit to your old stomping ground was a complication, then?"

"In a way, yeah."

"And who's *this*?"

The woman glared at Abel with a thousand tons of disapproval.

"Abel," he said, nearly choking on his name.

"And why is he here?" the woman asked Eddie.

"He got into some hot shit back in Arkansas," Eddie responded, "but I think he could be a really great asset for us."

"Asset?" Abel asked.

The woman thought Eddie's explanation over. Her jaw clenched for a moment before she let out a short chuckle and brushed past Abel. She bent down and picked up all his things and brought them into the cabin. "Right this way," she said, dissolving into the dark interior.

Abel shot a quick glance at Eddie.

"Why am I here?"

"I'm saving you," Eddie said. "Think of it as a favor. And also think of this as a new job opportunity. I know you were annoyed about applying for college, so this is how you skip that step entirely."

Abel mulled that over for a quick second before following Eddie into the cabin without another word on the matter.

While dim, the living area was neatly decorated with earthy oranges and greens that camouflaged nicely with the wilderness peering through the draped windows. The sweet, bitter scent of freshly brewed coffee wafted up Abel's nose, reminding him all too much of home. The way he would wake up for school each morning to the smell of cheap Folgers, his father pouring a steaming mug of it while his mother sat on the couch, putting out a cigarette the moment she noticed her son enter the room. Days were pleasant back then. Not great, but bearable. There had been enough joy throughout the day to cancel out the loathing, the sinister thoughts. The day after he'd stabbed Macy in the neck, he'd woken up in bed to that familiar smell of coffee. When he left his bedroom and checked the kitchen, no one was there. Only a ghost.

A ghost his mother ignored as she sat on the couch and smoked a cigarette without shame.

They walked past the eerily quiet living area and proceeded down a steep flight of rickety stairs. Abel could've sworn he heard distant chatter emanating from within the walls. A harsh fluorescent bulb hung overhead, illuminating a simple wooden door. The woman set Abel's belongings on the frigid concrete and unlocked the door. As it creaked open, Abel felt whiplash at the sight of what laid beyond.

There was a graying man with an eyepatch sitting at a folding table, a cup of coffee in his grip. The entire room felt as if it were from a completely different house, not even a cabin. The walls were stark white, the floor a shiny metallic gray. Six doors stood around the perimeter of the room, each one with a name tag nailed to the surface. Wyatt, Johnny, Xavier, Mateo, Valerie, and Zuri. There was a seventh door simply labeled "*GUEST*," which Abel assumed he and Eddie would reside in for the time being.

The older gentleman with the eyepatch gave Abel a stern look that sent shivers down his spine. The woman noticed his fright and remarked, "Oh, don't mind Johnny. He has a hard time being polite with so much of his head shoved up his ass."

"Go fuck yourself, Val," Johnny grumbled, sipping his coffee.

The woman—or Valerie, if one of the name tags and Johnny were to be believed—nudged open the guest room with her shoulder and threw Abel's things onto the floor.

"Home sweet home," Valerie said. She turned to Eddie, her tone solemn. "I need to speak with you for a bit. Come on."

Unsure of how to exist in this space, Abel shut himself inside the guest room. He could only take so much of that Johnny man's one-eyed stare for so long before his brain exploded from the stress. He turned on the light. It flickered before granting him consistent luminance. Other than his and Eddie's stuff, the room was barren save for a cot in the corner and a power outlet in the white wall. Everything felt grimy but sterile, like the smell of a car that was sold as new but had cumstains on the backseat.

He waited for an hour or so, twiddling his thumbs while staring at the two Winchesters on the concrete floor. Those rifles were (Abel hoped) the only evidence of his crime. Beside the rifles, he saw a brutal flash of Macy's bloodied corpse, lying contorted in the grassy knoll by Cemetery Hill like a dirty ragdoll. Next to her, his mother lay on her back, her haggard face seeming calmer without the stress wrinkles. Her hair was strewn about, intertwining with the blades of grass like a crochet quilt made from green and black threads. A thin trickle of blood seeped from her pursed lips. Her bulging eyes opened and stared into his, a grin now slashed across her face revealing pink teeth outlined with a darker red. She mouthed something inaudible, that smile refusing to slip. Abel leaned over the cot to listen, but the further he got to his mother, the more silent the guest room became. Still, he continued forward. As he approached, his mother turned her head, a glob of congealed blood spurting from her mouth, flecked with black tar. She reached out a hand and tugged at Macy's ear, pulling so hard that the skin and cartilage stretched like fleshy taffy. As the ear tore from the dead girl's head with a sickening squelch, Abel felt a sharp pain on the side of his head. His mother continued to quietly babble, the smile unflinching. He felt his head, the sensation of something wet hitting his fingers. In an instant, his mother disappeared from the floor and sat next to him on the cot. Her mouth was up to his ear, the lips moving without any sound. Sweat beaded on his brow. He didn't want to look at his mother, but she needed to tell him something. His fingers were covered in blood. *What the fuck?* he wondered.

Without warning, his mother raised her arm and jammed it into his head. He screamed; no one heard. Her fingers wriggled around inside his skull like tens of hungry eels slithering about for their next meal. She crunched and squished his brain into a fine paste. He felt it all as his senses faded and his screams evaporated into a terrified vapor.

When he awoke from this nightmare, Abel checked his ear. He felt the grooves of cartilage and knew he was physically alright. Someone knocked on the guest room door. Abel groaned, drenched in sweat as he walked over the bags containing the rest of his life and opened the door.

"You good?" Eddie asked.

"A little better," Abel said. "Still not good, though."

"That's fair. Val wants to meet with you upstairs."

Abel found himself back in the living area on the ground floor, the scent of brewed coffee beans notably absent in that now late hour. He sat on the sofa opposite Valerie, Eddie standing behind him as if he were his bodyguard. There was a Manila folder on the coffee table between Abel and Valerie. He couldn't keep his eyes off it. Something felt so intriguing about what laid in wait inside.

"Edmund filled me in on your situation while you were asleep," Valerie began, cutting the silence like a newly sharpened katana through a helpless watermelon. "You're quite the sharp-shooter, then?"

Abel didn't know whether that was meant as a compliment or a snide jab. This Valerie woman was so difficult to read with how much her face refused to twitch with any semblance of emotion.

"I didn't mean to kill her," he said.

"We've all made mistakes here, but that isn't the point. Edmund also told me about your mother. I'm quite sorry to hear about that, truly. When I started this line of work, it started as a way for me to escape the law as well. I had to leave behind my family and friends to come here and hide."

"Line of work?"

"We are the Coalition, Abel." He'd never heard of such a group, but the name had undeniable weight. "Underground operatives. We serve people with needs greater than our own. This entire business runs on the funds of the wealthy who have nowhere else to turn."

"Hired assassins," Eddie said.

Abel tried to suppress a laugh, but his resistance was futile. A fine spray of saliva jettisoned onto the folder before him. Valerie scowled and told Eddie: "I was getting to that part."

"You don't have to be cryptic," Eddie responded. "Get to the damn point. He's not some government spy. I told you everything you need to know. He has no one now."

No one? Abel thought. *Coffee in the morning, Mom on the couch, a day of school ahead of me, a pencil in some poor girl's neck.*

"We're hired assassins, as our friend Edmund so graciously put it," Valerie said. "If a wealthy donor needs someone axed, we're the ones to call. Now, I wouldn't be so upfront about this if it weren't for the fact that our marksman, Wyatt, isn't with us anymore."

"What happened to him?" Abel asked. It was easier for him to accept this absolutely insane situation if he asked questions. Surely, the lies would slip, and everyone would jump up in glee and yell *SURPRISE! THE JOKE'S ON YOU, ABEL!* if he kept speaking.

Valerie sighed and said, "He was hired for a hit in South Carolina. Some wealthy businessman who was eating into a wealthier businessman's client base. Things turned sour and Wyatt ended up not just shooting the guy but gunning down several more people to escape the nightclub he was sent to. The police shot him on sight."

A slam echoed from the kitchen. Eddie had abandoned his position behind Abel and punched the wall below a rack of hanging frying pans. Whoever this Wyatt person was, Eddie certainly wasn't taking the news of his death very well.

"All of this to say, we are in need of a new firearm specialist," Valerie said. "Johnny can't shoot for shit without his good eye, and the rest of us are either involved in demolition or infiltration."

"What about Eddie?"

"Edmund?" Valerie laughed. It felt forced, disturbing in its perfect hardy-hars. "No, that was never a consideration. He can be a bit... emotional."

Abel glanced at Eddie in the kitchen. His hands were pressed against the back of his head as he sobbed over his dead friend, his tears falling into the sink.

"I guess," Abel said.

"For that reason, I'm asking you to take up arms," said Valerie. "There's an election on the horizon and we're going to have a lot of customers. We'll need someone with a sharp eye and precise trigger finger. The others are out placing explosives at some conference in Virginia, but I'll ask the question on their behalf. What do you say? Will you join us?"

If this was all a ruse, Abel commended them all for a convincing role play. If this was real, however, he didn't know what to feel. His life had shifted so radically in the past 24 hours that the emotional whiplash still hadn't fully set it. A fun day of shooting the shit with his old friend had morphed into a treacherous deluge of accidental murder, new beginnings, and hard goodbyes. Goodbye Arkansas. Goodbye Mom. Goodbye dignity. As much as he had ached for the chance to kill alongside Mark for years, his actual first murder did not come with the satisfaction that he hoped for. All that was left in him was guilt and shame, trauma over what he had done and the consequences that would follow. But what better way for Abel to atone for his sins by signing onto a new life of debauchery?

Unaware of the terms and conditions of this offer, Abel agreed.

★ ★ ★

Mark couldn't wash that stupid grin off his face. He was on a tour bus headed to Joplin, Missouri, sitting in the back as to not draw too much attention to himself. *You should present yourself more*, he thought. *There's a world out there you didn't think was real, where people accepted you for who you are with thunderous applause. This is what you were born to do. Mom would be proud.*

Finely dressed older folks lined the seats of the front half of the bus, while that congressman Palmer and his two droogs sat only a few seats in front of Mark. He thought about sauntering to the front and congratulating them, but mostly himself, for a success well earned. The cheers had been his favorite part of the whole ordeal. All those people—as disgusting as some of them were—raised their voices in *agreement* with what he had to say. The things about his mother and all the lives he had saved after the fact. Things that he assumed would be taboo outside of Bernard weren't as frowned upon as he expected.

"Excellent work today."

Mark barely noticed Fitzgerald and Palmer had cozied up next to him, Palmer in the seat beside and Fitzgerald leaning over the back of the seat in front. Fitzgerald, while Mark had barely interacted with the man, was gleefully frothing at the mouth.

"I was a bit worried at first, but you really sold the show even before Robinson took the stage," Fitzgerald said. "That's *exactly* what the people want, Mr. Smith. Exactly what they need, even. A radical new face in the world of politics that isn't afraid to push the boundaries while also keeping true to the heart of America. Oh, it was a wonder to behold."

"I'm sure Robinson's little gift to you last night helped calm your nerves," Palmer added.

"What do you mean?" Mark asked.

"The girl, Mark. Don't you remember the girl?"

He remembered the girl in question. Long blonde hair, a too-young face, torn-off legs, all lying next to him in a hotel bed house-keeping was sure to have a field day with.

"Yes," he said, his grin fading.

"You know Robinson owns an entire brothel full of girls just like her?" Fitzgerald budded in. "All extremely young—"

"And extremely hateful toward him," Palmer interrupted. "Now, I've never seen where he keeps all the girls myself, but I can see it clear as day in their eyes: They're tired. So tired that they could just drop dead, I imagine."

It dawned on Mark that he was satisfied with Palmer's words. Maybe the dead girl in his bed had been contemplating suicide, if the congressman was to be believed. But what would a simple pol-itician know, and why would he be so apt to tell the truth? He took a glance at his reflection in the window, seeing nothing but his face against the darkness of summer nightfall. The smile was slowly returning, but the wrinkles forming at the corners of his mouth quickly made the joy subside.

"So why are you telling me this?" Mark asked, turning to the congressmen.

"I'm going to be frank with you, Mr. Smith," Palmer said, his voice smooth as warm butter. "Davey Robinson is a bad man. Terrible. He wrangles up these girls from all over the country and flaunts them around like prize-winning dogs. And we would hate to see him continue this frivolous lifestyle at the cost of innocent, young women's well-being. Wouldn't you hate to see what would become of them? Those pure, beautiful lives?"

"God forbid they start swallowing pills and dropping like flies," Fitzgerald said, a weird tone of sarcasm adding flavor to his words. "Talk about a suicide epidemic. Those poor girls."

They were talking *at* him, not *to* him. Mark didn't appreciate being babied by two United States congressmen, but their sentiment seemed sincere enough. They were giving him a mission. It was obvious. They skirted around outright telling him to murder Davey Robinson, but Mark understood the undertones of their speech. Robinson was a crook who harbored young girls into some sort of sex cabal and abused them into suicide. When they were dead, he would simply replace them with another beautiful girl. Mark knew for certain that Robinson had already found a replacement for the girl he'd murdered in his hotel room, and that the new girl would meet a horrible fate if he weren't there to stop it. Robinson had tried to reason with him by seducing him with one of those girls, but Mark wasn't stupid. He saw through everything.

He knew exactly what he had to do.

He would kill the Republican candidate for president of the United States, and it would save him a lot of pennies.

CHAPTER 9

The streets of Bernard, Arkansas were alight with anger. Being a small town in the middle of nowhere, the media had not bothered covering the protests and ensuing riots that engulfed the town in the days since Macy Thornton's body was found at the base of Cemetery Hill with two pennies nowhere to be found.

Bernard had a murderer on the loose, someone who wasn't Mark Smith, someone who the police similarly refused to open an investigation on. They had been so quick to apprehend Andre Williams for a harmless marijuana farm, but the murder of an innocent girl? All crickets from the police station. Simply another day in Bernard. People died all the time, why would this death be any different from the rest?

But the town's citizens saw through the deceit. They weren't idiots, as much as an outsider looking in would say otherwise. The Thornton family had been through so much in the past few years, whether it be the legal case against the Wattersons over their son stabbing Macy in the neck, or the chaos she had to endure in her own home after the matter was settled. Richard Thornton was an abuser, both of alcohol and of his wife and two children. The medical bills they accrued from the Abel Watterson incident had sent them into debt, the court case that was meant to mitigate the costs went south, and Richard was finally at his wit's end. He was a fucking doctor for God's sake! Couldn't they have given him an employee discount? The anger simmered in him like a slow-cooking stew, lying in wait for the perfect time to explode. And two days ago, the crockpot finally burst. Richard laid the belt on his wife, sending her to urgent care. He flogged their younger son so terribly that his arm fell out of its socket and his hip shattered. Some would have said that Macy was let off the hook. The worst pain she had received was a swift lashing to the back that tore her skin and left a trail of blood dripping into her underwear. After finding her mother lying helplessly on the floor, she dialed 9-1-1 and hid outside the house until the paramedics arrived. Once she knew her mother and brother would be safe from the tumultuous storm that was her father, she'd run. Ran so fast into the woods behind the Thornton home. She flew through jagged branches and poisoned ivy stems. She ran past her limit, barely able to breathe as she finally came to a clearing. The scar on her neck throbbed with an old pain, her ears filled with sorrow and near-to-bursting blood vessels, so clogged with grief that she never heard Abel Watterson and Edmund Wright firing Winchester rifles at a target just yards away. She had been so close to freedom, so close to escaping a life she never wanted to experience again. Nothing on her mind except for the places she would go, the people she would meet, the wonders outside Bernard just waiting for the taking. But as she took the first step outside the tree line, she felt white-hot lead pierce her trachea. As her vocal cords melted, she let out one final scream. In that scream, her hopes and dreams fizzled out like bubbles from a soda left open in the fridge. The places she would go to and the people she would meet disappeared from her timeline as her life was permanently extinguished.

Her killer had left her to rot in the tall grass beside Cemetery Hill. Atop that same hill, a little girl named Jordan—known commonly among Bernard residents as the Little Tomato Hurler—laid near the graves of Sophia and Mark Smith Sr. with a bullet lodged between her eyes. However, people did not give her untimely death any mind. Old Mrs. Donahugh, mourning her late husband a few yards from the murder site, spotted the girl. She informed the police, who immediately disregarded the tip when she mentioned the two pennies, a trademark of the infamous Hillside Butcher.

The protesters did not march through the streets for Jordan. The child was simply another natural occurrence in the wrath of one Mark Smith. They were smashing shop windows in Macy Thornton's name. How could someone *other* than Mark Smith do this to one of their neighbors? And why couldn't the police look past all the copper coins and see that they had a real problem on their hands?

"Justice for Macy!"

"Our pigs are deaf!"

"Say her name! Macy Thornton!"

"Defund BPD!"

"No justice, no peace!"

"All cops are bastards!"

No matter their differences in race, color, creed, sexuality, or political leaning, people from all corners of that small town raised their voices and arms to fight against injustice. The police on duty hunkered down inside their station, hiding under desks as the chanting grew louder and louder, guns unholstered and ready to fire. One officer held a metal crucifix around his neck, intoning a silent prayer with tears in his eyes. Another was fiending for a fight. He was new on the force and bootcamp had made him bloodthirsty. He wanted to know what it was like to shoot someone, to watch them reel back and fall, blood spurting from a tiny hole in their gut like a fountain of liquified strawberry jam.

As the protesters broke down the front door, this younger officer immediately rose from his hiding spot and opened fire. He sneered as he mowed down eight people, people that he recognized from grocery shopping or his walks around the park. He didn't give a shit about what they were angry about. They were just cannon fodder. But in his ecstasy, he forgot to reload his pistol, and by the time he realized the gun was empty, he was already dead.

Anthony Ratchet, a notoriously short-fused man, slammed a metal pipe into the murderous officer's head, forming a deep crater that cracked and split in gulleys of blood and yellow bone. With the department's only line of defense dead and gone, the protesters surged into the building like a swarm of wasps. No decency for the laws they had abided by all their lives, no humility in their cause. They toppled desks, stomped on officers' heads like rotten melons.

By the time the clock struck midnight, the Bernard Police Department had been eradicated, the building and all its employees. But the protesters weren't satisfied. Some drenched the outer walls in gasoline and set it ablaze. As the station burned down, a looming cloud of smoke shot into the moonlit sky, a beacon of mistrust and violence and a grave warning that no one heeded.

★ ★ ★

Tasha Duncan sat in the front row, eager to hear from one of her all-time idols, Dr. Harrison Wilmington. Hearing his TED Talks online had inspired her to pursue an education in psychology during her tenure at Syracuse University.

Well, she wouldn't have stayed in college past the first year if it hadn't been for Ashley. They met in a chemistry lecture they were both taking to fulfill graduation requirements. Tasha had immediately been infatuated with this curious girl who didn't seem to be from upstate New York. Her mannerisms were different. Many people at Syracuse were uptight but quick to buckle under pressure. Ashley, though. She was strong, intelligent, and funny. She didn't know how to formulate chemical equations, but she sure tried her best to pretend.

Tasha hadn't traveled as far from home for college as Ashley had—Tasha's family lived in Utica—but she empathized with Ashley whenever she seemed to be afflicted with an acute case of homesickness. They began their relationship as mutual cheaters off each other's exams, and that bond blossomed into a friendship that eventually exploded into a beautiful romance. A year into the relationship, Tasha discovered Dr. Wilmington's lectures, and the rest was history.

During the summer before their senior year, Tasha brought Ashley along to come visit her parents. At this point, Tasha knew about Ashley's disdain not for her own family, but for where she lived before moving northeast. Outside of Little Rock, there was nothing much for Ashley to do in Arkansas, and Tasha made it her mission to show her how lovely life could be with a bit of a change in scenery. Wilmington had advocated for changes in environmental stimuli as an ample form of therapy for ailing clients. And Utica was certainly different from the rural-ish area Ashley had grown up in; tall skinny homes were packed next to each other, every major fast-food chain was situated directly next to an Italian joint usually with "Tony" in the name, and everyone didn't know everyone. There was a privacy present in a larger town that smalltown America simply couldn't provide.

Tasha remembered sitting at the dinner table next to Ashley, Mr. and Mrs. Duncan sitting across from them, a large tomato pie the centerpiece of their late-night meal. Ashley's leg wouldn't stop jittering from how nervous she was. Tasha had snuck a hand over her thigh, and the shaking stopped. It was that damn look Ashley had given her that solidified everything for her. She was the one. The five or six boys she had relationships with in high school couldn't compare to the warmth Ashley Guthrie emitted with just a simple stare. There was an entire universe full of stars in her eyes, all twinkling with determination and comfort. The night had eventually devolved into a vicious round of Uno, but Ashley's ferocity as she laid down two Draw Four cards in a row was palpable. Not only was she gentle, but she could also put up a fight when necessary. It was no wonder that she would go on to be elected into the House of Representatives. Politicians needed to have brutal drive and enough kindness to serve the people. Tasha loved all that about her, and that's why it brought a smile to her face to see Ashley calling her as she sat in the front row of this conference hall.

Dr. Wilmington not only shepherded the modern environmental psychology movement but was a primary figure in mental health awareness within the federal government. His advice had harkened changes in substance abuse awareness in the Appalachian region as well as increased funding for mental healthcare in needy rural areas throughout the country. The fact that *she* was going to hear him speak in person was enough to make her burst into joyous applause as the doctor entered the stage. She sent Ashley to voicemail and typed a quick text as she sat back in her seat:

I'll call you back after this panel! Love you <3

Wilmington raised his hands as a sign of thanks. "You're too kind. Too kind," he mouthed as the applause slowly subsided. He was quite the older gentleman, standing at a meek five foot five, sporting a thick head of gray hair and thick-rimmed glasses. He waved once more before getting comfortable in a leather armchair.

The panel moderator sat in an identical chair to his left, a much younger man who looked barely out of undergrad.

Tasha was mesmerized by the presentation that followed. The moderator asked Wilmington questions that ranged from what kind of music he liked to what the meaning of life was. No matter how basic or difficult the questions were, Wilmington answered them with the same quick-witted gusto. Tasha simply couldn't believe this is where she was. When she returned to the capital, her first day back at the clinic would be spent incorporating the lessons she learned from this panel, she was sure of it. Plenty of insight on what it meant to relocate oneself, what a change of scenery could do for a person's wellbeing, how the world around us learned from our mistakes, and how we learned from the world's own mistakes. Tasha thought again of the first time Ashley had met her parents, how she had brightened up from the gloom of not wanting to return to Arkansas and feeling out of place in upstate New York.

The introduction panel concluded, and the moderator opened the floor for questions. Tasha bolted upright from her seat and paced frantically to the nearest microphone. Many others had the same idea, but she was alright with having to wait behind the five people already in line. There would be time.

Wilmington rose from his armchair, holding a portable mic. Tasha noticed a red, blinking light from underneath the doctor's chair, but surmised it was the Bluetooth receptor for the micro-phone. She was too excited to ask her idol a question that had been burning in her mind for damn near over a decade now. "How has changing the environment around you benefitted your own life?" she wanted to ask. His answer could be the key to not only bettering herself but bettering her future with Ashley. What would happen once Ashley inevitably wasn't reelected for her position in the House? Tasha had a hard time believing she would attempt to run for the Senate and instead pictured the two of them moving to the countryside and perhaps raising goats, maybe growing a gar-den full of nuts and carrots that she could use to bake Ashley as many carrot cakes as she wanted. It was the one thing Tasha had never heard Wilmington give an answer to, and she had to be the first to ask.

Four people in front of her… then three… two… one more. Tasha's bladder was full to bursting. She waited impatiently for the person in front to finish their question, for Wilmington to grant them his boundless wisdom. The audience clapped as Tasha finally stood at the mic. He was looking directly at her, his glasses reflect-ing the spotlight above.

She worked up the courage to pose the question. She thought of her clients at the agency right outside Washington. She thought of the friends she met because Ashley brought her to the country's capital. She thought of her mom, her dad, the quaint streets of her hometown, the fateful chemistry course at Syracuse. She thought of Ashley, pictured her as she always would be: A shining beacon of hope, love, and fortitude. This would be Tasha's gift to her; to show her she was determined to solidify their love through any means necessary.

She took in a deep breath as the bomb under Wilmington's chair went off.

★ ★ ★

The Joplin rally was a complete replay of the one in Tulsa. The same talking points—abortion, transgender youth, unsubtle microaggressions, Epstein files, the flourishing/dying economy—blared over the speakers to a crowd of people that looked more worse for wear than the Oklahomans.

The people of Joplin had been ravaged by a devastating tornado nearly seventeen years ago. The day before, they had gone about life as usual. Spending time with the kiddos on their day off from school, going grocery shopping for a new week's worth of meals, enjoying the sun before it was snuffed out. The destruction had been brutal, agonizing. Brick after brick, floorboard after floorboard. Everything in the tornado's path had been swallowed up and spit out like a wad of chewing gum. Homes, businesses, lives. It was the end of the world in southwestern Missouri. The Obama administration had assisted in rebuilding Joplin, damages that would end up totaling nearly three billion dollars, but that was chump change compared to the loon galavanting on stage.

The big shakeup for the Joplin rally was the introduction of one of Robinson's billionaire donors, a Silicon Valley shit-for-brains tech mogul with a square head and a patchy beard. He jumped into the air as an Imagine Dragons song played overhead. He giggled and made faces for the cameras, hoping that one of those snapshots would eventually become internet fodder. *For a guy so wealthy, you'd think he'd have enough money to buy some personality,* Mark thought. Unfortunately, this billionaire was just as dry as Robinson was. The humor of a rock. A repulsive smile that could crack mirrors.

There was a hint of confusion in the audience, baking under the evening sun. Why is this guy here? What's a glorified advertisement for electric cars going to do for me?

Mark had gone on stage a few speeches before the tech billionaire. His speech was mostly the same as the one from before, but Fitzgerald had amended his words, asking Mark to incorporate something about the lowly marijuana farmer that he had helped apprehend in Bernard. So Mark did, and the applause was much louder than the ones he received at the first rally. Either the people were really warming up to his ideas, or the echo in this venue reverberated more than inside the Tulsa venue. However, Mark didn't care about the answer to why the reception seemed warmer; his sense of pride and accomplishment trumped all else.

What he didn't enjoy, however, was what Robinson had to say at the tail end of the rally. "You're a tremendous crowd, thank you," he had said. "My only wish is to continue the work of our dear president so that you all can live in an America you deserve. No more gender politics, no more funding foreign wars. That tornado ruined many lives here, even took some from us. Look past your misery and vote for me in November! For a brighter future, I always say."

Mark knew Robinson had to die tonight, but that was simply the nail in the coffin for him. Asking for people to ignore their own sorrow so you can get some cheap votes in an election that doesn't matter? What a joke.

He attended yet another cocktail party in a horrendously lavish ballroom. Mark wondered if this place had been destroyed in the tornado all those years ago. Who was he kidding? Of course it had been. Hardship and affliction permeated in Joplin at a rate higher than Bernard's. The residents here were full of nothing but gloom and utter disdain for a god who chose them to be obliterated. *Once I'm done with Bernard, maybe I'll pack my bags and move here,* Mark thought. *This plague is spreading faster than I can keep up with.*

Most of the party's attendees were old, sickly so. Wrinkles so deep he could dip his thumb into them up to the knuckle. Chapped lips worn down from age and Great Depression-induced stress. Hunched backs so mangled and angular that Mark could set a tea saucer there without the guest noticing. He would hate to see himself grow this decrepit and useless, but the warning signs were already there, decaying his reflection in the mirror.

"Another brilliant performance, Smith!" Representative Palmer applauded, clapping Mark on the back.

"It was the same as the first speech," Mark said.

"We're glad you added that bit about the drug dealer," Fitzgerald chimed in, appearing out of nowhere along with "There's nothing more that our base enjoys than Black people being thrown in jail! I won't say I agree with it, but whatever gets us in their good graces is alright with me."

"They might enjoy transgenders killing themselves a bit more," added Hughes, his jowls flapping noisily with every syllable.

"I'm glad you all enjoyed it," Mark said, unable to take his eyes away from how disgustingly old Hughes was. "Is there anything else you need from me before I go back home? I've still got some business to attend to."

"Ah, don't worry about your hometown," Palmer said. "The National Guard is already taking care of *that* situation." Mark didn't understand what that was supposed to mean, but he took it as a joke that didn't land and let Palmer continue his spiel in a hushed tone. "Remember what we told you about Robinson, though. It surely would be a shame if he were allowed to continue in this race with all we know about him."

"I remember."

"Good. Well, he's over there if you'd like to chat with him.

He seems to be one girl short tonight, so maybe he'll enjoy your company in her stead."

Mark scoffed and pushed past the trio of congressmen. Who did Palmer think he was, pushing him around like a hound dog, sniffing for the next kill? He wasn't some animal to be guided on a leash, he was his own person, an individual star among a universe filled to the brim with galaxies.

He tapped Robinson on the shoulder, noticing how it felt like hard plastic instead of soft skin under the suit jacket. Robinson whirled drunkenly, facing Mark after a short stumble.

"Marky, my boy!" he slurred, champagne flute in hand. "Another tremendous speech today. You're a natural, a *real* natural. Not like those other creeps on stage. We keep 'em along for insurance reasons." He hiccuped and washed it down with the last of his beverage. "Total losers, if you ask me. But don't tell 'em that. Believe me, it'd be a disaster if they found out I don't give a shit about 'em. How's Lindy, by the way? I haven't seen her since Tulsa."

"Thank you, sir. I actually wanted to talk to you about her," Mark said, hoping Robinson's Lindy was the same dead girl from the hotel. "But we might need to go somewhere a little more private for that discussion."

Robinson sobered slightly, the glaze over his eyes evaporating. "Of course, of course. I know a spot. Come along."

Mark followed Robinson, wading through the elderly donors and government officials without losing sight of his prey. He wondered if Robinson had any idea where he was going. Did he know he was walking himself to his own execution? Did he believe a single word Mark had said in either Tulsa or Joplin? Or was it all theatrics to him? Only a man of his... *acquired* tastes would see the world as his dollhouse to play around with. That playtime would end tonight. For the girls. For the country, and maybe the world.

They climbed two flights of stairs, the commotion of the party fading gradually with every step. Robinson opened the door and entered a hallway decorated with gaudy orange and blue-stitched carpet and walls painted a dark forest green. Mark noted a glass case hanging from the wall reading "IN CASE OF EMER-GENCY" that housed a bright red axe. It called to him, but the glass muffled its voice. Impossible to hear, but raring to slice into flesh.

Robinson unlocked another door and beckoned Mark to en-ter. Ever the genius, Mark told Robinson he needed to tighten the laces on his dress shoes. Robinson flashed his disgusting veneers and disappeared into the room as Mark bent down to pretend to tie his shoes. When he was certain Robinson was far enough be-hind the door to not notice a thing, Mark bolted upright and slammed his elbow into the glass imprisoning his trusty weapon of choice. No alarm went off. The hotel probably turned off all the emergency sensors knowing how many politicians would be smoking inside the building tonight. Mark breathed a sigh of relief and gripped the axe tight. The smooth paint coating its handle was comforting, like a new teddy bear to a child on Christmas morn-ing.

He held the axe behind his back and slipped into the dimly lit hotel room. Women's undergarments were strewn about the floor like multicolored spaghetti strands in a boiling pot. The air condi-tioner was turned off, giving the room the sort of humidity one would expect from a sauna. It reeked of body odor and semen, that putrid mixture of salt and sex assaulting Mark's nose. Robin-son turned on a lamp at the far side of the room. The door closed behind Mark with a gentle click.

Robinson sat on the edge of the farthest bed from the door,

his back to Mark, staring at the window as if a thick curtain wasn't obscuring the world beyond. He set a hand beside himself and patted the duvet.

"Come here, Mark. Sit with me."

Mark felt his grip loosen around the axe, his sweat rendering the clean finish of the handle utterly tactless. He inched toward the candidate. Something in him shouted, *This is wrong! You need to stop this. He isn't miserable. He wants to better his country for his people, for his neighbors. Just like you… Just like you. Leave him be. Don't judge what he chooses to do in private.*

Mark stood at the other side of the bed, his legs refusing to take another step. Robinson snickered, but did not turn to face him. He kept his gaze locked on the closed curtains as he said, "Mark, what did you need to tell me?" When Mark couldn't find the words, Robinson added with a hint of menace: "Don't be shy."

"First, I want to congratulate you on all your success," Mark said, hating the words coming out his mouth. "Those rallies really are something. I've never seen so many people cheer for one person. It's magical."

"I'm sure you think that."

"Well, it's true." It wasn't true. Robinson's crowds were pitiful, both bored and never at capacity. "You have a good thing going on here, and I'm grateful you allowed me to be a small part of that."

"Cut the shit, Smith. Where's Lindy?"

Robinson sounded a lot more sober now. The room seemed to grow more sweltering with every passing second. Mark tugged at the collar of his dress shirt.

"We woke up the morning of the Tulsa rally. While I was freshening up in the shower, I heard her say she needed to meet with some family outside the hotel. I haven't seen her since."

"Do you think I'm an idiot?"

"No, sir."

"I know she's dead, Mark. Housekeeping stumbled on her remains after you left for the rally. One of my associates forwarded the information to me, saying you were the last person seen with her. Of course, I already knew you had spent the night with her, so my associate wasn't adding anything new."

"She's dead?"

"Of course she's fucking dead!" Robinson shouted, finally turning away from the window. His eyes were full of rage, the tanned creases around his mouth deepening into wrathful chasms. "I had cameras placed in your room! I saw everything! You think I was going to trust Palmer and his little group with your last-minute addition to my tour? They've been after me ever since I extorted my way into the Oval Office. And that's why I'm guessing you wanted to talk somewhere private. So you could murder me in cold blood. Like you did to my sweet Lindy."

"She wanted to die," Mark said. "I just helped her along."

"By ripping her legs off?! You fucking ate a hole into her stomach like a goddamn mole rat! I know I had slipped you some ketamine that night, but that shit shouldn't make you go *feral*. What the hell is wrong with you?"

You don't know the half of it, Mark thought.

Robinson resumed his position, staring at the curtains. They refused to sway, as there was no breeze in the room to warrant such movement. Another minute in this room would cause Mark to pass out from heat exhaustion. He wanted to chop Robinson's body clean in two, but the conversation was oddly interesting to a degree. He would wait, however long that meant.

"I had people on my team research your background today, after I saw the footage of you slaughtering one of my girls,"

Robinson said. His vocal cadence that mimicked the current president had completely vanished. The facade lifted. "They found connections between yourself and over 200 murders in your hometown. 'How could that be possible?' Some of my team asked that, but I knew the answer. It was possible because your town made it possible. You terrorized them so often that they grew complacent in their lives. But you were still stuck in a fantasy. Everyone there knew you were their Hillside Butcher, but you thought you were anonymous. In the shadows. Even then, no one did anything! Law enforcement ignored every murder you committed because they knew you wouldn't stop no matter where they locked you up."

"What's your point?"

"I want to know how you did it," Robinson said, lifting himself from the bed and walking toward Mark. His eyes lost that spark of anger and were completely drenched in fascination as if he were watching a spaceship soar past the stratosphere. "These crowds fucking hate me. They want their president back for another term, not some idiot parading around in his skin. I thought for sure they wanted to keep the same type of person in office forever, but I was wrong. They want *more*, the greedy fucks. As if mass deportations and banning gay marriage weren't enough. They want someone they can grow complacent with. Someone who'll commit crimes against humanity so often they become bored of it. How, then, do you do it? How do you make people bored with murder? How do you get away with it so easily?"

Mark was stunned, a deer in the headlights of a ginormous tour bus barreling toward him at 80 miles an hour. At this point he understood most—if not all—of Bernard knew he was the Hillside Butcher. He'd been able to see it in their faces. The anxiety they felt whenever he was within their vicinity. People shopping at Walmart giving him quick, worried glances and scampering away like terrified stray cats. People gathering around his totaled car, looks of confused pleasure on their faces, wondering if this would finally be the moment he died, and they could continue their business as usual. Even Abel Watterson, with his wide puppy-dog eyes and acne scars as crusty as homemade pizza, seemed to be weary around him. Adoration could only go so far before it descended into fear.

Even with the applause he had received at two election rallies, Mark was surprised to hear someone ask for advice, though the questions seemed to harbor some condescension. A presidential candidate was asking *him* about how he went about his business, business that was good, honest work. Mark never thought politicians could be either good or honest, but he appreciated Robinson's pleas for advice. However, appreciation wasn't going to be enough. Mark was past that now. People outside Bernard were beginning to understand his point of view, accepting him for all the goodwill he has given, all the righteousness of his cause.

Davey Robinson didn't have the spine to kill as Mark did. He didn't have that edge, that *drive* to succeed. He only wore the mask of someone who could do such things. Underneath that mask was something more frightening than anything Mark knew he had done. A leech that stole young women from their families and forced them to be his concubines. They were expendable to him, useless once their purpose was served. Mark thought of the dead girl from his bed—*Lindy*—and smiled. He had set her free, he could set the rest of them free, but he needed to destroy the source of the pain before going on that spree.

"You want to know how I slip through the cracks?" Mark said, his smile refusing to simmer down. "You want to know why I do what I do? How I do it? Everything you need to know is in my speeches. That's my entire doctrine. My code of honor. I do what I must for my community, whether they like it or not." He stepped forward, his nose practically touching Robinson's. Not the faintest scent of alcohol on the fraudulent man's lips. "Once you do something enough, people tend to accept it as a fact of life. My actions may be unorthodox to some, but my intentions are universal. No one wants to see their loved ones kill themselves. Humanity wasn't built for that sort of pain. We were built for a different kind of suffering. A merciful one."

Mark clamped his fingers around the axe's handle, tightening his grip so hard his knuckles nearly burst under the skin. Robinson's eyes widened, knowing all too well that his fate was sealed.

"I-If you kill me, my associates will be alerted," Robinson stuttered. "T-They'll send every hitman they can after you. You'll never know another m-moment of peace until the day you die."

"I'm well aware."

Mark lifted the axe and swung it down in a clean arc, plummeting the blade halfway through Robinson's left calf. The candidate howled as blood pooled around the axe, staining his haphazardly tailored navy-blue dress pants. Mark dislodged the axe, another wave of red fluid coming with it. He kicked the mangled leg so hard Robinson's tibia snapped in two. Robinson tumbled to the carpet, his left leg below the knee at a horrifically unnatural angle. Mark dropped the axe and bent down. He grabbed Robinson's foot and yanked as hard as his aging body would allow. Muscle tissue tore. The body's last defense before Robinson's shin was ripped in two with a sickening squelch. Robinson's screams grew more intense. They had begun as low howls, but now they transformed into shrill cries that tore the lining inside his throat.

Mark held the amputated leg, studying it as if for an upcoming anatomy exam. Skin flopped from the bloody stump like wet paper towels. Unable to control himself, Mark took a bite, tearing a clump of skin like the breading from a cooked chicken wing. Skin was usually plain in taste, but Robinson's obsession with spray tans gave it a uniquely bitter tang. It tasted like Lindy's lipstick the night he laid her. They had kissed and thrashed under the bed covers, taking in each other as if it were the last night of their lives. It would be Lindy's last night on Earth, but the sentiment still remained. Mark's brain had been firing on all cylinders as the ketamine coursed through his veins. He felt everything at once: Love, grief, pleasure, anger, euphoria, despair. He'd felt her emotions, too. That's why she had to die. There had been no other option. And it was this man's fault that she couldn't live a longer, more fruitful life.

Robinson's screams wouldn't quiet down, beginning to annoy the ever-loving piss out of Mark. What right did this man have to experience pain as any other human would? Mark took another glance at the severed foot in his hands before slamming it down on Robinson's skull.

There was a hollow thud. Robinson screamed louder. His face was soaked in his own blood. Blinding white teeth protruded from his mouth. Mark brought the foot down once more, smashing Robinson's teeth. Shards of porcelain fell down the man's throat; he began to choke as they sunk their prongs into his esophagus.

Mark continued to wail on Davey Robinson with his own torn-off foot. Sweat and blood beaded in Mark's eyes. It was so fucking humid in that room. But he wouldn't leave until the job was done. Not until those girls were freed, unshackled by the burden of being Robinson's consorts. They would walk into the boundless sunset with only Mark to thank for that opportunity, and the thought made Mark's smile grow wider.

Once Robinson let out a final guttural gurgle, Mark dropped the foot, reached into his pocket, and dropped two pennies into the cavernous pile of gore that, until recently, was Davey Robinson's head. They splatted in a viscous puddle of what used to be the man's eyes.

Mark didn't bother cleaning himself off. His bones ached from everything this kill took out of him. He cracked his knuckles, sighed, and left the hotel room in a hurry. The party wouldn't be complete without a serial murderer in their midst.

★ ★ ★

"Is this Ashley Guthrie?"

"Yes." Ashley wasn't in the mood to answer random phone calls in the middle of the night, but the screen had stated it was from an unknown caller ID, so she felt a weird obligation to pick up.

"Your number was listed as an emergency contact for one Natasha Duncan of 1201 Pennsylvania Avenue, Washington D.C.? Does this sound correct?"

The voice on the other end sounded so soothing, with the same low quiet tone of those ASMR videos that occasionally appeared on her Instagram feed. It was 12:08 in the morning. She'd already been asleep for two hours, and this mystery person was about to shove her back into her dreams.

"Yes, that's correct," she responded, rubbing some more sleep from her crusty eyes.

"Wonderful. Well… no, not wonderful. Forget I said that. Anyway, we're calling to inform you that Natasha has been involved in a serious crime."

Crime? The worst thing Tasha had ever done was enter the wrong Uber after a night out. What kind of shit could someone get up to at a psychology conference? Hypnosis? Conjuring spirits?

"Oh my God. Is she alright? I told her not to get too pushy with that Wilmington guy. Tasha's a complete sweetheart, but she forgets about personal space sometimes. Is she being held somewhere? I could drive over right no—"

"No, Ms. Guthrie. It isn't that." The voice on the other end paused. Ashley heard a sigh that seemed to last an excruciating eternity. *"Natasha passed away. She was at the epicenter of an explosive device that had been planted under our Dr. Wilmington's chair. I'm sorry for your loss."*

Ashley's heart sank to her stomach. A knot tightened around her throat. She was suffocating in the comfort of her satin bedsheets. Then the terror passed as she surmised what this midnight call really meant.

"You're a fucking piece of shit," she said. "Prank calling a government employee in the middle of the night. How the fuck did you get this number?"

"It's not a prank call, ma'am. Forensic agents identified her remains and Natasha's supervisor supplied her emergency contact information. We would have called sooner if not for the legal process required for such a case, and for that I apologize. All of us at the Conference of Psychological Associates are truly sorry for your loss. It can't be easy to process."

"No," Ashley muttered. "No no no no. You're lying... you're fucking lying."

"I wish I were, Ms. Guthrie."

Ashley rose from her bed. She felt weightless, as if her feet had dematerialized into floating clouds that carried her to the living room without her input. She pressed her phone so strenuously to her cheek that her jaw clicked. She held the last remnant of Tasha's memory to her ear, unable to let go. Her eyes were about to explode with how many gallons of tears pushed behind the sockets.

She remembered college. She remembered that chemistry class she never wanted to take. She remembered the beautiful girl with dark curly hair and a smile that could topple skyscrapers. She remembered coffee dates and movie nights. She remembered nights on the town punctuated by crude jokes and Amaretto sours. She remembered singing off key at a karaoke bar, only for Tasha to stand behind the mic and belt her heart out. She remembered matching tattoos and a necklace Tasha gifted her with a charm shaped like a spider. She remembered their first trip together to Utica. She remembered her parents, those charming souls that loved nothing more than their only daughter and wanted the best for her. She remembered feeling that she wasn't enough. She remembered...

"Are you still there, Ms. Guthrie?"

"Yes, I'm still here," Ashley said, making her best attempt not to choke on her words. "Have you contacted her parents?"

"They are next on the list of contacts, it seems. You were the first person we called. Should I hang up and give them a ring?"

"No! Don't do that." Ashley paused, a wave of profound melancholy flowing to the shore. She continued on when it ebbed to the sea. "I'll call them. They'd probably prefer to hear it from me than from a stranger."

"I understand. I'm sorry, ma'am."

Ashley hung up before she could hear more of the caller's unsettlingly pacifying voice. The living room was bathed in darkness, the only luminescence pouring in from the glow of the moon through the window. Surely this was all a bad dream. No... she didn't need to pinch herself to know that was a lie. Tasha hadn't texted or called after she'd promised to do so after Dr.

Wilmington's conference panel. That was very unlike her. She loved filling Ashley in on all the gossip she heard and the sights she saw. Ashley adored living vicariously through her, especially during times like these. She could shut herself down and live through Tasha one phone call at a time when House meetings made her want to tear her hair out.

But those two separate lives ceased to exist. It was only Ashley now, and she hated being alone. The wave of sorrow returned, but it was not a calm ripple. It was a tsunami, one that would never return to the sea.

★ ★ ★

Abel awoke to the sound of clamoring footsteps outside the guest room. Light seeped underneath the door, followed by indistinguishable conversation from voices he had never heard before. He rolled over in the cot. Eddie lay on the concrete floor with a thin blanket over his massive body. He snored like a lion with seasonal congestion.

Abel tiptoed to the door and put his ear against the wood.

"You should've checked how much charge was in it."

"I didn't know he was going to get out of his chair."

"What do you mean?"

"I manually set the detonation radius when that doctor walked away from his seat so the blast would reach him."

"But you blew up not just him, but a few people in the audience." Abel knew that voice to be Valerie's. "You're lucky you got out in time. We can't base all our hits on luck. You three know this."

"At least we got paid in advance. That client was desperate."

"And our next one will be more desperate," Valerie said.

"We've already got a request for a hit in two days."

Abel assumed this must be what the typical fallout of such jobs sounded like, people mulling over their mistakes and arguing without an end in sight. Eddie groaned in his sleep before returning to his rapturous snores. The conversation outside died down in response to the noise.

Abel returned to his cot and nestled under the sheets, unable to go back to sleep. He lay awake until the thin sliver of morning sunshine broke through the small window. Thoughts of death and destruction bombarded his mind, keeping his eyes open no matter how much he begged them to sleep. An image of how that explosion must have looked, the sudden burst of flames and shrapnel shredding through numerous victims. He thought of Mark, how the Hillside Butcher had been covered in blood while Abel was taking money out of the bank. Money out of his mother's account.

Oh, Mom, he brooded. *I'm so sorry.*

She was all alone in Bernard, so saddened by her son's sudden disappearance that she hadn't even thought to shoot him a text. Did she think he ran off and killed himself?

Did she care for the answer?

CHAPTER 10

★ ★ ★

The day after Davey Robinson was beat to death with his own amputated shin, Mark had never felt so alive. Any worry he had about being involved in politics vanished into thin air, like the waft of smoke from a cigarette in a light autumn breeze. The notion that he would return to his normal life in Bernard evaporated upon hearing the news of the riots in his hometown.

"They found the body of a girl by your namesake's cemetery. 20 years-old or so," Fitzgerald said.

"I had nothing to do with that," Mark said, the image of the tomato-hurling brat with a bullet in her head bringing a faint satisfied glimmer to his eyes.

"That's the point, Smith," Palmer said. "Your neighbors knew for sure you were not involved in this specific case, but when they called the local police, the department did nothing. They chalked it up to being another one of your killings, not someone else's. The townspeople threw riots, smashing windows, tipping cars, firing shots. They burned down the police department."

Mark felt assured of himself. Something deep inside him knew that Bernard would not last very long without his presence. So much hate and misery festered in that town, and he was the only one strong enough to be on pest control. Without him, the roaches dug into the hearts of his neighbors, sending them in a collective frenzy that resulted in a hapless death and a police squad reduced to ashes.

"It was bound to happen while I was gone," Mark said. "Have the riots quieted down since yesterday?"

"Not in the slightest," Fitzgerald said, sipping a dewy bottle of Bud Light. "If anything, the riots have gotten worse. There was a report from Little Rock that someone set a fire in the woods outside Bernard. The wind picked up, and the dry brush ignited. There's a wildfire spanning from your town to Friendship."

Mark mulled over that. He expected a bit of turbulence in town in his absence, but wildfires? Intentionally set wildfires? What were they trying to play at? The police department was gone. What else could they want?

"Is there any way we could keep the violence going but also contain it?" Mark asked.

"What are you getting at?" Fitzgerald's eyebrows furrowed, but Palmer stared wide in admiration, as if Mark were his baby taking his first steps.

"Maybe we could use Bernard as an example while also keeping the towns around it safe. You three have connections, I'm sure. Could you ask some of those National Guard people to hold the violence within the town's limits while also egging them on a bit?"

"You want to use them as an example?" Palmer asked.

"In a way, yes."

"The media would absolutely eat that up."

"Isn't that what politics is all about? The message?"

"Whoa-oh-OH!" Palmer reeled back in astonishment. "Where did *this* all come from, Smith? Have you been studying?"

"I've been an American citizen for 35 years. I think I've seen enough to get the general gist of things."

The two younger congressmen sat at their laptops and made many phone calls, all ranging from pleasant conversations with news outlets and screaming matches with event coordinators. The older congressman Hughes, who Mark had nearly forgotten existed until the elder man coughed a bit of phlegm onto his white shirt, scrolled endlessly on his phone, the volume set way too high.

By the end of the day, Fitzgerald had secured airtime for CNN, FOX News, MSNBC, and CSPAN. "They would *love* to have you on as a guest," he said. "A new, fresh face in the political scene always garners them the most ratings, no matter how… *unorthodox*… your beliefs are. People just love a new face to ogle." Palmer, on the other hand, booked a short round-trip flight from Kansas City to Washington, D.C. and was ready to meet with hundreds of Republicans around the capital, including the president.

"Don't worry about anything," Palmer said, resting a hand on Mark's shoulder. "I'll get all the dirty work settled. After I get back, you won't have to so much as lift a finger. This country will accept you like the darling you are."

★ ★ ★

The media painted the brutal murder of Davey Robinson as a massive blow to the bottom line of the Republican Party. Contrary to popular belief, that was not the case in Washington. Of the 206 Republican representatives in the House, nearly half of them were directly involved in the extortion scandal that catapulted Robinson to the top of the primaries. Those same representatives, along with all 46 Republican senators, backed Mark Smith as the understudy for Robinson's plight. It took Representative Finley Palmer of Arkansas a great deal of persuading (most of the persuading coming in the form of under-the-table bribes and reminders that Robinson's blackmail documents were safely in his hands now), but he managed to shoehorn Mark Smith into the presidential race within the eyes of his colleagues.

Well, all except one.

The president had finally been discharged from Walter Reed and was rotting in the Oval Office. Palmer thought it was oddly sweet how the geriatric boomers in America were as glued to their phones as millennials' children were attached to their iPads. When he entered the Oval Office, the president sat behind the *Resolute* desk—used by every president since Carter returned it to its rightful place after the Kennedy assassination—and watched clips of the latest *South Park* episode mocking his factually tiny penis. Palmer hated that he himself had seen the leaked nudes from a few months back. It truly was *that* small.

Two bodyguards greeted Palmer as he entered the garishly decorated office. Gold paint covered nearly every piece of decor, even the picture frame housing a copy of the Declaration of Independence that the president was certain was the real document from 1776 when it, in fact, wasn't.

"Good evening, Mr. President," he said with a slight bow of his head.

The president did not acknowledge his presence. The two bodyguards, both looking as if they would burst out of their tight suits at any given moment, chuckled. The Oval Office felt a bit eerie without Davey Robinson hovering over the president's shoulder, but Palmer quite enjoyed the silence. It was a welcome change for a dying president in a dying country.

"I came to discuss the election," he continued.

The president raised a small wrinkly hand and beckoned Palmer to come closer. He did, pulling up a chair that had been collecting dust under a portrait of Benjamin Franklin. The president clicked his phone off and set it screen-down on the desk. His sharp beady eyes met with Palmer's, the lids forever relaxed by the disease actively eating his brain.

"What about the election?" the president asked, his usually nasal voice hollow and dull from the pain medication.

"It has to do with Davey Robinson dropping out of the race. It's too late for the RNC to conduct another primary, so we'll need a quick turnaround on a new candidate before your base grows tiresome."

"Ah, I remember Davey. Tremendous guy! Absolutely stunning man. One of the best to ever do it. What ever happened to him?"

It had now been a week since Mark pulverized Robinson in a hotel room in Missouri. That information didn't seem to have made it to the president's ears. The man thought his right-hand man had simply fucked off on vacation and forgot to tell anyone.

"He dropped out of the race, as I said," Palmer punctuated, deciding it would be best to keep the ailing man in the dark. If his countless lapdogs hadn't broken the news, no one would. Surely someone had muted the words "Davey" and "Robinson" on his social media feeds. "But the Party has ruminated on who would be best fit to replace him in this race. That's why I'm here today. For an endorsement, or at least a promise of an endorsement. Whatever floats your boat, Mr. President."

"Which boat? I have five yachts off the coast of Florida. All the best in the world."

"I know, sir." Palmer wanted the conversation to end more than he needed air to breathe, but he persisted, rolling with the limp punches as they came. "It's just a turn of phrase. Older than you are."

The president took a large swig of Diet Coke, sighed with a faint burp, then clasped his hands, bruised with age. "I'm not *that* old, Mr. Parker."

"Palmer."

"Parker, Palmer, whatever. What are you proposing?"

"Most of our Republican colleagues in the House and the Senate have agreed that a swift change in candidacy is the best choice. The Democrats were allowed to squeeze in Mrs. Harris in 2024 without so much as a primary, so we feel that we should be allowed the same luxury." Palmer dug into his leather briefcase and fetched a Manila folder. He slid a document across the *Resolute* desk; a document plastered with images and intel surrounding Mr. Smith. "This is Mark Thomas Smith Jr. of Bernard, Arkansas. He gained prominence recently after he stopped and apprehended a notable drug kingpin in his hometown. Not only is he an advocate for working against drug-related crimes, but he also holds a firm stance on the mental health epidemic, particularly for those at risk of suicidal ideation."

"Less words, please," the president grumbled. "I can barely understand you with all this yap-yap-*yap*. You should know how much I hate when people talk in circles. Absolutely terrible."

Palmer wanted to rebut that statement, but—once again—he persisted. Persistence was the key to speaking to the glorious president of the United States. He talked in circles, made terrible decisions, and preyed on the weak in society, but you had to stay in his good graces so that you weren't at risk of being ostracized by his most loyal fans.

"I'm sorry about that, Mr. President. I'll get to the point."

"About fucking time."

"Mark Smith would be the perfect candidate to run in Davey Robinson's absence. He has no prior experience in politics, like you. He has years of baggage that supporters have instantly turned a blind eye to, like you. And he is very well spoken… like you."

"No political background?"

"Absolutely none. And he's sitting on a small inheritance fortune from his father. I feel like the stars have aligned in bringing him to our attention. He's a near carbon copy of you, but without the—*pardon my tongue*—wrinkles and corruption."

"I can be very corrupt, you're right. I'm about ready to fire my entire cabinet so they don't get any funny ideas about running against whoever has the Republican ticket."

Palmer instinctively glanced around the Oval Office, being sure there weren't any audio or video recording devices strewn about the gold decor. A leak to the press with anything the president was saying would surely land him his fourth impeachment, not that impeaching a president meant much anymore.

"Well, for your information, it would be very beneficial for you to lay off your entire cabinet," Palmer said, leaning close enough for his chair to creak. "We've talked some about baggage, but your cabinet members are the heaviest out there. Stripping them of their positions would make this election cycle roll over as smooth as it could get."

"I'll sign some papers and get them out of here," the president said, much to Palmer's surprise. He felt like a god manipulating reality to his own whim. The president, the leader of the so-called "free world," was under his thumb. This man who had been on top of the world not so long ago had kneeled before him, obeying his every request. Palmer wanted to laugh at the absurdity of it all, but the situation was too golden to ruin with his childish antics.

"To tell the truth, I've watched some clips of this Smith guy at those two rallies," the president continued. "With a little more practice, he could really be one of the greats. Not as great as me, for sure, but great enough to carry on my legacy. He reminds me a bit of my sons in that way, only I actually tolerate Smith. Did I tell you about the casino one of my sons opened recently? Absolute disaster. He didn't even reach out to me to sign any papers. People were stealing money from right under his nose."

"Yes, you told me," Palmer lied.

"Oh."

"Will you endorse Mark Smith for president?"

"Yes," said the president. "Can I get back to my phone now? I'm missing my favorite live stream. This woman reacts to every rose I send her. Gorgeous set of tits on her. Tremendous stuff."

★ ★ ★

As much as she hated to admit it, Ashley wanted to kill herself. Two funerals in the past month, both for the people she held most dearly in this world. She had been generally emotionless during her father's funeral, the tears only coming once she was on the road back to Washington, but Tasha's funeral broke her.

Her remains had been carted up to New York for the burial. There was no wake. There was nothing to put in the casket. She had been blasted apart, torn to shreds by shrapnel from a bomb planted under her idol's leather seat. The funeral was graciously held under a partially cloudy sky. Not too warm, not too cold, and without any rain to further dampen the mood. Tasha's parents bought a small plot at Cavalry Cemetery, a lush hill dotted with death, buried within the perimeter of luscious trees that had already begun to wither in time for autumn.

Another set of pallbearers lifted Tasha's casket onto the lowering device. Her father had been one of the pallbearers, and he was an absolute wreck. Tears slithered down his jolly plump cheeks like translucent salamanders. When the casket was secured, he returned to his wife, and they went into each other's arms. Ashley wanted to provide them with as much comfort as she was able to, but she'd already used up her diminished supply after the last funeral. She felt hollow, as if someone had shot her in the stomach with a cannon at point-blank range. Tears were seeping from her eyes, but they didn't feel substantial. They only felt like saltwater, falling in thin strips. A preacher sang somber hymns, a few family members told short eulogies between sobs, and the casket was finally six feet under the loose soil.

Most of Tasha's family had left the area by the time Ashley realized she also needed to leave the plot. Tasha's parents, Bill and Joy, came up behind her and held her shoulders. The earth at the foot of Tasha's headstone felt too slack, too new. Graves were meant to show age, to have years of dust and moss growing on the stone, to have green grass frolicking underneath. But the soil was wet and brown. It was all fresh, all too real. Ashley turned and sank into the in-laws that she would never have. Their faces squeezed tight together, their tears intermingling into one shared river.

But she was back in Washington D.C. before she knew it. Despite the severe lack of work being done within Congress, she had to be there no matter the circumstances. Tasha hadn't been family, not legally speaking. There was no marriage contract, not even proof of engagement. They were waiting for the worst the country had to offer to blow over before they could imagine their wedding. It never happened, though, and the thought of what could have been would haunt Ashley for the rest of her life, no matter how long or short that life would turn out to be.

She walked past the White House on her way back to her apartment. Landscapers had built an additional fence in front of the original after the president had passed legislation somehow barring people of color from working at PBS, fearful of any riots that would ensue from that surprisingly legal decree. But the lawn smelled crisp, that dewy scent of newly mowed grass tickled her nose, reminding her of home. Reminding her of her father, of his blood on the carpet. She had been powerless in seeking justice for his murder, and she couldn't bear to lift a finger against whoever placed the bomb that killed the love of her life.

A suited figure waltzed from the entryway leading into the White House. A lanky gentleman with a sharp undercut tapered into a low fade above the ears. He wore a stupid grin on his pale face, and Ashley knew that cockiness anywhere.

"Palmer?" she asked, quickening her pace.

Representative Palmer whipped around and met her gaze, his wide smile fading at the corners. "Oh! Congresswoman! Am I glad to see you," he said.

"What are you doing here? Shouldn't you be sucking Davey Robinson's dick on a tour bus?"

He chuckled low and slow without any humor. "I was just sucking our president's dick, for your information. He prefers more tongue when it's a man doing the deed, did you know?"

"Why were you there?"

"Why should I tell you?"

"Because you're an elected official in the state that I'm a legal resident of. Arkansas's voting body demands transparency."

"You drive a hard bargain."

"I'm not offering anything."

"Well, if you insist," Palmer said, rummaging through his briefcase. He pulled out a folder and handed it to her. The bottom flap was sticky and smelled like corn syrup. "Take a look."

Ashley begrudgingly scanned the documents inside. Flashes of her father's killer along with short biographies, medical histories, familial backgrounds. She didn't know Mark Smith was a quarter Lebanese. All the intel on Mark had been skewed in such a way that his murderous escapades were completely wiped out from the records. All those bodies had vanished, their only proof of death being the headstones atop Cemetery Hill in rural Arkansas.

"You showed *this* to the president? Why?"

"For an endorsement, of course. Why else?"

"You're joking."

"Why would I?"

Ashley wanted to take out her pepper spray and… well, not even spray it in the man's eyes. No, she wanted to take the little can and jam it in his eye socket, pushing it so deep that when she removed it, it would be covered in gray matter and blood.

"You can't have the president endorse two people for the same position," she said. "That's insane."

"Who said anything about two people?"

"You…" Ashley stopped herself. There was a lot of weight behind the words. *Two people.* "You mean to say Robinson dropped out of the race?"

"More or less."

"Stop being cryptic. We're colleagues. Tell it to me straight."

"I'd rather inform you somewhere more private," Palmer said, glancing up and down.

"There's no way in hell I'd let you coerce me into a dark closet and have you ogle my tits."

"I'm more of an ass man myself."

Primal instincts kicked in. Before Ashley had time to process her thoughts, she had already slapped Palmer square across the face, leaving a large pink welt on the man's cheek. He rubbed the area and chuckled.

"I heard Mark and Davey grew rather fond of each other," he said amusedly.

"Did he convince Robinson to drop? Or were *you* pulling the strings?"

"I may have pulled a string or two, but Mark Smith did not convince Robinson of anything. It was more of a persuasion, I believe. If you catch my drift."

"I don't follow."

"You were never the brightest, hot shot," Palmer seethed.

"I wasn't trying to be."

"Well, you're doing an awful job at that."

Palmer snatched the folder back from Ashley's grasp, stuffing it haphazardly into his briefcase. He sneered and turned to leave. Ashley had lost so much in the past few weeks, but she was not about to lose this. She slipped her fingers around the congressman's sleeve and jerked hard. He reeled back with a lot less anger on his face than she expected.

"What the hell are you trying to get out of me, Ms. Guthrie? Is it just some selfish detective sleuthing that you need to satiate your grief? I heard about your girlfriend. I'm truly sorry, but you cannot take it out on your colleagues, especially me. My plans for this election aren't something for a liberal such as yourself to stick their nose in. The cards need to be placed just right, or the tower will fall."

"You don't get to talk about her." Ashley wanted to place both her hands on Palmer's cheeks and twist his neck so hard it snapped. "I'm not asking for myself, or for some twisted sense of grief. I'm asking for the sake of everyone. Because if you're truly planning on what I think you are, you've damned us all. I cannot allow you to let Mark Smith become the president of this country, or *any* country."

"That worries you. Why?"

"You've read his files. Most of them are in that fucking folder. You know how dangerous he is. I know for sure you got him close to Robinson, so you had an excuse for the man to die. I don't need to watch the news to know that. But now, what if Mark taps into the same niche that the current president did? All the white supremacists and Neo-Nazis who don't realize they're getting fucked until they feel the aches in their asses the next morning. What kind of example will that set? How much longer are you going to stoke the fire until it burns you to death along with everyone else?"

Palmer gave a sarcastic pout, his bottom lip jutting comically. "So doom and gloom! Can't you ever be happy for once?"

"What is there to be happy about? You're about to shove a known serial killer into the highest office in the United States. That makes me pretty goddamn unhappy."

"It's only August. A lot can change in three months."

"Don't test me," commanded Ashley.

"And why are you so sure about Smith becoming our president? Shouldn't you be supporting the Democratic nominee? Are you scared your guy will lose?"

"No."

Ashley didn't care much for Reginald Foster, some business mogul from Omaha who was pushing fifty, both in terms of years and how many times he had visited Israel.

"Then why are you worrying? Let us run our campaign the way we want to. If your side puts up a good fight, maybe Mark will lose and return home, going back to his business as usual. Wouldn't you like that?"

The thought of Mark Smith wandering the streets of Bernard as he had for over three decades sent a shiver down Ashley's spine. Gallons of blood shed from his incompetent mind and sharpened axe. More bodies would never be enough for him. She wished he would have stopped the night before her father met his axe.

But then she thought of how Mark would be contained within just one town if he lost the election. It presented a trolley problem of sorts. Allow a small town in the middle of nowhere Arkansas to suffer, or permit Mark Smith to inflict that same suffering upon an entire country?

"You think that over," Palmer said, smoothing out his suit and walking away, leaving Ashley hopelessly alone and afraid on Pennsylvania Avenue.

* * *

Another shot rang through the trees. Abel stood behind a misshapen podium with the underside of a hunting rifle propped upon the flat wood panel. Hunched over, he squinted at the faraway flat metal target in the shape of a man. A gleaming dent protruded out the back where he had made his shot.

"Right in the heart," Valerie said from behind him, crossing her toned muscular arms. "Wouldn't be an *instant* kill, but it'd be quick, nonetheless. Great work."

Abel wanted to reply with his thanks, but he couldn't find those two simple words: *thank* and *you*. Instead, he nodded and loaded another .308 Winchester into the rifle and lined up his sights. He took a quick breath—just a short, singular puff that filled his lungs enough to steady himself—and squeezed the trigger.

The gun kicked back, and the sharp metal *twang* of the target being struck emitted from across the clearing. It swung back on its wooden balancing beams and returned to its prior upright position. A new dent had formed: a hole in the center of its forehead.

Valerie gave a short, succinct clap and blocked the sun from her eyes.

"Holy fuck, kid," she exclaimed. "That was one of the cleanest headshots I've ever seen. Who taught you? Really?"

Abel removed the bulky orange headphones from his ears and hung them around his neck. "I'm self-taught, I guess."

"No one learns how to hit a target five hundred yards away with a shitty hunting rifle without some practice, Abel. Stop messing around."

"I'm not! I used to go with my dad to a shooting range when I was younger."

Abel was shocked by how effortlessly he mentioned his estranged father to a woman he hadn't known existed two weeks prior. There was something oddly comforting about sharing stories with a small commune made up of contract killers.

"How young?" Valerie asked.

"First time, I was about seven or eight."

"And now you're… what? Seventeen? Sixteen?"

"Twenty."

Valerie's eyebrows lowered slightly as if being a skilled marksman at the age of twenty was exponentially less impressive than that of a late teenager.

"Regardless, I'm ashamed to have doubted you," Valerie said. "Whenever Eddie showers someone in praise, I have my doubts, naturally. You were friends with him. You should know how he can be."

"I know," Abel responded.

"All exaggeration and no substance. But even a broken clock

is right twice a day, I guess. I feel like I can truly welcome you to the team now."

Valerie offered Abel her right hand. The gesture felt too professional, standing in the middle of a glade on a sweltering early-August day with a rifle slung across his shoulder and her rock-hard abdomen peaking from below her cropped tank top. Was this how getting the job felt for everyone? Interview after interview, desperate for answers from employers while you struggle for a purpose. *Did I bypass all the bullshit?* Abel thought. *Did I make it?*

Abel slid his right hand into Valerie's grip.

They shook on it.

★ ★ ★

It didn't take long for Valerie to assign Abel for his first mission. He, Eddie, and Mateo had driven into New York City. The short amount of time it took to get there didn't surprise Abel as much as it should have. He had checked his location on his smartphone before Valerie confiscated it. The cabin was located deep in the woods on the outskirts of a quaint village called Franklin, which was lost in the sea of the New York wilderness everyone ignored because they were all focused on the commotion of the big city.

They set up shop in the barren penthouse of an apartment complex currently under construction. Abel had never seen buildings reach that high into the night clouds, their twinkling lights becoming stars as they pierced the fog. The penthouse, along with the rest of the building, was merely a concrete skeleton. No drywall, no appliances, and no windows. A cool breeze swept into what would soon be the living room, leaving Abel breathless. All his life, he thought he would never leave Bernard, let alone the entire state of Arkansas. But now he was *here*, in the Big Apple that everyone talked about but never visited.

"Stop digging in your ass and get over here," Mateo said.

Mateo was a tall, limber Latino with black curly hair and a wide nose that made it uncomfortable for him to use his binoculars. He peered across the wide avenue into the much taller apartment complex that stood there.

"Target's on the 32nd floor," he continued. "Johnny said she'd be home at around 9:30pm. She's a light drinker and will probably leave her Tuesday night out with her girlfriends early. She'll take a shower, do her skincare regimen, then lay on the couch until her husband arrives home from work at midnight." He lowered the binoculars and turned to Abel. "Hope this job isn't too difficult for you. You'll have an hour and thirty minutes to make the shot. I know that's surely not enough, but do make the best of it, small fry."

"Don't be a dick, Mateo," Eddie said, leaning on a pillar.

"I'm not! I'm just pissed that he got to join the Coalition in under two weeks. I wasn't allowed in until I lost my ear on a mock reconnaissance mission. And that was only after I'd basically been Val's intern for over a month!"

Abel hadn't noticed the nub on the side of Mateo's head where his left ear used to be, but now that he saw it, he couldn't look away.

"You gotta quiet down, man," Eddie told Mateo.

"Oh what? Don't want me waking the neighbors?"

Abel softly chuckled at that, earning a nasty look from Mateo. His eyes were black holes absorbing the light from everything around them.

"Let me do my job, and I'll let you do yours," Mateo grumbled as he resumed staring across the street.

Abel made an unfortunate habit of checking his watch every

few seconds. Time had slowed to a crawl, the seconds feeling like minutes and the minutes feeling like hours. He felt an itch in his trigger finger.

"Are you sure you wanna do this?" Eddie asked Abel, sitting next to him on the frigid concrete floor. The deep shadows permeating around them accented his distress.

"I don't really have much of a choice," Abel said. "This is all I have now. I can't go back to Bernard. I can't go anywhere. Everywhere is dangerous when you're a wanted criminal."

"That's fair. But seriously, how are you doing? You were pretty shaken up the whole car ride to the cabin. Are you still thinking about that girl?"

"Which girl?"

Eddie blinked, confused. "The one you *shot*."

Abel briefly recollected on the silhouette of a woman running out of the woods, bruises and scratches adorning her pale skin. The woman morphed into a metal target standing upright on a wooden pike, everything below its torso cut off for simplicity's sake.

"It doesn't matter," Abel lied. "It happened, it's over. I'm here now. I can't let any of you down."

"You barely know any of them," Eddie argued, his voice lowering to a whisper. "You *just* met Mateo tonight. You haven't so much as glanced at Johnny, and I don't think you know what Zuri and Xavier even look like."

"Like I said. It doesn't matter."

"It matters a whole lot to me, though."

It felt as if someone were using a feather duster inside his stomach. Abel's cheeks grew hot, not understanding why he felt the way he did. Something about mattering meant to the world to him, and the world barely knew him. Not yet, anyway.

When 9:30 rolled around, the target arrived. She removed her red heels and unclamped her dangling gold earrings. After stretching her arms above her head, she lurched forward, her cheeks puffing out like a squirrel with one too many acorns in its mouth. She scampered to the bathroom to presumably spill her guts into the toilet.

"Can't wait to see the look on Johnny's face when I tell him he was wrong about the 'light drinker' bullshit," Mateo mumbled.

The Coalition had provided Abel with a much nicer gun: a military-grade sniper rifle with a scope that zoomed so far into the target's apartment that he could see her individual strands of red hair. The target exited the bathroom plopped onto the king-sized mattress that took up near the entirety of the bedroom. The large windowpanes allowed Abel to see everything, since the owners had neglected to invest their wealth into blinds, curtains, or both.

"Remember: You have time to make the shot between when she lies on the couch and when her husband comes home at midnight. That's nearly two hours. Don't waste them," Mateo said.

Abel began to feel annoyed at the constant nagging. No wonder Valerie assigned Mateo to lead the charge. He sure had a mouth on him, and a smartass one at that. He seemed to enjoy hearing himself talk as much as Mark enjoyed killing. For a moment, Abel nearly saw Mark in Mateo's figure, both being as tall as they were. But Mateo was much more well-spoken. He had to be, of course, because how could a man who loves to talk not know how to speak? On the other hand, Abel had to admit Mark Smith had been a bit of an idiot. Were there reasons for his idiocy? Probably, but Abel didn't want to know why. Something about tragedy striking his family and the old paper mill being reduced to a moss-covered husk of its former self. But haven't we all been there?

The target finally emerged from the bathroom, her hair damp from a long shower. She wrapped the strands into a neat cone with her towel and secured it tight around her temples. Abel checked his watch. 10:12. An hour and 48 minutes until the hubby came home. The Coalition's paycheck counted on the man finding his wife dead instead of alive. Chop-chop.

She flopped comically onto the couch, her feet hanging suspended in the air a few seconds after her ass hit the cushions. She was in position. All Abel needed to do was shoot her in the head. A bullet between the eyes. Simple enough.

But something tugged at him. A spirit of sorts, but not of the dead. His mother begged for him to stop this nonsense, to come home. She was sorry. Oh, so sorry. *I should've been a better mother. I should've forced your father to stay. I should've loved you and cherished you and raised you to be a better man.*

Abel breathed in a shallow gasp and pulled the trigger. He expected a loud *boom* from the rifle but was instead met with a short *crack* as the suppressor smothered any semblance of noise. A small circle shattered into the windowpane across the street, the bullet whizzing through and into a velvet armchair at the back of the living room. The target bolted upright and began to scream so loud he could hear her over the traffic multiple stories below.

"Abel!" Mateo scolded.

"I got it," Abel said, loading another .308 into the rifle.

He gasped another breath and fired.

The target's head jerked back, her mouth jutting open in a violent, silent screech. The towel fell from her head as she toppled onto a glass coffee table, meeting the floor in a shower of piercing snow.

"What the fuck was that?" Mateo yelled.

"He did the job, didn't he?" Eddie remarked.

"Yes, but not *well*. Val's gonna get an earful of this."

They packed up, left the unfinished apartment complex, and drove through the night back into the New York wilderness. As Abel sat in the back of the gray sedan, he listened to the rush of wind as cars passed from the other side of the road. Quick flashes of headlights before snapping off once the vehicles slipped by. He rummaged through the fabric pocket stitched to the back of the passenger seat. He pulled out a red pocketknife, flicked it open, pulled up his shirtsleeve, and etched two short parallel lines into the meat of his forearm, enjoying the pain despite the dull blade

If his mother wanted to apologize, she would've done it long ago. She wanted him to grow up, to leave the house. While she was thinking of college, life had different plans. It didn't shock Abel that he felt nothing for the target's death.

It was all a job, and a well-paying one too.

★ ★ ★

Mark sucked in his gut, pleasured by the sight of his protruding stomach disappearing underneath his dress shirt in the mirror.

"You're on in five," a thin brunette said, peaking into the dressing room. She had a blob of her red lipstick plastered to her front teeth.

"What do you need that clipboard for?" Mark asked, slipping on his suit jacket. "Are you an intern? You can't be older than 22."

"With how much they're paying me, I might as well be an intern." She chuckled, caught herself, and lowered her head to break eye contact. "But anyway, five minutes."

"Thank you."

Mark couldn't keep the image of that woman out of his mind, even as he sat across the long desk from Wilson Byrne. The man wore a head of full silver hair and thick-rimmed glasses that made his eyes look two times bigger. Mark remembered seeing a much younger version of this man on CNN when his mother had been glued to the television during chemo. Between then and now, Byrne had turned heel and chased a much larger salary at FOX News.

Studio J felt like the old paper mill. Iron scaffolding hung from the ceiling and employees constantly walked in from one unseen corner and out the other. There was a feverish energy embedded within every square inch of the interview room, and through the brouhaha, Mark spotted the brunette lady waltzing by, yelling something probably important into her bulky headset. She became lost in the ocean of chaos before Mark could really get another good look at her.

A neon "ON AIR" sign blinked on, the cameras flashed red. Wilson Byrne wiped sweat from his porous forehead. Studio J was infested with humidity and disposable vape smoke, and Mark could tell the otherworldly heat could be too much for a New Yorker used to overbearing cold for a good chunk of the year. Mark felt fine, though. A little moist in the armpits, but otherwise good. Byrne, on the other hand, looked as though he was on the verge of a heart attack.

"Are you alright, sir?" Mark asked.

"Just shut up and make this quick."

Mark imagined Byrne being ripped in two by a ferocious Minotaur. His elderly guts and bones would crack and squish along the gnarly tearing point, skin stretching and giving like the cheese inside a panini as someone digs in for a bite. The man clearly wasn't well. Death would be a mercy compared to whatever shit he was dealing with currently.

Within an instant, Byrne's face shifted from worrisome to jubilant. He turned from Mark to the largest camera in the room, planting his hands on the blank papers before him. There was a rose gold wedding band on one of his fingers. Mark thought it looked more like copper than anything resembling gold.

"Welcome to Night Watch," Byrne told the camera. "I'm your host, Wilson Byrne. We have a special segment planned tonight, as we have a controversial figure in the 2028 presidential race sitting across from me in the studio. Mark Smith? Would you please introduce yourself?"

Mark's mouth went dry. Byrne's stone-cold stare froze him to his chair. There was a nation full of viewers behind the camera, all waiting for what he had to say. The concept of that many eyes on him was terrifying, that many eyes perceiving him. How many of them could notice the hint of a double chin under his head? How many would notice he hadn't had a haircut in over two weeks?

"Hello," he coughed. "I'm Mark Smith, and I am the new Republican candidate for president of the United States."

"Your rise to the top has been tumultuous, to say the least. Davey Robinson, the earlier candidate, was a controversial figure as well. How would you say your relationship was with him before he bowed out of this race?"

"I had only met him two weeks ago," Mark started. He glanced past the camera and spotted Fitzgerald and Hughes sitting in a dark corner. Fitzgerald watched intently with damning eyes, while Hughes tapped at his overly bright phone screen. "I began speaking at his rallies because it was a new opportunity for me. I have so many ideas, and I thought, 'What better way to express myself than in front of thousands of people?' Davey was very welcoming to my joining the tour, but I could tell from the moment I met him that his heart wasn't in it."

Byrne gave a dishonest laugh and said, "You must have made quite the impression on him. How do you feel about the endorsement that came your way earlier today? The president is not known to endorse many people. Presidential pardons? Sure, but not endorsements."

"It was an honor to hear, for sure. I've always admired the man, and to have him endorse me as his successor meant everything to me." He couldn't believe any of those words left his mouth, but they were what the teleprompter said, so he had to read them.

"Are there any issues that you relate to the president on? Any topics you would like to align yourself with?"

"I would say—"

The main camera's red light flicked off as a brawny man with a headset and clipboard shuffled over to Byrne. He whispered into the interviewer's ear. Byrne's eyes went so wide they almost fell out of their sockets.

"What kind of sick joke is this?"

"Your wife, sir," the brawny man said. "She didn't make it."

Byrne flicked his hand, shooing the man away as fast as he came. The teleprompter had stopped scrolling, ending at the bottom of the screen with the words **I WOULD SAY I ALIGN**. Byrne removed his glasses and threw them across the room, hitting a camera operator in the dick.

"I need to go," Byrne said, his head in his hands. "Fuck this."

Byrne rose from his seat without so much as another look at Mark. He stomped out of Studio J as his eyes grew glassy with tears. Mark didn't know until later when he slept with the brunette girl—whose named happened to be Janet—why Wilson Byrne had cancelled the interview and fled the studio.

She said, "His wife had been shot before the interview. She survived the attack but died on the way to the hospital. He already knew about the first half when you were up for Night Watch. Not the second part, though."

"That's terrible," Mark whispered, his lips salty with sex-induced sweat. "Do you think he'll be okay?"

"Not sure."

"Maybe I could help."

"No, Mark." Janet rolled over underneath the covers, her bare breasts sliding over his shaved, damp chest. "Please don't kill my boss. I need the paycheck, small as it is."

"You know about that? The murders?" Mark wasn't sure why he felt embarrassed to talk about his life's work. Something about this woman brought the inner child out of his bedrock heart.

"Of course I do. Everyone does," she said.

"And you aren't against it?"

"You're making the world a better place, right?"

"That's the idea."

"I'm a little pissed that the interview was cut short before you could give your stance on anything. More people need to hear what you have to say. It's inspiring stuff."

"Inspiring?"

"Well, yeah. I'm not saying *I* would ever kill someone, but I'm glad someone's actually taking a stance for what they believe. We're sorely lacking that these days. Everyone's so afraid to be noticed. We're in an epidemic of nonchalance. We need someone like you, no matter how violent."

Mark felt heat rising in his cheeks and penis.

"Do you want to work for me?" he asked, the thought coming to him only after he had said it. "I can pay more than those FOX idiots."

"I thought you'd never ask."

Janet planted her lips on his, and they fucked for the third time that night without protection.

CHAPTER 11

★ ★ ★

Rain spewed from the gutters in miniature waterfalls. Droplets splattered on the windowpane; little pinpricks of water tainted from pollution tapping the glass like thousands of infants' pudgy fingers.

Ashley sat on the couch; the same seat she watched Mark Smith make his first speech on. Her mind rattled. The Solar System was constructed completely at random. The Sun was just massive enough to sustain millions of orbits, the Moon at just the perfect distance to keep the tides in check. If Earth had formed a few miles further from the Sun, it would be too cold for life to survive. None of this would have happened. All their silly little problems would never have had the chance to bloom, the solutions just as meaningless.

Thunder clouds obscured that sun, rendering its light pointless. Ashley had seen the government as the central point for all life to revolve around, a bright star with enough mass to warrant its importance. But as the years drew on, that fantasy began to diminish. In the past few weeks, exponentially so. Her fiancée exploding into meaty chunks because of a terrorist's bomb. Her father falling victim to the boogeyman. That same boogeyman running for president.

It was absurd, illogical. Complete horseshit.

Nothing made sense, yet that was sensible.

She wanted to get up. She wanted to haul her sorry ass off the couch and into a tailored suit. She wanted to walk to the House floor and join committees, write legislation, and vote for what was right. She wanted so much out of this job, and she wanted the United States to receive help from her tenure. The country was broken, but not beyond repair. She went to college to study for this moment, to hold the wrench that will tighten the loose bolts that barely held America together.

Her phone vibrated on the armrest. She checked the screen, saw Christopher Shaw's name, rolled her eyes, pressed to answer, and put the phone on speaker. "What?" she asked, mildly shocked by how bitter she sounded.

"*Is now a bad time?*" Shaw asked.

"When has it ever been a *good* time?"

"*I'll take that as a no. How have you been?*"

"Worse."

"*That's fair, Ashley. That's fair. Have you thought about my proposal?*"

"What proposal?"

"*I emailed you some documents about… let's see… three days ago.*"

"I was at Tasha's funeral, Chris."

"*Oh! Right, sorry. Well anyway, they're pertaining to the Government Protections ad hoc committee. If you want to take a look while I have you, that would be great.*"

"I'm not on that committee."

"Yes, I know. But I need your input on something. It's a bit more serious than I was expecting and I need a fresh set of eyes looking at it."

Ashley rubbed the drowsiness from her eyes and opened her email. She scrolled to the messages from three days ago and saw the mail from Shaw, titled "GP Files."

"Why are you sending me classified documents over Gmail?" she asked. "There's no encryption. You don't want to pull a Hegseth with stuff like this."

"I know, but you have me blocked on Signal."

Ashley didn't even know you could block people on Signal, but she tucked away that tidbit for the next time Hughes decided to unwelcomely ask for lewd photos.

"Oh, I'm sorry about that."

"It's no problem. But please read over the documents I sent you. I really really really need your thoughts on what's being proposed. They might be of use to you, or they might not be. That's what I'm trying to figure out."

"I'll look into it."

"No, please do it now."

"I have to go."

Before Shaw could convince her to stay on the line, Ashley hung up. The rain continued to pitter-patter on the window. The capital was awash with a tense dull grayness that made her palms sweat. She looked at her phone, the email still pulled up, and slid the message into the archive folder.

★ ★ ★

As a summer rain poured in D.C., the sky was uniquely barren of clouds in the New York wilderness. Abel couldn't sleep last night, despite wishing the hit on that woman wouldn't affect his psyche too much. The image of her head caving in from the bullet's impact played repeatedly, as if someone had the television remote attached to his brain and kept pressing rewind.

He spent the rest of the night and most of the early morning laying in a grassy patch behind the cabin and under the stars. A brood of lost cicadas chirped as he stared into the blackened sky. In every star, he saw another, and the two points of light glared at him like glowing eyes. Faceless, but not without wrath. Only when the sunrise came did the faceless eyes cease, and the day began anew.

A twig snapped behind him. He twisted his neck and spotted a pair of black boots laced a quarter way up the shins. Eddie bent down and took a seat next to him.

"Sorry about Mateo," Eddie said, his voice raspy with sleep. "He can be a handful sometimes."

"It's alright," Abel said, not knowing if that was entirely true. "I was bound to make a mistake. I'm not gonna fault him for getting on my ass."

"You should, though. He stepped over the line."

"And *I* missed the shot."

"But you hit the next one. Be proud of that."

"It's kinda hard to be proud of much when what I did got someone killed."

Eddie scoffed. "When did you get so soft?"

"I didn't."

The two of them sat for a minute or three taking in the cool morning air before it gave way to the humid soup that was late summer oxygen. When the silence became more deafening than the cicadas, Abel asked, "Who was that woman, anyway?"

"The target? Just some lady with a rich old husband. Why?"

"Was she guilty?"

"Of what?"

"Of anything."

Eddie paused for a moment, combing his fingers through his beard. It was still damp from the shower but smelled faintly of peppermint. "It doesn't matter whether or not she was guilty," he said. "We were hired to do a job, and we did it. That's how the Coalition works. That's how it's always been. We don't have the authority to ask questions. We do what we're paid for, and that usually involves killing people, yeah."

"It just doesn't feel right."

"It never does." Eddie scooted closer, the peppermint scent of his beard oil growing more pungent. "You know, when I started here, I felt the exact same way you do. Scared, confused. But eventually I realized that this is all I had left. The only thing keeping me going. If it weren't for the Coalition, I'd probably be wasting away as a cashier… or dead, probably."

"But you don't do the actual killing. You just keep watch."

"I think it's more than that. I keep you all protected, and that means the world to me, I guess. I don't mind being inactive or whatever. As long as I'm with this crew, I'm good."

"Have you ever killed anyone?"

Eddie paused again, lifting his eyes as if the answer were written in the blue sky. "Yeah, but it was an accident. It was my uncle, actually. He was such an asshole. One day he came to visit in California and started getting flirty with my dad. That night, I heard noises from the basement, so I grabbed my parents' handgun and walked downstairs. It was pitch black down there, but I could hear something going on. Almost like a fight was happening. You know, with punching n' shit. I called out, and the basement went quiet. Then I heard footsteps coming toward me, and I tensed up. My finger pulled the trigger, and I shot my uncle in the heart. He was naked, my dad was naked. They'd been fucking down there while my mom slept alone upstairs.

"So anyway, yeah. I've killed someone. Maybe two if you count my dad killing himself afterward. It took a while for me to process it all, but I'm in a much better place now, I think. I bulked up, grew out my hair, and got a job I love. I barely think about what I've done anymore. Killing isn't my thing, personally, but it can be yours."

"I don't think it is," Abel said.

"That's bullshit. You've always been interested in that stuff. Remember all the ISIS beheading videos you used to send me on Instagram?"

"It was just a phase." Abel thought about how enamored he had been of Mark Smith, following him around like some sort of witless sidekick to a superhero. "I think I grew up or something. I don't know."

"But you were so excited to go shooting a few weeks back," Eddie argued. "You always invite me to play *Counter-Strike*. You love the hunt. You always have."

"I don't want that to be all I am."

"It isn't."

Abel felt a twinge of tension between the two of them. That peppermint scent grew to toxic proportions, stinging his nose. He wanted to wrap his arms around Eddie's bulky frame, to breathe him in, to kiss his neck.

"Then what am I?"

"A badass, man," Eddie answered. "A complete and total badass. Sure, you missed that first shot, but that second one. Oh, bro. Straight in the face! Huge goddamn hole in that target's head. Right in the center too. You're a badass, and you should be proud of that. Not many men nowadays can say the same for themselves."

Abel took in those words like an amoeba absorbing another

single-celled organism, feeding on his own kind in a way that benefits nobody but himself. His life had been a train wreck. It started off strong, but then his father left, the bullies at school grew more vicious, and his mother barely acknowledged his existence. He had been on the path of uselessness, a path that would probably lead him to four years at a bum-ass college, then some dead-end job as a middle school janitor or a garbage collector. No further growth, only the same shit day in and day out until the day he lay in bed and never woke up again.

Now, his path was simple.

Continue the killing. The *work*. The *job*. Then bathe in the money until your dying breath. Purpose was a funny thing to ponder, but Abel's purpose was set. Being a badass was surely better than a lifetime of student loan debt.

★ ★ ★

Janet wept when Mark told her how much her salary as a campaign assistant would amount to. "I could pay off all my student loans," she stuttered through phlegm and tears. "I could rent a… No, I could *buy* a house. Are you sure about this?"

"Yes," Mark said, unsure why she was crying.

"One million dollars is a lot, though."

"I have a few extra lying around somewhere."

"Thank you."

Janet scooped him up in a tight squeeze that was almost too violent to call a hug. An air bubble popped between his ribs that granted him the most pleasure he had felt since Davey Robinson's death. Mark pushed Janet away, and her face went from being overjoyed to momentarily confused.

"What's wrong?" she asked.

"We'll have to keep it professional during the campaign, though. Palmer told me that an affair with my assistant wouldn't look good in the polls. I don't know much about all that, but I'm going to have to believe him on that front."

"An affair? But you're not married."

"It would be a political affair."

"What?"

He placed his hands on her shoulders. Even with this wrench thrown into their infantile relationship, she still marveled at how much taller he was than her. He clocked that shimmer of subservience, the desire to be dominated.

"We can start things publicly again after I win the election," Mark explained. "We just need to make it to November. I'll make it up to you. I promise."

She smiled at that. "Alright, but I'll have you know something: I hate broken promises. Don't make me hate you."

Janet left the hotel room in New York City wearing the same tight suit she'd been wearing in Studio J the previous night. She would walk into the FOX News headquarters and demand her immediate resignation. She would then return to the hotel and sign documents Fitzgerald had begrudgingly prepared.

"We could've just given you one of our interns as an assistant," the congressman had mumbled, the pages slowly inching out of the printer. "Why this random woman?"

"I had a hunch," Mark had said.

His hunch should've been obvious to anyone who knew him. There was a reason Mark had grown so fond of Janet in such a short amount of time. She bore an uncanny resemblance to his late mother, and he saw that as a sign from whatever higher power watched over him. He started this campaign with his mother in mind. The killings, the blood, the guts. All for her.

"I hope I don't regret this," Fitzgerald had said, handing over the contract, still warm from the printer.

"You won't. I promise."

Mark spent the rest of his time in New York visiting other news stations. They all frothed at the mouth with anticipation. How often would the perfect interview fall into their lap? A man from the middle of nowhere rising to the top of the ballot only on the promise of demolishing the suicide epidemic? A man whose loose ties to former candidate Davey Robinson couldn't be ignored. What about the alleged crimes in his hometown that were too juicy to leave on the table?

His interview with MSNBC bored him to tears. They asked questions such as "What are your goals for your potential presidency?" and "Why politics? Why not the farm?" Before Mark had the chance to correct the interviewer that it was a paper mill and not a farm, Janet swooped in and answered the worst questions with startling precision. He hadn't known it, since his only experience with her had been in bed, but Janet was a masterful liar. She conjured up explanations that he had never dreamt of stating aloud. She twisted questions to her whim, making the answers about illegal immigration when the question was about his favorite pastime.

CNN was a completely different beast. When he sat down with Anderson Cooper, he felt nothing but an overbearing anxiety. The anchor, despite his clearly feminine bone structure, was as intimidating in person as a raging bull in the arena. Mark felt the urge to hoist up a red cape, surrendering to the power this white-haired man held.

"Our current president recently endorsed Davey Robinson as the Republican candidate for this election," Cooper said. "But after Robinson's untimely disappearance, the president granted you another endorsement. Do you think he made this change in good faith?"

Mark struggled to find anything in the English language that could answer that question. Janet hadn't been allowed to enter the interviewing space for aesthetic purposes, since CNN preferred to keep only the interviewer, interviewee, and a single cameraman in the intricately decorated room. There wasn't even a table between the two of them, only empty space occupied by nothing except a buried sense of disdain from both parties.

"I believe the president makes all his decisions in good faith," Mark finally said. "His endorsement of my candidacy is no different."

"That leads into the next topic of discussion," Cooper said. "You state that all his decisions are made in good faith. Would you say the same about his tariff policies?"

"What's a tariff?"

Cooper looked dumbfounded.

Oops, Mark thought. *I should've let Palmer explain this shit to me.*

"It's a tax on imported goods. The president's frantic tariff policies caused the prices of everyday goods such as groceries to skyrocket. The consumer eats the cost to import. Would you say that decision was made in good faith?"

"I usually only buy lettuce, bread, and sandpaper from Walmart, so I would say I haven't noticed any higher prices. Where are you getting this information from?"

"The Consumer Price Index from the Bureau of Labor Statistics."

"That's a lot of words," Mark laughed.

"Do you find the higher prices funny?"

"No." Mark coughed the laughter out of his system, realizing his mistake. "No, I do not."

A look of bewilderment washed across Cooper's face. His eyebrows furrowed as he coughed into the crook of his elbow and continued, "Was the president's decision to redact his own name from the Epstein files also in good faith?"

"I can't comment on that. I haven't read them."

"No one has. The White House is still holding onto those."

"Oh, alright."

"What about undocumented immigrants? Was it 'good faith' for the president to send ICE after people who pay taxes, live honest lives, and commit no crime?"

"Doesn't sound right," Mark said.

Instead of bewildered, Cooper began to look intrigued. He leaned forward. "Do you denounce the immigration policies of our current president?"

"No comment."

"What *can* you comment on?"

"Suicide."

Cooper shifted in his seat, clearly uncomfortable with where the conversation was headed. "That's something you had preached about on Robinson's campaign trail. Would you care to elaborate?"

"I kill people to save them from killing themselves. It's simple, really."

"That's something you've mentioned many times. Is it a turn of phrase from your hometown?"

"No," Mark said. "Well, not that I know of."

"Then how are the American people supposed to interpret your words?"

"At face value."

The interview continued for another fifteen minutes. Cooper had gone completely silent as Mark explained some of his favorite murders. He mentioned the clothing iron he had used to smash and cook a girl's face with. He mentioned the fire extinguisher incident involving another news reporter and her cameraman lackey. His favorite kill by far was on a homeless man who had recently hitchhiked into Bernard from Charleston, South Carolina. Mark had lured him to the old paper mill with the promise of free heroin. Once the homeless man arrived, he was met with Mark stabbing him repeatedly in the face with a used syringe until he died from shock, his face dripping in skinny crimson streams from hundreds of holes no bigger than pesky blackheads.

"How'd it go?" Janet asked as he left the room.

"Better than expected."

Anderson Cooper exited after him and barreled over to the nearest restroom. As Mark heard a fit of dry heaving echoing from the stalls down the hallway, he sighed and motioned Janet to follow him out of the studio.

Palmer, who had finally returned from the nation's capital, sat at the reception desk, his head buried in a stack of a hundred or so legal documents. When he noticed Mark, he quickly shoved the papers into his briefcase as if he were a child trying to hide evidence finding him guilty of stealing from the cookie jar.

"Long time, no see!" the congressman said. "I trust you've heard the news."

"The endorsement? Yes, I've heard."

"No, not that. I expected you'd already heard through the interview circuit. Have you heard about your hometown?"

"I don't think I have."

"Remember when I mentioned the National Guard had been deployed to quell the violence? Well, my sources informed me that your fellow neighbors have torn half of the fleet limb for limb. Literally! It's a madhouse down in Bernard."

"That's terrible," Mark mumbled.

"You don't have to lie, Mr. Smith," Palmer playfully scolded. "I know that fills you with a great amount of pleasure."

Mark twitched a smirk. He did quite enjoy the mental image of the people he swore to protect taking after him to murder other miserable people in his absence.

Palmer continued, "The president has deployed another fleet of National Guard troops. Can't beat them with one, you have got to send in another. Keep throwing nukes at them until they stop throwing rocks."

★ ★ ★

Ashley spent the next day doomscrolling through Instagram. When the mindless memes and political stories became too much for her waning mind to handle, she moved onto TikTok, where she was met with more of the same, only with the added detractor of an advertisement every other video. A teenager attempted to sell an oversized plush shaped like a goose, another waxed poetic about tight tank tops that smoothed out his protruding steroid-infested nipples, and another looked orgasmic while sniffing a candle that allegedly smelled like Dr. Pepper. She then made a pit stop on Twitter or X or whatever, immediately got annoyed by a user claiming that the newest Pixar movie made a mockery of September 11th, and made her way over to Facebook.

She scrolled for a while until her feed was engulfed in community posts from Bernard. She clicked on the page and was met with photos of local businesses burning to the ground, videos of kids as young as 10 plucking out the eyes of helpless National Guardsmen, and written posts that called for safety, mercy, and everything in between:

I can't find my husband! Eric went to Walmart to grab another six pack, but never came back. If anyone has seen him, lmk!

       — Tiffany Redwood

Is there a hospital closer to us than Little Rock Memorial?? My wife threw her back out ripping one of them DC cops' legs off and she needs care immediately. Any suggestions?

       — Pat McMahan

My kids haven't been able to sleep in DAYS... Whoever is setting off grenades down White Street, please STOP NOW!! The kids need to be in school tomorrow morning, and I can't have them blown up! THX!!!!

       — Kelsi Wiesenthal

Free piano in good condition. Must be able to pickup.

       — Steve O'Leary

The piano was nearly perfect. Ashley wondered why Mr. O'Leary would give away such a fine instrument for free. The other posts—and many, many more—were also quite concerning, but she'd had enough death and bloodshed to deal with in recent months. That damn piano, though. Now *that* was outrageous.

She closed the app before she had the chance to wallow in her father's rambling posts, public messages that she had thought were abrasive before his death but found oddly charming in their new state. They were now a window into his soul, a glimpse into his life before his fatal mutilation. Complaints about rowdy neighborhood children, questions about whether Dollar General was open, requests for a fly swatter from anyone willing to be a good Samaritan. But Ashley turned off her phone before her curiosity got the better of her. Her tears were in short supply nowadays.

Bernard died the day her father did. There was no reason for her to return. They could nuke themselves into atoms for all she cared. The town had given birth to Mark Smith, and that was enough of a sin to warrant the destruction they found themselves in now. Years of tormenting that—admittedly creepy—child, morphing his mind into a twisted amalgam of terror and violence. He was bullied in school; Ashley had seen it, being a year above him. He'd been much taller than his peers, his face riddled with acne, and his parents rich as people could be in a backwater town. *Moneybags, daddy long-legs, Yellowstone,* and *beanpole* were among the more creative insults along with the standard gibes such as *asswipe, fuckwad, shithead, faggot,* and *retard.* Ashley had never gotten involved in the tyrannizing, but that might've been just the problem. If all the anti-bullying seminars in high school and college taught her anything, it was that being a bystander was just as bad as being the perpetrator.

Ashley shook her head. It was all bullshit. She couldn't sink into her couch like the world's heaviest, saddest potato and blame herself for the most egregious case of unaccounted serial murder in the country's history. Mark Smith had much more going on outside of Bernard High's walls. His father was rumored to be abusive, his mother had cancer and died by suicide. Both very normal reasons for why a growing boy would resort to murder as a form of pain relief.

She looked toward where her analog clock hung on the living room walls, realized it was too dark in the apartment to see anything, and fought herself as she rose from the couch. Day had slipped into night before she had the chance to notice.

She made herself a frozen dinner (shrimp fettuccine Alfredo, a college favorite) and ate it in silence, the only sound being the limited traffic on the D.C. streets outside. She finished the last morsels of noodle and dumped the empty tray into the trash can. A momentary glance at her couch sent a chill down her spine. She grasped the gold spider around her neck, feeling her heartbeat.

Her phone rang. Cristopher Shaw. She let the marimba ringtone play out before the screen went dark again.

★ ★ ★

Abel hadn't seen a ghost in three weeks. The visions of people he'd lost—his father, his mother, Macy Thornton, the newscaster's wife—vanished little by little until those apparition became nothing more than dust in the wind. He'd been on fifteen missions since his first hit, each kill easier than the last. It was all for the money, and money trumps all, even the law. Even morality.

September was briskly approaching, and as summer dimmed into fall, the number of calls the Coalition received grew from one or two per week to about one every other day. Something about the leaves withering from green to brown made these customers bloodthirsty, and that was alright by Abel's standards.

"Another hit," Valerie said as she barged into the cabin's basement. "Congressman from Arkansas. Someone wants him dead for fifty grand."

"Fifty grand? For a fucking politician?" Johnny asked, scratching his eyepatch with contempt.

"That was the starting offer," Valerie assured, "but I got that bumped up to two hundred. With this election coming up, people are getting desperate to change the tides."

"Good for business," mumbled Zuri.

Zuri and Xavier had finally arrived at the cabin the week before. Their location had been compromised after law enforcement

216

was tipped at their presence after they detonated a bomb that vaporized a congregation of Neo-Nazis in northern Idaho. The twins had to lay low in nearby Montana before hitchhiking back to New York, an arduous journey that lasted two grueling weeks. Despite Zuri being a woman and Xavier a man, they were clearly of the same kin. Their skin was a deep mocha shade, decorated with wide black eyes and full lips that always seemed impossibly moist. Zuri looked like Xavier with cornrows, and Xavier looked like Zuri with short locs and a high fade.

Aside from their similarities in the looks department, they also seemed to share one mind; a singular consciousness that allowed them to never disagree on anything.

"Yeah, definitely good for business," Xavier predictably said.

"Is it a Republican?" Mateo asked Valerie.

"Does it matter?"

"No, but I'd like to know how satisfied this kill will make me."

"You know that's not how any of this works," Eddie reasoned.

"Shut up, big boy," Mateo retorted.

Eddie crossed his arms, making them look twice as large as they were.

"The client had a special request for us," Valerie said, peering at Zuri and Xavier. "I think you two will really enjoy this."

The twins leaned forward in their foldout chairs, wonderment shining in their abyssal eyes.

"Make it messy."

CHAPTER 12

★ ★ ★

Mark met the Democratic candidate on a late August night at a party organized by lobbyists from Spotify and Lockheed Martin. His name was Reginald Foster, an African American gentleman who was nearly as tall as Mark himself, if only shorter by an inch. His face was round with cheekbones that bulged into two brown balls whenever he smiled.

"Mr. Smith," Foster said, presenting an outstretched hand. "It's a pleasure to finally meet you."

"The same to you," Mark responded.

They shook for a second longer than what was comfortable. Foster squeezed for another second, popping Mark's knuckles, and finally let go.

"You're the talk of the town," Foster said. "Everyone has something to say about you online and off. You're quite the character."

"What're they saying?"

"Oh, nothing too bad. Just that you're a fraud."

The initial facade of camaraderie vanished into the classical music emitting loudly from the grand hall's overhead speakers. Foster's wide smile dipped into a more serious look of contempt.

"I don't know what your game is, Smith," Foster said, jabbing a stout finger into Mark's chest, "but I want you to know that there's no chance in hell the American people will allow someone like you to lead them. You represent everything wrong with this country."

"How so?" Mark was genuinely curious.

"Well, there are rumors circulating that you are serious about your claims of murdering those you deem unfit for society, for starters. You go up on these stages and sit in front of interview cameras and spew this nonsense about male loneliness or whatever the hell you think is important to people. What about healthcare? Income taxes? Foreign wars? Do you have any opinions on those things? Any solutions? Or are you just along for the ride?"

"Shouldn't we just enjoy the party?"

Foster didn't simply laugh; he *roared*. Roared like a lion becoming a bit too excited while watching a standup comedy routine. "We just met, Mr. Smith. Don't you think we should settle some of our differences before having to argue with one another for the next two months?"

"You could try being less rude about it."

"Me? Less rude? You really don't know anything, do you?"

"I guess not."

Foster's eyelids lowered in abhorrence. He scratched the side of his nose and folded his arms over his broad chest.

"What did you do to Davey Robinson, Smith?" Foster asked. "It's alright. You can tell me. I'm not wearing a wire or anything. You can be completely truthful with me. I won't tell."

"Robinson was a dear friend of mine who made it very clear behind closed doors that he wanted to drop out of the race. As for where he went after his rally in Joplin, I don't know. No one knows."

Foster's eyes lowered even more, his pupils becoming so hidden that he looked almost as if he would fall asleep standing up. "You really are something else," he roared once more. "This debate'll be a cakewalk."

"In whose favor? I can't tell. I'm too *stupid*."

Foster awoke from whatever judgmental trance he found himself in, his eyes now blazing in fury. He placed both of his large hands around Mark's arms, squeezing so tight that Mark could feel his pulse throbbing in his veins.

"Don't be a smartass, Mark," Foster seethed. "This is my race to win, and your hillbilly antics aren't gonna sway the public. They'll see right. Through. You."

"Hey hey hey! What's going on here?"

Representative Palmer compressed himself between the two candidates and struggled to push them apart. Once Foster finally released his strong grip on Mark, Mark stumbled backward a few steps before regaining his composure. Foster dusted himself off as if Mark were a contagion that needed to be sanitized from his suit.

"We were just having a chat," he said.

"Looked like a violation of civil conduct to me," Palmer remarked. "Why don't you get back to your friends over there?"

He pointed to the bar area, at which sat half a dozen elderly white men laughing over flutes of champagne. One of them turned, a Lockheed Martin pin affixed to his breast pocket. Foster huffed and fled the scene without saying another word.

When the coast was clear, Palmer turned to Mark and said,

"Please forgive Reggie. He can get very passionate about stuff like this. He'll calm down by the time the debate rolls around, the brute." He fetched a disposable vape from his pocket and took a long drag, the tiny light on the bottom of the device glowing bright as the motors inside produced enough toxic flavored gas to satiate the congressman's nicotine addiction for a while longer. "I need you to come with me. Fitzgerald, Hughes, and I need to discuss some important matters upstairs while we're all here together. Come along."

They took a gold-plated elevator up to the fifteenth floor of the equally gold-plated skyscraper. The president had graciously (if not against his will) allowed the party to take place at his luxury hotel in the heart of the Windy City. Mark wondered on the way up why a president would need such an extravagant hotel in his name, and not just in Chicago, but in multiple metropolitan areas around the country.

Upon exiting the elevator, Palmer and Mark winded through confusingly laid out hallways and eventually found the room they were looking for just before they became completely lost in the gilded labyrinthine hellscape.

"We need to discuss the logistics of the next two moths," Fitzgerald said after everyone was settled inside the empty conference room. "September should be a breeze, but October is where things could get dicey."

"Dicey?" asked Mark.

"I'm not particularly a man of superstition, but October always spells bad news for campaigns on either side of the aisle. Teddy Roosevelt was shot during a speech in October 1912, Hurricane Sandy nearly knocked Obama out of the race in 2012, our current president almost lost in 2016 when a clip surfaced of himself saying he was so famous he could grab women by the pussy without consequence. Things come out of nowhere, but you always need to be prepared."

"So, what should we do?"

"We need to have backup plans," Palmer said. "Believe it or not, Hughes is rather skilled in that department. Would you like to give some suggestions, Hughes?"

Congressman Hughes startled awake when Palmer tapped him on the bony shoulder. The man looked about ready to meet his maker, but his face contorted into a look of deep seriousness despite his age. He coughed and asked, "What are we talking about?"

"October surprises," Fitzgerald and Palmer said in unison.

"Ah, yes."

Hughes struggled to his feet and meandered to the front of the conference room, the twinkling lights of nighttime Chicago setting the background for his presentation. He looked paler than usual in his gray suit jacket, the washed-out fabric accentuating the wrinkles creasing his loose facial skin.

"I was a campaign advisor for Richard Nixon during the '68 election," he grumbled, his medieval voice brimming with loose gravel. "The war against the Vietcong was much of the reason Nixon won, but not without some bumps in the trail. Reagan was a huge personality. One of the greats, I will admit. The primaries we obviously don't need to deal with. We skipped that step entirely. But there is the problem of, uh… What's his name?"

"Reggie Foster," Fitzgerald said.

"Foster, mhm. He may present a problem for us in terms of staying power. He's a Black from the Midwest. He'll appeal to the poor left, both in racial optics and by simply living in Nebraska. He's as down-to-earth a candidate as the Democrats could select. But there's a hitch. He isn't really salt of the earth. Oh, no no no.

He's a wealthy businessman with ties to landlord operations and the Israeli state. He likes to keep those two things hidden, but if I learned anything from Nixon's victory, it's that anything can happen, and *anything* can be brought to light. Even the darkest bullshit in Foster's little closet."

"What do we have on him?" Mark asked.

"Well, we have the aforementioned ties to Israel, a nation that only eight percent of polled Americans support currently," Palmer explained. They had clearly rehearsed this beforehand, even down to the accents on certain syllables. "We also have his collusions with landlords in and around the Omaha area. As the current mayor of the city, he hikes rental prices to pocket the extra funds for his business ventures in Silicon Valley. Some new AI startup that wants to rival Sam Altman and all the other tech freaks on the West Coast. Those two things would surely put a dent in his campaign, but nothing too serious, unfortunately."

"This country runs on emotion," Hughes said. Mark felt a sense of whiplash from how intelligent the usually senile old fart sounded. "The American people do not need these 'culture wars' anymore. No more hashtag MeToo. No more Black Lives Matter. What they need is a leader who will open their eyes, to make them see that the American dream is right in front of them. All they need to do is reach out and grab it from the jaws of defeat. Everything surrounding Foster will come to light in due time, but our little secret will tip the scales."

"That being?" Mark asked, growing impatient.

"Pornography, Mr. Smith," Palmer grinned. "Foster has computers full of child pornography. Our interns have already forwarded the files to news outlets across the country. *That* will be our October surprise. A big, heaping pile of child pornography with Foster's name scribbled all over it."

"If Foster's a child molester, why don't I just kill him?" Mark asked. "Pedophiles are the most likely to kill themselves in prison."

"He's not *actually* a pedophile, Mark. Well, as far as we know, he isn't. But the public doesn't know that. We will have the news outlets drop the bombs in October to fuel the general October superstition. And when Foster attempts to clear his name, he will look even more guilty."

"Is that fair?"

"Does it matter?" Hughes asked, stretching his arms out as if he were Jesus on the cross. "It's politics. That's the name of the…"

★ ★ ★

Abel lay on his stomach, his eye essentially glued inside the sniper scope. He watched two men—one in his mid-fifties, the other so old a light breeze could reduce him to dust—enter the conference room four blocks down the road.

"You need to be careful with this one. Super high-value target." Mateo said.

"I know I'm supposed to be careful," Abel said, his gaze focused entirely on the two men in suits nearly a mile away.

"Are you sure? I'm still not forgiving you for that fuck-up job in NYC."

"You're still hung up on that?" Eddie asked from far behind.

Instead of the usual construction site the Coalition found themselves in for missions, they had opted for a swanky hotel suite in the heart of Chicago. With the lights dimmed, of course. Operations related to governmental personnel always brought the risk of higher paid security having eyes like hawks. Even from their faraway distance, the likelihood of a bodyguard spotting a suspiciously bright window a mile away wasn't zero.

They had moved one of the queen beds toward the window for Abel to lay on, keeping his vision level with just above the windowsill. Mateo spun around in a creaky desk chair while Eddie blocked the door with his broad shoulders, checking through the peephole every minute or so for passersby.

Abel watched the conference room with an unwavering eye. The two men lazed about in their rolling chairs, the older of the two looking quite uncomfortable with how comfortable the chair made him feel. By special request, the client had asked for the assassination to be carried out in the presence of a full party, so Abel was contractually obligated to wait for more people to storm the conference room inside the gleaming golden building across the way.

But Abel wanted to just take the shot. His mouth had gone dry in anticipation. In the past few weeks, he had discovered more about himself than the first twenty years of his life could offer. He wasn't keen on the actual killing part of all this. What he enjoyed most was the calm yet succinct way the trigger of his rifle felt under his finger. Just a simple action, pulling the trigger. A light press, then a short click, and then whatever was at the tail end of the barrel would explode in a red haze.

He watched as the main door in the conference room opened. Two more men entered. "*The target will be accompanied by three colleagues, where they will develop plans pertaining to this year's presidential election,*" the client, their voice garbled through encryption software, had said. "*Make sure they are all attentive. We want them to watch. We want them to realize the error of their ways.*"

The first man looked nearly identical to the fifty-something from before, but the second man looked more familiar, something

Abel found deeply unsettling. He recognized that clean face, the basic swoop of his brown hair, the height at which he towered over his colleagues. The man from the television, the one in the hospital bed. A savior, a god. Or someone who used to be.

Mark Smith was in that room, and he was to be a witness to Abel's wrath. Abel salivated, his dry gums moistening as the tensions grew. He smiled, sucked in a short breath, and felt the trigger click beneath his finger.

★ ★ ★

Before Hughes could finish his statement, his head exploded like a grapefruit in the microwave. His blood splattered across the glossy table, jettisoning in all directions, splashing into the eyes of his two Republican colleagues and the star of the show himself, though Mark certainly did not receive as much of the spray, to his dismay.

Hughes collapsed forward, his outstretched arms flopping to his hips. The cavity that used to be his face slammed wetly onto the table. Loose skin melted into the laminated wood. His gray hair flipped over his bald spot and soaked in his pooling blood.

The congressmen sat in shock, their eyes wide in terror. Not a sound in the room. Well, expect for the dripping and pouring sounds from Hughes's corpse. Mark thought it sounded like a babbling brook, the type of calm water that flowed through the little trench he had dug by the lake behind his parents' home as a child. The sound soothed him, but not Palmer and Fitzgerald. Their eyes were locked on the grotesque image splayed before them. Palmer's mouth was agape, his screams suppressed by his lack of thought. What was there to think about? Nothing mattered in the presence of such a brutal death. Nothing except the denial that it had happened so close to you. So close you could reach out and touch it, sinking your fingers in the squelching gore like Little Jack Horner sticking his thumb in a plum pie.

Mark wished he'd been the one to kill old Hughes. The man was beyond his years despite the rather insightful speech he had orated in his final moments. Life had served him well, but Mark could always sense a deeper feeling in the congressman. That feeling of being spent up. Nothing left to give to the world. If old age hadn't taken him, it surely would've been suicide.

Palmer was the first to break from his daze. He closed his mouth, tasted the bits of bone and brain on his tongue, and immediately began dry-heaving off to the side. His wretches woke Fitzgerald up from the same stupor, but he thankfully didn't have his mouth open during the brief carnage. Instead, his forehead had been slashed by a flying bit of bone debris, and blood oozed from the gash through his eyebrows and onto the bottom half of his face. He wiped vigorously with the sleeve of his suit but to no avail, as his suit had already been soaked in blood.

"Who the fuck did this?" Palmer asked with a low burp. "Who the *FUCK* did this?"

"I… I don't know," Fitzgerald blabbered.

"Are they going to shoot *us*?"

Palmer's question sparked fear in the both of them. They rushed from their seats and slammed open the double doors. Mark stayed behind and calmly rose from his chair. He walked to the other end of the table. He put a hand on Hughes's shoulder and flipped him over. He felt the urge to throw two pennies into the late congressman's toilet bowl of a face but knew he had no right to. This hadn't been his kill. He was jealous, and overwhelmingly so.

"Penny for your thoughts?" Mark asked, the words so foreign yet so familiar to his tongue.

He reached a hand into the hollowed skull and gripped a thin shard of bone poking from the yellowed cranium. He applied pressure until the piece snapped off like a section of a Hershey's bar. He wiped it on his pants and put the triangular shard in his pocket.

"Penny for your life," he intoned.

★ ★ ★

Ashley made up her mind. News of Congressman Hughes's assassination hit her like a cargo jet filled to the brim with the nuclear warheads Mark Smith would certainly have access to if he were to win the election. Whatever Shaw had needed her for, Ashley was ready and willing to listen. The world was growing anxious, stressed enough to snipe down a sitting member of the House without so much as a warning. She couldn't spend another day cooped up in the apartment. She had begun to hear whispers in the night, faded voices of people long past. Her father, her lover, all the countless victims of the Hillside Butcher. People that she interacted with in her nearly four decades of life. Classmates, college roommates, neighbors, friends, colleagues, enemies, everyone. They berated her.

Useless.

Stupid bitch.

Quit your job.

You got a nice rack. No use in letting it go to waste.

It should've been you at that conference.

Worthless cunt.

Amid all the hate that kept her awake at night, there was always one central figure to blame. A hollow shape, a black hole of a silhouette, blotting out the moonlight. Mark Smith. He was the reason for all this. The reason for all the suffering, not just hers. If he were to be elected, to take the oath, to sit behind the *Resolute* desk. Oh God, she didn't want to imagine that scenario, as real as a possibility it was. Democrats were more loyal to arguing with each other than simply banding together and supporting a candidate. If the current president's base got behind Mark Smith, he would have no problem steamrolling Reggie Foster in the polls.

She sat at the kitchen counter, her phone screen up, waiting for the inevitable call. Shaw had made a habit of contacting her at eight o'clock every night for the past two weeks. No sense in believing he would suddenly forget the ritual tonight.

Ashley warmed a cup of peach tea in the microwave when the phone finally rang. Eight o'clock on the dot. Shaw was nothing if not consistent. She steeped the brew at she answered the call.

"Hello?" she greeted.

"*Ashley! I knew I'd finally reach you!*" Shaw shouted. "*How have you been? I've been so worried about you. We all have.*"

"We?"

"*Oh sorry! The other members of the committee. We've been discussing logistics and the like for the last few weeks, as I'm sure you know.*"

"Is that why you've called me every day? To check on me?"

"*I mean, that was* part *of it. The other reason is that we would like some of your expertise on a subject that is imperative to the operations of this ad hoc committee. None of us are from rural areas, you see. So, we may benefit from your perspective.*"

Ashley could tell when Shaw told half-truths. His voice would raise an octave at the end of each sentence while still adhering to the rules of his usually deep tone. But she was bored and terrified and comically lonely, so she humored him.

"Us? Are you all together right now? It's a bit late."

"*Yes, we are. I'll send you the address for you to come to.*" A pause, then a hint of worry from Shaw. "*If you're not busy, of course.*"

"Never been less busy. Just send me the address and I'll be there as soon as possible."

That last part had been her own version of a half-truth. She arrived at the provided address as soon as she felt strong enough to leave her apartment, which wasn't for another twenty minutes. But she eventually found herself in an Uber, staying mute in the backseat despite wishing to have a conversation with the driver. Talking to *anyone* would have sufficed, but her continued grief had other, more silent plans.

The address Shaw texted her was for a residential apartment building on the north side of D.C. This confused Ashley to a degree when she glimpsed the place's digital location, and she grew more confused when she stepped out of the car and stood before the building on the knobby sidewalk. The air was crisp as an apple picked straight from the orchard, a calm breeze attempting to simmer her disquietude. It felt strange to breathe in the world outside her apartment after many long days of solitude, yet she thought it would feel more enjoyable. Alas, that could never be the case. Not in the nation's capital especially.

She buzzed the intercom, heard the front door click open, and allowed herself inside. The stairs weren't as creaky as the flights up to her own apartment, and she wondered whether the people who lived here happened to be in a higher tax bracket. On the third floor, she found the door labeled 302 and knocked quiet enough so that the next-door neighbors wouldn't file a noise complaint.

There was a shuffling of feet behind the door followed by several deadbolts being unlocked. The door slowly opened a crack, a face not belonging to Shaw appearing in the small sliver. The single chain keeping the door from fully opening was so tight it looked like it was ready to uncouple from the wood.

"You're alone, correct?" the man asked, the one eye Ashley could see bolting frantically from left to right. "No wires? No microphones?"

"I'm… I'm alone, yes," Ashley said.

"Strip."

"Excuse me?"

"Strip down. I need to be sure about the wire."

"Whoa! Hold on! What're you doing, Tim?" Shaw asked, angry as all hell as he stomped into view behind the man. "Just let her in."

"I'm not taking any chances."

"We took a chance in getting her here. Trust her, please."

There was a painful pause that thickened the atmosphere like tar. The man—Tim presumably, even though Ashley couldn't pinpoint whether she'd seen him before—mulled over the possible consequences of letting her into the apartment, his eye looking toward the ceiling as if the answers to all his problems hung there.

"Fine," he said, slamming the door.

He unshackled the chain and reopened the door, grabbing Ashley by the arm and hoisting her inside the apartment.

It was dimly lit inside, the only luminescence emitting from a few lamps with shades that were in desperate need of dusting. In the faint glow, Ashley recognized a select few of the Government Protections committee's members. Representatives Howard, Garrison, and Whitmore, all of whom were male, sat on the sofa, wearing plain tees and slacks. The people other than Shaw and Tim, however. Those two weren't very distinct in her mind. An elderly man and an even older woman, both decked out in full formal wear as if the clothes were superglued to their bodies. Ashley shook the older members' hands.

"Penelope Marigold," said the woman.

"Senator Rushakoff," said the man.

A senator? If they hadn't already been meeting outside of the Capitol Building, Ashley would've been put off by this development. The Government Protections committee had been formed as a separate group, not a joint committee. Why was this man here? And furthermore, who the fuck was this Penelope character?

Ashley sat on the chevron rug with her legs crossed before her myriad of thoughts could overwhelm her further. But as hard as she tried, she couldn't stop at least one question from exiting her mouth. "Whose apartment is this?" she asked. Her inquiry was ignored straight away as the committee began chattering.

"What's our next move?"

"Next move? Can we not celebrate before we start thinking about the future?"

"The future is now."

"I agree. We need to act fast with the election approaching."

"It's in two months. That's plenty of time."

"Plenty of time for anything to happen."

"May I have a refill on the wine?"

"No, Penny. Be quiet."

"Would you like to chime in?"

Ashley had zoned out for a while, the conversation going in one ear and out the other. Only when she was asked to speak did she come back to Earth. She glanced around the room, the low groan of heat lightning in the distance rattling the various glassware inside the china cabinet down the hall.

"I'm sorry, what were you saying?" she asked.

"What're your thoughts on the situation?" asked Representative Garrison, obviously annoyed.

"The situation?"

"With Government Protections. With Hughes out of the

picture, this will cause a ripple in the Republican base."

"Fear is a wonderful teacher," said Tim.

"What are you talking about?" asked Ashley. Another rumbling from somewhere off in the Virginian wilderness. Something so unnatural about thunder without rain.

"Christopher," Garrison said, scowling, "did you not tell her about what we do in this committee?"

Shaw froze up, a bottle of Coors Light pressed against his lips. He took a large gulp of whatever had entered his mouth and coughed. "I guess I forgot to mention it," he said.

"What the hell, Shaw!" Whitmore berated. "So we need to fill her in on *everything*? Is that correct?"

Shaw shrugged his shoulders, avoiding Ashley's gaze.

"If it's something serious, I'm bound by oath to hear it," she said to the group. "Both to the Constitution and to the country."

"Well, seeing as you've so graciously accepted our invitation after many weeks of ignoring Representative Shaw's calls, we may as well trust you with the information we have," Whitmore said.

"Can we *please* check for a wire?" Tim asked, a thick film of sweat glossed over his brow.

"And can I please get some more wine?" asked Penelope Marigold.

"Hush, woman!" Senator Rushakoff demanded. He turned his focus to Ashley, his snow-white eyebrows furrowing like two large caterpillars performing a mating ritual. "Ms. Guthrie, the Government Protections committee was formed to protect the sanctity of the United States' general elections. After what has occurred within this decade, the formation of this group was more than a necessity. As you may well know, this ad hoc committee has been in effect since 2027, over a year ago now. Ad hocs are never supposed to last this long. But with our Republican colleagues providing roadblocks to all our legislation, we haven't been able to pass anything, let alone debate on topics. This is true in the House, and it is even more so in the Senate. On a good day, we have twenty-six senators. Not fifty, which is the required amount for litigation, as we all know. Government Protections began to pen laws that would limit the power presidential candidates hold between the time of election and the day they are inaugurated. However, we have had more troubling developments occur within the last few months. Developments that we have been told you are indirectly connected with."

"Troubling developments? Such as?" Ashley inquired.

"Davey Robinson barging into Washington with a briefcase full of damning evidence on top government employees, including the president himself," Rushakoff continued. "Him hanging those documents over their heads as blackmail. Him becoming very close with the ailing president, tricking him into agreeing to an endorsement. Robinson spewing nonsense at campaign rallies, picking up young women on the road, and forcing them into his various sex rings. Robinson disappearing in Missouri, where a prominent new face in his campaign quickly stole the title of Republican candidate from him. That new candidate being a criminal, and a violent one at that. One of the deadliest serial killers in American history. That new candidate being someone from your hometown."

"What's your point?"

"The point is that you have information pertaining to Mark Smith that would prove beneficial to our cause. We've already planted the seed for his campaign's demise, but we need the water and sunlight to help it grow. That can be you."

"I can't help but wonder why you're being so vague. What exactly do you people do here?"

"We protect the government, of course. And in turn, the country, and then the world. We simply must tip the scales in the right direction. That's all."

Ashley had come here to agree to whatever schemes Shaw had been incessantly calling her for. The life and color had been sucked out of her world, leaving a hollow void where her heart should have been. But now she wasn't too sure. There was a threatening aura surrounding the government officials sitting in a circle around this living room. Another blast of heat lightning shook the linoleum, and Ashley knew what they had done.

…with Hughes out of the picture…

"Did you… did you send a hitman after Hughes?" she asked, already knowing the answer.

"You catch on well," Garrison mumbled.

Whatever shreds of her heart were left in her chest plummeted to the bottom of her stomach. She wanted to vomit. Knowing that these people who had sworn to protect the United States would do such a thing. It made her lightheaded and full of rage. These same people who promised to better the world for people like her, people like her father, people like Tasha.

"How could you?" she seethed through gritted teeth. "How fucking could you?"

"We didn't use taxpayer funds," Senator Rushakoff assured. "The payment was all out of pocket. No loose ends."

"That's not the fucking point!" Ashley shot upright from her cross-legged position on the rug. "You paid money to have a sitting member of Congress assassinated! It doesn't matter which side they're on; you committed murder. First-degree, too. And you, Shaw." She turned and pointed a finger at him. He almost choked on another swig of Coors. "You were in on this? I asked you so many times, 'How's the committee going? Have you all come to any decisions?' And you always said, 'It's going fine.' Well, excuse me, but *I* don't think this is fine. Any sane person would say the same damn thing!"

Shaw propped himself on the glass coffee table and balanced on his feet. He set the half-full beer bottle down and raised both his hands, his palms facing outward like a mime becoming aware he was trapped inside an invisible brick wall.

"I was going to tell you," he said. "Honestly. There were just so many logistic hurdles that couldn't allow me to disclose anything until now. I'm sorry. We all are."

"You aren't sorry for shit."

The group had grown cold, seemingly unable to predict Ashley's outburst. They had been under the assumption that she would simply waltz into their elaborately cultish apartment space with a grin on her face and a cheer in her step. Who wouldn't in their eyes? Their committee was tainted with the blood of an innocent, no matter how deplorable Hughes had been.

American blood.

Murder.

Treason.

"What we're doing is for the benefit of the common citizen," Senator Rushakoff explained. "A few deaths to prevent the deaths of millions. It's a worthy sacrifice. Mark Smith must not be allowed to take the Oval Office, no matter what it takes."

"No matter what it takes," the room replied in unison.

"What we need from you is information," Rushakoff continued. "Any information you may have on Smith that is not listed in his files. Vignettes from his childhood, where he played around after school hours, anything about his home life. Hell, even if he owns a Pomeranian rat dog, we need to know. Help us help you. Help us save this country."

"Why don't you just kill Mark?" Ashley asked, surprised by how blunt the question sounded. "Why all the antics? Just hire your little hitmen to take him out and *poof.* No more problems."

"You know that won't solve anything, Ash," Shaw chimed in, rather solemnly. "If we go for his head now, someone else will come along. There are over 300 million people in the United States. They'll find someone else, someone worse. For now, we need to keep him in the race but mark him with death. Strike fear into the Republican base. Send a message that says, 'No, we will not allow murderers in Washington. Pick someone better.' And they will, surely."

Ashley had to admit the plan—no matter how morbid—was solid. Take out the hired assassins, and you have a plan clearly created by people directly tied to the government. Little hits here and there to gather suspicion, and a healthy dose of hysteria as a result. Not so much that it makes the country explode in violence and mass mania, but just enough to scare worthless people away from the presidency. People like Mark Smith, like a feral rat scampering away in fear of a lit torch. It was foolproof.

She was pissed at Shaw for lying to her for so long. She was pissed at her Arkansawyer colleagues for allowing such a degenerative candidate to weasel his way into the presidential race. She was pissed at the current president for destroying the system so much that people like Mark Smith were even permitted to run. She was pissed at the justice system for granting the president immunity from his previous 34 felony convictions. She was pissed at the world for standing idly by while the country she loved stridently burned to the ground.

But simply being pissed wouldn't change anything. She would be no better than the useless drivel spewing from millions of people on the internet. Hollow complaints with no substance, no call to action. This would be her action. Her purpose. For Tasha. For Arthur. For the life she would never have again. For the lives of others that will benefit from what the Government Protections committee has already put into motion.

Now was her time to finally prove herself. She couldn't be the worthless cunt her constituents saw her as. She couldn't trip and fall in the last sprint of the marathon. Nearly two years of no motion in the House would be atoned for in this gloomy apartment. America would survive. A few little sins could go a long way no matter how sick they made her feel.

"Where should I start?" Ashley asked.

PART THREE

★ ★ ★

THE BLOOD OF
PATRIOTS

CHAPTER 13

★ ★ ★

Democracy is a fleeting thing. It is thought of as a phoenix, burning bright in the night sky in the minds of philosophers. But as we all know, the phoenix's life is finite, as are all things. Eventually its fire will peter out, all the fuel burning up, all its oxygen spent.

What of the rebirth, though? What of the promise of resurrection? If democracy is equated to the myth of the phoenix, wouldn't that mean all empires would die but someday rise from their own ashes? Germany fell after two world wars, decaying from the inside by way of Nazism, but rebuilt in the decades that followed, becoming a nation that acknowledges the past, but strives to move forward. China rose and fell over and over again, dying with the decimation of one dynasty and resurrecting with the beginning of a new. So many examples from history. People with enough willpower to see the good and faithful in their nation and help to rebuild. Glory to the chieftain, honor for the dead.

The United States of America is also a fleeting thing, but it is not a phoenix. An eagle would be more apt. The country was born, grew, lived its life as long as it could, and will eventually die. 250 years would be an overly fruitful life for an eagle, and it's also long enough for an empire. The United States was never supposed to last as long as it did. In due time, a leader would come around with enough hate in their heart to bring about the end times. People believed the current president would present the crumbling of the Stars and Stripes, removing the load bearing Jenga block at the bottom of the tower, allowing the structure to fall. But they were wrong. He was too weak, too submissive. He bowed his head to foreign dictators. Stuck up his nose to the world leaders who only wanted what was best for America and for the planet. Irrationality is an incurable tumor for those seeking power. The worst leaders make judgments based on their own needs, not the needs of the people they serve.

Mark Smith was different. The people who rallied behind the current president were doubtful of him at first, more so than the ever so boring Davey Robinson. His qualms with the state of mental health in America fell on deaf ears. Suicide epidemic? Sure, buddy. People killing themselves was contagious. That made sense. Anyone with brains knew that suicide was a hoax created by the psychiatry industry to sell more medication. And therapy? No, get out of here. Therapy was a Ponzi scheme that benefited the therapist more than the client. At least, that's what most red-hat-clad supporters believed.

But when he had joked about murdering those who showed signs of major depressive symptoms, some people began to perk up their ears. The joke was funny at first. Hilarious, even. No sane man would ever condone violence on a stage campaigning for the next president of the United States. However, Mark Smith was no sane man. Just like the current Commander in Chief, he was irrational, unruly. But he had a point. A point that many people could agree upon.

To stop an epidemic, you needed to segregate the source, and the source came in the form of sissy liberals who were too busy labeling themselves as mentally ill to care about more important things like tax benefits for the rich and prison time for the homeless.

And who could refute the evidence of Mark Smith's good deeds? The small town of Bernard, Arkansas was on fire in his absence. Everyone knew about it. The violence hit the news cycle with similar force to the Haitian-immigrants-eating-cats-and-dogs story from the 2024 election cycle. Bernard had been a quiet, complacent town. The same type of town that hosted farmers' markets, threw seasonal festivals with beer kegs and haphazard parades, and had rapport amongst its neighbors so strong they didn't bother locking their front doors at night. Mark Smith had been the catalyst for that peace, picking people off one by one with his trusty axe whenever a hint of sadness permeated into the quiet air. He was unbiased yet caring for his fellow man. Weed out the misery, lower the rate of suicide, and increase the percentage of the population who appreciated life and didn't waste the country's frugal resources.

When Davey Robinson vanished ("…to an island off the cost of Cuba," as a zonked Joe Rogan said into his podcast mic), it was generally agreed upon that Smith would be his replacement in the race. His presidential endorsement sealed the deal, much to the pleasure of the Republican base and the horror of the Democrats. As August bled into September and September became awash with autumn leaves, protests feebly crept into focus. People of all walks of life—except conservative, naturally—held up signs that decried Smith's candidacy without a proper primary: *"TRUST WHAT PROCESS?" "HANDS OFF!! OUR ELECTION,"*

"BRING BACK HARRIS," "MARK SUCKS COCKS," and *"KEEP YOUR ASS IN ARKANSASS,"* to name a few.

Notably, nobody in all the crowds across the country's largest urban centers mentioned Smith's comments on literally, not figuratively, murdering his neighbors under the false pretense of martyrdom. Liberals focused on the legal principles of how a candidate should be chosen. They focused on the straight, white, maleness of Smith, how he took that opportunity from a much more deserving person of color. "This is not normal," they would share on social media without much else in terms of activism. They focused on all the minor issues at hand, ignoring the major topic of serial murder as if it were the plague. If they dared mention the Hillside Butcher, they would grow uncomfortable. What is the point of a protest if not to be comfortable?

These protests grew in frequency, blossoming from the largest cities and budding in more rural and suburban areas. Violence sprouted its maniacal petals from there. In Lincoln, Nebraska, a man donning a red hat plowed his pickup truck through a crowd of protesters. The man later claimed, "I was protecting my third amendment rights to free speech."

"First amendment," a news reporter corrected.

"What do you know, fuckin' tard."

In a small community of southern Illinois, far from the bustling streets of multicultural Chicago, a fistfight inside a local pub exploded into a riot that caused the mass destruction of over twenty homes. A disgruntled resident had been planning on planting bombs throughout town and saw the ensuing turmoil as a wonderful excuse to get the job done.

In Eden, Utah, an abortion clinic became overrun with pro-life protesters. They had been strengthened by Mark Smith's words of wisdom, deciding it would be best for those vile child murderers to be dealt with swiftly. This resulted in the mass murder of twelve nurses and the clinic's secretary, all under the age of thirty. The pro-lifers were not charged with any crimes, only let off with a warning by the local police force who later gunned down a Black man who had called the department for a welfare check on his neighbor.

The world took note of the worsening state of America. As a major source of income to most foreign nations, they all had the right to be worried. As the General Assembly of the United Nations met in September in New York City, most noticed a glaring omission in the lineup of leaders present. The chair for the United States sat empty despite the conference being held in the country itself. Many countries had sent their actual leaders to the Assembly instead of ambassadors due to the U.S. president's erratic behavior and the even more erratic election.

Between sessions, some world leaders communicated behind closed doors. They spoke of their worries that the United States was ready to close their own Iron Curtain. They worried about trade agreements and foreign policy. They worried that if Mark Smith were to be elected president, the United States would secede from the world and cut off all ties.

"Without America," the prime minister of Japan said, "who will buy all of our products?"

"This cannot continue," said the Indonesian president.

"Agreed," said the prime minister of Lesotho.

Times were as turbulent as a passenger jet attempting to land in the middle of a hailstorm. No one could distinguish their right hand from their left. Phone calls to the American president went straight to voicemail, his press secretary refused to answer any questions starting with *what* or *why*, and a serial killer was rising in the polls without any idea of how to run a country.

Democracy is a fleeting thing, but it can be salvaged.
One mangled corpse at a time.

★ ★ ★

Abel and Eddie donned New York Yankees caps and medical masks as they entered a Wegmans supermarket. The smell of the deli section clawed its way under Abel's mask, forcing his mouth to water. Meats and cheeses, fresh from the slicer and in bulk, seduced him more than the most beautiful man with the most beautiful chest ever could. No, woman. He meant to think about women. Big, beautiful women and their large voluptuous breasts. Yeah, that was right.

The Coalition had been living off canned goods and coffee grains for the few weeks following the murder of Congressman Ronald Hughes. They were in hot water despite residing over a thousand miles away from Chicago in the New York State wilderness. Valerie had put the cabin on lockdown as the news broke, shattering the nation. The oldest sitting congressman in the country had been slain in cold blood, the killer on the loose.

Little did law enforcement know, the killer was busy choosing between Gouda and Swiss at a deli station in Pennsylvania.

"Could you just pick one already?" Eddie asked, his mask holding on for dear life as it struggled to contain his beard.

"What do you think everyone will like?"

"Don't think it matters. Cheese is cheese."

Abel gave up the chase and asked the worker behind the glass case for one pound of sliced Gouda. Eddie chimed in, asking how much it would cost for an entire bird's worth of the wrapped smoked chicken. "We don't sell the whole chicken," the employee said tiredly. This wasn't the first time he'd been asked that question. "Would you like five pounds of sliced meat instead? That's the best

I can do for you."

"Fine."

The worker went to town with the slicer, sliding the cylindrical block of cheese and ginormous bulk of chicken back and forth, each new slice flopping out the machine like soggy sheets of paper in the rain.

They continued their journey through the supermarket, grabbing as much food as the shopping cart would allow. The funds from the congressman killing had been wired into their accounts the night before, and they were starving. Cans of carrots, green beans, asparagus, corn, and cranberries. Boxes of gourmet multicolored pasta shaped like mini–Eiffel Towers. Glass bottles and aluminum cans of green tea, beer, Sprite, and pineapple rum. They picked up bandages, gauze, and rubbing alcohol in case of emergencies, as well as stopped by the household essentials.

"Could use a pillow," Abel said.

"We all could, dipshit," Eddie smirked.

In the line to the AI-automated checkout lanes, Abel spotted the tabloid magazine rack next to a small fridge full of Starbucks Frappuccinos and five flavors of Redbull. He picked out a magazine at random, flipping through the pages without reading them. The pages smelled like home. Mom sitting on the couch, smoking a cigarette, scanning the celebrity drama as the cigarette burned down to its filter. He wondered how she was doing, if she was on the couch just as he imagined. Alone, unmoving, uncaring. Oh, Abel's gone? How long has it been? Nevermind that, I need to get back to Gail Collins' op-ed on Perez Hilton's sex tapes.

Abel closed the magazine, but before he returned it to the rack, he spotted something unusual. There was a different magazine under the one he'd taken. He grabbed that one and stared in bewilderment at the cover.

Two men glared into the camera, their portraits hastily photoshopped together to appear as if their backs were turned. One of the men was middle-aged and Black, fitted in a beige dress shirt, navy blue tie, and a mahogany suit jacket. The other man elicited a response from Abel, harkening back to the circular image of his sniper scope. The three congressmen in that conference room in Chicago, one with his head blown into a red mist and the other two cowering in fear. And then there was Mark Smith, who sat completely still with the older man's blood dripping down his face.

That blood wasn't on him now as he stared blankly through the magazine cover at Abel. He flipped to page five to see the article chronicling the tumult of this year's presidential election.

"President?" Abel asked himself.

"Huh?" Eddie mumbled distractedly.

"Here." Abel showed Eddie the magazine, pointing to Mark's printed face. "I know that guy. Remember that guy who killed all those people back home? There must've been at least a dozen murders when you lived there."

"Yeah, I remember. What about them?"

"That's the guy."

"Lemme see that."

Eddie grabbed the magazine. *God, this line is taking forever*, Abel thought as Eddie nearly tore the front cover from its staples. Eddie scanned page five, his beard furrowing and consuming his mouth, leaving most of his face devoid of features underneath all that hair.

"Seems like there's been a lotta shit going on since Valerie hired you," Eddie said. "Read this."

He passed the magazine back and pointed to a passage a few paragraphs down from the top:

Mark Thomas Smith (R-AR) has sparked some hope into the deflated Republican Party. With news of the current president being on death's door, red states have thrown their complete support behind Smith, who promises to continue the 'good work' of the current president while also implementing his own ideas for change.

A former assistant to the president—who wishes to remain anonymous—chimed in on the sudden and steep rise of Mark Smith in the national polls: "I've seen this all before," they said. "A hot shot steals the campaign from more worthy opponents, but just at the last minute, he fumbles. No amount of inspiring violence among the American people will persuade normally sane voters to put him in office. Must we really make the same mistake again?"

Our source reported Smith has inspired violence, which is factually true. Numerous cities across the nation have succumbed to riots and other forms of mass violence. The only question is: Are people willing to stop? Or has it gone too far?

"What the hell," Abel whispered. "You don't think any of that is *our* fault, do you?"

"Why would it be?"

"I don't know. We're kind of a part of the violence, right? I shot that government guy in the head."

"That was just a job, Abel. Nothing crazy about it. You clock in, do the work, and get paid just like anyone else."

They eventually paid for the groceries with their blood money, drove two hours back to the cabin, and received the first assignment after the Coalition's long hiatus. A wealthy widower living in a mega-mansion off Tampa Bay. Abel thought he could use some sun and smiled at the thought.

★ ★ ★

Mark hid in the shadows behind a motel dumpster, the lights glowing from the Days Inn sign above forming a darkened trapezoid in its wake.

The woman in the flowing white dress slipped off her high heels and walked barefoot to her room for the night, her feet slapping against the filthy asphalt of the parking lot. Her head was held low, hair drooping over her face in long wisps that looked like a frayed floor mop. Despite the hum of the Days Inn sign, Mark could hear the woman's soft sobs as she stuck her room key into the lock.

Mark shuffled from his prone position and tiptoed toward her as the door closed on squealing hinges. He flew through the night like a vampire bat homing in on its prey. His mouth watered in anticipation, his grip bracing his axe. The door closed with an unsatisfying click. Another equally unsatisfying click followed as the deadbolt snapped shut.

It was no matter, though. Mark had employed the old rock-in-the-windowsill trick. He peered through the pulled curtain and made out the fuzzy figure of the woman as she lumbered to the bathroom. When that door closed, Mark dug his fingers under the windowsill and pulled up, struggling against his shoulders as they nearly popped from their doddering sockets.

He climbed into the room, the hems of his pants legs nearly snagging on a loose splinter. He got to his feet, not minding the figures in the dark corners, and sat himself in the small closet across the short hall from the bathroom. The woman exuded weighty sobs that echoed behind the door. Surely, she would wake the neighbors, and no one wanted *that* to happen. Mark licked his lips. The sink began sputtering water with just enough lead in it to be unnoticed by the Environmental Protection Agency. When the woman closed the faucet, the bathroom door opened just a crack. Mark stared through his own crack in the door, his mouth refusing to cease dripping saliva. She wiped mascara from her cheeks, sniffled quietly, then left the bathroom, unaware of the monster lurking within her closet.

She plopped onto the bed, springs squeezing under her weight. She lay there in relative silence, not even bothering to flick on the television and watch *9-1-1* or *Family Guy* or whatever other shows motels usually had access to.

Her soft cries reminded him deeply of his mother's. The way she would limp back to the master bedroom after another visit with the belt from old man Mark the First and close the door behind her, believing the two-inch-thick wooden panel would suppress the sounds of her despair. It never did, and Mark heard every wail, every weep, every tear. "You must be strong, Markie," she would say, ruffling his boyish hair. "The world needs strong men. Not like your father. We don't need more devils. Be an angel. A strong angel."

Mark snuck out of the closet and hunched down, approaching his target with the utmost caution. She laid above the covers and duvet, her white dress coating the mattress like a fresh blanket of snow. His mother had worn a similar dress, only that one had flowers hemmed into its fabric, while this one was quite boring in comparison. Straight pieces of white, nearly transparent, revealing smooth peachy skin beneath.

He began to stomp, making his presence known. The woman started, her frightened face cleanly illuminated by faint moonlight. She screamed as Mark hurdled onto the bed, planting his knees on her legs and pinning her arms to her sides. She thrashed like a worm on the end of a fishhook, shrill shrieks punctuating her every movement. Mark put a finger to his mouth, smiling as he shushed. *This is the natural course of life*, he thought. *You're born scream-ing, and you die the same.*

He raised the axe.

"Please please please!" the woman begged.

Please please please, no Mark! Stop it! It hurts!

For a fleeting moment, the woman's face—so delicate, so beautiful—metamorphosed in the face of his dying mother. A gaunt face with sunken cheeks and hollow eyes. She begged for mercy. Not from Mark himself, but from his father. Begging for release from the life she never wanted.

Mark winced and let the axe fall between the woman's eyes. Her screams and pleas terminated. The metal severed her neurons. There was a sickening crunch as the blade cracked bone, split skin, poured blood. Discontent with the mess, Mark pressed his palm against the back of the axe head and pushed. It sunk deeper, squelching with bodily fluids both red and crystalline. Her head split further, a fathomless gorge tearing her nose and lips in two. Blood gurgled in her throat, some lucky escapees trickling down her cheek.

Just as Mark reached into his pocket for two pennies, a flash of light brought him back to reality.

"No no NO!" shouted the director, slapping him with a baby blue folder that had its fair share of bloodstains. "This is the *third* time, Smith! What did I tell you before? DON'T kill them! We can edit that in post with CGI."

Mark looked back at the woman, an actress who had been the understudy for the understudy, both of whom died in similarly gruesome ways at the end of Mark's axe.

"She was unhappy," he said.

"She was *acting*, you piece of shit."

The director, a short man with thick rimmed glasses and jowls that sagged below his jaw, told the camera operator to send for the producer. A new candidate from the commercial's auditions would be needed for tomorrow night. The director sighed heavily then returned to Mark, who had become busy jamming two pennies into the latest victim's open skull.

"This shoot was supposed to last a single night," the director said, sounding slightly calmer than before. "You've turned it into three, and now probably four. Our budget didn't account for biohazard disposal."

"I can just dig out of my own funds," Mark said, hopping off the bed. "It's no problem, really."

"I know you can pay for addition budgetary concerns. That's not the main issue. You need to get a grip. Please don't kill the next actress. If you need mental health consultation, the crew can accommodate for that."

"I'll pass but thank you."

The director tightened the black cap atop his head and sighed once more. "Be here again tomorrow. Same time. You have the part down perfectly, but it's just the final shot that needs… tuning."

★ ★ ★

Ashley had told the Government Protections committee everything. Every minute detail. No stone left unturned. She chronicled every juicy bit of backstory related to Mark Smith. His upbringing, his family's paper mill, the possible causes of his erratic mental state, and his calling card were all discussed among other things.

There had been so much to tell that Ashley talked for more or less five hours. Many committee members fell asleep during the word vomit; all except Shaw, who remained attentive until the very last sentence.

Ashley felt a strange wave of nostalgia wash over her mind. She walked into a local coffee shop on the first day of October, grateful that her legs could assist her all the way there from her apartment. The smell of coffee beans and sugary syrups reminded her of home, a phenomenon she thought most of Americans experienced. The fresh scent of roasted coffee, but more importantly the person who had been stirring that brew. Her father sipping his coffee without sugar or creamer while her mother's hairdryer blasted down the hallway and to the right. "Good morning, sweetheart," he would say between sips. And they were always good mornings, indeed. And Ashley was determined to make another good morning today.

October had begun without so much as a peep from Mark Smith's campaign circle. No updates on rally dates, no threats to murder the mentally unwell, no testimonials from assistants who adored working for him. It was a peaceful day in D.C., and Ashley intended to keep it that way. As she sat at a table with her cold brew, she gazed out the window and admired the beauty of Washington. Trees losing their green and replacing it with rich earth tones. A gentle breeze rustling those leaves, allowing them to fall to the streets below where a car or bicycle will lap them up under their wheels. She watched a young mother and father wheel their newborn in a stroller. There was an older gentleman walking his German shepherd. An Indian man sold hot dogs from a quaint stand across the way, smiling infectiously to each potential customer that passed. This was the America she wished for. A country where people were free to roam the streets without fear. A place where comfort was the norm and not a luxury and being kind to your fellow neighbor came naturally instead of from a mistranslated Bible quote.

Another call from Shaw pinged on her phone. She ignored it

and continued to sip her drink, taking in the simple beauties of her nation's capital. Ignorance wouldn't save her, though, as Shaw called her again. Then again. And again.

Fuck, she thought.

She clenched her jaw, held the phone to her ear, and asked, "Hello?"

"*Are you busy?*" Shaw asked, sounding out of breath.

"Maybe. Why?"

"*I need to speak with you in private. It's important.*"

"Can it wait?"

"*Of course it can't.*"

Ashley glanced around the coffee shop, watching customers chatting to one another. Life was moving ahead despite whatever serious situation Shaw was worried about. She guzzled the rest of her cold brew like a racehorse drinking water from the hose after a grueling day on the track. She packed herself up and left the café in a rush.

She met Shaw in an alley blocked off with highlighter yellow police tape. He leaned against a moldy brick wall and smoked a cigarette, something Ashley had never seen him do. His hand trembled as he took in another puff of smoke.

"I need to show you something," Shaw said, peeking over her shoulder as if someone were watching them from a distance. "It's insanity."

He fumbled for his phone and flipped the screen toward her. He implored her to press the play button of a video obscured by a blank first frame. Hesitant, she pressed play and listened as a gruff voice narrated a political advertisement. Pretty standard stuff, if a little on the dramatic side. "America is dying," the narrator said as a woman in a white dress stumbled toward a dimly lit motel. "The Biden administration allowed prostitution to run rampant. Sex crimes not only demoralize the victims but decrease the morale of our nation's beautiful women."

Ashley scoffed at the unfounded jab toward the Biden administration. The current president—who had been elected after Joe Biden bowed out of the 2024 race—had pushed legislation for the nationwide legalization of prostitution as a ploy to steer the public away from asking about the Jeffrey Epstein files. The orders came out of nowhere, but the president's erratic behavior was commonplace by that point, so no one had batted an eye.

The woman in the ad entered the motel. The camera zoomed back from the closed door and settled behind a dark figure perched behind a dumpster.

"The mental health crisis in America has soared due to these Marxist ideologies," the narrator continued as the figure walked toward the motel. "Women feel comfortable having their hearts broken. So-called transgenders infest the streets, preying on your children. But only one person can save the American people from certain doom."

The figure hopped through an open window. A light shined on its face, revealing the haunting image of Mark Smith.

"Mark Smith is the candidate for the people," the narrator stated triumphantly. "No more bullshit. No more lies. No more suffering. Elect Mark Smith for president this November. You won't regret it."

The final few seconds of the commercial were set to The Killers' "Mr. Brightside." Mark leapt from a nearby closet and homed in on the woman in the white dress. He pinned her down, screaming and crying as Mark silently told her to hush. He raised his axe, and as it plummeted toward the woman, the camera stayed pointed at the ceiling, an explosive river of blood shooting up from where the axe likely landed. "This ad is paid for and endorsed by Mark Smith," a robotic voice read from tiny letters at the bottom of the screen.

Ashley felt numb, a feeling she was all too used to at this point. She handed the phone back to Shaw, who placed a shaking hand on her shoulder. With her head bowed low, she fought back the urge to remember her father and what Mark had done to him. It was so hard. Too hard. Grief had its filthy fingers all over her again, squeezing so tight her innards would escape in heaps of sludge from her mouth.

"They aren't airing this, correct?" she asked, hoping for a no.

"They are," Shaw said.

"This is bullshit. There's no way television stations would allow something like that. It *is* insane. You're right about that."

"What if I told you this is a heavily censored version of the commercial? What if I told you the uncensored version shows the lady's skull being chopped? The one I just showed you will air on Cartoon Network, Nickelodeon, Disney XD, all those kid-centric channels. The uncensored version with actual *live* murder will be on everything else. It performed well in test groups, apparently."

"I don't care about test groups, Shaw." Ashley didn't know how much more inhumane shit she could take. Another lapse would surely shoot smoke out of her ears. "What are *we* supposed to do about it?"

"Well…"

"The answer is 'nothing,' Shaw. Nothing. It's October now. The election is almost one month away. Whatever the Republicans have up their sleeve, we need to be better. If they're being provocative, we blow up a building. If they're spewing hate, we throw that shit back in their faces. Rules don't apply anymore. You of all people should know that."

Shaw did a double take. He didn't seem to want Ashley to

notice the slight widening of his eyes, but she did. She wasn't stupid. Since he was vulnerable, she decided to plunge the knife and twist.

"I satisfied your little group's bloodlust, alright?" she said, stepping close. "But what have you all done since then? Probably sent hitmen after another person who—while bad enough—does not deserve to die. How can you all call yourselves servants of the American public if you use their good faith as leverage for white collar crimes? If you want to disrupt this election, you need to play by the new rules, not the old. I don't like Reggie Foster, but most others don't seem to mind him. Make them mind. Push him into the zeitgeist. Weird ads, public stunts, anything. What the Republicans have is someone who has very public baggage. That's what makes him interesting; *more* interesting than Davey Robinson ever was. Play with the cards you have but cut the assassin shit. Mark Smith needs to be kicked out of Washington before he even has the chance to step into the Oval Office, I agree. Any sane person would. But don't stoop to his level. Don't commit murder."

Shaw, whose mouth had gradually grown agape as Ashley spoke her piece, gritted his teeth and formed a halfhearted smile. "We already have, Ashley," he said. "Hughes is dead, and many more will be too. We must fight fire with fire, just as you said. An eye for an eye."

"He's killed so many people. Do you mean to say you'll match his murder rate?"

"If that is what it takes."

Ashley reeled back, horrified by the implication of those six words. Countless more politicians dead, and for what? To maybe (only perhaps) secure a fruitful election result for Foster, a man who was falling behind in the polls by three whole points? This wasn't what had been taught to her during United States history class in high school, or in her numerous college seminars detailing the founding and cultivation of the nation. Politicians weren't murderers. Well, except for Aaron Burr… and Duncan Brown Cooper… and Byron Looper… and, shit maybe there were more than a few cases.

"You need to find another way," Ashley mumbled, her anger slowly diffusing. She applied pressure to her temples and breathed out deeply. "Hiring hitmen may seem the right thing to do, but it's not. It's the *lazy* thing."

"You're in no position to tell the committee what to do," Shaw hissed. "You're compromised now, just like the rest of us. The best thing for you to do is keep quiet and out of sight. Let this thing run its course. I don't want you getting caught in the cross-fire. Not to say it would come to that, but just in case: lay low."

"Fuck you, Shaw."

Ashley gathered saliva and spat it out. The milky glob splattered on Shaw's shoe, but Ashley didn't have time to admire her work. She was already halfway down the alley, back into the blissful autumn breeze.

CHAPTER 14

★ ★ ★

Representative Finley Palmer refused to leave his house. He kept the curtains drawn, his profile low. The living room was completely off limits for both himself and his wife. Too close to the front window. Too close to the street. Someone could be on the second floor of a home across the road; a sniper pointed out the windowpane with its sights trained on him. Instead, he hunkered down in the basement, lazing about on an old armchair with a beer in one hand and a television remote in the other.

He watched the news. Didn't matter which channel. His eyes had been glued to the screen for so long they were on the verge of bursting into flames and melting down his cheeks. But he couldn't look away. He needed to be present, in the know. Without information, who was he? Just another fuckup of a politician who serves his time and vanishes into the ether without leaving his mark? That could never come to be. He watched news coverage of the riots erupting across the nation, both for and against Mark

Smith. He suppressed a smile as he saw an Asian twenty-something hoist a large cardboard cut-out of Smith's face above a raucous crowd. *Without me, none of this would've happened,* Palmer thought, unsure whether the assumption was pessimistic or its opposite.

A knock at the door.

Palmer reached over his stomach and felt the grip of the pistol he hid in the armchair's cushion. Another knock. "Come in!" Palmer shouted, his finger on the trigger.

The door flew open, and he was elated to see the knocking hadn't come from an assassin who had broken into his home.

"Are you coming up for dinner?" Veronica asked.

"Is the coast clear?"

"Sure, Fin. Come upstairs."

Dinner was a bowl of tuna casserole with a side of pickled beets. Veronica was never the best at cooking, a fatal flaw in her duties as his wife, but Palmer gobbled down whatever she cooked simply to keep her happy. However, she cooked a mean casserole, and he was thankful for a good meal after the hell he'd been put through in recent weeks.

"Someone was hungry," she commented.

With a mouthful of noodles, Palmer snorted laughter. He shoveled another bite into his mouth.

Swallowing, he said, "You put mushrooms in this?"

"Thought I'd spice things up a bit."

"Tastes good."

"Thank you."

Palmer was halfway done with his bowl before he noticed Veronica hadn't touched her food. He asked if she wasn't hungry and was met with a sigh.

"What's wrong, baby?" Palmer asked.

"Nothing's wrong with me."

"Then what is it?"

"You, Finley. *You're* wrong."

"I don't know what you mean."

"Look at yourself!" Veronica jabbed a finger across the table, nearly spilling the pitcher of water that sat there. "You never leave your little mancave, you look like shit, you smell like shit, and… oh for fuck's sake! You're wearing a bulletproof vest at the dinner table!"

Palmer had slipped on the Kevlar vest just in case someone wanted to fire a cheap shot through the window above the kitchen sink. He never trusted those neighbors anyway.

"It's just a precaution," he reasoned.

"You need to get ahold of yourself."

"I'm as ahold of myself as anyone."

Veronica scoffed. "Keep telling yourself that."

"Your food's getting cold."

"Screw the food! You make me feel useless, Finley. Day after day I come home from work and there you are, sitting in the basement with your gut hanging out and the television speakers on full blast. You won't let me help you, and it's exhausting."

"Imagine how I feel."

"I know, honey," Veronica said, placing her head in her hands. "I know it's hard to process all that shit with Hughes. I know he was a mentor for you, but you need to let that go. He served his purpose. You don't want to disappoint him now. Especially not with this election coming up."

"I can't leave the house, Veronica. There's a target on my back. Don't you understand?"

"Fine."

Veronica stood with her bowl and walked it to the trashcan. She dumped the contents into the bin and placed the empty bowl in the sink. She ran the faucet and began scrubbing and scrubbing until her fingers became pink and raw. Palmer watched with fascination. He'd never seen her so upset before. Was it something he'd said?

"I'm going to go back to my hole," he said, standing. "Holler if you need me."

"I won't bother," Veronica said, eyes unwavering from the sink and its suds. "Go have fun."

Palmer went back downstairs without saying another word. He grabbed another beer from the mini fridge and plopped his ass down on the armchair, unmuting the television as he did. In his hiatus from the campaign, he had told Smith to make his own tour around the country, picking up opportunities as they came. There was a rather humorous commercial showing Smith chopping up a helpless young woman with an axe. There was another photo op in the suburbs surrounding Kansas City, Missouri. The only thing Palmer had advised him not to do was go past the Rockies. Didn't need the liberals out there growing more restless than they already were with Reggie Foster breathing down their necks. California was an entirely different beast that their campaign simply would never be able to handle.

Palmer's fingers brushed past cold polished metal. He pulled his pistol from its makeshift holster inside the chair's cushion, studying its shine in the blue glow of the television. So much harm could come from a single bullet. One precise shot to the prefrontal cortex would wipe all thoughts from his mind. Thoughts of Hughes's brains splattered all over that conference room table. The blood of another man in Palmer's mouth. That acrid taste of metal on his tongue. Bits of raw meat squishing between his teeth. Remains of a man only moments before alive and well, now sliding down his throat.

He keeled over and vomited his barely digested casserole, the phantom flavor of Hughes lingering on his tastebuds. Wiping the remaining spittle from his lips, he contemplated calling Fitzgerald, asking how the man was taking things. They'd both gone into hiding after the assassination, Palmer back to Little Rock with his wife and Fitzgerald alone in Fayetteville. He wondered what Fitzgerald was up to, or maybe if he had already come to terms with things and rejoined Smith on the campaign trail. He desperately wanted to whip out his phone and dial up his number, just to hear the voice of his colleague, a real man. He couldn't be in this house with his wife any longer. He never hated her, would never say such a thing, even behind the curtain. But she could be a bit too feminine at times, for lack of a better term. Nagging, complaining, bitter.

After a brief commercial break advertising mesothelioma lawsuits and Ozempic, FOX News returned for its six o'clock evening newscast. The first headline of the show stated, "CANDLELIGHT VIGIL HELD FOR CONGRESSMAN ASSASSINATED BY LIBERAL EXTREMIST." Palmer studied the screen as footage of a heavily fenced-off area underneath the Washington Monument was decorated with red, white and blue flowers of varying artificiality. Suited figures—both men and women—paid their respects with a lit candle, the warm glow illuminating the base of the monument with an ominously inviting glow. A framed photo of Hughes sat amidst the organized chaos. He looked younger, happier. He died doing what he loved.

He served his purpose.

Palmer gulped down half his beer and felt the urge to cry, whether from the sting of the carbonation or from his deep-seated emotions, he couldn't tell. What he did know was he didn't want to let Hughes down, to not finish what he started. How embarrassing would that be? To set the country down the path of no return and bow out before the grand finale? If his plan of cutting America off from the world would come to fruition, he would need to be at Mark Smith's side.

He stood up, making sure to avoid the puddle of vomit seeping into the carpet, and dialed Fitzgerald.

It was time to get back to work.

★ ★ ★

Abel loved his job. Sure, it had taken a while for him to adjust to the ins and outs of what was required of him, but now that he was reaping the monetary rewards of his endeavors, he had a new problem: he simply couldn't say no to an assignment.

"I'll come with you," he said at the central table in the cabin's basement. "I can help with recon."

"No, Abel," Valerie stated. "This is strictly a demolition assignment. Xavier, Zuri, and Mateo are on the job."

"We'll deploy you when the time is right," Johnny grumbled, his raspy tone filled with more gravel than usual. "Sit this one out, rookie."

Abel sat back in his chair, disappointment weighing on him like a ton of bricks. His mind raced, trying to figure out a way to convince everyone he could go on with this operation. He was addicted to the money, that much was certain. The concept of taking another person's life for thousands of dollars at a time numbed him to the ethics behind it all. People were dying because of his actions, but they provided a hefty wallet full of cash, so who was really winning there? He needed more than anything to continue working, no matter how small his role would be. Without this job, his life would be over.

Once an idea sprung from his brain like a dolphin from the ocean, Abel turned to Valerie and reasoned, "I really think it'd be good for me to watch Zuri and Xavier do their thing. Who knows? Maybe they'll both be unavailable for a demolition assignment someday. Who would replace them? Please just let me go—"

Eddie, who had been standing taut behind him for quite a while, placed a hand on his shoulder and squeezed. *Shut the fuck up*, his grip seemed to say.

"It's alright, Abel," Zuri chimed in before Valerie could say her piece. "Xavier and I can teach you some other time. We're not very good at being instructors in the field."

"Yeah, we like to focus on one thing at a time," Xavier added.

"Listen to your fellow Coalition members," Valerie said to Abel. "Trust that they'll return to allow you to learn what they do. For now, though, we need you to stay here in case someone calls for a neat kill instead of a messy one."

Zuri rolled her eyes and Eddie's grip loosened.

"Don't worry, Abel," Mateo said. "You'll have many more opportunities to fuck up simple shots. And personally, I can't wait to watch."

"Shut up, man," Abel mumbled, bowing his head.

He felt embarrassed. Just a whiny kid who thought he was better than everyone else, thinking he was great enough to simply be shoved into every position either offered or not to him. It had been nearly three months with the Coalition now. Why couldn't he be higher on the food chain? He'd gone through so much. More than the other assailants, for sure. Dad leaving, neglectful mother, murder attempt at school, actual murder that forced him out of his hometown of twenty years. Tragic story for an even more tragic boy. A complete and utter tragedy that he was born like *this*. Looking like this… creature. Pimple-faced, slightly underweight, completely unsociable. Not the work of art that was Mark Smith.

That day when he had stabbed Macy Thornton in the neck was the most thrilling day of his life. The ability to cause such harm to another human being without much consequence had filled him with a rush no hard drug could replicate. The subtle pop of her skin as the pencil plunged into her neck meat. The blood oozing around the pencil. Her clawing at her throat, unable to breathe. Abel had been in control of whether she lived or died, and it felt good to have that authority.

What Mark had done for him that day would live in Abel's mind for the rest of his life. Abel was just another kid on the street to him, but Mark had seen the blood splattered on his face and said, "You have spirit, kid. I could use someone like you."

Someone like him.

What a triumph it had been to leave Bernard City Jail with a new friend to call his own, but it was all for naught. Mark had remained aloof despite the platitudes. He would kill another helpless victim, and there Abel would be, waiting like a lonely pooch at the rail station for its master. He would ask for the gory details, studying Mark's anecdotes and facial expressions, willing to mimic those actions in the Hillside Butcher's field of work. But when he would ask Mark if he could accompany him on the next hunt, Mark would say, "No. Fuck off," and slam the door in his face.

Abel, blissfully enamored by the tiniest hint of attention, had taken those fuck offs as a joke. Snide remarks were Mark's pseudo love language. Abel hadn't thought much of Mark in recent weeks, the memories only really returning to him at first when he saw the Butcher down the sniper's sight, and second when he saw the magazine at Wegmans. Abel had purchased the tabloid and read it on the way back to the cabin. The further he made it down the page and onto the next, the more hate filled his heart. Eventually, as they pulled onto the rocky driveway, Abel had read the article twice over, and his heart couldn't take it anymore. It burst in the passenger seat and dripped with sorrow, loss, and hollowness as he shuffled his feet back into the cabin's murderous sanctum.

His fingers twitched on the table now. The Coalition kept their conversation going, paying him no mind. He was a ghost, a game hunter in the foggy brush. Physically there, but mentally absent in the minds of his cohort. He stood up with such speed that his chair fell on its side with a metallic clank. Before he knew it, he was in the guest room, lying on his cot, eyes shut tight so that the rage couldn't trickle out.

★ ★ ★

Ashley had that nightmare again. The one where she stands on the sidewalk of an empty street devoid of movement and light.

Fog covers the landscape in a billowing shroud. She is walking along the road, careful not to trip and fall into oncoming traffic, not that there would be any traffic in such a desolate place, but she is cautious. Far in the distance, there is a flashing light like that of a plane's signal pretending to be a star. She walks toward the light, unsure if she is getting any closer. She persists. There is no wind on this road, no leaves rusting in the tall trees, no sound except for the clacking of her shoes. Like a moth to a flame, she moves toward the peculiar flashing light. What else was she supposed to do? Waiting for a bus in the middle of nowhere seemed to be a great waste of her time.

Despite the haze, she feels as if she is traveling uphill. Her calves ache from the effort of walking. Left foot, right foot, left foot, right foot. The rhythm becomes monotonous. She must reach the light.

She persists.

Her persistence is rewarded with a scream. Not her own, but that of someone or something past the thick brush of trees. It echoes in the vast wilderness, and it sends a shiver down her spine. The air around her becomes cold. Not deep winter cold, but the strange frigidity that bares its teeth between Halloween and Thanksgiving. A dry cold that feels wrong without snow to accompany it. Her breath seeps into the air, the mist mixing with the everlasting fog.

Another scream, this time longer than the one that came before. She can faintly make out a single word.

Help.

She takes another glance at the light that refuses to come closer, wishes she would stay out of trouble and keep on her path, and ducks into the forest.

The screams have less silence between them now. They are a run-on sentence, desperately in need of punctuation to give the reader a chance to breathe. "I'm coming!" Ashley yells.

"*I'm coming... coming... come...*" her voice echoes back.

More screams laid bare in the mist. Ashley quickens her pace, pawing through loose branches, her legs still aching from the trek up the road. "HELP ME!" the voice from beyond pleads. It sounds familiar, more feminine than masculine. It's shrill and wavering, a new carbon copy of her own voice.

A new light appears then. Where the one down the road blinked white, this light changes and morphs in a pale orange glow. The screams grow louder and louder until all Ashley can think about is the pain in those two words.

Help me. Help me. Help me.

She nearly trips over a tree root before the fog parts, and she stands in an oasis of sheer clarity. A wall of fog creates a circular perimeter around the area, and in the center of it is a blazing bon-fire. No signs of potential campers, no lawn chairs, no instant coffee, no tents. Just a fire. It crackles and pops, embers soaring into the pitch-black sky. The screeching had ceased the moment she crossed the hazy threshold. Everything was imbued with a deafening silence. The forest should never be this quiet. There should be branches tickling each other, owls taking flight, cicadas humming their grating tune. But there was nothing except her own heavy breathing and the snapping bonfire.

"Atone," a voice says, deep and vacant.

"What?" Ashley asks.

She expects a new response but is met with the same word.

"Atone."

Ashley steps back, feels a branch snap under her shoe. There is no sound, only the kinetic feeling vibrating up her legs. She fran-tically looks around. "Who are you?" she asks.

No response.

In an instant the bonfire, once so grand and destructive in its beauty, peters out. She is left in complete and total darkness. She looks up. The stars have been blotted out. If not from the fog, but from their own destruction. Each mass of solar energy blown out like candles from a birthday cake.

"Atone."

"Atone for what?" Ashley yells.

As quickly as the fire goes out, a new sensation enters her body. A sharp pain emanates from her back and through her chest. An old-timely lantern comes to life above her head suspended in midair, allowing her to glimpse the damage.

A hunting knife with a blade the width of three fingers squeezed together juts from her sternum. Blood coats the tip of the blade with an oily luster. She wants to turn around. So desperately wants to turn around. Her legs yearn to do the work, but her mind will not allow her. Instead, she gasps and plummets to the forest floor.

The pain is agonizing, even in the dream. A burning sensation blooms as her heart struggles to pump life. She rolls onto her back, the knife's handle pushing under her weight, the blade crawling deeper through her chest. She struggles to plant herself up on her elbows, to take one good look at her assailant. Yet the forest is empty. No one put that knife there except for her.

The trees part like a theater curtain presenting a play's opening set. The fog dissipates, and in the distance, she can discern the flashing light from the road. Bathed in moonlight, the light blinks atop Cemetery Hill. But it isn't the only one. Another light appears, then another. Soon enough, the entire cemetery is aglow with flickering radiance. Too many to count. Must be in the hundreds.

"Atone."

Ashley lets out a yelp and twists her torso. Blood spurts through her shirt as the knife contorts her body. Another spasm of grueling pain.

There are footsteps now, low and drumming. Two dress shoes planted right beside her. The figure squats down, places a delicate hand under Ashley's chin, and lifts her head toward him.

"You must atone for the sins of our maker," Mark Smith says, a wide grin plastered on his face that barely reaches his eyes. "You see them?" He points through the parted woods toward the flashing lights. "Those are the people I have saved. But there can be so many more. All you need to do is get out of my way."

"N… *no*," Ashley sputters, blood leaking from the side of her mouth.

"You'd do well to say yes."

He rises, his knees cracking from the effort. An axe appears as if from thin air in his hands. Mark smirks, raises the blade, and sends it down, severing Ashley's head from her neck.

* * *

Ashley woke up soaked in sweat and piss, raking at her neck. Her throat was gone, all gone. Air was nothing but a luxury she sorely took for granted.

As she woke further from drowsiness, the clawing stopped. She stared around the bedroom. Mark wasn't there. No, of *course* he wasn't there. He would have no use for breaking into her apartment and slaughtering her like a pig ready to be processed into an unholy obelisk of deli meat.

But Mark targeted the weak, the vulnerable. He had a keen sense of when people were at their lowest, a skill that would have been more beneficial utilized in a therapeutic setting. Instead, he decided to take that gift and use it as an excuse for mass (albeit rather slow considering the decade-spanning nature of it) murder.

Ashley carefully removed herself from bed and turned on the bedside lamp. Yep, she soiled herself. A pungent yellow stain adorned the sheets exactly where she had awoken. She gathered the sheets and placed them into the wash. As the linens tumbled about in their metal tube, Ashley climbed into the shower. It was difficult for her to not think of Janet Leigh in *Psycho* while she scrubbed herself clean.

Rinsed and dried, Ashley sat at the foot of the bed and refused to go back to sleep. She'd had that nightmare before, but only in fragments. Tonight provided the wider scope of her psyche's hellscape. Bernard's countless dead lighting up Cemetery Hill, Mark commanding her to atone, the overwhelming burden of the fog.

She needed Tasha with her then. Tasha had always been so enchanted by the concept of dreams. If she were here, Ashley would ask her to decipher everything while it was still clear in her mind. But she wasn't here and never would be again. Ashley choked a sob as her heart broke for the millionth time.

"I'll make everything up to you," she whispered to Tasha's ghost. "I'll make things right."

It was an empty promise, meaningless in the grand scheme of things, but it felt good to set an objective during a time where goals were frowned upon in favor of hasty actions. But how was one supposed to go about fixing something so substantially destroyed? The 2028 election cycle was a trainwreck, and the country would suffer if they chose the wrong person. How could she stop such an unbridled force of nature? She pondered cornering Mark in a green room behind the debate stage, using a switchblade to persuade him to quit while he was ahead. Images of her father's name etched into Mark's stomach. That made her feel adequate. It wasn't a principled thought, but it brought a hurt smile to her face.

She sat at the edge of the bed until the sky outside her window burgeoned from black twilight to orange dawn. She spent that time kicking her bare feet gently back and forth, her heels tapping the baseboard.

All you need to do is get out of my way.

A blazing bonfire.

A knife in the gut

An expanse of twinkling stars atop a hillside cemetery.

Ashley knew she could not sit idly by. She swore an oath to her constituents that she would be on the frontlines of progress. If those plans were to never reach the light of day, she did not deserve to be in the position she currently held. Simple as that. But she could not resort to violence. Fuck Senator Rushakoff. Fuck that entire committee. She would reason with Mark; convince him that government work plainly was not cut out for him and his… *talents*. She would find him backstage at whatever presidential debate occurred and coax him out of whatever heightened grandiosity he felt.

She googled information regarding the big debate, finding that it had been scheduled for October 10th at Washington University in St. Louis. Fully awake and uncaring of the looming presence of sleep, Ashley booked a round-trip flight to and from Lambert International Airport.

She would find a way to set things right.

For her father.

For Tasha.

For everyone who died before, and those who would come after.

CHAPTER 15

★ ★ ★

Violence erupted at yet another rally, and Mark could not be happier if he tried. There was a strange beauty in spotting the first punch fly, escalating into an exquisite symphony of terror. He hated to be escorted off the stage, to miss the ensuing chaos as it unfolded. He saw a supporter steal a protester's sign, snap the wood post, and stab the makeshift stake into the protester's eye socket. Blood sprayed, mixing with the falling American confetti in a frenzied weightless dance.

Mark hadn't expected such a show from the Mormons but found himself pleasantly surprised. Salt Lake City had truly hosted the best campaign rally yet, and the delight he felt seeped into his bloodstream and stiffened his cock.

The two burly security guards motioned him to his changing room, and inside were Palmer and Fitzgerald. Fitzgerald seemed not to notice Mark's entrance, instead enraptured by whatever he was typing on his MacBook. Palmer, on the other hand, noticed immediately, rising to attention like a plebe on his first day of bootcamp. The congressman forced a smile then hoisted Fitzgerald up from his chair. "We trust the rally went well," Palmer said, his voice bobbing and weaving between anxious and joyous.

"It did," Mark responded. "I didn't even have to mention undocumented immigrants this time!"

"*Illegal* immigrants, Smith. We don't want people seeing them as human. Calling them undocumented grants them a humanity that will weaken our chances at the ballots. We've gone over this."

Mark scowled, saw Palmer flinch slightly.

"I'm only nitpicking because the debate is so soon," Palmer reassured. "We only have three days to show the country who you really are, and I need it to be perfect."

"Right."

He snarled like a rabid dog and lunged at Palmer with his hands extended into claws. Palmer jumped back with a yelp. Mark chuckled and left the room. Something was off about the congressman, had been since both he and Fitzgerald returned to the campaign trail after the incident with Hughes.

Later that night, Mark slipped out of his shoes and laid next to Janet in their hotel bed. The billowing light of fires across Salt Lake City gave the dark room a faint warm glow that rippled like ocean water.

Janet had been a naughty girl before he was due to be at the main stage. She had kept advising him to "rethink his strategies" and "evaluate his allegiances." Mark could hardly hear himself think with all the senseless nagging, so he did what any other man would do and strung her to the bedposts with industrial-grade rope and duct taped her mouth shut.

He was surprised by how beautiful she looked in the pale firelight. Her breasts sagged over her rib cage but still retained their supple roundness. He traced the circle of one breast with a finger, feeling the tiny hairs lining her soft skin. Her chest rose and fell, deep in slumber. Her wrists and ankles were welting from an apparent struggle to set herself free. That was her fault, of course. She would realize the error of her ways soon enough.

Mark traced another circle and slapped Janet across the face. Her steady breathing choked for a moment as she awoke from a quickly forgotten dream. The fear slowly but surely creeping into her eyes as she remembered she was tied and bound to a bed was something special to behold. Mark had already been hard after the rally, but *this* was on a whole other level. Sexual desire mixed with a burning lust for struggle. And she was so quiet. He had appreciated her comments and critiques at first, but he could take it from here. Those crowds full of cheering Americans were proof of that.

"Hush now," Mark whispered, planting the same finger that caressed her breast on her taped lips. "Do you promise to keep quiet?"

Sweat dripped down her forehead like rain off a car's windshield. Janet nodded, overwrought with a primal desire to be set free.

Mark tore the duct tape from her mouth in a singular swift motion. She yelped in pain, the rectangular area where the tape had been puckering her pale white skin a pink resembling peony petals. Her lips pursed as if to form words, but Mark grabbed her by the cheeks and said sternly, "You promised."

Janet eased up, her shoulders lowering. Mark slowly removed his hand from her face and stared longingly into her eyes. She attempted to give him the same look, but terror had become as natural to her as breathing, and she could barely hold a feigned smile.

"The rally went very well tonight," Mark said as he untied her wrists. "You should've seen the riot that broke out. It was really something else, I tell you. Blood spewing all over the place. Into people's eyes, their clothes, their hair. That's the America my mother dreamed of. I want that too."

The moment he finished untying her wrists and ankles, Janet squirmed out of the bed and tumbled to the floor, skittering away like a cockroach. A naked cockroach with pretty tits, but a cockroach regardless. She sat with her back to the wall, panting. Once her breathing slowed, she gulped and attempted to speak.

"You never told me what happened to your mother," she said, cringing with every syllable as if Mark would shoot her dead at the sound. "I'm… intrigued, I guess."

Mark tilted his head like a dog hearing the squeaky bit of a chew toy. He crawled off the bed, swaying his hips in a manner he hoped looked sensual. "She's the reason I do all of this," he explained. "I've told you this before."

"But what happened?"

"To her? She hanged herself. Between the chemo and my father's belt, it was all too much for her."

"Is that so?"

"Yes."

Mark pinned her against the wall, his breath spilling onto her neck. Janet pushed back as far as she could, believing that if she tried hard enough, she would phase through the wall and make her escape down the hallway. He kissed her neck then, and she could only think of him as a vampire going in for the kill. It would be so easy to die, she thought. So easy to let this man take her life and allow her to be released from this hell she confidently sold her soul for.

"You love me, don't you?" Mark asked between pecks.

"Yes," Janet choked.

"How much?"

Mark sat up and reached into his pocket. He produced a wallet filled to the brim with wads of cash. Twenties, fifties, hundreds. He pulled out a hundred-dollar bill and presented it to her. "Would this suffice?" he asked.

Janet hated herself for nodding. What would her parents think? She had followed this man across the country with the promise of money and sex. Her interest had been piqued because of how taboo his stances were on certain topics, but she couldn't keep living like this. Though, she also couldn't show Mark any sign of distress. If she slipped just once, she would be on the chopping block. Not just for her generous paycheck, but for her life. Mark was a charming man to a fault. She needed to remain happy to stay alive. Simple as that.

She nodded, and he slipped the bill into her mouth. The sour cotton paper scratched her tongue, but she allowed the additional raise to her funds. She couldn't go back to FOX, and she *definitely* couldn't go back to her minimum wage job at the shabby bookstore in her hometown. She needed to make it past the election before she could escape. Until then, smile and nod.

"Want more?" Mark asked, presenting another Franklin.

"Yes, please."

* * *

Salt Lake City was only the newest in a long line of vicious outbursts resulting from Mark Smith's plight across the United States. In addition to the escalating violence in America's urban centers, the riots that ensued from Smith's rallies sent the politically adjacent death toll into rates not seen since Abraham Lincoln's time. Another civil war was brewing in the country, and if only they had eyes to see the errors of their ways, maybe they could apply pressure to the wound before the Union bled out.

Bernard, Arkansas suffered the worst from the erupting chaos across the country. A small town had been physically wiped from the map, the only hints of life being structures burnt to a crisp, corpses littering the vacant streets, and a cemetery atop a hill that remained miraculously untouched. And since no one who had escaped the town was willing to come forward with damning information pertaining to Mark Smith's bad deeds, he was virtually let off scot-free. No whistleblowers from the now-defunct police department, no sob stories from locals affected by the murders.

Nothing.

As the 2028 presidential debate approached on a fateful mid-October night, rumors circulated of St. Louis police conspiring to escort Smith from the building and throw him into a jail cell. Progressives online were obviously excited by the prospect of justice finally being served, but Representatives Palmer and Fitzgerald knew better.

"No need to worry yourself," Palmer told Mark. "Our interns at the Capitol planted that rumor all over the web. Having a rumor like that be common knowledge helps more viewers tune into the debate. Rest assured, there is no conspiracy being planned against you."

If only that were true.

★ ★ ★

After surviving a flight that had been delayed twice before takeoff and experiencing nearly an hour's worth of turbulence, Ashley Guthrie finally landed in St. Louis, Missouri at the crack of dawn on October 10th. Finding her meager luggage on the conveyer belt was tough enough, but finding a shuttle out of the airport was a nightmare. Families in soccer mom minivans hogged spaces at the pickup lane better reserved for much larger vehicles to occupy. She really was not in a rush to get the Washington University, but anxiety had that funny way of toying with the minds of its victims, making them believe every second was a matter of life and death. It was imperative that she found Mark Smith before the debate. She could not waste a single second.

A yellow shuttle bus adorned with black polka dots like a cow with jaundice veered around the corner and swiped a roadside parking spot from another disgruntled family of four. Ashley hoisted her backpack over her shoulder and climbed in, greeting the driver with a brisk nod and finding a seat toward the back of the bus.

She had never been to St. Louis despite the city being just up the Mississippi River from the east side of Arkansas. The sun peaked over the horizon as the shuttle driver swerved onto the freeway. Its light glinted off the top rim of the Gateway Arch far in the distance, giving the structure a beautiful sheen not unlike angels' halos. The Arch jutted from the skyscrapers roughening the vista, a warped semicircle watching over a city lauded over a century before as the city of opportunity. The launching point for Lewis and Clark's expedition into the newly acquired Louisiana Purchase. It was hard to believe that the highway Ashley rode upon now had once been a lush forest overlooking a quaint fur trading post, but progress was inevitable, and the results were both mesmerizing and hard to witness. The first integrated kindergarten in the United States was founded here in 1873. The first of the modern Olympics held in the country took place in St. Louis at the very university she was traveling to. The first interstate high-way was built here, despite the economic hardship that followed.

The roads were constructed through poorer communities, forcing them to accept a life of homelessness their generations would inherit for decades. People fled the city for greater economic opportunities elsewhere, leaving the city behind to rot. Crime became rampant, police brutality skyrocketing even further. Something so wondrous and promising had been diminished to a stereotypical version of what Ashley's Republican colleagues liked to refer to as "liberal cities." She wished she could do more for the people of Cardinal Nation, but hopefully her talk with Mark would ease the pain. She wanted that at the very least.

"Last stop, ma'am!" the shuttle driver hollered.

Ashley had been dozing off again. She gathered herself and her bag, slipped the driver ten dollars, and hopped out the bus. Urban air wafted up her nose, the sound of sirens in the distance whistling like agitated baby whales.

She opened the map app on her phone and was met with an endlessly spinning loading icon. No signal in the middle of a goddamn city?

Perfect.

She picked a direction she thought was south and walked that way. Passing shops both flourishing and long abandoned, Ashley was reminded of similar streets in upstate New York. A local coffee shop would go out of business, only to be replaced by a Dunkin' Donuts in the blink of an eye. Only here that replacement would never come. Not for a while, anyway.

Her eyes stayed trained on a shattered windowpane instead of the sidewalk in front of her. Something flat hit her square in the stomach, and she stumbled backward, her gaze torn from the deserted shop.

A trash bag full to bursting toppled from the shopping cart she carelessly strolled into. The woman pushing the cart gave Ashley a sorrowful look as she bent over to pick up her belongings.

"No, let me help," Ashley insisted.

"You're very kind, miss."

Ashley struggled against the trash bag, underestimating how heavy its contents were. She eventually placed it atop the mounds of other knickknacks inside the cart. Intrigued, Ashley reached through the grill and pulled out a wood-carved bald eagle no more than three inches tall. Its wings were outstretched as if the inanimate object were trying to intimidate her.

"I used to make carvings," the woman said. She brushed a thick strand of matted graying hair from her mouth. "Hubby and I owned a shop a few blocks thataway."

Ashley continued to study the little wooden statue while listening intently to the woman's rough yet endearing voice. "Well, it's very beautiful," she said. "When did you make this one?"

"Oh, that must've been around 2001. Hubby and I got obsessed with all that patriotic bullshit. How couldn't you? All anyone could talk about was war and revenge and all that."

"I'll pay you for this one. The eagle."

"You've paid enough. Thank you for picking that bag up for me. My back isn't the same as it used to be."

"But *I* bumped into *you*," Ashley reasoned.

"People make mistakes. I'm just happy you atoned for it."

Atone.

That damn word again. It was tattooed to her brain, permanently etched there so that whenever she closed her eyes, her dreams would be nothing but that word. *Atone, atone, atone.* Atonement. What did she need to make amends for?

"Thank you," Ashley said to the woman.

The woman nodded with a smile wider than her circumstance. She gripped the cart and went on her way, leaving Ashley with the miniature wooden eagle. Ashley clutched the figure to her chest and walked in the opposite direction, sneaking another glance at the mysterious woman, but she was already gone.

★ ★ ★

"Remember everything we have taught you," Fitzgerald implored.

"You do remember, correct?" Palmer asked.

"Everything I already knew and more," Mark said.

"Repeat what we said."

"Deny allegations." Mark still hated using *alleged* in any form. The word dampened his contributions to society, but if it allowed him a greater chance of taking the Oval Office, he might as well play along.

"And what else?" Fitzgerald asked, chewing a fingernail.

"Make subtle yet vicious jabs at Foster whenever I can," Mark continued, "appeal to the sensibilities of the conservative base, and do not mention Latin America."

"And what if you do not know the answer to a question?" Palmer asked, his eyes brightening as if a lightbulb flashed behind his pupils.

"Ramble about something else."

"Perfect! You're ready."

Palmer and Fitzgerald took turns patting Mark on the back before quickly shuffling out of the dressing room. With the door shut behind them, Mark checked the digital clock above the mirror. Its glowing red numbers read seven o'clock. In one hour, the debate would begin, moderated by newscasters from ABC network. Palmer had attempted to snag reporters from FOX instead, but severe worry from television executives on biased questioning to the candidates swiftly put that scheme to rest. It was all for the best, Mark assumed. More people would tune in for an unbiased debate. The rumor of his imminent arrest already boosted the projected viewership, so this would be icing on the cake.

A knock echoed from the door a few minutes later as he was examining the corners of his mouth for smile wrinkles. He grunted and answered the call. On the other side of the door was a face he didn't think he would see so soon before his all but guaranteed inauguration ceremony.

"Are you going to let me in?" Ashley Guthrie asked with no hint of good-natured humor in her tone.

"Yes, of course."

Ashley brushed past him and whistled amusedly as she studied the room with its many mirrors on the walls and changes of formal clothing on the sturdy racks. Mark wanted nothing more than to ask her why she was here, but he had a faint judgment as to the answer to that question.

"It's cozy in here," she commented, her eyes avoiding his.

"WashU makes it feel like home."

Ashley made that sort of halfhearted laugh that only made its presence known through a short burst of air through the nostrils. "Home," she reminisced, turning to face him. "Do you miss it, Mark?"

"What? Home?"

"Yes."

"I do."

"Don't you wish you could go back?"

"From what I hear, there isn't much left to go back to." Bernard was the first casualty of his mission, and he hoped many more towns would fall. It was his God-given right to carry out that destructive path. "Well, everything is gone except for the cemetery. I find that very fitting."

"How so?" Ashley asked. Her arms were crossed, but one hand fondled at a slight bulge underneath her suit jacket and toward the side of her ribs.

"No matter how destroyed that town becomes, my legacy lives on."

"Do you remember our conversation the night you murdered my father?"

Mark looked back on that night with both horror and gratitude. Horror in the fact that he had finally been caught in the act, but gratitude in the events that transpired in the days, weeks, and months afterward. The car accident, the hospital visit, the news reporter, the cameraman he pumped with fire extinguisher fumes. Without his encounter with Arthur Guthrie and his politician daughter, none of this would have happened. So why did he feel a simmering rage seeing her now? He could have chalked that feeling up to his regret over not killing her, or the way her snide remarks had cut him like a knife with thousands of tiny, serrated barbs.

"Who let you in here?" he asked.

"Answer my question first," Ashley demanded.

"Yes, I remember."

He found himself staring at her chest once more, but she had taken the liberty of covering up her cleavage. Damn her. He couldn't even see that spider necklace he had noticed that fateful night.

Ashley spotted his eyes wandering down there and snapped her fingers as if she were a pet owner beckoning their precious animal.

"Stay with me here, Mark."

"Sorry."

"Remember what I told you about the whole town noticing you since your father died?"

Mark could remember that night like his reflection in a mirror. Everything was so vivid: the blood, the guts, the television blaring the nightly news, the can of Coke hissing and popping in the kitchen, the nervousness he felt, a first in his career.

"Not clearly, no," Mark lied.

"You were never some masked vigilante in the streets, Mark," Ashley said, ignoring his feigned incompetence. "Everyone in Bernard was aware you were the Hillside Butcher. Every resident, all their children, even the police. They all knew. You were a *legend*, Mark. The office of president, though. That's not a place where legends are born. That's where they go to die."

"Are you threatening me?"

"Scared?" Ashley asked slyly.

"No, just concerned."

"So many good people have become president and lost their goodwill with the public the moment they placed their hand on the Bible and took the oath. Jimmy Carter was a wonderful human being, but a terrible president. Now everyone remembers him for his awful term and not the philanthropy he did before and after. Joe Biden could have lived the rest of his life being Obama's charismatic vice president, but his public image was squandered by four years of nothing happening. Our current guy could have been remembered as that businessman with the reality show, but he *had* to go into politics and will be forever known as one of the worst presidents in American history."

"Okay?"

"What I mean to say is you can either continue this campaign and never be remembered for what you did in Bernard, or you can drop out and continue to live in infamy," Ashley proposed. "It's your choice."

Who did she think she was, coming into his private room and

demanding he drop out of the race? Who was she to offer him a choice as if he had to comply? Mark took a quick glance at the fire extinguisher hanging by the door, remembered the mess he had made of that cameraman, and locked his eyes back onto Ashley.

He scowled. "That's why you broke into my dressing room? To give me a choice that I'm obviously not willing to make?" He stepped closer, towering over her. She did not budge, and that filled him with more rage. "You're just a sad little congresswoman who is too grief-stricken to think straight. You lost your father, and I'm sorry about that, but you have no right to barge in here and tell me what to do."

"I've lost more than just my father," Ashley said sternly.

"I'm sure you have. Now get out of here before I do something drastic."

She would not move. Mark felt the urge to tap her shoulder in case she had suddenly calcified into stone. She did not blink, did not breathe. With her chin held high, Ashley Guthrie made Mark feel small. All with a single stare. It was aggravating how good she was at intimidation for someone so much smaller than him.

"You and I are more similar than you think," she finally said, easing Mark's nerves a bit. "We've both lost our parents; we are hopelessly lost in our own grief. We grew up in a small town in Arkansas and experienced the same day-to-day that everyone else did. We lived and breathed the smoke from that paper mill. But you know why our lives diverged so heavily from one another? I'm not a murderer, and that's the truth of it. I've never chopped someone into little chucks. I've never shot a little girl in the head. I've never had a primal sense to evade the police. Because *I* haven't done anything wrong. But *you* have enough blood on your hands to last for generations. Why continue this stupid charade with

Washington and politics and all that junk? Don't you want to go back to the shadows? Don't you want to be remembered? Not seen?"

Mark wanted nothing more than to be remembered—no, rewarded—for his martyrdom. He equated himself to Jesus Christ in that way. A man who walked the earth and performed miracles for the sake of humanity's salvation. A man who was not only etched into the stonework of history, but had an entire religion based on his accomplishments. Ashley had no idea what she was talking about. That much was clear. The greatest heroes were the ones who lived in the public eye. What use were his hundreds of murders if the people could never attach a face to them?

"I'll think about it," Mark said. "Now get out."

A look of triumph flashed onto Ashley's face. She turned and left the room believing in a false sense of hope. Mark had made his decision long before she had spoken the choice into existence.

CHAPTER 16

★ ★ ★

He read the magazine article repeatedly as if his life depended on it. Mark Smith and Reginald Foster. Two of the youngest presidential candidates of the twenty-first century, Mark being the youngest overall in the country's history.

Jealousy was a strange thing. If Mark had been planning on becoming the president, why hadn't he asked Abel to help him along? Why did Mark always find him so useless? Abel knew in his heart that he wasn't useless. Ever since Wyatt's passing, Abel had filled his position at the Coalition and proved himself worthy of the sharpshooter's crown. Abel had worth, just as any other person did. Why couldn't everyone see that? Abel was a blind spot in their lives' highways, a dangerous thing to ignore when switching lanes.

Zuri, Xavier, Mateo, and Eddie were all out on their roadtrip to the Midwest, leaving Abel alone with Valerie and Johnny. He didn't mind sharing a space with Valerie, but Johnny on the other hand. Johnny scared the shit out of him. There was something demented hiding underneath the man's eyepatch. Most likely it was only an empty eye socket, but in Abel's nightmares he imagined that hole in his skull to be a miniature cannon, one that had its sights set only for Abel. It was only a matter of time before Abel said the wrong thing at the central table and was promptly shot between the eyes.

For this reason, Abel left the cabin's guest room as quietly as he could manage. Johnny laid sprawled across the table, snoring with such vigor that a snot bubble popped every time he breathed out. Abel tiptoed up the stairs and into the living room.

The familiar scent of freshly brewed coffee. Mornings before school. His father reading the newspaper. His mother cleaning the dishes. Sunlight, fresh air, a life ahead of them all.

Valerie stood by the kitchen stove and watched as coffee dripped from the machine into the hazy glass pot. Abel took a seat at the counter and watched intently. He folded the magazine as best as he could and shoved it into his cargo pants pocket.

She heard the crumpling of glossy coated paper and turned, her hand hovering over the pistol strapped to her hip. Upon realizing it was only Abel at the counter, she eased up and walked toward him.

"Sleep alright?" she asked.

Her motherly tone set him on edge. There could have been a life before this Coalition business where Valerie was a mom of two, where she could take a morning walk before work without fearing her head would be blown off by the FBI or CIA. Maybe that was where she was before this. Or maybe she was born into this line of work. Hard to say.

"Fine, yeah," Abel said.

"You're not still angry about the excursion, correct?"

"I wasn't in the first place."

"You've got a good eye, kid. But you have an awful poker face."

Abel covered his mouth, then segued that motion into a subtle scratch of his chin. Razor bumps and pimples grazed past his fingertips.

"I was a little mad," he admitted.

"'A little' is an understatement."

"It's no big deal. Honest."

Valerie leaned over the counter. The scar bisecting her eyebrow looked more pronounced this morning. What had usually been faint and beige looked rawer and pinker in the sunlight.

"I promise there'll be more work for you to do, Abel," she said. "There's always a job to complete in our business. Always someone who hates another person enough to put a hit on them. I want to keep good rapport within the Coalition, because if we start to lose trust in one another, this whole operation goes under. Do you understand?"

There was nothing threatening in the question. She was less a drill sergeant and more an elementary school teacher making sure their students understood the rules of multiplication. Calm but stern. Caring but direct.

"I understand, Valerie."

"Good."

She walked back to the coffeemaker, pulled the pot from its receptacle, and poured its contents into a plain white mug. Without looking over her shoulder, she asked Abel, "You want some?"

"Sure."

They sat side by side at the kitchen counter, wordlessly sipping their steaming cups of coffee as the brilliance of early morning faded into the typical bright of the lunch hour. When Valerie finished her mug, she gripped Abel's shoulder and said, "I'm glad you're on our side."

She set her mug in the sink and went downstairs.

There'll be more work.

More opportunities to prove himself. More ways to assert his dominance over a society that wronged him. Wronged his mother and father. Wronged his hometown. Wronged the country.

He would make his mark.

The only question was how.

★ ★ ★

While Abel finished his coffee in the New York wilderness, Ashley Guthrie landed in St. Louis. Now in the later hours of October 10th, Ashley sat toward the back of an arch of chairs surrounding two podiums and a desk in the middle of a small Washington University auditorium. It was the same room Senator John Kerry and President George W. Bush had their second debate in 2004, back during a time in which presidential debates were civilized and free from whiny bickering between the candidates.

The room felt strangely nostalgic to Ashley. Its blue walls and red carpet were cleaned spotless yet still smelled of mildew and closet mothballs. The stage lights above felt like dozens of pocket-sized stars ready to burst into spectacular supernovas. More people filed into the auditorium with their heads held high. Representatives, senators, friends and family of Reggie Foster, and the current vice president. He plopped into the front row and clasped his hands together. The vice president's leg shook if struck by a magnitude 6.0 earthquake. Ashley thought she would also be nervous if she were being tossed from maligned president to maligned candidate like a hot potato. She had heard rumors that since

Mark had not chosen a running mate, Palmer had bribed the vice president into joining the race. Ashley was not sure if people liked him enough to accept him being tacked onto another campaign so soon after the last one, but his being there confirmed much of the rumors. He was trying to keep his position no matter what it took. Being named directly under a serial killer on the campaign trail meant nothing to his ego.

With everyone in their seats, the lights dimmed, the cameras began recording, and the ABC news reporters introduced themselves.

"Good evening," said the male reporter at the central desk. "My name is Daniel Crawford and thank you for joining us for tonight's ABC News presidential debate. We want to welcome viewers watching on ABC and around the world tonight. Mr. Mark Smith of Bernard, Arkansas and Mayor Reginald Foster of Omaha, Nebraska are just moments away from taking the debate stage in this unprecedented race for the Oval Office."

"And I am Whitney Johnson," said the female reporter. "Tonight's meeting could be the most consequential moment in either candidate's campaign. With Election Day less than a month away, this will be the quickest turnaround between first debate and election results in United States history. Mr. Mark Smith runs on an unprecedented campaign after Davey Robinson, the previous Republican candidate, dropped out of the race in August. Since then, this race has taken on a completely new dynamic."

"And that brings us to the rules of tonight's debate," Daniel Crawford said. "Ninety minutes with two commercial breaks. No topics or questions have been shared with the candidates or campaigns. The candidates will have two minutes to answer questions, two minutes for rebuttals, and one minute for any follow-ups or clarifications. There are no pre-written notes for tonight."

"In a change from the 2024 debate, there *is* an audience present tonight," Whitney Johnson said. "However, the previous rule of the microphones being turned off if it is not a candidate's turn to speak will remain in effect. Mr. Smith won the coin toss; he chose to give the final closing statement of the evening."

"Now, let us welcome the candidates to the stage," Crawford concluded. "Mr. Reginald Foster and Mr. Mark Smith."

The two candidates stepped out from opposite sides of the auditorium dressed in their best suits. They met in the middle of the room and firmly shook hands. That handshake marked the last inkling of decorum for the rest of the night.

* * *

"Good evening to you both," said Whitney Johnson. "We hope for a spirited and thoughtful debate tonight."

Mark found the comment insensitive. This female reporter probably knew full and well Mark was about to offer nothing new. That smug expression on her face told him everything he needed to know and then some. She and her male counterpart sat at a long desk across the space from him and Foster. Judges ready to fire away, sentencing Mark to the pits of political embarrassment. He imagined himself chained to a table, a pendulum blade swinging lower and lower from above until it sliced through his abdomen. The reporters nodded to both himself and Foster, but Mark did not return the empty hospitality. He stood with his hands gripped to either side of his podium, knuckles paling white in anticipation.

"Let's get started," said Daniel Crawford. "We will begin tonight with the topic that most polled voters believe to be the number one issue in our country. Transparency from the presidential office has been a hot subject for many years now, stemming from voter distrust in our previous two presidents and their waning health. Mr. Foster, we would like to ask you how you plan on creating a greater sense of transparency and honesty from Washington if you were to be elected president? You have two minutes to respond."

Foster cleared his throat and leaned toward his microphone. "I would like to start by saying what everyone is thinking. The current president of the United States is a crook. Plain and simple. He ran on empty promises that never saw the light of day. He promised lowered taxes, higher wages, the release of the files pertaining to the Jeffery Epstein case, and safer borders. All of those promises, and many more, were quickly forgotten about the moment he took office. And what were Americans hit with in response? Higher taxes in the form of exorbitant tariffs, no movement in Congress for raising the national minimum wage, a country no safer than the countries immigrants come to us from, and a stern refusal to release the Epstein files. Everything in the White House is a secret, an iron curtain, if you will. If I am to be elected president, I will be sure to be open and honest with the American people. All campaign promises I have made will be enacted during my term. If the people are to vote for me, then it is my duty to abide by their decision."

"Thank you, Mr. Foster," Crawford said, turning his attention to Mark. "Mr. Smith, I'll give you two minutes."

Mark felt the room freeze. Dust motes that had once swirled without pattern before now hung suspended in the air. The breath in his lungs sat like cinderblocks in his stomach. His left eye twitched, and then he spoke. "I cannot stand here and agree with Mr. Foster's first comment," Mark jabbed. "Our current president is not a crook. That is a baseless argument. Sure, he was a wealthy businessman before running for his terms in 2016 and 2024, but

Reginald Foster has a very similar background. He stands over there and talks about transparency as if it is second nature to him. But what about your trips to Israel, Mr. Foster? What about your collusions with the predatory landlords in your home state? Personally, *I* wouldn't feel safe in a country run by a man with so much baggage. If I were to be elected president, I would make damn sure that the American people knew who I was even before my inauguration. And some say I have already done that. I hope the ballot boxes run red with the blood of patriots. I yield my time."

"May I refute his claims?" Foster asked the moderators, his eyes widening in shock.

"Yes, Mr. Foster," Johnson said. "You have two minutes to state your rebuttal."

"Thank you." Foster turned to Mark, his gaze shooting blistering heat into Mark's stomach. "It's true that you've been mighty honest on your short campaign trail, Mr. Smith. And I applaud you for that. But can you stand there now and truthfully believe what you have told the American public continually has benefited them in any way? You speak of murder and violence upon your stages. Not the love and freedom our country was built upon. Frankly, I find it absurd that I'm even sharing a debate stage with this criminal."

There was a thunderous gasp in the audience. This confused Mark regardless of whether the gasps were directed toward himself or Foster. He always viewed himself as a criminal. There was nothing shocking about that claim. Mark emitted a soft chuckle as Foster continued to berate him.

"Would you like time to respond, Mr. Smith?" Johnson asked.

"No, it's quite alright," Mark said, waving the question away as if it were a pesky fruit fly tormenting his kitchen sink.

"Related to a topic Mr. Foster brought up," Crawford said, "our next question has to do with the economy. This current presidential term has brought about tariffs that have brought hardship to the common working American. Reginald Foster has recently stated that he plans to immediately put in place a national minimum wage of $15 an hour, up from the current $7.25. Mr. Smith, what do you have to say in response to that?"

Ah yes, the economy. Something Mark Smith did not give two shits about. He had been living vicariously through his parents' inheritance since his father died. Not a care in the world for the cost of things. He quickly formulated his response and let it rip.

"I can say I have been rather fortunate. Much more fortunate than others. I inherited a large sum of money from my parents after they both…" Mark squeezed his eyes shut to produce a fake tear, but nothing came, and his eyes remained dry as the Sahara. "… tragically passed. But I know that my circumstance is something that many more people *could* experience. That is why I will propose that if you are struggling to make ends meet, I will be the president to call upon. If your parents or guardians are at risk of suicide, why wait? Call the Department of Homeland Security and have the FBI kill them both, reap the monetary benefits, and live more comfortably!"

That silence again. The audience was not impressed, the moderators were not impressed, and Reggie Foster was the least impressed of them all. The man was blushing in vexation. He tore his mic from its stand and yelled, "You think this is a joke?" despite it being turned off.

Crawford began, "According to the rules, you must wait your tur—"

"But we'll let *this* slide?" Foster asked, pointing at Mark furiously.

"Please settle down, Mr. Foster," Whitney Johnson pleaded.

Foster breathed in, held it for five seconds, and loudly sighed it all out. He returned to his position behind the podium and apologized for his outburst, clearly not meaning a single word of the apology.

"Mr. Smith, you may continue," Crawford said.

"Thank you." Mark smiled as wide as he could without the cameras picking up on his forehead wrinkles. "What I mean to say is that there is an entire world of economic growth out there, the seeds planted in the fathers of our sons and the mothers of our daughters. Not just inheritance money, but also life insurance claims. Property is left to the children once the parents die. If more people could save their parents from suicidal damnation, the country could be a richer place. A *powerful* place. More powerful than any nation in modern history."

"Your two minutes are up," said Crawford. "Mr. Foster, you have two minutes to respond."

Foster hung his head low over the podium, shaking it back and forth as if silently disagreeing with a flake of dust that had landed there. He lifted his head after losing twenty seconds of his allotted time and said, "I won't respond to any of the useless nonsense coming from my opponent over there, but I will respond to the overall question. The tariffs were one of the worst economic decisions any president has made since Reagan's trickle-down push. As president, I would immediately put in an executive order that halts all tariffs on goods imported into our country. This would not only lower the cost of goods for U.S. citizens but also strengthen our ties to foreign nations. Cheaper groceries mean happier people, and I would be a happy man if I was the man those people could look to for support."

The moderators thanked Foster, turned to Mark, and asked if

he would like to amend his previous statements. Mark declined, and the debate continued.

"Our next question brings us back to a more intimate view of our nation," Whitney Johnson said in her newscaster monotone. "Racial tensions in America have slowly been on the rise, with recent research pointing to the decision in the 2016 election as the root cause of the divide. What would you like to state to the minority groups in America who feel that their rights have been slowly but surely stripped away? Are there any changes you propose to enact once in office? Mr. Foster, you have two minutes to respond."

Sure, give the Black person the first chance to answer a question about racism, Mark thought. *How the hell am I supposed to follow* that *up?*

Reggie Foster went on a spiel about his difficult childhood. How his parents raised him as best they could in a poor neighborhood bordered by a gentrified neighborhood in downtown Omaha. Mark had to admit, the anecdote about Foster starting a lemonade stand directly on the divide between communities fiddled with his heartstrings, but it just wasn't fair. Mark was White, and he was proud of it. But he never murdered people based on their skin color. He had killed everyone. Whites, Blacks, Asians, Latinos, even a Native American once. *Maybe* scalping the native was a bit culturally insensitive at the time, but Mark had good intentions. Mark had to think of any way to veer this conversation off the rails, to avoid the question to not embarrass himself in front of the entire world. As Foster finished his argument with a call to reinstate D.E.I. initiatives across the country, Mark's heart dropped when the question was turned to him.

"Mr. Smith?"

"Huh? Oh, right." Mark checked the large timer behind him. He had lost half a minute to his infinitely churning mind. "Racism is bad. Sure, I've killed a Black person before, but I didn't feel *good* doing it." He did feel good doing it, but he wouldn't outright state that on the world stage. That would be humiliating. He was spiraling. He couldn't think of what to say. All those cameras staring at him. All those people perceiving him both in this auditorium and at home on the couch. There was a time when that perception would fill him with an overwhelming sense of pride, but now it made him want to explode. He remembered Foster's childhood sob story from minutes before and went with that. "I grew up in a backwater town called Bernard, Arkansas. My father owned a paper mill that was the main source of economic growth in the area. He employed the best people of all shapes, colors, and sizes. It was a beautiful thing to witness that sense of community. If I were to be your president, I would make sure the country ran like my father's paper mill. With equality, hard work, and joy."

He had no idea how he pulled that statement out of his ass, but the audience seemed to be warm to his words. Foster looked flabbergasted, and Mark guessed that was a step in the right direction. His opponent did not look as abhorrent as before. His smooth dark skin hugged his face with a less agitated tightness.

"Mr. Foster, would you like to respond?"

"No. Please proceed."

"The political assassination of U.S. Representative Ronald Hughes of Arkansas sparked outrage and worry throughout the American public," Crawford said. "Mr. Smith, your campaign has expressed anger over this scandal despite your many comments revolving around the morality of murder. Would you care to provide an explanation?"

"Yes," Mark said, excited to finally talk about something interesting. "The assassination of Representative Hughes was a tragic loss. There is no other way to describe it. When his head exploded across the conference room we were discussing in, I could feel nothing but an instant sense of grief. This was a man who—along with Representatives Palmer and Fitzgerald—found me in Arkansas and believed in my mission enough to usher me into this campaign. Political violence is wrong… but only to a degree."

The audience seemed to simultaneously lean forward, the room closing in around them. He had them now, caught them by the throats.

"Hughes was an old man. An old, sad man. His death was tragic, as I said, but it was also natural in a sense. He was miserable being stuck in that elderly, wrinkly body. Whoever fired that shot into his brain honestly did him a service. If he had not been put out of his misery sooner, he surely would have killed himself. And *that's* what I'm running on, as you all know. Do I support assassination? Not always. But sometimes it can be justified. Not as justified as whoring people out of their money through deceptive landlord practices, but I digress."

Mark spotted Palmer and Fitzgerald standing in the dark behind the back row of chairs. Fitzgerald relentlessly chewed his fingernails while Palmer looked directly at Mark and drew a finger across his throat. *Oh shit*, Mark thought with a start. *Was I supposed to deny* those *allegations?*

"Mr. Foster, you have the floor."

"And I'm glad I get to relieve you all from the utter bullshit spewing from Mark Smith's demented mouth," Foster said. "My message is clear. I want our country to return to a sense of unity. Without unity, there is divide. And with divide comes the violence we see today. Not just in the assassination of a congressman, but in our own communities. The recent mass murder at a Planned Parenthood in Utah, another riot in Texas resulting in the deaths of fifty schoolchildren, or the pickup truck plowing into a crowd of people protesting *this* man." He pointed once again to Mark, his voice growing deeper and more formidable. "These acts of violence are because of Mr. Smith. Culprits directly cite him as their inspiration for the heinous acts they commit. I beg my fellow neighbors who support this man to rethink their morals. A man this unhinged should not oversee anything, let alone an entire country."

Mark rolled his eyes, hoping the camera caught that sarcastic motion.

"Would you like to respond, Mr. Smith?"

"No."

Murmurs throughout the auditorium. People were wondering why Mark was rushing through the debate. Did he not want the public to hear his takes on any of the topics?

No, he did not want them to hear.

He wanted them to trust him enough to allow him to prove his worth once he stepped into the Oval Office in January.

"And our final topic of tonight involves the ongoing conflicts between Russia and Ukraine, and Israel and the Gaza Strip," Johnson said. "Multiple attempts to quell these conflicts have been enacted by the current administration to no avail. Many Americans find the refusal to end wars as opposed to starting new wars to be demeaning to the concept of the United States as a whole. How would you ease the public in these matters, and what would your plan be to stop these senseless wars? Mr. Foster, you have two minutes to respond."

"Simply put, the war between Ukraine and Russia should not have happened," Foster said. "But it also should not have *continued* under the current administration. The incompetence in our nation's capital has allowed thousands of Ukrainian and Russian citizens to die, and I vow to take a stand to President Putin when the time comes to finally end thi—"

"You're leaving something out," Mark mumbled just loud enough to catch Foster's attention and no one else.

"Finally end this," Foster continued, giving Mark a vicious side eye. "I plan to also meet with Zelenskyy to discuss the United States' contribution to ending the war, whether that be though continued combat or through peace agreeme—"

"Running out of time," Mark mumbled again.

"Would you shut up?!" Foster roared.

Half the audience chuckled at that, the other half sitting taut with their brows furrowed and their arms crossed in defiance to the Democratic candidate's outburst.

Mark himself could not help smiling at the absurdity of the situation, but now Foster was in the palm of his hand, and he took control. Mark walked over to Foster's podium and snatched the microphone.

"Reginald Foster, I agree with your stance on Ukraine," Mark said, hoping that was the right thing to say, "but I cannot help but mention your blatant omission of the conflict in Gaza."

Foster grabbed him by the shoulder and yanked him back to the podium. He fought for the mic like an infant begging for his pacifier. Mark clenched his open fist and slammed his knuckles into Foster's nose, a rush of euphoria blessing his nerves as the Democrat's bone and cartilage snapped underneath the pressure of the punch.

Foster reeled back, hand covering his broken nose. He grunted and yelled something incomprehensible. Still wielding the mic, Mark pointed to Foster and said exactly what had been rehearsed.

"You are an agent of the Israeli state, and you have no

business in the White House." The words rolled effortlessly off Mark's tongue, the statements coming to him as naturally as air to his lungs and blood to his heart. "If you must decide between your allegiances to two separate states, how can you lead one of them? I would not trust a man to be in office for a country he has only half his faith in."

Security guards stormed the center stage, but they were no match for Foster's strength. As two guards grabbed his arms, he tore free and barreled toward Mark. Mark held up his guard as the auditorium erupted in chaos. Foster went in for a punch, his knuckles connecting with Mark's left cheek. Mark tasted blood in his mouth, savoring that sweet metallic taste. He laughed and swung back, his arm swishing over Foster's head as the man ducked low. The security guards struggled to tame the two candidates, Foster full of hatred and Mark cackling with spraying blood and childlike whimsy.

Foster laid another blow onto Mark, and when Mark saw a bright flash of light, he imagined it was his eyes playing tricks on him due to the sudden impact of flesh on flesh.

But Mark wasn't the only person to see that unforeseen blast. Ashley Guthrie saw the flash of light as well, all at once reminded of her constant nightmares and of the bomb that killed her fiancée. The light engulfed the left corner of the auditorium in a sphere of violent flame. Then came the shock wave, the bang, the crash, the limbs, the blood, the gore. Foster hurled his body over Mark to protect the both of them from the ensuing blast. Most of the spectators further from the explosion dropped to the floor. Ashley watched unblinking as a bomb destroyed the Washington University auditorium, nearly forgetting the embarrassing excuse for a presidential debate that just occurred.

Zuri and Xavier, watching the debate from the rafters above, quickly scurried out of the auditorium through an air vent and escaped with Mateo and Eddie back to the New York cabin.

Another job well done.

On to the next.

CHAPTER 17

★ ★ ★

Thirty-five dead. Thirty-five.

Firefighters discovered the charred remains of a detonated pipe bomb beneath the rubble along with all thirty-five of the dead. Thirty-five bodies. No, thirty-five *people*. Another thirty-five people to add to the kill count. Whose kill count? Mark didn't plant the bomb there. The police were too scared of him to ask, anyway. Mark worried about whether the dead had been unsatisfied with their lives or not. If they were depressed, he would be glad to see them go, but he knew that could never be the case. There had to be at least one happy person in that crowd, and that person was dead. That wasn't right. It went against his very sturdy moral compass.

"You alright, Smith?"

Mark glanced up and said, "What do you want?"

"To talk."

Reginald Foster sat next to him on the back bumper of an

ambulance wearing the same crumpled shiny space blankets wrapped around Mark himself.

"Haven't we done enough talking?" Mark asked, annoyed.

"No, I mean *real* talking. What we were doing in there was a farce. Think of it like theater. We were performing for the public, hopping around on television like breakdancers on acid. To be honest with you, brother, I didn't mean most of the shit I said back there, and I hope you didn't either."

Foster put an arm around Mark's shoulders. Mark felt the urge to squirm away but kept his ground.

"For real, though. You killed it up there," Foster continued. "For a second there, I thought you were really being serious about the whole murder thing. Have you ever tried auditioning for Broadway? You'd be a natural."

"No, I haven't." *This is insulting*, Mark thought.

"But look at all these people you've riled up."

Foster motioned to the small crowd of protesters lined up behind the ambulance. Their signs and masks and combat outfits were cute to a degree, but nothing that made Mark feel particularly threatened.

"That's a real gift in the political space," Foster continued. "The ability to spark so much outrage. It's how you stay in the news, and it's how you get more votes. Honestly, I wish I was as divisive as you, but the scriptwriters wouldn't allow that unfortunately."

Mark gave a halfhearted smirk and lowered his head in thought. He did not care much for the election at the moment. What he did care about was the explosion and whoever set the bomb in that auditorium. They must have planted it under someone's seat before everyone piled in for the debate. But how could someone slip in undetected with Secret Service agents prowling the premises? Everyone who had attended either paid to be there or were personally invited by either candidate. All except…

"Ashley," Mark whispered.

"What was that?"

"Nothing."

Mark rose from his stoop and let his space blanket calmly crinkle to the asphalt. He surveyed his surroundings, desperate to spot the person who had been hot on his tail ever since their encounter in July. Flashing red and blue lights obscured his vision as he walked with a limp through lines of medical and police vehicles. The protesters continued to shout their dismay. "Hands off our election! Mark sucks cocks!" they screamed in relative unison. It would be so easy to grab a service pistol from a nearby cop and gun them all down. Make the rowdy night a bit quieter.

He asked an officer if she had seen an average height woman wearing a sport coat with a spider necklace. When that officer shook her head, Mark went to the next officer, and the cycle continued for a while until—at the exact moment he was on the brink of completely losing his mind—there she was.

★ ★ ★

Ashley sat bundled in her own space blanket and sipped a thermos full of steaming hot black coffee. The brew gave her the jitters, but she did not mind. Witnessing a bomb detonating merely yards from her had her shaken up enough as it was, so a little extra caffeine wouldn't hurt.

A hand curled around her shoulder. As the mystery assailant began to turn her towards them, Ashley's survival instinct kicked in, resulting in a swift spasm of her arm holding the thermos. She splashed the scalding contents of the cup into the torso of whoever had grabbed her, and they screamed, "What the fuck?!"

Mark Smith let go of her, but he had already been agitated before the coffee seared through his dress shirt. He winded back his arm and slapped her across the mouth. A burst of pain sprouted on her cheek, and she gave a small yelp.

Already forgetting about the coffee, Mark jabbed a finger into Ashley's stomach. "How the fuck did you get into the debate tonight?"

"I paid," she said, holding her cheek. "How else was I supposed to get in?"

"And who let you behind the stage?"

"Security let me through. I told them I'm a government employee. That's all."

"And *why* were you here?"

Ashley knew she had come to St. Louis as a last-ditch effort to make Mark see any semblance of reason before taking his campaign too far. His arrogance would get the best of him, and the whole country would suffer the consequences if they elected him as their president. Sure, she regretted flying in *now* because of the terrorist attack, but her reasoning was sound. But was it sound enough for someone as insane as Mark Smith? Probably not. She mulled over her options and quickly decided on what to say next.

"To speak with an old friend," she fibbed.

"Oh really?" Mark crossed his arms.

Ashley stood up to even the playing field. "Why else would I leave Washington? I get very sentimental about hometown affairs, and someone from Bernard running for president? Wow, that's just something else. If I missed this historic moment, I don't think I could live with myself."

She almost hated the lie more than the man she told it to.

Almost.

"You're fucking with me," Mark said sternly.

"I'm not."

"Then explain why you were playing around with that detonator under your coat the whole time you spoke with me."

"Detonator? I…"

She placed her hand over the inner pocket of her suit jacket. The fabric went down onto her skin with nothing between it and the shirt beneath. The eagle. The wood-carved eagle the homeless woman had gifted her earlier that day. She must have lost it in the commotion of exiting the auditorium. There had been so much fire. So much blood. It had all regrettably reminded her of Tasha. Those final agonizing moments of her fiancée's life. Ground zero of an explosion targeting her lifetime idol.

Dr. Wilmington. A staunch advocate for mental health resources in rural areas, as Tasha had once raved about over a spaghetti and meatball dinner. A man with close ties to Democrats for that very reason. But also, a man who sat upon more wealth than some Silicon Valley tech firms. A man who had been caught funneling funds to Republican candidates across the nation despite outwardly seeming to be more left leaning. Someone who would be a ripe target for an operation focused on weakening the longevity of Mark Smith's presidential campaign.

That fucking committee planted another bomb at another national event.

Shaw.

Fucking Shaw.

"Oh," Ashley said, trying her hardest to not stumble on her words, "it was a little figurine I got before the debate. I must've lost it in the scuffle."

"I'm sure."

"You don't seriously think *I* would do this?"

"I don't know what to think about you anymore."

"You're fucking insane for thinking I'd be behind something as horrific as this."

"Am I?"

Ashley was ready to call over the officers chatting to other survivors. There was a crazed lunatic on the loose and he was ready to steal the presidency. He was ready to blame her for enacting mass terror without any proper evidence. And, despite her better judgment, Ashley knew there was a chance they would believe him. Why? Because they were afraid of him. They saw through his schemes, his outward confessions of brutality toward the innocent.

Her breath had been stolen. Air was nothing more than a concept. Mark walked over to the nearby officers. They recoiled as if they had spotted a rattlesnake underneath an abandoned suitcase in the desert. Mark talked to them. Ashley watched. That is all she could really do. Her ass was glued to the curb. The weight of the world on her shoulders. And through all that fright and helplessness, she couldn't help but wonder why she felt so guilty. Guilty for *what?* She had flown in to convince him to drop out. To watch a presidential debate for the first time in person. To take her mind off her father, Tasha, the Government Protections committee, and the dismantling of her beautiful country brick by brick. Watching something adjacent to what she loved: helping people. Being a cog in the governmental machine was something she was born to do. It was her purpose. And whatever Mark was telling those officers was sure to destroy that last bit of motivation she had to carry on.

But she couldn't run. Running would make her look suspicious. Would automatically brand her as a criminal. A quick hit-and-runner. Detonate a bomb, blend in with the survivors, and flee the scene. *No*, she thought. *Don't think like a criminal. You aren't guilty. You have nothing to do with this.*

The officers appeared before her, seemingly out of thin air. She stared at them. They stared back.

"Ms. Ashley Guthrie?" one of them asked.

"Representative, but yes," she corrected.

"Alright, *Representative* Guthrie. Would you mind coming along with us?"

"What for?"

"A matter has been brought to our attention by a credible source. We need you at the station for some questioning. Nothing serious."

Nothing serious. What a joke.

"Sure," Ashley said.

And that was that.

Mark watched the officers guide Ashley to their car. She climbed into the back seat, and the cruiser was off before Mark had the chance to wave her goodbye. He knew full and well she hadn't caused the deaths of all those people. Frankly, he appreciated the blood and guts despite the depravity of the situation. They added a bit of flavor to a rather boring night of debating.

He also knew he was now in a position of authority that made his say absolute. No questions asked. Walk up to a cop and tell him you think that woman over there detonated that bomb. Watch as the cop's eyes glaze over in fright, ready to say, "Sir, yes, sir!" no matter the context.

He was sad to see her go, but he *loved* to watch her leave.

Hopefully she would walk the Green Mile.

Say hello to Arthur for me.

★ ★ ★

The investigator clearly did not hear a word she said. He jotted some notes down on his yellow legal pad as she pled her case. That this was all a big misunderstanding. That she was being framed. That she would never think for a half a second about enacting violence on any scale, especially to the degree she had witnessed firsthand both in Bernard and at Washington University.

The investigator nodded in agreement even when she had not said a word. He continued to write in the legal pad, angling the paper just enough so that Ashley could not discern what he wrote. With tears in her eyes, Ashley asked, "What are they planning on doing with me?"

The investigator—a rotund older man with an unfortunate beer belly and a bald spot that reflected the overhead light brighter than the moon reflected the sunlight—finally looked her in the eye. She hated the sense of relief that washed over her then. Her legs stopped jittering for an instant, but they resumed their *tap-tap-tapping* once the investigator said, "I am not of the authority to make such judgments. All I know is that you will be held here for the remainder of the week."

"Held here?" Ashley shouted, her voice an echoed boom in the tightly enclosed interrogation room. "Is that really necessary?"

The investigator lifted an eyebrow. "Yes."

"Can I at least see what you wrote?"

"No."

Ashley slumped back in her chair. She was ravenously hungry, but asking for a bite to eat from this man would be as useless as asking a desk lamp to recite the Declaration of Independence. Her forehead dripped sweat. It was the middle of October, and she was perspiring enough to fill a lake.

After an agonizing minute of silence, the investigator made a few more notes and stood up from his chair. "I need to speak with a colleague," he said. "It will only be a moment."

As he left the room, Ashley caught a glimpse of what he had been writing. There were no words, only a crude doodle of lizard.

She sat alone in that room for two hours, 46 minutes, and 21 seconds. She only knew this because her early onset insanity crept into her veins and all she could focus on was the ticking analog clock above the door. Her mind had grown tired, numb. This was all a tactic, a final ploy to get her to submit. Something they were all in on. Mark, Palmer, Fitzgerald, the entire Protections committee. She was sure of it. Beat her into submission until she peacefully walked away.

The investigator eventually entered the room once more, this time with a fully outfitted police officer at his side. Badge number, sunglasses despite the midnight hour, taser on one side of his utility belt, holstered service pistol at the other. He held a pair of handcuffs and presented them to Ashley.

She couldn't submit.

She needed to stay strong.

Not just for herself.

But for the country.

She willed herself to stand from the chair, her ass aching from prolonged immobility. She stared at the cuffs. Watched as they glinted in the light. Pure silver. Like the necklace around her neck, Tasha's golden spider dangling at the end of it.

She presented her wrists.

★ ★ ★

Ashley spent the next two weeks in those cuffs. They paired nicely with her new orange jumpsuit. It had initially smelled of fresh linens, but that faint aroma washed away as the days passed.

The initial court hearing went as smoothly as one could go.

"You are being tried for the murders of thirty-five citizens, some of which were government officials," the judge stated, "as well as conspiracy to assassinate a sitting member of the U.S. House of Representatives."

"I didn't do any of it," she mumbled, her voice in outer space.

Her court-appointed attorney nudged her shoulder, silently mouthing, "*Shut up.*"

They took her from the courtroom, back to a cell, where she would wait for the next time she entered the court.

Two days later, she sat in the courtroom surrounded by the loved ones of the people lost in the Washington University bombing. Sniffles, tears, full-on sobs of anguish. She remembered a time in which crying meant something. Where tears falling down one's face signified a deep and painful sadness, one that burrowed so deep it couldn't be extracted by simple means such as self-medication or suicide. An eternal mourning that time would never heal. No amount of water dripping for her eyes could bring back her father. Tasha would be forever a ghost, damned for the sin of being in love with her.

Ashley did not understand why the loved ones were allowed to speak as if they would offer valid testimonies. They did not witness the carnage like she did. They only felt the aftershock. A feeling in one's gut that signaled doom over the horizon. But they did not see the sudden flash of light, feel the blistering heat, smell the stench of sulfur and blood congealing in the air.

But despite all the anguish, Ashley was spared the death penalty, an outcome she had been considering progressively more the longer they held her behind bars. She would not have minded a quick end. Lethal injection would be better, but maybe she deserved a firing squad. Or maybe a public hanging. Anything able to be conducted on the town square would suffice. But no, the judge sentenced her to life in federal prison.

Was that so bad, though?

She could finally escape the hell of living in the United States. Live in her own enclosed space for the rest of her days. Read all those books she would never get to, watch movies she had not seen, and meet people she would never meet otherwise. All behind those walls, away from the chaos brewing out there.

In her first day at a women's only federal prison, Ashley was visited by someone she wanted to choke. Congressman Shaw sat in the stool on the other side of the plexiglass, looking less sorrowful than he deserved. Ashley picked up the phone and waited for him to do the same. When he did, he let out a dramatic sigh and pressed his free hand to the glass. Ashley recoiled as if someone had sneezed in her direction.

"I'm sorry, Ash," he finally said.

"Don't call me that."

"Sorry."

"Why are you sorry? You didn't put me in here."

The sorrowful gaze along with Shaw's hollowed eyes instantly vanished. He looked like a completely different person from the man that had sat himself there only moments before. He locked his eyes onto hers and said, "We're out of time, Ashley."

"We?"

"The committee. The election is next week and… well. Smith is the projected winner. By a mile. There have been smear campaigns for both major candidates, but none as harsh as the ones against Foster. It's ludicrous."

"I don't care about any of that," Ashley said. "What else do you have to talk about? I don't have all day."

"I would think you would. You *are* in prison, after all. What do they have you doing in there? Mopping?"

"Visiting times are limited, dumbass."

"Oh right. Of course."

There was a long pause then. One so long Ashley hoped it would cut into their time just enough to force her to leave the booth. She knew she could just ask the guard to let her go, but there was still an inkling of curiosity inside the former congress-woman.

"I want to thank you," Shaw said.

"For what?"

"For being our fall guy. Or… fall gal? Whichever works. The committee had Secret Service agents on our asses about why our team had been stalling. Whoever's left of the president's cabinet was worried we were staging a coup."

"You kinda were."

"Yes, but not in the traditional sense."

"So, you all were the ones who planted that bomb at Washington University?"

"Did you just now understand that?"

"No, I knew. I just wanted to hear it from you."

Shaw leaned his elbows on the counter and sighed again. It was all the confirmation Ashley required. The reason the trial went by so quickly was probably because Senator Rushakoff paid the judge to get it over with. They needed a scapegoat for their most treacherous scheme, and Ashley had simply been at the right place at the right time. Lucky her.

"What else do you have planned, Shaw?"

"You don't have to be formal with me."

"I barely know who you are anymore."

"Don't say that. I was only doing what I had sworn to do. To protect our nation by any means necessary."

"And you wrote our fate in blood," Ashley said. "You threw your colleague in jail to protect your own image. And for what? So you can suffer out there when Mark Smith becomes president? And I get to watch from afar in here?" She chuckled unhappily. "It should be you behind bars. I should be the one suffering for the sins of my hometown. I let this monster grow. You should have let me handle things my own way."

"You know words are never enough."

"But you went straight for the bullets. Assassinating people never silences them. Their legacies live on in different ways once they're gone. You don't take life, you make martyrs. Instead of pressing mute on these people, you're shoving a megaphone into their faces and begging them to scream. It's dumb as fuck."

"Mark Smith will die," Shaw said, clearly ignoring everything Ashley had said.

"And I hope he does. But you don't know what you're getting into. If you send a hit on him, you'll create ten more people just like him. The cycle will never end."

"Keep telling yourself that, Ashley."

Shaw slipped the phone onto its handle and rose from his seat. With pure rage in his eyes, he left the visitation room without a goodbye. Ashley gawked at the sheer stupidity of a man she trusted to be right and just. To be willing to put his welfare on the line for the United States, just as she did. He and that entire committee weren't trying to be heroes.

No.

They were bloodthirsty.

Nothing would satisfy them until they took down their greatest trophy of all, and Ashley hated herself for feeling sick to her stomach over the thought of Mark Smith being gunned down within the next week. She hated him. She *loathed* him. But no one deserved to die like that. Not even him, despite all his sins.

Ashley ate lunch in the mess hall, a gourmet meal of sludge slurry and an overripe apple, and returned to her cell. It was cozy enough for her diminishing mental state, but surely not cozy enough to last her for the rest of her life. Maybe she would get out in thirty years with good behavior. The judge had not ruled that out. He had not stated it as a fact either, but Ashley needed at least a shred of optimism to bear her new life.

She took a nap, was awoken by a guard tapping her baton on the cell bars and went into the basement laundry room to fold neatly cleaned orange jumpsuits. There was a strange precision in the folding, the satisfying crease that would form when she laid the clothes down flat on the stainless-steel table. She could do this forever. Maybe.

Lots of maybes today.

And many more to come.

When she returned to her cell once again, she was shocked to have a visitor. A man clad in a tight black suit and egregiously slicked back hair. He turned to reveal himself as a guard slammed the cell door behind her.

"You've been busy, Ms. Guthrie," Representative Palmer said cheerily, his arms outstretched as if for a hug.

"What the hell are you doing here?" Ashley asked, more annoyed than angered. "Don't you have a campaign to run?"

"It's going well enough that I seem to have accrued some free time. How have things been?"

"Shit, Palmer. It's been shit."

"That's good to hear."

"If you came here to berate me about government related crap, I don't want to hear it."

"No no. I didn't come for that." Palmer reached inside his suit jacket and pulled out a folded sheet of lined notebook paper. "I wanted to personally deliver this to you. Don't read it now, but I wanted to gift this as a sort of... how should I say... farewell present? Here."

He handed it to her, but when she crossed her arms in refusal, he backed away and set it on her bunk.

"Do you have a roommate?" he asked.

"No. They wouldn't let me since I allegedly blew up 35 people."

"Oh, yes. That's right. Silly of me to ask."

While Shaw had been one of the people she wanted to strangle the most, Palmer was certainly also on that list. She imagined reaching out like a hawk closing in on its prey, squeezing the life out of him. Watching the whites of his eyes disappear in an ocean of burst blood vessels. It would be a fitting end for the congressman, to be choked to death by the person he thought was too weak to govern.

"Is that all you wanted to do? To give me a piece of paper?"

"Yes. That's all."

Was he expecting something in return? A hug? A peck on the cheek? He and most of his Republican colleagues had sexually harassed her enough inside the Capitol building. Was this his last perverted ploy before leaving her in prison for the rest of her life? It would be such a godawfully cruel joke if true.

They stood there for quite some time, studying each other's movements, Palmer quietly enjoying the discomfort while Ashley wanted to melt into the drain in the middle of her cell. A prisoner screamed for help down the long hallway, motioning the guard to bang her baton on the cell. "Would you two get this over with?" she shouted.

Palmer flashed a smile and strolled to the cell door. Before leaving, he turned to Ashley and gave a mocking, dainty wave like Judy Garland would give to the camera at the end of one of those ancient motion pictures.

When he was gone, and when the prison went eerily quiet, Ashley sat on her bed. She refused to look at the paper. The unknown of what was written on that page turned her stomach into knots. Palmer had been so insistent on delivering the paper himself. To make his presence known, as if to tell Ashley, "The world is better off with you in here. We'll be keeping an eye on you." It was a power play. They were on the House floor debating the intricacies of the death penalty. Should we? Could we? Too many questions, not enough action.

But that was someone else's problem now.

Ashley couldn't bear the mystery surrounding that folded slip of paper. She made out indents in the page, markings made on the inside that Palmer wanted Ashley to see. A simple note, an ominous warning, a plea for silence.

She held the page in her hand, feeling the weight of it. Paper wasn't supposed to feel this heavy. The weight of the world in the palm of her hand. Her fingers trembled as she unfolded the note, straining her eyes to read the hastily scribbled script.

Dear Ms. Ashley Guthrie,

You may be wondering why I was so quick to blame you for those deaths. "Mark is obviously the crazy one! Why isn't he the culprit?" you may be asking. The answer is simple, really. I needed someone to blame, and in a lapse of judgment, you were the one that fit the bill. While I thought your life sentence was a bit harsh, I fully understood the judge's decision. 35 people is a lot (not as many as I have killed, but that is a whole different thing). Hopefully you take this time to heal and reckon for your sins against me and my message.

Regardless, I hope to see you again once this is all over. Take all the

time you need, so you can properly grieve all you have lost. I wish you well,
Ashley Guthrie. You are the best of us.

Yours,
Mark Thomas Smith, Jr.

Ashley tore the letter to pieces, letting the shreds scatter onto the cold cement floor. "That fucking dick," she whispered, holding her head in her hands.

That urge came crawling back. The desire to wind her bedsheets around the towering bedpost and shove her head through the loop. To feel the air slowly seeping from her lips as her throat clogged shut. Her eyes popping from their sockets like grapes under a hydraulic press.

She peered across her hollow cell, smelled the rank stench of mildew and human feces. Would any of this be worth it? To be tucked away from the rest of the world, safe from the ensuing carnage? If she were to get out early, would there be anything to go back to?

America would be a bed of ashes.

She had never been more certain of anything.

Her father and Tasha were unfortunate casualties in the timeline that inevitably ended with the destruction of an entire nation.

Ashley stared at her bed sheets and wondered if she would be the next. She would have a lot to atone for.

CHAPTER 18

★ ★ ★

Joaquin Fajardo Guzman was only here because his scholarship required it. A year-long internship in Washington D.C. to satisfy his graduation requirements. The opportunity had been exciting the summer before, but now every day felt like a new hell.

Constant calls from his boss, incessant nagging for fresh pots of coffee, and judgmental stares from the most elderly people he had ever seen. The Capitol felt more like a nursing home than a place that determined the rights of over 300 million people. He could handle the calls and the coffee runs, but those damn lead-paint stares were creepy as all hell. And he knew it wasn't because of the clothes he wore or the way he walked. It was because of that slightly brownish hue to his skin. He was an alien to them despite never knowing a home other than the United States.

But he rolled with the punches, because there was no way he was going to tack another year to the end of his degree at Sanduhr University. One such punch came at seven o'clock on the dot on a random October Tuesday when his boss called him once again.

"*Juan!*" Congressman Finley Palmer shouted from his end. "*Please let the media know the files are good to go live! It's time for that October surprise!*"

Now? Seriously?

Congressman Palmer had forced Joaquin to fabricate dozens upon dozens of documents pertaining to the apparent child pornography Reginald Foster had possession of. Joaquin had no idea whether Foster actually had child porn on his computer, but Palmer assured that everything he would type up would be proven true in one way or another. Not wanting to risk losing his internship position, Joaquin had opened a Microsoft Word document and typed away, weaving facts about Foster's personal life with that of whatever pedophilic antics he could think of. The work was laborious and tiresome, but he eventually finished the file and shipped USB thumb drives to multiple news outlets across the country.

It was time now. Only a week out from the 2028 presidential election, and Joaquin knew he was about to drop a nuke on the projections. Mark Smith and Reginald Foster were basically toe and toe in the polls, but not for long. Twitter, Facebook, Instagram, and all the other social media platforms would catch wind of this. And, like COVID in 2020, it would spread without mercy. Foster's political reputation would die before it had the chance to do anything meaningful. No more promises of a better economy. No more promises to raise the federal minimum wage. All of that would be out the window as his campaign scrambled to control the wildfire.

"Are you sure, sir?" Joaquin asked.

"*Yes! Send the emails now!*"

Palmer hung up and Joaquin walked at a brisk pace through

the Capitol Building to Palmer's office. Once inside, he flicked on the lights, made haste in brushing past the American, Israeli, and Russian flags mounted on display, and logged onto Palmer's desktop computer.

In a few keystrokes, Joaquin was prepared to hit send on the email that would destroy a man's life. One single email that would drive a stake into the heart of the Democratic Party for decades to come.

Joaquin hadn't wanted to be placed with a Republican for this internship, seeing as they spent every day of their lives petitioning for people like him to be deported regardless of citizenship status. He would've rather been paired with Ocasio-Cortez, or Dexter, or Lee, or McIver. Literally anyone else as long as they weren't planning to undermine the sanctity of the American government (or lack thereof; it was hard to tell sometimes).

His finger hovered over the Enter key. Doubts filled his head to the point of explosion. He wasn't even being paid for any of this. He could simply shut off the computer and walk out in the dead of night. No harm done. Well, no harm done except for the harm done to his chances at graduation.

Fuck, he thought. He was so *fucked*.

He would make a mockery of his heritage, his people. How could he go home for winter break and look his mother in the face knowing he was the reason another fucking Republican with no political experience was elected president? He would never again deserve the tamales and carne asada. He would never deserve to attend his little sister's quinceañera. He would never be able to go deer hunting with his dad or take his girlfriend to the movies or go soundly to sleep at night.

But that nagging feeling. That pull to do what was best for his financial future. You had no future in the United States without a fat paycheck. And that was why he was where he was. So he could graduate from a fucked-up college to get a fucked-up job that fucked up everyone's lives.

Joaquin pressed Enter.

It was done.

Goodbye, Reginald Foster.

That political science degree wasn't going to earn itself.

★ ★ ★

Valerie hung up the phone with a grim look on her face. Well, more grim than usual. Abel was both terrified and exhilarated to hear what had made her so uninviting.

She went down to the basement and Abel followed. When he found an empty chair around the main table, Valerie planted her hands down and hung her head low. *This is gonna be good*, Abel thought.

"I just got a call from a high-profile client," Valerie said, that grimness refusing to leave like an unwanted houseguest. "The same client who ordered the bombing in St. Louis, the hit on that congressman in Chicago, and the bombing in Virginia. With the election coming up so soon, you can probably guess where this is going."

The room went silent. Everyone held their breath, even Johnny whose lungs were on life support from decades of smoking cigars. Could this really be...? No, it couldn't be. That would be insane. *More* insane than the concept of a group of hitmen patrolling the country in search of targets both high and low in profile. If Abel's scrambled mind was correct, this could only mean...

"We're gonna kill the president?" Zuri asked in a hushed murmur.

"We're gonna kill the president," Valerie repeated.

This was it. Finally, Abel would be able to prove his worth. No more mistakes, no more hesitation. Just unadulterated violence in its purest form. A bullet to the skull of a top dog in the United States. This was all too good to be true, so Abel popped the question with a gigantic grin on his face: "Stealthy or messy?"

"Stealthy," Valerie said. "But we need a plan. We've been called upon to do hits on foreign presidents and prime ministers, but we have *never* been called to do a hit on a candidate so close to their election. I'll leave most of the logistics to Mateo and Johnny, but I will say this outright: we will need all hands on deck for this job. Everyone needs to be there. Security could be either very relaxed or very tight, and I'm not taking any chances."

"Understood," Johnny muttered.

"So, we're not taking out the current guy?" Xavier asked.

"No, just his successor," Valerie denied.

Xavier's smile quickly faded.

After the meeting, Abel returned to the guest room with Eddie. Eddie sat in the corner while Abel made himself comfortable atop the cot. It was finally happening. Sure, he had had his fair share of assassinations during his time with the Coalition, but certainly not enough. This was it. The big show. Abel could hardly contain himself but remained composed so that he didn't embarrass himself. He wanted to shout his excitement from the roof of their remote cabin, to waltz into the next town over and tell everyone he came across that, "Yes, I'm going to kill…"

Kill who?

Not the *actual* president. Valerie had made that clear. With an election on the horizon, were they seriously being tasked with… what? Taking out the guy who wins? How would they already know so soon? Abel and the rest of the Coalition (except Valerie for obvious communication requirements between clients) were forbidden from keeping their cellphones. No phone meant no internet, and no internet meant no knowledge. Abel was aware because of that digest magazine that Bernard's very own Mark Smith was in the running, but there was also the other guy. But that was where his knowledge ended. He had no idea who was ahead in the polls. A slight twinge of nervousness infected Abel's previous elation, spreading like a virus until anxiety was all he could think of.

He stopped biting a fingernail he hadn't realized he'd been chewing and left the guest room. Everyone was gone except Johnny, who Abel wouldn't be surprised to learn he had been superglued to his chair. He tapped Johnny's shoulder and asked, "Which candidate are we taking out, exactly?"

"The red one," Johnny said, jotting notes on a legal pad.

"What's that supposed to mean?"

"The Republican, idiot."

"That being?"

"Mark Smith from Arkansas. Now leave me alone. I'm busy."

The light vanished from the room. Abel felt weightless. Every ounce of care he had lost for Mark Smith in the past few months flooded back in an instant. He remembered the day he stabbed Macy Thornton in the neck; the day Mark saw him out of the police station.

You have spirit, kid.

Abel was unsure now if he could do what was being asked of him. There was too much history. So much lore that it could possibly spill out as he aimed down the sights and pulled the trigger. He could *miss*, for Christ's sake. And that wouldn't do.

But there was no one else here to do the job as well as him.

This would be how he proved himself.

To be remembered.

★ ★ ★

Christopher Shaw hung up with the lady from the Coalition and laid his phone face down on the coffee table. His hands trembled as he rose from the carpet, nearly slipping off the edge of the low table. But he managed to get to his feet without much pressure. The Government Protections committee stared at him, smiling in obscene ways without the joy spreading to their eyes. They scared the shit out of him all the time, but this time was horrific.

What had he done?

The dim lamplight of the apartment cast them all in a faint glow that barely accented their facial features. It was as if he were gazing upon a room full of ghosts. They were already dead. All of them, whether they knew it or not.

Ashley had taken the fall for this treachery, this treason, but something inside Shaw ached. Maybe he hadn't eaten a nutritious meal in quite a while. Four months now. His days were punctuated by sips of beer and shots of the harder stuff. He didn't know how much longer he could keep a straight face among these animals. These lions dressed in sheep's clothing. Senators and House Representatives masquerading as righteous individuals.

He imagined Ashley behind that plexiglass. The vacant stare that served as her only expression. The quick trial had taken the spunk out of her. Any semblance of the Ashley from before had vanished the moment the judge laid down the gavel. She would spend the rest of her days in that federal prison for something she never did.

It had to be necessary, right? There was no way *he* would want to go to prison. He had too much work left to be done. They all did. The loss of a single congresswoman would not tip the scales that much, surely.

"You did the right thing," Senator Rushakoff said, clearly noticing Shaw's discomfort. "They'll etch your name into history books for your bravery."

Shaw sat with the sentiment for a moment, letting it stew in the thick apartment air. The sun had set during his call with the Coalition. Not that he noticed. The world had become a dark, dark place already. The loss of sunlight scarcely made a difference.

"It had to been done," added Representative Garrison.

"One last stand for democracy," Rushakoff said, lifting his drink.

The rest of the committee did the same in uncanny unison.

Shaw stared at his half-drunk bottle of Coors on the coffee table. Right next to his phone. The phone he used to order Mark Smith's execution.

Maybe it was for the best. Or maybe not.

Shaw lifted his bottle and took a swig.

But he needed to make another call.

One last stand.

★ ★ ★

Reginald Foster never stood a chance.

Once the articles dropped, social media predictably did the rest of the work. Drove the final nail into his campaign's coffin. The files were long enough that most people neglected to read past the title page, if they even opened the attached documents at all. The title read: "CASE FILES RELATED TO ALLEGATIONS AGAINST PRESIDENTIAL CANDIDATE REGINALD FOSTER." It was a simple enough hook but did not divulge the horrors laid within the rest of the file.

According to news outlets, Foster was a family man. He

enjoyed a healthy marriage with his wife of twenty years, giving life to two beautiful children in the process. He earned his wealth through businesses pertaining to the abundant apartment complexes around the Omaha area. In his free time (and he had *lots* of free time, since most Americans argue being a mayor means you do not actually have a "real job"), Foster dabbled in watercolor painting. Many of his works amounted to amalgamations of random colors that never came together to form something resembling art, but a few other works were as clear as day. Paintings of trees, of the Omaha skyline, of lakes and beaches and family vacations. One painting was of what appeared to be his two children as infants naked in the tub, though the lack of skill in the painting process made the distinction controversial in and of itself.

The files chronicled Foster's alleged other hobby, that of his indulgence in the realm of child pornography. While the file purported that entire hard drives of the inappropriate material were confiscated from Foster's campaign laptops, the actual photographs and videos were not shown for obvious legal purposes. The facts were laid bare, though, as the documents narrated in stark detail how deep Foster's addiction went. Leaving campaign events for hours at a time to sit on the toilet and watch the content, fantasizing about the videos during important meetings, and bragging about his collection to notable colleagues in the election cycle.

Users on X, formerly known as Twitter, responded to the news articles in varying ways. While people who leaned more toward the left of the political spectrum showed clear revulsion to the accusations, people of the right were relishing in it:

> **not surprised. have you heard the way he laughs? clear pedo behavior**
>
> — @LittleChrisFucker

I can excuse Mark Smith's murders, but I draw the line at Reggie Foster touching kids

— @MAGAFishBait

We got the Foster files before the Epstein files??? Wtf gives?

— @Gabby10479367920

hilarious that a democrat would finally follow in bill clintons footsteps but without all the secrecy good job bozo

— @TheNickeling

When the current president posted his disdain on a social media app he had created to champion free speech, he wrote:

The ever so terrible Reggie "Wedgie" Foster is a PEDOPHILE. I've always trusted the REAL NEWS in our Beautiful country and today they have done America a GREAT service. Foster is the WORST candidate in united States HISTORY. Worse than "Sleepy" Joe if you can believe it. I can never imagine what goes through the Head of such a DISGUSTING human being. How was he allowed to run?? I can tell you why... it's because the democRATS are desperate! No one wanted to step up, so they sent they're first bench warmer. What an EMBARRASS-MENT! Do NOT let the radical left win this election. If you are a patriot who loves children as much as I do, vote for MARK SMITH! President ****** * *****

Needless to say, Foster could never come back from this scandal, no matter whether it had been fabricated by Washington officials.

Mark Smith was still reeling from the court's decision to lock Ashley Guthrie in prison for life. He hoped his note to her would quell her definite suicidal ideation. He trusted that his words would be comfort enough to put her at ease for the decades to come. Those lonely and isolating decades. But she was not the focus now. He locked her memory into a jewelry case in his mind and shoved it into the closet, making room for the next problem on his checklist.

It was the night before the election. November 6, 2028. A cool Monday evening with winds that howled between the buildings of the nation's capital. He stood outside the lobby of a downtown bed and breakfast staring up at a window that had just gone black. Foster and his family had slipped into bed. His two little girls nestled under the covers, dreaming those sweet dreams only children could conjure. His wife curled up beside him, worrying not only for her husband's career, but for his sanity. And then there would be Foster himself, laying on his back, his eyes glued to the ceiling. Mulling over what had happened. Why him? Who would fabricate such drivel, and better yet, who would send that shit to the press? He was probably thinking of killing himself. A saner man would have done it already. But Mark knew better. Reggie Foster was different from his contemporaries. He had a strong will, and that was dangerous. It made him unpredictable, and unpredictability would lose Mark the election.

Couldn't have that.

Mark entered the inn and sauntered past the sleeping desk clerk. He rode the elevator to the third floor and went to room 326. The scandal had rid Foster of his security detail, as nobody in their right mind would think to work for a known sex offender. And since the inn was a bit older fashioned—lacking all the bells and whistles of keycards and deadbolts—Mark quietly let himself in. It brought him back to the days in which people in Bernard refused to lock their windows. What a blessing they had been to shepherd his talents onto the national stage.

The daughters were sleeping soundly on the foldout couch, their mother and father resting in the king size bed. Foster looked much more content with life than Mark had expected, but not for long. Mark reached into his sack of delights and pulled out a fire poker. He pressed the sharp end onto the mound of blankets covering Foster's thigh. Vibrations shot up the metal pole into Mark's fists as the poker broke skin and slid into Foster's leg muscle. *Heavy sleeper*, Mark thought amusedly. The white sheets began to soak red as blood spurted from the Democrat's leg. Mark felt the fire poker protrude from the other side of the thigh and skewer the mattress beneath. He pushed it deeper until the handle was the only thing sticking out.

The air conditioning units kicked in, blasting freezing air up his shirt. He shivered and got into position in the middle of the tight room. He reached into his sack and retrieved the same pistol he had used on that tomato-hurling little bitch in Bernard. With the barrel pointed at Foster's eldest daughter, Mark clicked on the bedside lamp and shouted, "Wake up, sunshine!"

Foster's wife shot up straight with a scream, not because Mark was in the room, but she had woken up at eleven in the evening. She rubbed that sleep from her eyes and finally noticed Mark. Her eyes widened, but her open mouth let out no sound. Without breaking eye contact, Foster's wife shook her husband vigorously. "Reggie," she said, her voice wavering. "Reggie, wake up. Wake up!"

Foster's eyes opened a crack, and when he attempted to roll onto his side, he realized he couldn't and opened his eyes more to investigate. When he noticed the handle of the fire poker sticking out of his thigh, he shouted incomprehensibly and tried to move to no avail. Mark heard meat squelching, metal scraping against the bone.

"Please don't kill them," Foster's wife pleaded with tear streaming down her dark cheeks. "Please, please, please don't. They didn't *do* anything!"

Foster neglected to say anything, only seethed through the pain bursting from the nerves in his leg.

"Don't struggle, Reggie," Mark told him. "You're only making the hole bigger."

"Leave them alone!"

The two daughters rose from sleep because of the sudden ruckus. They did not shout or reel back like their parents, only sat there confused yet full of wonderment. Who *was* this strange man? Why are Mommy and Daddy crying?

"Reginald," Mark said. "Look me in the eye."

He did, unblinking. His face was drenched in sweat, the salt from his tears nearly invisible on his slick skin.

"That's good," Mark continued. "That's very good."

Without warning, Mark fired. The recoil sent a shockwave through his arm, the sound of the pistol firing shaking the entire room. The eldest daughter's brains splattered across the back of the couch, some of it splashing onto her younger sister's face. *Now* she started screaming. Right on cue.

"NO!" Foster's wife screamed, making to rise from the bed until Mark aimed the pistol at her.

"Get back, bitch!" he shouted. "I'm not DONE!"

She slowly curled back into the bed. Reginald was breathing heavy now, his skin paler than before. He was losing a lot of blood. Mark had to make this quick, it seemed. He aimed the pistol at the younger (now only) daughter. She was shivering either from the air conditioning or the dead body sprawled next to her. She would be free now. Free from pain.

Mark fired once more, hitting right between the little girl's brown eyes. Her locs recoiled as her head spilled a blood and bone stew.

"Now come over here," Mark told Foster's wife.

She did as she was told. Good girl.

"Pick them up," he said.

She hesitated, her muscles tensing.

"Why so afraid? You don't like children? I know your husband does."

"That's… that's not…" Foster attempted to speak.

"Pick them up, whatever your name is," Mark told the wife.

"W-Wendy," she stuttered.

"Go on now."

Wendy scooped up the smallest girl first and brought her to the king size bed. Propping her against the headboard, Wendy moved on to the eldest daughter. But when she picked her up, more bloody chunks of brain spilled out the hole in the back of her head and onto her mother's arms and chest. Wendy essentially threw the girl onto the bed and keeled over, vomiting all over the floor and crying while doing so.

It was a pathetic scene. Mark needed her to get over it quickly before the real fun began. He aimed the pistol at the entire Foster family now, the two dead and the two almost dead.

"I want you four to get nice and close like you love each other," Mark smiled, pulling a digital camera from his back pocket.

Wendy's bottom lip trembled as she slowly wrapped her arms around her daughters' corpses, bringing them close. Reggie leaned as close as he could without the fire poker causing more damage to his thigh. They truly were a beautiful family. Picture-perfect in terms of that all-American nuclear family stereotype. Loving husband and wife with two gorgeous daughters. Mark wanted to capture this moment forever.

The camera flashed and Mark slipped it back into his pocket. He then reached into his sack and retrieved a simple kitchen knife. It had been a while since he used one of these, so he had sharpened it to perfection before heading over to the inn. He stepped closer to the bed, blood now dripping from all four corners of the duvet.

"You watching this, Reggie?" Mark asked jokingly.

"Please don't," he begged. "We haven't done anything wrong. Those articles were faked. I don't know how, but they were."

"I know they were, but let's not talk politics in front of the wife. That would be rude."

Mark reeled back his arm and slashed. The knife slid elegantly over Wendy's trachea. She gasped, and her next breath sent blood gushing down her neck. Now her breathing was sharp and guttural, like a ventilation system with one too many rats crawling around inside. She tried to cover the wound with her hands. Applying pressure was the easiest way to stop bleeding, she knew. But the blood continued to flow through the gaps between her fingers. Her eyes nearly bulged from her head before rolling into her skull. She and her daughters flopped like fish to the floor with loud thuds, hers louder than the other two.

Wendy gurgled a desperate breath before Mark kicked her in the head. The noise stopped.

"Now we can talk," Mark said.

"You're a monster," Foster seethed.

"That may be true, but it's also my job. You don't fault the artist for their critics, do you?"

"Those files were *faked*, Smith. Don't you get that?"

"Oh, I know. Palmer got those whipped up a month or two ago. It was always part of the plan."

"My career is over because of you," Foster snarled.

"Nothing more to live for, it seems."

Mark threw the knife aside and grabbed his last weapon from the sack. Old reliable. His trusty axe, shined and sharpened for optimal chopping.

"You don't know what life is, Mark," Foster tried to reason. "People are insane. They're complicated. They can feel happy, sad, nervous, confident, all at the same time. That's what it is to be human. I thought everything you said at those rallies was a sick joke. No real person could say all that shit and mean it."

Mark did not respond, only sneered.

He reached across the bed and shoved Foster off. When the man dropped off the edge, his leg was the only limb left, nailed to the bed like Jesus to the cross. Foster screamed for help.

"Please! Please! Anyone! Help!"

"Should've picked a better hotel," Mark said.

He began at Foster's incapacitated leg, chopping without precision. A lop here, another there. Tonight was not about cleanliness. It was about passion, rage, hunger. Blood flew to all corners of the room. The television, the curtains, the carpet, the lamps, the desk, its chair, the family's belongings. Everything stained with Reginald Foster's bodily fluids. Mark did not say a single word. He grunted and spit like a rabid Saint Bernard tearing apart a helpless squirrel.

His arms ached from the effort of raising the axe high above his head and letting it fly down over and over again. But when Foster was nothing but a slurry of finely diced human flesh, Mark packed his various weapons into his sack, reached into his pocket, and placed eight pennies into his latest victims' gaping orifices.

★ ★ ★

The Coalition arrived in Washington D.C. moments after the brutal slaying of Reginald Foster and his family.

They set up shop in an abandoned parking garage with a clear view of the Capitol Building and the surrounding Pennsylvania Avenue area. Zuri and Xavier sat perched on a concrete barrier like falcons on a power line, chatting about something Abel did not care for. They talked about how exciting it was to become the next John Wilkes Booth or Lee Harvey Oswald or at least abet in the crimes of the marksman.

While Abel shared similar excitement, the dreadful gloom of bittersweetness overtook his thoughts. Mark had been instrumental in Abel's development, whether the man liked it or not. Abel could not help but feel like a traitor despite the necessity of the work. Someone had phoned Valerie asking for this task to be carried out for an extremely large sum of cash, and Abel would be remiss to not put Mark down like a terminally sick dog.

Abel found Eddie tucked behind a concrete post and sat next to him, smelling the faint aroma of his father's ocean spray cologne, that nostalgic scent of better days.

"You alright?" Abel asked.

"As alright as I'll ever be," Eddie said, his eyes remaining fixed on a nondescript trash bin instead of Abel.

"You don't seem alright."

"Then why did you ask?"

"Because I care about you, man. You've barely talked in weeks."

"It's none of your business, okay? Leave me alone."

Abel had the distinct ability to *not* leave people alone when they told him to, so he stayed sitting until Eddie decided to speak again.

After a long moment, Eddie finally sighed and said, "I just

don't want to disappoint my mom, you know?"

Abel understood the feeling, so he nodded.

"Sure, she's made some dumbass life decisions, but I can't fault her for that," Eddie continued. "I've been thinking about Wyatt a lot. You know, the guy before I brought you in. It's so fucking unfair that he had to go out like that. Full of bullet holes n' shit. They could barely identify his body after that goddamn shooting. And it made me think, *What if that happens to me?* I don't wanna go out like that. I love the job, and I love the people here, but I can't imagine how disappointed Mom would feel seeing her son in the news not just for dying, but for helping murder someone. She had to deal with Dad taking the easy way out already. I just… I just don't want to put all that on her again."

"You won't," Abel said.

"You sure?"

"I am."

★ ★ ★

Once the backlash against Reginald Foster had reached its peak, the election of November 7, 2028 reached a unanimous and equally controversial conclusion: Mark Smith was declared the 48th president of the United States in a landmark landslide vote.

Election maps on CNN, AP, FOX News, MSNBC, and many other news outlets were completely swathed in red. Even states that historically swung blue voted for the grassroots candidate from Arkansas. California, New York, Illinois, among others. Not since Ronald Reagan had an election been called so early. Polling projections called the election in Smith's favor by the time the sun set on the East Coast.

Representative Palmer sat in the back of the conference room snorting another line of cocaine when everything was said and done. Republican congressmen whooped and hollered as confetti exploded throughout the (thankfully windowless) room.

"In an unprecedented blowout, Mark Smith has won the presidency," one news anchor said from one of the many flatscreens lining the perimeter. He did not seem the very least excited, but Palmer was ecstatic.

Good Lord, what a night tonight was.

It was here.

It was finally happening.

With a president so goddamn unlikeable, who would even dare think of entering the country? Legally or illegally? It didn't matter. With a serial murderer sitting in the Oval Office, Palmer hoped the prospect of immigration would die as quickly as the people Mark Smith had brutalized over the past ten years.

He snorted another line as Fitzgerald sat beside him.

"We did it, Palmer," he said, patting Palmer on the shoulder. "We really fucking did it."

"I didn't think it would happen, you know?" Palmer said, wiping the excess coke from his nostril. "How could a *felon* become president?"

The two of them heartily laughed at this, smacking the table with open palms while the rest of the room danced and cheered for another election well won.

"What now, then?" Fitzgerald asked.

"Well, I guess we bring Smith out for the pleasantries. Victory speech, whatever. You want some of this?"

"No thanks, Palmer. I already smoked half the pot Whitmore smuggled into here."

"Didn't hurt to ask."

Palmer put one last line up his nose, roared like a ferocious lion, and joined the celebration at the front of the room.

God, tonight could not get any better.

★ ★ ★

Lights. Cameras.

He knew his mother would be proud. He did it all for her. The murders, the campaign, everything. He wondered if she knew her son would go on to do great things. Protect and serve his country in the name of the late Sophia Smith, gone too soon through the circumstances of chemotherapy and domestic violence coalescing into her hanging from the ceiling.

Mark was still covered in the Foster family's blood. The quadruple homicide left him feeling more alive than he ever had before. He had not bothered taking a shower, let alone put on a new set of clothes. He wanted to walk onto that stage dressed in the blood of his opponent. To show the world that he really meant business.

Cheers rang throughout the streets of D.C. Police blockades were set up along the block to keep supporters in and protesters out. Those protesters had set trash fires everywhere, it seemed. The dim glows of different flames burning in disdain for him. Mark appreciated the police for always being by his side, for seemingly turning a blind eye to his apparent "misdeeds." He knew those Bernard police officers were long dead and gone, but he intoned a silent prayer to them as Palmer and Fitzgerald made the opening statements at this election victory event.

Spotlights beamed down onto the two congressman, the stage around them wrapped in various tapestries of red, white, and blue. They spoke of Mark as if he were a God, the American people's messiah. Mark pinched himself backstage. Maybe this was all a dream. A *really* good fucking dream. People like him were never supposed to be handed responsibilities such as these. A kid from a backwater town whose social life was admittedly not the greatest. A kid whose parents were his only source of comfort… until they weren't.

His father had been hopelessly drunk the night he died. Mark thought that was the reason killing him was so easy. His father had somehow made his way home from the local bar, parked the car in the garage, but did not kill the engine. Instead, he fell asleep, drooling over himself like a toddler after drinking an entire bottle of formula. The dog had been barking at the door leading into the garage. It was around midnight, and Mark—who was 25 years-old and still living in his family's home due to not going to college or having a full-time job—rubbed sleep from his eyes, wondering what the hell the dog was barking at. When he opened the door, he saw the car parked there, the garage door still open, the engine still rumbling.

Something had come over Mark in that moment, seeing his father sleeping in the driver's seat. So pathetic. So weak. *This* was the man his mother had killed herself over? What a waste of a beautiful life. When Mark had been lost in that Missouri science center all those years ago, watching his pennies spin around and around down the rim of that bowl, he had been enraptured by the simplicity of it. The physics that allowed a simple coin to spin endlessly with only the barest of movements to set its course. "A penny for your thoughts?" his mother had asked when she and his father found him, tears in her eyes and nothing in his. She must have said that as a joke, one to ease the tension after a grueling day of feeling like a failure as a parent. Losing your only son in an unfamiliar place surrounded by unfamiliar people. She had hugged him close, so close that he could feel her limp heartbeat through her blouse. But that little joke had stayed with him. *A penny for your thoughts?* Yes, a penny for one's thoughts. And a penny for their life. Yes, two pennies. One to quell your emotional state, and another asking permission to take your life. It was genius. Too good to leave discarded.

When Mark had seen his father passed out in the car that fateful night, he thought of a penny. No, *two* pennies. How exquisite they would look inside his father. One to dampen the emotional burden of causing the love of his life to suffer, and another as payment to take his life. Mark had found a power drill, cautiously opened the car door, and pointed the bit at his father's temple. The man snored—or choked, more like—and leaned to his side, but he was still asleep. Which was good. Better to go out dreaming than in the waking world.

Mark pressed the drill to his father's skull and powered it on. The bit swirled relentlessly as it clawed through skin and bone, ripping and tearing as it made its way toward the brain. But Mark did not wish to make this clean, so he jiggled the drill around to make the hole wider. Wide enough to slip a coin into. Blood sprayed onto Mark's face, some of it jetting into his mouth. He licked it from his lips as he continued his work. His father's eyes opened for a moment; the pupils locking straight onto Mark. Almost as if his father were aware of the violence occurring. Almost as if he wanted to get one last look at his son before going to hell.

Fueled by an overwhelming sense of resentment, Mark had stopped jiggling the drill and pushed it further. It wasn't just blood now. It was brain. It was hair. Everything that stored Mark Smith Sr.'s DNA flew in chucks throughout the car and half the garage as his son pushed the drill further into his skull.

Mark had let out a primal cry as he strained to get the drill in more but was met with a hollow end as the drill pushed out the other end of his father's cranium. Blood oozed from the man's eyes, dripping onto his lap like vicious tears. He had been met with no resistance, no signs of anguish. Almost as if his father wanted him to do it. To put him out of his misery.

The rush Mark had felt when he slipped those two pennies into his father's skull was unmatched by any sporting event or masturbation session in a public restroom. He had felt the rush pump into his bloodstream, clogging his veins with an unbridled arousal.

Lights. Cameras.

Oh, what a joyous night. Mark stood behind the stage's backdrop waiting for Palmer and Fitzgerald to finish up their little speeches. They were unsurprisingly good at buttering Mark up before serving him to the world on a hot platter. "He's a man for the people!" Palmer shouted into the mic. "And the people chose right!" The crowd of supporters in the front raised their voices in praise, while the crowd of protesters in the back continued to shout their disgust. Both the positive and negative cheers blended into one booming voice, one that shouted his name.

"Mark Smith! Mark Smith! Mark Smith!"

"And without further ado," Fitzgerald said to them, "the next president of the United States!"

Mark straightened his dress shirt as well as the crusty, dried blood caked on the fabric would allow him. He combed a hand through his wavy hair, put on his widest smile, and walked onto the stage.

The crowd was much more massive than he could ever have imagined. So many people. More people than the entire population of Bernard. Phones held up to the night sky. Cameras flashing milliseconds at a time. A vast ocean of blinking lights and enraptured voices. All cheering for him. All cheering for the future they wanted. A future they *needed*.

"Hello, you beautiful people!" He shouted.

The crowd erupted in applause.

"*You* did this! I love you all for that! This campaign was put together with table scraps, and it wouldn't have been possible without people like you to see it through. So thank you, from the bottom of my heart. Thank you."

Mark glanced up for a moment down Pennsylvania Avenue. There was something reflecting the lights from the stage. Up there, if you squinted at just the right angle, something flickered in that faraway parking garage like a flame born anew. A young flame, eager to engulf its prey.

★ ★ ★

Abel's nerves were on fire. Mark stood on that stage looking the happiest he had ever been. He waved to the crowd, they waved back, he shouted his thanks, they shouted their admiration. It was a constant cycle of dopamine that kept Mark's stage presence healthy and alive.

Sweat beaded on Abel's forehead, dripping slowly toward his eyebrows. He kept his eye squished into the sniper scope to keep the moisture out. He could not, under any circumstances, fuck this up. The whole team was watching. Waiting. The Coalition was in its full force to see this job taken care of as discretely as possible. No second chances. This bullet had to leave the chamber and sore straight between Mark Smith's eyes. No ifs, ands, or buts about it. If Mark did not die the instant Abel pulled the trigger, what would Abel have left to live for? A life marred by a damnable guilt, a weight of uselessness bearing on his shoulders that threatened to push him beneath Earth's crust.

No, he couldn't have that.

Not with his entire career on the line.

Valerie and the rest hadn't explicitly stated their shared concern for Abel's subpar performance in terms of hitting his target, but Abel knew they were all thinking it at the very least, if not gossiping about it behind his back. He deserved to be talked about without his knowledge. He knew that. He was a piece of shit redneck who didn't know shit about espionage and murder. A pencil in his classmate's neck said otherwise in terms of attempted homicide, but his only kill before the Coalition was that same girl, and even then, that had been an accident. A tragic, honest mistake.

So now Abel stared down the scope and watched Mark soak in all the love he had accrued. The smile upon his face. One Abel had wished would be placed upon him. "Oh, hello Abel! Nice running into you today!" Mark would say. But he never did. He would talk down to him, tell him to fuck off.

But Abel wasn't fucking off.

Not now.

Not ever.

When he pointed that glowing red reticle onto Mark, he felt like a god. A higher being with the power to smite down anyone with the flick of a wrist. Dissidents be damned. The fate of the world rested on Abel's shoulders, and a fat paycheck waited for him too.

His finger wrapped around the trigger, he breathed in, breathed out. Felt the air rush in and out, making him one with the universe surrounding him. Breathing in the urban air of the nation's capital. Tasting the sweet scents of banana strawberry vapes and oven-baked pastries. Old rubber tires and damp asphalt. Cold air for a cold night.

Then a shot was fired.

But Mark didn't go down.

No…

Oh God.

He missed it, didn't he?

Oh, *FUCK.* How was he supposed to explain this?

Abel refused to remove his eye from the scope, refused to leave this tunnel vision view of the world and enter a reality in which he didn't blast Mark's head off with a high caliber round. Whatever sweat had already accumulated over his brow began to swell and came crashing down like Niagara Falls. Down from the stage, Mark peered up and… was he *looking* at Abel? Surely not. But possibly: *Yes.* Abel's heart raced, then another shot rang out.

But he had not fired that one.

And he was starting to grow suspicious that he had not fired the first one either.

Another shot.

BANG!

Abel removed himself from his perch and whirled around, witnessing with great horror the carnage befalling the Coalition. Men in police uniforms shot and killed Zuri, marking a wet meaty hole between her eyes. She lay limp on the ground, Xavier next to her in tears. Then Xavier went down, his brains splattering on the concrete. Johnny whipped out a revolver and screamed, "Come at me, commies!" His revolver, paired with his eyepatch, was no match for those officers, though, and Johnny was gunned down in three quick bursts. *Pop pop pop.* Mateo, ever the loyal gentleman, slipped into the shadows and began to make his grand escape. But whoever these officers were had planned for this, and one of them looped around the same corner as Mateo and caught him by the neck. The officer threw him over the concrete ledge, and Mateo became nothing more than a thin layer of strawberry jam on the sidewalk tens of stories below.

Valerie came up behind another officer with a serrated hunting knife, screaming like a hawk and closing in like a tiger. But of course this officer was only one of the many who had ambushed the Coalition, so a different officer made quick work of her. He punched her square in the jaw and popped a cap in her as she tumbled to the floor.

Eddie, Abel thought.

"Get him," one officer said, pointing to Abel.

As the officer walked closer, Abel could make out the words patched to his right breast. They were all Secret Service agents, go figure. Someone had snitched. Ratted out the Coalition. It was done. Finite.

Had Eddie cheated on his group? His home? The Coalition had provided him with security, payment, and familial bonds. But it clearly had not been enough. Whether or not Eddie had warned Washington about the hit on Mark Smith's life, Abel had a hard time forgiving him. This was supposed to be *his* chance to shine, not Eddie's.

Abel raised his arms in defeat, allowing the Secret Service to lock his wrists in chains.

★ ★ ★

"Settle down. Settle down."

The gunshots in the distance had put the crowd on edge. It made sense. America had an apparent problem in terms of gun violence. School shootings happened nearly every single day, so the idea of going to a public event always came with the caveat that, yes, you were at risk of being shot in the face if you left the house. Guns were as normalized in America as peanut butter and jelly sandwiches.

"It's all part of the show," Mark said, his arms raised as if the gesture would calm down thousands of people he had never met. "It's the start of a joke. You'll see the punchline very soon. Just wait a moment. I promise it'll be worth it."

That little spark of light reflecting from the parking garage a few blocks down immediately vanished the moment the first shot echoed down Pennsylvania Avenue. With that glimpse of his potential killer extinguished, Mark wore a grin so tight his cheekbones were in danger of popping out of his skull. The killer had been there, just as the informant had predicted. And it was just what Mark's allotted team of Secret Service agents needed to intervene. Everything continued to work out just as he wanted. Days upon weeks upon months of blood, sweat, and tears coalescing into a final moment. A period at the end of a sentence. The water draining after a flash flood.

Twenty minutes later, as the chattering and murmuring throughout the crowd quieted down enough to be tolerable, the Secret Service agents brought out the gurneys. Mark stood with a stupid grin on his face, counting the gurneys as if he were counting sheep hopping over the fence in his dreams. *One gurney, two gurney, three gurney, four.* Bodies wrapped in tarp, blood dripping from the metal bars they were tied to, creating patterns of red dots along the concrete like snakes chopped into bite-sized pieces.

"These are examples, my fellow Americans," Mark said into the mic, pointing to the five gurneys. "Examples of what should be done to people who disagree with my ways. Examples of what happens when patriotism is scoffed at. How can America survive if dissidents such as these are free to walk the streets? To go to your restaurants? To attend your holy churches? The answer is no, not at all."

The Secret Service agents folded back the tarps, revealing the bodies within. All four of them were drenched in fluids, arms and heads wrapped in thin layers of blood like red-tinted shrink wrap. Brain matter tumbled from one body and landed on a crowd member's sneaker. On the Jumbotron hanging above the stage, these images were broadcast to those not within sniffing distance of the corpses. Everyone was to bear witness to their possible futures. Futures that would only befall them if they stepped out of line.

People from both the supporting and protesting sides of the crowd projectile vomited, chunks of their previous meals spewing endlessly through the cracks between their shoulder-to-shoulder neighbors.

"But we aren't done!" Mark continued, soaking in the brewing carnage. "While one slipped away, we *did* capture the man responsible for nearly taking my life. While you all were too busy either cheering for or slandering my name, this man sat inside that parking garage—" Mark pointed toward the structure down the avenue. The entire crowd swiveled their heads back as if possessed. "—aimed a firearm at my head and intended to pull the trigger. But he didn't, and I am proof of my opposition's incompetence. I am the Hillside Butcher, and I cannot be stopped. This is my purpose."

Two more agents brought the potential shooter on stage, his arms hooked around theirs, his head sagging over his weak shoulders. Greasy black tendrils of hair flopped to and fro, and that smell. God, that smell. One too odorous, too powerful to be detained by deodorant.

The agents kicked the shooter to the floor. Mark silently applauded Congressman Christopher Shaw for ratting this attempted assassination out. His frenzied phone call after Mark had slain the Foster family had come as a terrifying surprise but became a surprise more akin to that of an unexpected birthday celebration.

"Look at me," Mark commanded.

The shooter slowly lifted his head, mountainous ranges of acne peeking from underneath the skin. This couldn't be… no, it was.

Abel Watterson met his eyes with both horror and shame, the dichotomy of the two emotions mixing as well as barbecue sauce on strawberry ice cream. The kid was sweating more than Mark had ever seen before. He could fuck Janet five times in a row and still not accumulate the amount of sweat pouring from Abel's face. It was obscene.

"This is our man," Mark told the crowd, motioning them to look at the scrawny kid knelt before him like a peasant to his king. "This is the man who thought killing me was necessary. No, the *right* thing to do. But you see, killing is something that needs to be calculated, but not cold. If there is coldness in your heart when you take a life, there is no point. The life you stole cannot be yours to steal. There needs to be compassion in your blade, empathy in your swing. Because without caring for the victim, there can be no point."

A Secret Service agent brought out an axe and handed it to Mark. It was decorated for the occasion, painted in the colors of the American flag and bedazzled along the handle with glittering silver gemstones. The protesters in the back of the crowd stared in shock as if to ask why or how this could be happening, and in a public place, no less. But the supporters in front—the people who truly cared for the health of their great nation—looked like college sports fans. They were cheering, hollering, roaring, barking, growling. One lifted a cardboard cutout of a chainsaw and began whacking the person next to her with it.

★ ★ ★

With his hands cuffed behind his back, Abel shifted his body to the audience as if he wanted this to happen. He did it without a word, but with a fuck ton of shame plastered on his face.

This was it. This was the conclusion his life had been barreling towards. No light at the end of the tunnel. He didn't deserve that. He was nothing in the grand scheme of everything. Abel's father had made the right decision in leaving him and his mother behind those many years ago. Better to leave the trash out to rot on the curb than have it sit and fester in the living room. Maggots. That's what they were. Disgusting, vile maggots that squirmed on your rotten steak cuts and grew into flies, the same flies that eventually found the dead and lay their eggs in their eye sockets. Abel knew he was a symptom of a disease. It was clear now.

These people here, this audience.

They were cheering, but not for him.

It was all for Mark.

Just as it would be. As it should be.

Abel felt the vibrations of Mark's footsteps as the man circled around him, closing in on his prey. Abel licked his lips, wanted to close his eyes, but didn't. It was dazzling, like pixels on a screen. Millions of little dots of all colors coming together to form one image so extraordinary you wouldn't dare to look away. If he was to die with this sight as his last, maybe death wasn't so bad.

Mark planted his feet to Abel's right, lifting the glimmering axe toward the sky. Hundreds of beams of fractured light shot from its silver jewels. Mark flashed Abel a grin, and it was the first genuine smile Abel had seen from him in his entire life.

Abel returned the favor and awaited the end.

★ ★ ★

I could use someone like you.

Mark had said that to Abel the day they unfortunately met out-side of Bernard's police department. The kid was covered in the blood of his classmate, and the sight had made Mark yearn for a possible childhood in which he killed people sooner than 25. That was why he had said those things about Abel having spirit, having guts, being potentially useful in some nondescript future scenario.

Here was the nondescript future scenario.

Abel would be Mark's beacon, his example for the world.

If you fuck with the United States, you fuck with Mark Smith.

And if you fuck with Mark Smith, you get the axe.

The thunderous sounds of the roaring crowd drowned out, only replaced by a faint hum like a jet ski far out in the distance. Mark looked Abel in the eye. Abel looked back. Mark smiled, un-sure as to why, and Abel smiled back.

Gross, Mark thought.

Then he lifted the axe high, caught the light just so, and came down swinging.

Abel let out a short scream that almost sounded like *"NO!"* and was swiftly silenced. The blade sliced directly through his open mouth, carving a path straight down the creases at the cheeks where the upper and lower lips meet. Blood instantly poured onto the axe in thick, oily drizzles. But the axe hadn't gone all the way through. Mark felt it stop dead on something tough. *Must be the spine*, he thought. He took in the sheer spectacle of the kill. Abel on his knees, still twitching as if those jittering movements would somehow save his life. The collective gasp from the audience. The painful silence of a nation shocked by the brutal nature of what they were witnessing. Bodily fluids coating the lens of every cam-era catching this wicked scene on video, some of them showcasing directly onto the Jumbotron above.

Whatever was left of Abel gurgled another pint of blood. It gushed from muscle tissue in the face that Mark had never known was there. Chipped bits of bloodied teeth sat on the horizontal axe blade, simmering like cow bones in a beef stew.

Mark held an immaterial wealth of power, holding Abel's corpse up on its knees with only an axe to keep him balanced. He glanced at the audience, seeking approval for the deed well done. They glanced back. No, *stared* back. Appalled or in awe or both at what they were seeing. Is this what they wanted? Is this all Americans needed? A little bit of violence?

Well, there was more where that came from.

Mark grabbed Abel by his greasy hair and removed the axe, Abel's tongue and gums going away with it. They plopped to the stage in pink, gooey clumps. The acrid smell of human waste torched the air. Mark breathed it in, savoring the flavor of his destructive blessing.

Straining against his shoulder that desperately wanted to dislocate from its weak and old socket, Mark wrenched the top half of Abel's head from the bottom. Muscles and nerves twisted against him. This was no natural way from the human body to be dismantled. But Mark tried again, gritting his teeth as he pried the half skull from the forces holding him back.

The nerves gave way, snapping like clipped piano wires. Tendrils of flesh flew in all directions, desperate to latch onto something a little less dead. Pain swelled in Mark's back, the humble beginnings of a hernia. The pressure built higher until, finally, the piece of Abel's head completely tore free, half of his spine slithering up with it.

The rest of Abel's body flopped with a sharp thud, the lower part of his jaw spewing blood like a Yellowstone geyser laced with cherry Kool-Aid. And Mark Smith held his prize up to the night sky for all to see. He grabbed the mic from a bloody puddle, wiped it on his already bloodstained shirt, and shouted: "This is what happens to those who oppose me! This is what needs to be done to ensure a prosperous nation. Some may say the United States is a failing empire, and they may be right. But *I* can get us back on track. This is only the beginning."

His supporters applauded so loud their voices shattered the sound barrier. The protesters had left their self-imposed posts and ran off screaming in terror, only adding their voices to the current rapture.

Confetti cannons blasted red, white, and blue streamers throughout the block, "Y.M.C.A." thundered from the speakers, and everyone began to shout Mark's name.

Mark beamed. He turned Abel's head toward his own, looking the kid in his dead eyes. Mark dropped the mic and used his free hand to fetch two pennies from his pocket. He slid one into Abel's left eye, and another into his right. Two new copper eyes stared back at him, their embossed portraits of Abraham Lincoln standing guard.

EPILOGUE

★ ★ ★

"Please raise your right hand and repeat after me."

Mark Smith did as he was told, sneering as he did so. His right hand in the air, his left placed upon a leatherbound Bible.

"I, Mark Thomas Smith, do solemnly swear…"

"I, Mark Thomas Smith, do solemnly swear…"

The Capitol Building was decorated with red, white, and blue banners. Two ginormous American flags—one depicting the current fifty stars and the other showing the Betsy Ross original with its thirteen—hung from the ledge just underneath the building's rotunda. A crowd, unlike anything Mark had seen before, filled the space between the Capitol and the Washington Monument. People seemed to stretch for miles down that strip of grass, all of them cheering their gratitude for their new fearless leader.

Mark felt quite young standing amongst the general body of the United States government. He was a healthy 35 years-old compared to everyone else's insistence on being fifty year or (in most cases) older. The little pains in his back and shoulders diminished as he gawked at the brittle bones and wrinkly faces of his government, his cabinet, his new friends.

"...*that I will faithfully execute...*"

"...that I will faithfully execute..."

It was a beautiful day for an inauguration. As he recited the Oath of Office, Mark took in the D.C. skyline. The sky was painted a pale blue dotted with white puffy clouds. The sun overhead, Mark wished his mother were here to see this. The beautiful day, the many festivities, the red carpet, all of these in honor of her perfect son. Mark gripped Janet's hand. She did not grip it back, simply let her fingers hang limp in his grasp. It was no matter, as he kept telling himself like a prayer. She would come around to him. She looked so much like his mother.

"...*the office of president of the United States...*"

"...the office of president of the United States..."

He pondered what he would accomplish during his first day in office. The current (for the next minute or so) president would greet him despite everyone believing and hoping the old man would be dead by now. They would shake hands, pass by one another, and Mark would sit behind the *Resolute* desk with his head held high. He would sign orders demanding all American citizens disclose their mental health status to government agencies. This would allow a streamlining of the execution process. He would then block all immigration into the United States. The country had enough of its own problems to deal with; no need for additional problems to bog everyone down.

"...*and will, to the best of my ability...*"

"...and will, to the best of my ability..."

After all was said and done, Mark Smith would truly be the people's president. They would all adore him whether they wanted to or not. He would never claim to be a king, but he would surely think that of himself. He would retool ICE into a more rogue operation. A tool of the government to enact violence on a wider scale. No more unmarked vehicles and masked officers. Now was the time for full transparency, and the people were going to get what they asked for. ICE agents in suits, badges proudly displaying their names and organizations. If someone were considered suicidal, the agents would barge into their homes and take them out. It was simple, effective, and a much better use of taxpayer dollars than the frivolous deportation crap from the earlier administration.

"...*preserve, protect, and defend...*"

"...preserve, protect, and defend..."

No one would ever have to face the horrors Mark went through in his youth. No one would bear witness to the suicides of their loved ones. Easier to skip the grief altogether. Some people would obviously be against the idea, but they would come around. They all would. A little bit of fear never hurt anybody. Fear is the catalyst for complacency, as shown by how the people of Bernard had treated Mark. Now, he would spread the wealth throughout the country, and they would thank him dearly.

Mark wished he could feel remorse for what he did to Ashley Guthrie. It wasn't her fault that her father was severely depressed enough to fall victim to his axe. It wasn't her fault she was at the wrong place at the wrong time, both in Bernard and at the debate in Missouri. He wished her well as she served her sentence in federal prison. Hopefully a few decades behind bars would teach her the true meaning of loss, and she would finally come around to the country Mark will create.

A faint glimmer of sorrow washed upon Mark for someone else, though. As he finished the Oath of Office, his final thought was not of his mother, his father, or even Ashley and the remaining survivors of the destruction of Bernard, Arkansas. It was of Abel Watterson, the kid who wanted so desperately to be like him. But no one was like Mark. No one could ever dream of being such a thing. Murdering him in front of that crowd was a message. No, a warning. A warning to all those who dared go against what he planned to do. Mark kept Abel's severed head safe in a freezer in the basement of his new home in D.C. as a reminder of what he would carry out. It took everything in Mark not to thaw the head and eat the remains. He needed to savor the moment and savor the future.

"*…the Constitution of the United States.*"

"…the Constitution of the United States."

The crowd below cheered as Mark neared the end of the oath. The crowd further toward the Washington Memorial was not so keen on the reception. Picket signs and megaphones shouting their disdain and calls for immediate impeachment. They would come around. Or they would be dead. Either was fine by Mark. With the final line of the oath nearing its oration, Palmer and Fitzgerald nodded their agreement from across the aisle. Mark smiled then, feeling happier than ever. There would come a time when he would gladly chop the two miserable congressmen into tiny bits of bloody meat but now was not that time.

This was *his* moment.

He would not let the country down.

Mark took two pennies from his wallet and slipped them neatly between the worn pages of the leatherbound Bible.

"*So help me, God.*"

So help us, God.

June 2024 — September 2025

Lexington, KY

Charleston, IL

AUTHOR'S NOTE

This novel began its life shortly after I published my previous novel, *Scyphozoa*. I spent the summer after graduating from the University of Kentucky working at a local independent bookstore, raising my basset hound puppy, preparing for graduate school, and writing short stories. One of those stories was simply titled "Butcher," and it followed the downward spiral of a serial killer finding out no one gave a shit about his crimes. A brief, humorous tale satirizing the notoriety these types of murderers receive, but nothing more than that. Unfortunately, something was missing. I couldn't figure out the puzzle; couldn't find that final piece that put the whole thing into perspective. So I tucked the idea away and moved onto other projects in the meantime.

In the fall of 2024, I started and didn't finish many attempts at my second novel. A religious horror, a sci-fi horror, a murder mystery. All great ideas (I think) but simply not the right stories for the right time.

Then the 2024 U.S. presidential election happened, and what a disappointment it was. A convicted billionaire won with more hate in his heart than the last time he won. What could go wrong?

A lot, it seemed.

Economic instability, ICE raids, border patrol, AI slop posted from the official White House social channels. I'd become so fed up with the insanity that I turned back to my laptop to alleviate the stress. In March of 2025, I stumbled upon my work on "Butcher" from the year before, and I knew I finally found that final puzzle piece.

And now you've read it, or I hope you have. If you haven't, what are you doing here? The author's note is in the back of the book for a reason! Anyway, I would like to explain myself, because I do realize that *The Hillside Butcher* is insane.

I neglected to give a name to the president described throughout this novel. He is exactly who you think he is. Taking away his name stripped him of his power, and that's exactly how it should be. For a man so obsessed with attention, the least I could do was take that away from him. I did the same with the vice president to keep things fair and honest.

The assassination of Turning Point U.S.A founder Charlie Kirk occurred the week I completed Chapter 18 of the novel. It was a shock to the country, and even more of a shock to Kirk's mainly conservative base. Political violence has no place in this country, no matter who the violence is directed toward. No matter the hateful rhetoric, no matter the backward beliefs. I immediately clocked the connection between Kirk's assassination and the themes of the book I was on the cusp of completing. And that made me feel sick to my stomach. Not just because of the real-life horror of the one death, but also the fact that I hadn't felt that same visceral reaction to the school shooting that had occurred at the same time in a state hundreds of miles away. As Americans, we have become desensitized to gun violence. It happens every day. It shouldn't, but it does. My heart bleeds for the parents who bite their nails every morning they send their children to school. That's an existential terror I hope to never experience. Abel Watterson is an amalgamation of all the confused rage brewing within our nation. He is a loose cannon. He is raised in an individualistic culture that seemingly left him behind. He wants to be more. And what is the best way to gain recognition in an objectively violent nation? Murder. That's the headspace many of these mass shooters live in. They want to be seen. To be heard. And buying guns and ammunition is the easiest way for them to go down that path. I hope someday our government realizes that gun reform is the only way to stop this senseless violence. Mental healthcare, while I am currently in school for this very subject, can only go so far.

You probably have more questions, but I don't have any more answers. Sorry! I'll leave the rest of this book up to your own interpretation. I hate when authors overexplain their work. It's insulting to the readers' intelligence. You're a smart and beautiful human being, and I wish to respect that.

I would like to express my gratitude to the people who encouraged me throughout the process of writing *The Hillside Butcher.* Firstly, I would like to thank Kamilo Davila, who this book is dedicated to. You got me through the most difficult four years of my life, and I will cherish your kindness and friendship until the day I die. There's also some usual suspects that deserve to be acknowledged: Tricia Bertke, Ricky Camacho, Nathan Ellis, Kevin Endrijaitis, Keaton Fuller, Will Hatten, Mattye Jackson, Lucas Kinzer, Carson Kitts, Joshua Koch, Julia Kollitz, Jake Lynn, Jacob Phillips, Morgan Rhodes, Jonathan Schares, Thommy Snow, Brayden Sosa, and Kyla Stevens.

Thank you, Mom and Dad, as always.

For the amazing cover artwork, thanks to SORRISO.

And of course, thank *you*. Yes, you. Thank you for reading the insane ramblings of a twenty-something struggling through his last year of graduate school. I'm so grateful to have a small audience who cares enough to read the words I write. You're awesome. Keep being you, but please seek counseling.

The Hillside Butcher was written to the music of King Gizzard and the Lizard Wizard, and was edited to the music of Magdalena Bay, specifically their 2024 album *Imaginal Disk*.

And finally, I will repeat what I did at the end of *Scyphozoa* and acknowledge the books I read while I wrote this book. You may have spotted bits and pieces of these authors' amazing works throughout my novel, and I hope you check them out.

The Angel of Indian Lake (2024)................Stephen Graham Jones
A Burning (2020)..Megha Majumdar
Bury Your Gays (2024).................................Chuck Tingle
Camp Damascus (2023)..................................Chuck Tingle
Crooked Kingdom (2016)..............................Leigh Bardugo
Crying in H Mart (2021).............................Michelle Zauner
Dark Matter (2016)......................................Blake Crouch
Death Spell (2025)...................................David Sodergren
Demon Copperhead (2022).......................Barbara Kingsolver
Don't Fear the Reaper (2023)..................Stephen Graham Jones
The Eyes Are the Best Part (2024)...................Monika Kim
The Fireman (2016)...Joe Hill
The Institute (2019).......................................Stephen King
The Invisible Life of Addie LaRue (2020)..................V.E. Schwab
The Long Walk (1979).....................................Stephen King
Luminous (2025)..Silvia Park

Mickey7 (2022)......................................Edward Ashton

My Friends (2025)...................................Fredrik Backman

My Heart Is a Chainsaw (2021).................Stephen Graham Jones

Never Flinch (2025)....................................Stephen King

Nuclear War: A Scenario (2024).......................Annie Jacobsen

The Only Good Indians (2020).................Stephen Graham Jones

Rotten Tommy (2024)..............................David Sodergren

The Running Man (1982)................................Stephen King

Six of Crows (2015).....................................Leigh Bardugo

Sky Daddy (2025)..Kate Folk

Sunrise on the Reaping (2025).........................Suzanne Collins

This Thing Between Us (2021)..........................Gus Moreno

Uzumaki (1998-1999)....................................Junji Ito